BARGAINING POWER

Also by Deborah J. Natelson:

The Land of the Purple Ring
The Midnight Files

BARGAINING POWER
Copyright © 2019 by Deborah J. Natelson.

Cover design by Nada Orlic.

Map by K. Futterwacken,
https://mischieviousfairie.wixsite.com/kfutterwacken

Thinklings Books
1400 Lloyd Rd. #279
Wickliffe, OH 44092
thinklingsbooks.com

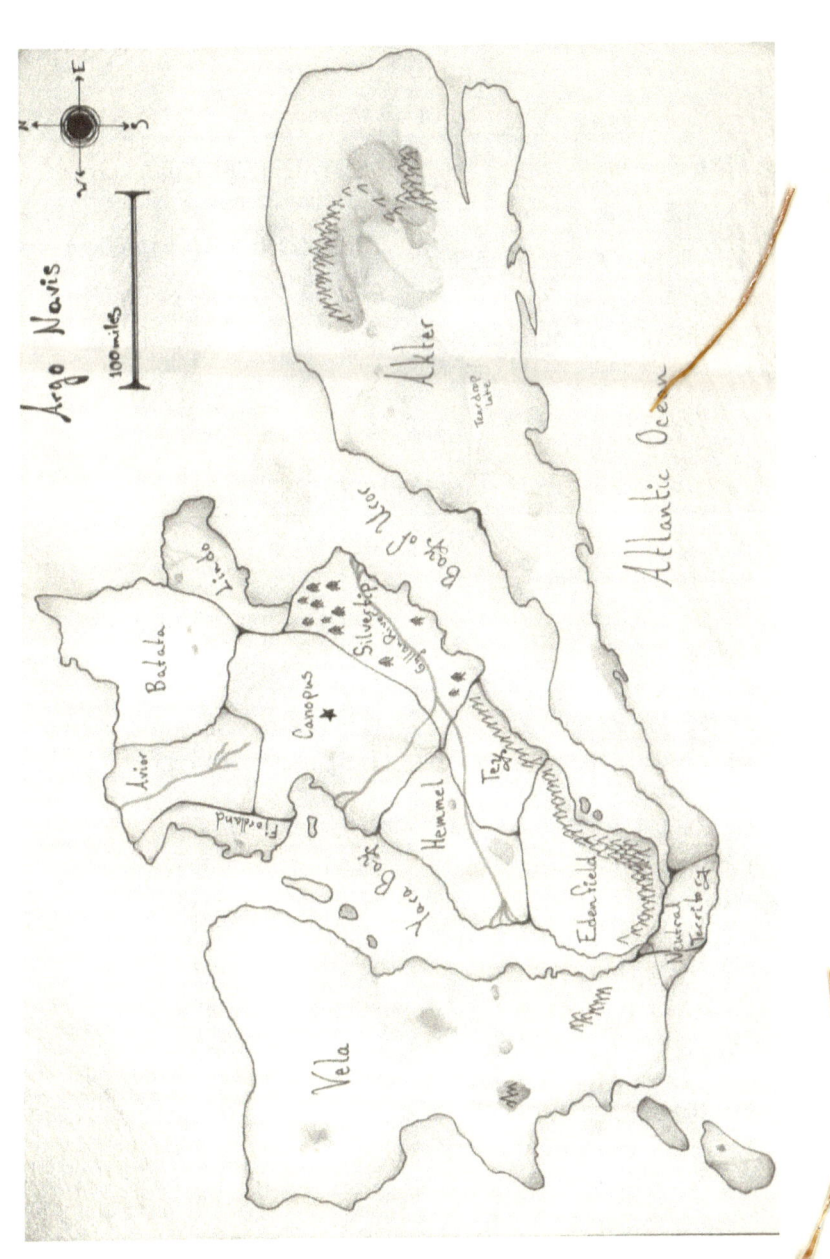

The Royal Court
(black & white)

KING Emil II

PRINCE Emok

CHANCELLOR: Lord Rodrigue Thomas

CHAPLAIN: Rev. Abraham Beck

ROYAL SECRETARY: Lord Évariste Mendes

SEIDKONUR: Madame Ebba Lundquist

SKALD: Keir Skuli

The Prefectures

AVIOR
Prefect: Lucio Winter
Ivory & sapphire blue

BATATA
Prefect: Joel Pinho
Beige & dark brown

CANOPUS
Prefect: Therese Ferro
Wine red & gold

EDENFIELD
Prefect: Bo Holst
Midnight purple & ice blue

FJORDLAND
Prefect: Calixto Victor
Colors: Indigo & rose

HEMMEL
Prefect: Claes Bager
Pumpkin orange & russet brown

LINDO
Prefect: Graça Silveira
Turquoise & dark gray

SILVERTIP
Prefect: Otto Ostberg
Silver-gray & leaf green

TEY
Prefect: Tobias Nilsen
Cardinal red & sky blue

Translator's Note

The primary language of the Island of Argo Navis is Plishan, a complex amalgamation of Portuguese and Norwegian with fragments of French, Japanese, and English.

Argo Navis doesn't show up on most maps, not even satellite images, and so most of the world doesn't know it exists. Argo Navis's isolation is further emphasized by the surrounding ocean, which is extremely treacherous. Ships that manage to cross to it seldom return, and those that do are crewed by confused sailors who can provide no clear picture of where they've been or how to get back there. This explains a great deal about ships from which cargo disappears and why the people of Argo Navis have access to some modern technology.

The curious nature of this geography has enforced a distinct history on the island: It is populated almost exclusively by the descendants of people who meant to end up somewhere else. In several cases, we can guess who these people were. At some point, there was definitely a Norwegian (or possibly French-Norwegian) expedition to reach the South Pole that became trapped on Argo Navis. (Keep an eye out for mentions of *flyte* or *flyting*—a game of insults extremely popular in the fifth through sixteenth centuries in the Norse, Celtic, and Anglo-Saxon worlds.) We additionally can guess that part of Carina's and Vela's high Brazilian populations moved there after the Portuguese arrived in Brazil, some four hundred years ago, because Portuguese is the language that influenced Plishan.

Not much is at present known about Argo Navis, but it is my hope that, by translating this account and sharing it with the general public, I may inspire further academic interest in its unique history and culture.

BARGAINING
POWER

Power Trips #1

Deborah J. Natelson

Thinklings Books, LLC
Wickliffe, OH

Chapter 1

FRATRICIDE

No king can maintain his power long without the consent of his people and the support of his lords. And by "lords," I'm including—you know, just to take a random example—Gil Winter, Prefect of Avior, whose car had been circling the Carinan Security Service building for the past eighteen minutes.

"Would you look at that," I said. "He's parking."

"At last," my boss said, putting his pencil down atop the cipher he'd been unraveling. "Stay sharp, Mercedes. If you are gone more than twenty minutes—"

"I won't be," I promised.

"I will call," he said steadily, almost ponderously, and I smiled. There wasn't much even a high-ranking member of the Security Service could do against a prefect; but then, there wasn't much Sr. Nordfeld couldn't do, once he'd aimed his marvelous brain at the task. I let that comfort me as I passed through security and stepped out into the chilly autumnal smog.

On the sidewalk by the sleek sapphire-blue limo of Avior Prefecture, a man waited. He was massive: nearly two feet taller than I and three times as broad, with hands like shovels and a chin to match. His ivory-and-sapphire uniform and the stars decorating his collar labeled him head knight: Avior's second-in-command, answerable to no one except his prefect.

"Miss Cartier?" he demanded.

It doesn't do to mess with head knights any more than to mess with their prefects. Besides, I had an image to maintain. I clutched my handbag timidly and bowed, not making eye contact. "I am she."

The head knight nodded politely and opened the limo door.

I rocked back as perfume and alcohol gusted out. Red leather seats glistened under dim LEDs, which fit exactly what I'd heard about Gil Winter. But the smells were old and stale, and no rave music thundered at me, and that didn't fit in the least.

"Get in, please," the head knight said, looming close behind me.

I bobbed another timid bow and in no way pointed out that this was Silvertip Prefecture, not Avior, and that he had no business ordering me around. Instead, I got in the limo like a good little personal assistant. And when the door shut behind me, it was no harder than necessary. And when the lock clicked, it was only because we'd begun moving.

"Miss Cartier," said the man in the shadowy, lime-and-raspberry-lit depths of the limo. "Thank you for joining me."

The voice was . . . almost familiar. Strange. I'd have thought I'd have known Lord Winter's voice from television. I'd have thought, in person, that it would sound charming and confident.

Keeping my expression neutrally polite, I peered down the throat of the limo, trying to see past the distortion of the neon lights. But try though I might, I couldn't make out my host's face until he leaned forward. *Then* I inhaled sharply.

He was five-foot-seven, forty-six years old, and had the unhealthy, prematurely aged skin of a man who lived off mayonnaise and potato chips and didn't believe in fresh air or sunshine. Unlike his brother, who had a certain rough charm, this was the sort of man most women instinctively avoided—unless, like this man's wife, they were so desperate for elevation that they would sell themselves to the Devil if he came knocking.

I dug my fingers into red leather. The temperature had jumped about twenty degrees. "I don't understand," I said distantly. It was an automatic response, a placeholder while I struggled to wrench my rational mind back into place. "What is this? I thought Prefect Avior wanted to talk to me. Are you bringing me to him?"

My host watched with detached interest. Dim lights carved out the hollows around his eyes and stained his teeth. He had no reason to hurt me. No reason to think I knew anything. He said, "*I* am Prefect Avior."

"What?" I shot back. "No you aren't. I know what Gil Winter looks like—I used to live in Avior Prefecture. What's really going on? Who are you?"

My host laughed, genuinely amused. "Gil," he said, "was my brother. I'm Lord *Lucio* Winter, the new Prefect Avior." He displayed his heavy signet ring, and I scooted close enough to see. He smelled of incense, sulfur, and body odor. And upon his finger, sure enough, was the engraved Avior bat.

Softly, I asked, "Gil Winter is—dead?"

"He was bound to die eventually," said the new Prefect Avior. "It's no secret that he drank like a storm drain. The wonder is that he didn't totter off a balcony years ago."

He spoke casually, as if his brother had meant no more to him than a drop of rain to the ocean. My eyes flew up to his, and behind his words I saw the glee of violence, the thirsty self-satisfaction of triumph. And in that moment, I knew as clearly as if he had confessed it in court that this man had killed his brother—and that my life depended on him not realizing that I knew it.

Sweat prickled my eyes like tears. I clutched my hands before my sternum. "You poor thing!" I cried, three parts nice and seven parts stupid. "You don't have to be brave for me; I can see how deeply you're hurting. I'm so, so sorry."

"A thousand thanks," he said, "but I didn't actually drive a hundred miles to Silvertip to talk about my brother."

"Of course!" I exclaimed. "I'm sorry, I didn't think—I'm sorry."

Avior cleared his throat. When he spoke again, he'd infused his tone with false jollity. "You're not in trouble, Miss Cartier—I promise. I came because I wanted to talk to you."

He's putting me at my ease, I thought absurdly, and let the nervous giggle escape unchecked.

"I believe—correct me if I'm wrong—but I believe you went to university in my prefecture. You studied—what?"

"History, my lord."

"Ah, yes! I remember now. I saw one of your papers on warfare. Hardly an appropriate topic for a girl!"

The title of my 80,000-word dissertation had been, "The Applicability of Ancient Tactics in Modern Warfare." It had taken me two years of concerted research to write.

I shrugged and tittered again.

"How did you end up as a cryptanalyst's personal assistant?" Avior asked. "If you didn't want to marry straight out of school, you could always have become a teacher. Or were you planning to join the military?"

He was joking, but enlisting was exactly what I'd planned. I'd have done it, too, only I'd failed the vision requirement and didn't have the cash for eye surgery. That's why I'd gotten my current job: to save for it. I had put away enough money nine months ago, but somehow, I'd never gotten around to taking the next step.

"Oh, no!" I exclaimed, channeling one of my brother Francis's girlfriends—#14, I thought: the one who'd thrown up from watching us play Zombie SlashHouse III. "I could never join the military. Wait . . ." I placed one delicate hand to my lips. "Oh, that's not why you came, is it? But, you see, it's different on paper. You don't have to see the—the—the blood and—and all the rest of it."

He patted my hand kindly. "No, no. I only wanted to understand you—to understand what could have drawn you to your current position. I thought it might have to do with your employer. Jon Nordfeld sounds like quite an extraordinary man."

"Oh, yes!" I cried, cycling to Francis's Girlfriend #29, the enthusiastic one. "He's brilliant, truly. Amazing. I've never met anyone like him."

Avior nodded encouragingly. "I can see you're a perspicacious young lady. Go on."

I twirled my hair, deciding where to begin. "Well . . . he's brilliant, like I said. You can't be in the same room with him for ten seconds without seeing that. It's in his eyes, you know? And . . ." I stole a quick, shy look at him. "And I've never had any problems with him. He's never—never come on to me, if you know what I mean."

"You're a very pretty woman, Miss Cartier."

His approval meant so much.

"He sounds," Avior coaxed, "like the sort of man who likes to talk about himself."

I shook my head in chagrin. "Hardly ever. He's incredibly private. I've worked for him for three years, driven him to and from his apartment building every day—and I've never even seen inside the front door!"

This part was true, unfortunately. My boss had made it extremely clear from the start that we were to have no contact outside of work, and that I had no right to any of his personal information. I didn't know how he spent his free time, although I suspected he read a great deal. Nor did I know if he had any family, whether he lived alone, or where he'd grown up. Flattering attentiveness could get him to expound upon any other subject, but his personal life remained a void.

"Sometimes," I sighed, as vapid as the hated Girlfriend #42, "I think I'll never understand him. He's too smart. It's like he's beyond normal people. But you don't mind, do you?" I added earnestly. "You won't be disappointed in him, I promise. He always delivers."

The change might've been funny, if it weren't so terrifying. In an instant, Avior went from friendly to draconic: tension stretching his torso taut and contorting his fingers into claws. His voice rattled harsh and low, and I shrank from him as he demanded, "What has he told you?"

"I—I thought—" I stumbled, fighting to keep my real alarm separate from the pretense. "I thought that's why you wanted to talk to me! Because you want to hire him to—to break codes and ciphers for you and—I'm sorry! I won't say a word. I promise. Please don't be angry with me."

Avior's expression cleared as I spoke, and he resumed his avuncular guise by patting my hand again. "Quite all right, Miss Cartier. I'm not angry. I should have known you'd guess. I said you were perspicacious!"

I went weak at that, as much in real relief as in false, but he pinned me back down with a frown. "There is one other matter," he said, and steadied his nerves with more patting. "It's awkward and embarrassing, but during your time in Avior, you must have heard the slander my enemies spread about me. The nonsense about demonology."

I had, as it happened. Frequently. One of my classmates had

grown up in the neighborhood of Avior Manor, and had told us about the time her beloved dog had disappeared, along with every other pet in a half-mile radius. I also had it on good authority that Lucio's obsession was the reason Gil had originally been the one chosen as prefect, although Lucio was the older brother.

There hadn't been any recent scandals, so Lucio must have learned caution—but since my boss had contacted him by posing as an expert on a demonology forum, I suspected caution was the only thing he'd learned.

"It's fine," Avior assured me. "I'm used to it. Their lies have even proven somewhat useful, because I end up hearing about the crazies who really are interested in such superstitious nonsense. You'd be shocked at how respectable some of them seem, before you know the truth about them. I even heard that Jon Nordfeld—"

I snatched my hand back. "How dare you!"

"I didn't finish."

"You didn't have to!" I cried, too enraged to respect the rules of rank. "And if you think for one moment that I will sit here and listen to you slander the most respectable, gracious, gentlemanly man on the planet, then you can think again!"

"He never mentioned—"

"Certainly not. And I'll thank you to keep your nasty implications to yourself. For shame!"

Avior studied me, taking in the heaving chest, the brimming indignation and righteous offense, the way I didn't shy from eye contact.

"My apologies," he said at last, "but as prefect, I must ask these things." He leaned back and tapped three times on the driver's barricade.

I slashed my furious glare over to the seat opposite, squeezing my handbag hard as the limo slowed.

"I hope," Prefect Avior said as the limo settled to a stop, "that you'll keep this conversation privileged."

"I know my duty!" I flashed at him and then relented from anger to mere stiffness. "I didn't mean to offend you, my lord. I mean, I realize that you did need to ask."

"I did," he agreed, "and I thank you for taking a weight off my mind. Have a nice day, Miss Cartier."

"You too, prefect. And . . . and I *am* sorry about your brother."

The limo door opened, and golden-white light rushed its rhombus upon the seats. I scooted down and let the head knight hand me out of the neon-lit stale smoke and onto the sun-warmed sidewalk. After nodding politely, I walked directly back to the Carinan Security Service building, not looking around until I reached the door. Then I paused and watched the limo drive away, a glittering sapphire worm among black beetles. I wasn't feeling wistful; I just wanted to make sure it really left.

It did, and I went in.

There is something wonderfully calming about the ritual of making tea, although I slopped boiling water onto the tray and rattled cups in their saucers. That's adrenaline for you: terribly inconvenient when it's not busy saving your life.

Anyway, a little hand-trembling didn't matter, not now that Avior couldn't see me. So I let the cups clatter as I carried the tray back to the office and set it on the desk.

My boss took one look at me and said, "Something is wrong."

I'd eat glass before looking foolish in front of him. I sat on my hands so I didn't jiggle, and I gave a full report. My memory's not perfect, but I wouldn't be forgetting that conversation for a long, long time.

"Did he suspect you?" my boss asked, when I was done.

"No."

"You're certain?"

"I'm certain."

He relaxed back into his chair. "Good. Then we can proceed as planned."

Chapter 2:

BURGLARY

That was Tuesday. The rest of the business week passed in a flurry, but a flurry of the ordinary sort. We did not solve the new cipher—yet—but my boss concentrated on it while I handled the more ordinary work.

Friday evening, in a daze of too many hours of unwinding ciphers that had undergone some particularly grotesque mistakes, I staggered home: away from the parking garage, across my apartment complex, up the concrete stairs—and straight into a choking cloud of garlic and chili oil.

"Luc!" I tried to yell, and devolved into hacking coughs. Stuffing my sleeve over my nose and mouth, I bulled across the living room to throw open the balcony door, then charged to the kitchen window, the stove fan, the overhead fan, and—

"Where's the box fan?" I demanded between coughs. "You know it's meant to live by the balcony, Luc. So you can open the door and turn it on when you cook toxic foods. Like we agreed."

Luc, who can eat wasabi straight and has lungs of titanium, gave me an amused glance and continued transferring noodles from the sizzling wok to his plate. "I made plenty for you."

"Box fan!"

"It's cooling Elspeth. *Don't* move it. I need to take her apart; she's been gathering dust."

"I thought that was Kirsty," Francis said, toweling off his hair as he

16

ambled in. "Good evening, Mercedes. I see you've arrived just in time for food." Shower heat lingered in his cheeks and puffed his fingertips. Francis bathing on a Friday evening might mean a date, but it had also rained today, and rain meant a muddy construction site, so there was hope that Girlfriend #44 had dumped him.

Francis tossed the damp towel on the sofa and made a beeline for the food. "Do you mind closing the balcony door?" he asked me. "It's freezing in here."

"Are you in*sane*?"

"She's in a bad mood," Luc informed him *sotto voce*.

"Impossible," Francis proclaimed. "She's late. That means she got to spend extra time at work, and you know how she loves her work."

"Adores him," Luc agreed. "I mean 'it.' It's so . . . stimulating."

"Now, now, Luc. She doesn't appreciate us being flippant about it."

"But we're only flippant because we don't understand him!"

"There is a solution to that," Francis said, tapping his chin wisely. "We must get to know him. We should invite him to dinner! You could cook him something impressive, Luc. Or do you think Mercy would rather serve him?"

"I'm not inviting him," I said. "Besides, he wouldn't come."

Luc swung an arm around my shoulders. "Faint heart never won fair boss man."

I pushed him off and busied myself getting a plate.

"At least tell us his name," Luc persisted. "I have mad internet stalking skills."

"What's in here, Luc?" I asked, poking around the wok. Luc is a superb cook, but he does like to experiment. "These aren't shrimp."

"I wanted to try snook. Focus, Mercedes. You were about to tell us your boss's name."

I threw a chunk of snook at him. He caught and ate it.

Despite the teasing, chili oil, and parade of insipid girlfriends, I liked living with my brothers. After six years in university, where I had my roommates variously under my thumb and twirled around my little finger, it was refreshing to live with people who were neither intimidated nor impressed by me, and whom I could be sure were honest. Best of all, I could flyte as hard as I liked against my brothers without damaging any delicate egos. The fact that Luc was about a thousand times better at cooking than any of my previous roommates (or I) certainly didn't hurt.

Our apartment was on the outskirts of Silvertip City—for reasons lost to time, both the capital city and the prefecture are called Silvertip—and entirely satisfactory. It's a petite three bedroom, two bath with a big enough kitchen that Luc didn't complain as long as neither Francis nor I tried to use it while he was cooking. Between us, we could have afforded something bigger, but there didn't seem to be any point: none of us was a packrat, and only Luc spent the majority of his time there, destroying his spine over various computers.

Working from home won Luc the right to decorate and redecorate the apartment to his heart's content, which meant I'd grown used to an ever-rotating collection of Celtic metal, Celtic Christian, Celtic rock, and just plain Celtic band posters. I could barely tell one from the next, though I nodded sagely when Luc patiently explained the difference between one selection of long-haired, kilted redheads and the next.

Francis had only once shown any interest in decorating, when he'd hung a framed Psalm 23 near the front door. As for me, I'd spent weeks hunting down the pinkest, sparkliest unicorn poster this side of the rainbow, and had centered it above the TV. When anyone (usually girlfriends of Francis, but occasionally of Luc) asked about it, I proclaimed straight-faced that it was my favorite piece of art in the whole wide world and that I had an identical one at work.

"So, my furry little guinea pigs," Luc said, rubbing his hands together and bouncing his eyebrows, "what do you say to—"

"No," said Francis, around a mouthful of his third plate of noodles.

"I agree," I said. "If this one doesn't have a rocket launcher, it's not worth playing. Really, Luc, I don't care if that game was set in a medieval forest-castle-moat-fairy kingdom. Rocket launchers are essential."

"Rocket launchers are overrated," Luc said primly. "In this one, your only weapon is a butter knife. You see, you were using it to spread jam on toast when the zombie apocalypse—" He laughed at our expressions. "Fine, it has a rocket launcher. I want feedback primarily on scratch and decapitation effects."

"For realism, comedy, or squick factor?" I asked.

"You tell me," Luc said. "I want honest reactions here."

"What do you say, Mercedes?" Francis asked, swallowing his last forkful of noodles. "Team up and take him down?"

"It's not a team game!" Luc protested.

"Partners," I agreed. "Until I turn on you and rocket launcher you to bits."

"Until you try, you mean."

I winked at him, and we headed to the living room to perform a serious analysis of Luc's digital artwork.

Among its other charms, the apartment I share with my brothers sits on the upper of two stories, directly above an older lady with a pug and a serious cigar addiction. At this very moment, three hours after we'd finished dinner, she was out on her balcony, puffing hard over a bodice-ripper and oblivious to everything.

From the living room, shrieks and zombie noises blasted. Most of the noise emanated from the TV, but maybe twenty percent of the shrieks were from Francis and Luc, who'd be ducking and head-shotting shambling corpses into the wee hours of the morning.

Safe in my bedroom, I shucked my dress suit in favor of a soft maroon turtleneck, navy split skirt, and soft-soled black tennis shoes. A charcoal wool coat with matching gloves and hat shoved in the pocket finished the ensemble. My skin and hair are dark enough that, unlike my boss, I wouldn't have to go full mummy mode—so no ski mask needed.

Thus suitably attired, I pulled on my backpack and lifted my window open. With some maneuvering, but far less noise than staving off the zombie apocalypse, I popped out the screen and slid it under my bed. Then I climbed onto the window sill.

It'd been years since I'd last snuck out of my bedroom window, and grown women are a lot less springy than teenagers. It took much more grunting than I expected to squirm onto my belly, pull the window mostly closed, dangle from my fingertips, and drop down to the grass. There'd be no climbing back up this way, but even my brothers should be asleep by the time I got back—unless Francis's insomnia got him, in which case I'd have to do some fast talking.

Wincing over my shins, I hobbled off to the bus station. It was ten minutes away, and twenty minutes after I reached it, I was boarding the last train south.

Dust and concrete, gasoline and metal: these are the smells of train stations to me. Onboard, those smells fade in the background, overwhelmed by luggage, trampled carpet, old sweat, and sanitizer: cold, humid smells that render food unsatisfying and stretch minutes into hours. Books become harder to read and less interesting when you try; games lose their excitement; and your fellow passengers are the dullest creatures on the planet.

I shall never understand why I enjoy traveling by train.

I elbowed my way down the train cars, starting in first class, eying the closed food trolley and its inaccessible coffee, and finally finding my boss in the last car.

His backward-facing double seat shared a table with an empty forward-facing double seat, over which he'd spread his coat to guard it from occupation. Artificial light bounced off his sandy-brown hair (thinning slightly above the forehead) and made clusters of half-hearted shadows at his feet. Aside from his eyes, there was nothing in his appearance to draw attention, nothing that indicated he was anything other than—well, than the boring mid-level pencil pusher my brothers thought he was.

I folded his coat and sat across from him to wait for his attention. A finger rose off the top edge of his book to ward me off. By the look of it, he was adding another obscure language to his collection. My boss collects knowledge like Luc collects Celtic bands.

I used the pause as an opportunity to take stock.

My boss had dressed sensibly and plainly in dark gray sweater and trousers, and the meticulous pile beside him included dark green scarf and hat, and black leather gloves. The edge of his briefcase peeked unobtrusively from beneath the pile.

He had chosen our seats well. I could see almost everyone, and he no one, and no one but our nearest neighbors could see us. Even the toilets lay in the opposite direction.

The train was about a quarter full: couples tucked close in conversation; college students visiting home for the weekend, laughing together near the front of the car and playing on their phones; lone businesspeople staring mindlessly out their windows or stuffing themselves with junk food; one elderly lady intent on her knitting and another submerged in a mystery novel. The lateness of the hour spared us small children; the youngest I spotted looked about fourteen, earbudded and asleep.

The train juddered to life, and my boss lowered his book, not marking the page anywhere except in his memory. "You had a pleasant evening, I hope," he said. I translated this as: *Did anyone notice or follow you?*

"Francis stole my rocket launcher," I said, "but I found a flamethrower and burned him to a crisp before dying of my wounds. You?"

"I paid the Craftsmen a visit," he said placidly, tucking the book into his pile. "Everything has been completed to my exact specifications. Inside my coat pocket, please."

I hesitated for one astonished second, thinking he meant me to pull out the equipment then and there. But the pocket held only a checkered ash-and-rosewood case, eight inches by four by two, expensive and old. I looked at it sorrowfully, resigning myself as I handed it over and he set up the board.

Chess is the classic strategy game: two sides do battle with a collection of pieces able to move in preordained fashions. Each side is equal in theory, save that one must go first, but in practice the players are never equal, and one must always lose.

I never was one for turn-based games. Why would I sit there, twiddling my thumbs while my opponent attacked me? While white is endlessly contemplating whether to move his bishop or his castle, I'll move my troops to surround him and pick off the king from behind. And where are my archers? An arrow could definitely curve over that single row of pawns, and problem solved.

But maybe I only think that way because I'm no good at the game.

"I do not like it either," my boss told me, "but it is essential to understand nevertheless. A good chess player uses tactics at two levels: the level of individual moves and the level of the whole game. Computers can mimic this, to an extent. A good program can determine which move is technically best in any specific situation and make that move. A *very* good program can calculate the probability of its opponent's follow-up move.

"But a good chess player can predict even further, can understand his opponent's psychology beyond the constraints of probability. Most chess players have favorite opening moves and use them—or variations on them—over and over. If you play enough, you see patterns not only in the moves your opponent uses, but the *sorts* of moves he uses. Once you understand how he likes to combine and respond to moves, you will be able to predict, even before the game begins, exactly how your opponent will perform and exactly which moves you will require. If you predict thoroughly enough, you can even instruct someone else on which moves to make in which order, allowing them to win the game without you being present—or them understanding what they are doing."

I nodded. "Which is why it's tactically idiotic to follow your opponent's rules, if you know your opponent can calculate like that."

"Everyone follows rules, Mercedes."

"Precisely why I'd rather not. If my choice is between using my opponent's tactics or winging it, I'd rather wing it."

"Then you would lose," my boss said, and emphasized his point by boxing in my king. "Proper strategy makes work lighter, not heavier. Working within preset guidelines allows you to cheat time limitations. Not only will you have fewer permutations to compute *in situ*—"

Like I was capable of computing chess permutations.

"—you will be able to use your knowledge of your opponent's tactics against him more effectively, something impossible if you introduce random factors into the equation. Use his momentum to let him maneuver himself into his own destruction."

"Is that what Senhora Ahlgren does?"

I'd hit a sore point. Sra. Ahlgren is one of the other cryptanalysts, and she beats my boss at chess nine times out of ten, although he never makes a technical mistake. She's a world-class grandmaster, which doesn't make it any easier for him to bear.

"As I said," my boss replied, putting my queen out of her misery, "I do not like the game—and no, not only because she occasionally wins."

I made a vaguely affirming noise. I thought the conversation was over, and it was for that game and the next one. But two games later, he picked it up again.

"Consider the chessboard before play begins," he said, putting the last pawn into place. "Two colors, each in its place. Two rows on each side, identical in setup. Perfect balance, perfect harmony, perfect order. Then the game begins, and what happens?"

"Black sticks its head in the sand while white attacks."

"Exactly: one side moves; the other does not. Balance is lost. The pieces intermix. Some are removed from the equation. Pawns turn into knights. Chaos ensues. One side wins by destroying the other—restoring balance by way of annihilation."

"You could refuse to play," I pointed out.

"I could," he agreed, "except what then? Someone sets up the board, moves a piece. Order is lost, and I can restore it only by playing the game to completion."

"To annihilating the enemy."

"Or to being annihilated myself."

"Which is better than a little disorder?"

He inclined his head, and we played on in silence. I was a far superior player to when he'd first brought out the chessboard, about a year ago, which didn't stop me from losing soundly.

I sighed and knocked over my poor abused king for the sixth time in six games. "If you ask me," I said, "chess is a poor analogy for the conquering of a kingdom."

"You do not see any parallel between the strategy of generals on the battlefield and the movement of pieces?"

"Sure I see a parallel," I said, "but battlefields aren't the only way to defeat the opposing king and put oneself in power. For one thing, the conqueror may come from inside the country instead of the next kingdom over."

"Careful, Mercedes."

I shook my head to show him that I wasn't about to blab anything I shouldn't, and clarified, "I mean, it's not how *I* would go about making myself king—even if I had my own army, which I don't."

My boss's eyes sparkled with uncommon mischief. "It would be far easier for you to marry the king."

"That wouldn't make *me* king, only consort—and he already has an heir."

My boss nodded, giving up the point but countering, "You could be the power behind the throne, which is much more effective and much less dangerous than sitting upon it." He held up one of my pawns—white this time—and placed it on his side of the board. "Queen me. An excellent analogy."

I put another pawn next to his. "King me," I said. "Except you can't do that in chess, can you."

He took the pawn and began setting up the board again, so he could trounce me a seventh time. Like he needed the practice.

"As I see it," I said, "there are two ways to make yourself king: by force or by invitation. Using force requires an army behind you, and unless that army is so overwhelmingly enormous that the other side surrenders immediately, you're looking at heavy casualties, broken morale, and unstable politics. You leave the losing side terrified and the winning side in danger of rebellion. If you make yourself king that way, you'd better be darn sure of your power, the loyalty of your subordinates, and your ability to protect yourself."

"A king only rules by consent of his people," my boss murmured, for the moment distracted from beginning the game. "Go on."

"That leaves invitation. Don't make yourself king—convince everyone else to make you king. A propaganda campaign helps, but you need something to back it up. Say the country has an imminent disaster—you can create one if there isn't anything available. Solve that disaster, and everyone is happy, you're lauded as a hero . . . and you've got a foothold. Time for a new crisis that only you can solve."

"Like the Roman dictators," my boss said.

I blinked at him. I'm mostly accustomed to my boss's tremendous breadth of knowledge, but since military history and strategy are *my* area of expertise, I'd thought for once—

"In times of crisis, the Senate would elect a temporary dictator," my boss explained, taking my surprise for confusion, "that is, a military commander, for a term to solve the crisis. Typically, the dictator—Julius Caesar did this—would solve the problem and then refuse to give up power."

"Basically, yes," I said. "Except that instead of seizing power as they did—which goes back to making myself king—I'd simply keep the crises going until they begged me to stay for good. Between solving crises, my propaganda campaigns, and a few surgical assassinations, I'd become and remain king through popular demand. We're assum-

ing, of course, that I have the intelligence, knowledge, personal cha-
risma, and lack of morals to achieve this."

My boss smiled indulgently and moved a pawn. "All in all, wonderfully analogous to chess: moving people in predictable patterns
toward a final goal."

"Personally," I said, "I prefer capture the flag. Or murder in the
dark."

This train ran right to the border, which it reached at 2:58 a.m. There,
adventurous souls could hire ponies and guides to take them across
Plisp to Vela or Akter. Personally, I've never seen much appeal in traveling that way—through the wastes and past the wind-warped trees of
the neutral territory connecting our nations—when there are perfectly
serviceable ferries. But maybe one day I'd buy a really good wind-
breaker, travel to the southernmost outcropping of Plisp, and look
toward the South Pole—just to be able to say I had.

My boss and I weren't traveling as far as the border tonight: we
reached our stop at 2:25 a.m. Frigid night air whipped my breath away
as I stepped out onto the platform, and I instantly wished I'd brought a
ski mask after all. We were a good 150 miles closer to the Pole here,
and I hadn't realized how big a difference that'd make. I turned up my
collar and jammed on my hat before looking over to my boss, who was
calmly hiding his luminously pale face under a woolly green scarf.

No one else had alighted with us. There wasn't anywhere to miss
them; the platform was only a platform, without a ticket booth or shelter anywhere to be seen. No one in their right mind would arrive here
at half past two in the morning, with no light beyond a single orange
lamp and no possibility of a taxi.

As the train rumbled off, I hiked up my backpack and followed my
boss down old wooden steps and toward the town beyond.

"Town," by the way, is a misnomer. Edenfield Prefecture's capital
is by far the dinkiest in Carina. It's called Gjerde, and it has 171 inhabitants, most of whom spend three-quarters of the year away on border
duty. The train station was built about a century ago by some optimistic but unrealistic soul who'd placed it a mile outside of town to allow

for expansion.

He'd have been better off laying the tracks through the center of town to allow for contraction. Edenfield has the smallest population of any prefecture but the third largest landmass (after Canopus and Batata). The bays separating Carina from her neighbors are at their narrowest here, which means that Edenfield effectively borders Akter and Vela on three sides. Those able-bodied men and women who aren't lumberjacks are border patrollers—some knights, some lower-ranking prefectsmen, all underpaid and overworked.

Hopefully, that meant there would be few to no knights guarding the prefect's manor. That, along with the prefect's general character, the manor's isolation, and the distance from Avior and Lindo Prefectures, was why my boss had chosen it.

I could have done with it being less cold, though.

Gjerde hadn't sprung for streetlamps any more than its train station had, so our way was lit only by a half moon and a sky full of stars—plenty of light to see by, but not enough that we had to worry about being seen.

The town came and passed in a single block of houses, a church, and a general store, and then the road narrowed to a paved lane. Woods crept in on either side—beech trees with plenty of room for gloomy paths beneath their ancient trunks and not much in the way of undergrowth. The sort of woods that are great for walking through and terrible for hiding in.

We'd completed our third mile, and I was warm going on hot, when the paved lane spilled into a wide gravel loop. The tree line spilled away too, as if pushed back by trolls to make room for a lawn on either side of the manor.

Edenfield Manor. I'd never seen it in person before, but I couldn't have mistaken it for anything else. It loomed out of the darkness, white-painted wood interrupted by dark crosshatching and curtained windows. My initial impression was that the manor stretched into the distance, staggeringly enormous, ferociously forbidding.

"It is built into the hillside," my boss murmured, almost too low to catch. "There is the knighthouse." He pointed left, and I picked it out with difficulty.

"It looks empty," I commented, no louder than he. The knighthouse had been built to match the manor and stood slightly detached from its northeast corner. It was unlit and smaller than my apartment, both of which facts struck me as promising.

My boss contemplated the manor, comparing it to the information he'd dug up on it and drawing various conclusions. Then he nodded and indicated the left side.

My eyebrows went up. Personally, I'd have picked the side without the knighthouse, but no doubt he knew something I didn't. Anyway, this wasn't the time to argue about it.

I headed due east into the trees, on the theory that staying behind a layer of them would make me less visible than striding directly across the lawn. Plant debris softened my footfalls, and the gentle sounds of a woods at night shielded me—though I suspected no one was watching anyway.

I circled the lawn until I came up against the hillside. It was mostly dirt and rock down here, but it climbed suddenly and steeply—too steeply to easily scale—and it stretched up into the line of mountains that protected the south and east edges of Edenfield from Plisp's brutal winds. The manor wasn't so big, in comparison.

Starlight gleamed off three windows on the ground floor, two more above that, and two on the top level. The crosshatching stuck out enough that I thought I could climb it to an upper window, especially if I left the backpack behind. On the whole, though, I preferred sticking to the ground floor.

I edged along the side of the manor and pressed my nose to the first window. Moonlight shone through the curtain crack, illuminating a slash of rumpled bedding. An ear to the window confirmed that it was occupied by either a vacuum cleaner or a sleeper who snored like one.

I moved on to the next window, which was to the same bedroom, and then to a third. The curtains on this third were properly closed, but an ear to the glass met with silence. Either the room was empty or the sleeper didn't snore—and the latter was almost as good as the former. Snoring means shallow, unhealthy sleep that's easy to disturb. Silent sleepers are deep sleepers: easier to wake than the dead, but not by much.

I ran my fingers around the window frame and grinned. It must've been older than the rail station, and no one had bothered to upgrade it. Who'd break in to Edenfield Manor?

Glad my boss couldn't see me (he thought I was looking for unlocked entrances), I jimmied the window, swept aside the curtain—and found another bedroom. Twin beds, unnecessarily disturbing lemur clock, and . . . no sleepers. A children's room without children. The current prefect had never married.

In other words, a perfect room for clambering into.

There wasn't any light to speak of in the hallway, but I didn't dare use my flashlight yet. I felt my way along the wall to each room, mentally mapping and cataloging. I listened intently before opening doors, and none were locked.

It didn't take long to establish that the east wing was the family suite. In addition to the bedrooms—the occupied one surely belonged to Lord Bo Holst, the current Prefect Edenfield—I found a study, various closets and bathrooms, and stairs to the cellar.

(I didn't go down. The gust of damp and mold told me everything I needed to know.)

Between east and west wings was an open area: foyer to the north, sitting room on one side of the front entrance, and coat closet on the other. Opposite were the main stairs and the dining room, which connected to the kitchen.

The kitchen began the west wing, which also included servants' quarters (occupied by elderly breathing—the Gulbransens, according to my boss), servants' stairs, conference room, and two-car garage.

No one was awake on the ground floor, and if anyone was awake on the others, he was staying awfully quiet.

I felt my way back to the front entrance and peered out the peephole before silently unlocking the door and pulling it open. My boss arrived a few seconds later to slip inside and follow me to the conference room. He used the flashlight—he's not the kind of man who goes fumbling through the dark, and taking his sleeve would have been an unpardonable liberty. Anyway, I was sure enough by then that no one was about to catch us. But I did hold off flicking on the overhead light until I'd secured the shutters and curtains. Then, without hurrying— there wasn't enough time to make mistakes—my boss set up the equipment while I watched.

"I found the basement," I told him while he worked. "It's extremely damp."

Too damp, in fact, to plant spy equipment with any expectation of it still functioning in two weeks' time. I can't pretend I was sorry about that. Basements might be more suitably creepy than other rooms, but I hate them. Always have.

"We will use the attic then," my boss said. "Lead on."

I returned the windows to their previous state and guided him to the main stairs.

Every prefect's manor is designed to host the yearly prefects' conference, which means nine spare bedrooms: enough for eight visiting prefects and the king. The prefects aren't allowed to bring extra personnel, not even their head knights. The king can bring anyone he wants, but if that's more than a few bodyguards, they'll have to camp outside or stay in town.

I expected the extra bedrooms were what we'd find on the second floor, and I was right: eight nice but simple suites, one lavish suite, and a back area with servants' stair, laundry room, and linen closet. The main staircase ended on the second floor, but the servants' stairs continued up.

Eureka.

The attic had clearly been designed with serving quarters in mind, probably to cope with extra staff during conference time, but the accumulation of dust spoke of decades since Edenfield could afford such luxuries. There were a few pieces of extra furniture, mostly threadbare, and a small collection of trash from neglected years gone by. The area by the stairs was the only reasonably clear space in the attic—although the dust ensured that we'd have to be wary of leaving traces.

As in the conference room, my boss worked precisely and assiduously, triple checking everything while I kept watch. It was nearly five in the morning when he finished. I felt dirty, satisfied, and like I might topple over if I let my eyes close for too long. I thought about the hour-long walk back to the train station, how cold it was, and how much I didn't want to sit on the platform for half an hour waiting for the train.

"There should be an extra bedroom in the family wing," my boss told me.

I caught my eyelids sagging, squeezed them shut and open, and made myself stand straight. "That's right. It's how I got in."

"Good. Plant this"—he handed me a device about the length of my thumb, with a memory card and a speaker—"in the bottom drawer of a dresser. I will erase my traces here and meet you by the road."

I hiked up my backpack, pulled my hat back on, and headed down the servants' stairs, through the kitchen and dining room, into the main area, and toward the children's room. I was about to pass the prefect's bedroom when the front door clicked open.

I blame my fatigue for what happened next. I thought at first it was my boss leaving, then realized it couldn't be: whoever it was was coming *in*. It wasn't anyone who should've been here, either. The innocent use light switches, not flashlights, and they don't creep into manors at night in socked feet.

It took my brain so much time to process this that I didn't hurry on to the children's room: I threw myself across the hallway into the room opposite the prefect's and quivered behind the door, watching through the crack.

The flashlight was more like a penlight, a narrow beam that stayed steadily before even feet. The intruder wasn't hunting around: he or she had a definite goal, and knew how to get there. And by "there," I mean "this way."

I shrank back, realizing that I'd chosen Edenfield's office to hide in. The room that, no doubt, held the most sensitive documents.

I scurried around, desperate for a place to hide. The closet? Under the desk? No *time*. I dove behind a wingback chair and huddled against the soft old fabric.

The footsteps stopped outside the door, and the beam of light flicked off. A pause, the faint rattle of . . . a turning doorknob?

That wasn't right; I'd left the office door cracked open. Was the intruder in the room with me, closing the door? The sounds were too distant. Then where—?

The prefect's bedroom.

I shoved a hand over my mouth to stop myself from exclaiming. Was this—could it be another assassination? But who would want to kill Prefect Edenfield?

I crept out from behind the wingback chair, feeling my knees creak, and squinted through the door crack. The intruder was definitely in the prefect's bedroom; he or she had left the door slightly open.

I licked my lips. I should do something. Yell and turn on the lights, stop the intruder in his or her tracks.

But ... me, against an armed intruder? With only a sleeping prefect on my side? *There* was a recipe for suicide. I needed law enforcement. The reeves ... what, in the distant town? Or maybe the study phone had a direct line to the knighthouse ... which I was pretty sure was empty. Besides, the phone would be noisy, and if I used my phone to text, I could look forward to a few decades in prison for breaking into a prefect's manor, and it would be too late to save the prefect anyway.

The prefect's door opened wide again, and out came the intruder, moving with the sort of catlike stealth that told me a one-on-one would definitely have ended badly for me.

A scarce ten seconds had passed. With great care, the intruder shut the door and padded off, penlight steady, steps sure, never knowing I was there.

I waited, heart in my throat and ears peeled, until the front door opened and closed again. Then I kept waiting, in case he came back. A minute, two, and I couldn't bear it any longer. I sidled across the hallway and eased open the prefect's door.

I'd been wrong, before. He didn't snore like a vacuum cleaner: he snored like an airplane engine. Whatever the intruder had done, it hadn't been murder.

So that was that. But I couldn't stop wondering about it, while planting the receiver in the children's room, during the whole cold walk back to the train station. And for once, my boss didn't know any more on the topic than I did.

INTERLUDE

King Emil settled himself gingerly into a gorgeously plush armchair, its rough skeleton hidden beneath countless layers of padding. His care was extreme, but not as extreme as was his habit, because today he'd realized that he was (probably) not made of glass.

The realization had struck him with the first rays of morning light. He'd stared raptly at those rays as they streamed through the window, as they'd turned motes of dust and dead skin into glittering sparks, as they'd spread languorously over the sea-weathered knuckles of his hand—spread that far, and no further. When he lifted his hand, he saw the shadow it cast.

Emil's eyes turned wonderingly back to the window. Light had no trouble passing through it, because glass was transparent. Even colored glass filtered light through. But his hand cast a shadow. He was not transparent; light could not pass through him. Therefore, it logically followed that he could not be made of glass.

Was it possible? Emil drew back his silk bed sheets and approached the mirror, delicately avoiding the corners of the mattress. He'd had the bedposts removed ages ago, and his mattress was wholly down, without any structure inside, but he did not trust it. He did not trust the mirror either, and he stopped three feet short of it to examine himself.

The mirror confirmed it: he was not transparent. If he had had more prominent ears or a flashlight to hold behind his fingertips, he might have come to a different conclusion; but he had neither of these, and so he pronounced himself *not glass* with all the ebullience that caution would permit.

It would not do to test his theory too far, in case it proved false: the consequences of such a mistake would be dire. But even so, it was with a lighter heart and a heavier step than yesterday that King Emil allowed his valet to usher him to breakfast and thence into the care of his chancellor and his chancellor's regrettable regimen of morning meetings.

"What first?" he asked, comfortably snuggled into his plush armchair.

"Your high marshal has completed his report," replied the chancellor.

"Hasn't he given up looking for trouble?" asked the royal secretary, the third and final person in the room.

The chancellor sent him a moue of disgust. "Looking for trouble is his job."

"And he savors it so."

The chancellor dismissed this comment by turning back to the king. "Sire, may I bring him in?"

Personally, Emil agreed with the royal secretary's analysis of the high marshal—a man who was, to the king's mind, crafted of stainless steel and therefore a dangerous man to approach too closely. But his chancellor had long ago ground kingly duties into Emil's mind, and so he said, "Bring him in."

The high marshal, captain of the kingsmen and head of Carina's military, had held his position for six years and looked the part. He stood a head taller than anyone else in the room, and his torso filled out his stiff white uniform impressively. His face was lean and rather handsome, and his eyes conveyed moderate military intelligence. At the chancellor's invitation, he marched into the room and dropped to one knee a calculated ten feet away from the king—distant enough that even Emil could not feel threatened.

"Rise and speak," Emil said.

The high marshal snapped to his feet. "Sire," he announced, "fresh reports from Lindo Prefecture."

Slivers of displeasure punctured Emil's good mood. "Go on."

"Renovations on Lindo Manor continue apace," the high marshal announced—he was the sort of man who announced everything. "Secrecy greater than ever." With martial precision, he went on to enumerate what his agent, tucked up cozily with Prefect Lindo, had discovered. Most was highly suggestive, but none of it, Emil established with relief, was definite or convicting. True, it was strange that Lindo had chosen now to install a maze of secret passages ... but private escape routes were nothing new for prefect manors; they all had them. As for the added defenses, trick staircases, murder holes, traps, cubbies ... sure, they were melodramatic, but they spoke of paranoia, not treason.

"People are always complaining to me about our neighbors' growing hostility," the king commented. "Lindo Manor isn't far off the Bay of Uror; if Prefect Lindo believes the reports, this must be her attempt to shore up her defenses against Akter. It's ridiculous to think she'd go to such excesses to murder me. She's a sensible woman, and I am but one man—even if I am king."

"Revenge is a powerful motivator," said the high marshal. "Prefect Lindo would not be the first person to go overboard to ensure success—and Prefect Lindo has never been known for the subtlety of her anger. Hear me, Your Majesty: my agent is certain on this front. Prefect Lindo is planning treason, and almost certainly in the form of an assault upon your person."

King Emil was not subtle in his anger either. His eyes blazed, and his hands balled into fists. "For a lowly agent to accuse a prefect is beyond presumption!" he cried. "Where are her proofs? That Graça prepares her manor for the conference and for her own defense? What prefect would not do as much? That she has emotions—that she burns with fury at herself and at me? Anger is not disloyalty, and hers is well earned!"

"My agent insists," the high marshal persevered, "that this anger is of the dangerous variety." He returned to one knee, extending the steel rods of his arms at Emil. "Sire, we implore you not to underestimate her."

A delicate cough captured the king's attention, and he turned to his royal secretary. More and more, over the years, Emil had placed his reliance on the royal secretary's sound advice, even to the extent of inviting him to meetings that had traditionally been restricted to the chancellor. Only the chancellor had dared question this, and then only once. "Our royal secretary is to be our voice to the people," the king had explained on that occasion. "It is his place to convey our will; and so, he must know what that will is. It is your place to administer that will—not to question it."

"Lord Secretary," said the king, on this present occasion. "Speak."

"With respect, Your Majesty," said the royal secretary, "although sensible when calm, Prefect Lindo is famously of a neurotic tendency, which explains much of her sudden angers. Yet she seldom remains angry long, and too many years have passed for her to now hold any irrational belief that you were responsible for her sister's demise. If it be true, as your high marshal and chancellor would insist, that her preparations reflect something other than fear and stress, let them represent her apology and her assurances of fidelity: she is eager to ensure Your Majesty's safety, and thus she prepares her manor against outside attack. Her renovations should be applauded, not deplored!"

"High Marshal?" King Emil prompted.

The stainless steel soldier hesitated, reluctant to contradict the royal secretary. "My agent is good," he said. "I haven't witnessed the situation first hand, but the possibility she has made a mistake—"

"Is greatly heightened," put in the royal secretary, "by her being a spy. She has been trained to be suspicious and to see conspiracy everywhere. Is it any surprise that she does?"

"Spies are trained not to blind themselves against conspiracy, not to see it where it is not," said the chancellor, and Emil found his gaze sliding that way. There was something, he'd often thought, between these two—some rooted dislike, although rooted in what he could not say. Jealousy or competition? Or maybe their constant disagreements originated more simply in a difference of character: the royal secretary's drama, panache, widow's peak, and unfortunate taste for red satin-lined opera cloaks gave him rather the look of a cartoon villain. By contrast, the chancellor's sensible gray tweed and measured tones pronounced him a restrained and honest man.

Strangely enough, this restraint was the very reason Emil did not wholly trust his chancellor. It seemed to him that the man was trying too hard. A truly honest man wouldn't have to put on a show of stead-fastness; he would twirl his mustache and cackle without fear of judg-ment. Only a man with something to hide would flagellate himself into wearing tweed.

The chancellor continued. "This isn't the first time we've sus-pected the prefects—and Prefect Lindo particularly—of plotting against Your Majesty. It fits the pattern."

"Patterns," scoffed Emil. "We will not move against Prefect Lindo without absolute proof."

"Then let us get you that proof," the chancellor urged. "Send me with a contingent of kingsmen, and I will bring it to you. Or send the valorous high marshal."

The royal secretary stroked his pointed beard. "Extreme measures, my lord—far out of proportion with the evidence of the report, which is neither impressive nor convincing."

"I find it to be both."

"Gentlemen, enough," Emil commanded. "We appreciate your vehemence on our behalf, but we'd prefer your wise suggestions. We would seek proof, but not in such a manner as to offend, provoke, or accuse."

The royal secretary bowed. "Your Majesty is wise not to antago-nize Prefect Lindo. A simple approach would be best—although its primary benefit would be to set my lord chancellor's mind at ease, so he can concentrate on his actual work. Why not summon Prefect Lindo and simply ask her about these"—his fingers flicked contemptu-ously at the high marshal—"rumors? When she denies them, allow her to renew her oath of fealty to Your Majesty. That should more than suffice."

"A woman who has broken one vow will break another," the chan-cellor pronounced gravely.

"We will have you recall that this woman is a prefect, Lord Chan-cellor," Emil snapped, "not a commoner, and demands the respect of her station. Our royal secretary's suggestion pleases us."

The chancellor's lips compressed, as humorless as his tweed. "I beg you, sire: take no risks. Meet her not alone. Prefect Lindo can re-cover from any offense you give, real or imagined, but you cannot recover from death."

"If she is indeed faithful, as she surely is," the royal secretary retorted, "dealing such a great offense might change that."

"Then she is not a worthy prefect."

"And that is your response? To scorn her? Are your coffers so great, my lord, your knights so plentiful that you could guard our borders against the combined powers of Vela and Akter, should it come to that? Can you replace her?"

"I would rather attempt to replace Prefect Lindo than His Majesty."

"Enough!" Emil bellowed, slamming down his open palm on the plush arm of his chair and pushing himself to his feet. "We have made up our mind, and we will not have you bickering like children before our high marshal! Lord Secretary, summon Prefect Lindo to attend us tomorrow. Lord Chancellor, arrange time in our schedule. Now, be gone with you both!"

His advisors bowed, one pleased, one not, and took the high marshal with them.

Emil did not observe them go; the entirety of his mind had turned to horror. It had dawned upon him that sometimes glass vessels were filled with another substance, such as colored sand, and that this substance would hide the glass's transparency.

He stared aghast at the hand he had slammed down, paralyzed by how close he'd come to spilling the precious grains inside.

Chapter 3:

UNDER-THE-TABLE DEALING

My boss announced, "I will drive myself today."

I stopped, one arm in my coat sleeve, to stare at him. He did not appear to be ill. His fair skin had not deepened into the particularly disturbing bluish shade it'd had when he'd come down with pneumonia or the greenish-yellow one it'd had that awful time I'd gotten us food from the Curry Bowl. Besides, on the former occasion, he'd had me drive him to the hospital and deal with the formalities, and on the latter he'd barely left the bathroom once before midnight. On neither occasion had he offered to let me go home so he could drive himself and save me the trouble of waiting—not that I'd have taken him up on it, if he had.

"Marta will provide you with a copy of the bus schedule," he went on, locking his drawer. "The 2A bus will stop across the street in six minutes. Take that, then transfer to the 12. You have plenty of time to make it."

As far as I knew, he couldn't even drive; I'd never seen him behind the wheel. He owned the car I drove him in, a luxurious vehicle he must've been on the waiting list for forever to get. Its only minor inconvenience was that the wheel was on the left, and I'd always assumed he'd left it that way because he wasn't the one driving. Certainly he hadn't driven since hiring me. He hadn't had the chance: the car lived in a parking garage two blocks from my home, the better for me to chauffeur him back and forth to work.

I'd never asked what he did on the weekends. Stay home? Take taxis? I tried to picture him on the bus, and my brain shorted out. Seeing him use his every-bell-and-whistle phone was weird enough.

"Is there a problem, Mercedes?" my boss asked, uncharacteristically tart. "You have turned into a goldfish."

His eyes were shifty. Since when had he been afraid of making eye contact? Something was definitely up, and asking would only get me stonewalled. But I had an advantage: he didn't want me to know what was wrong, and would avoid admitting anything was wrong, if he could.

"Less like a goldfish and more like a light bulb," I said. "See, I can only imagine one reason you'd consider sending me on a long, winding bus ride as a favor: you plan to be out really late. So late that even the bus would be faster. Which is very considerate of you, except that on this particular evening, I'd do just about anything to be out a few extra hours."

He seemed ready to answer and shut me down, so I hurried on with a mix of half-truths and round-eyed desperation.

"Luc's on a cooking strike. I know that doesn't sound that bad, but you've never seen what Francis does to the kitchen. *Especially* when he's been broken up with. Doesn't matter if he's dated the girl for one evening or six months; he's just as bad. I can't even sneak in and grab cereal, not unless I want to be shouted and wailed at and used as a crying pillow through half the night. I'm hardened to it by now, but it's still pretty horrible. I was going to go home and face it, because I'm not quite mean enough to actively go out again to avoid him, but if I had an excuse—" I spun the keys around my finger and then clutched them, gazing hopefully, shoulders compressed down, hair falling over my neck. "Please don't make me go back to that. I'd rather drive you around all night long than pretend I'm sorry Her Vapidity left him."

My boss is not a man who enjoys other people's outbursts of emotion. His usual response to one of Sr. Basile's fits is to say something harsh and find any excuse to leave. He's also classically trained to respond to feminine vulnerability. I could never play him as hard as Prefect Avior and have him believe it, but I could see him wavering.

"Besides," I added with a shy, puckish smile, "endangering the lives of pedestrians is a job for a professional."

He folded. He didn't give me the address—in retrospect, I'm not sure he knew it—but every few minutes he told me to turn left or right or stay in such-and-such lane, and did it nearly as well as my GPS. Aside from guiding me through the mind-boggling traffic patterns that Silvertip City had paid some fool to design, he didn't say a word, and he didn't look at me.

That was almost as worrying as the idea of him driving. The morning drive is his time to read the newspaper; the evening drive is his time to exposit on whatever he's been learning about. He'd been telling me about Coptic recently, although I'd sensed a shift toward the gravitational influence of astral bodies on the feasibility of space travel.

Don't ask me how those two are related.

But my point is that the way my boss was staring wordlessly at the road, without even that faraway look he gets when working out a cipher in his head, was about the most disturbing thing I'd ever seen.

"I have a meeting," my boss said, interrupting my silent brooding.

"A meeting, eh?" I said, with exaggerated sage nodding. "I too drive in circles, snakes, backtracks, and zigzags when going to meetings. Every day, in fact, on my way to work. Seriously, Silvertip. What were you thinking?"

"The meeting," he said, "is located in a private auction house. Entrance is by invitation only."

Translation: I wasn't invited. I grinned over at him anyway. "I'd certainly hate to go in and interrupt all that important bidding on marvelous works of art, ugly antiques, and future horror movie props," I told him. "I don't mind waiting in the car. Maybe I'll find a really sketchy talk show to listen to. I never get to, when you're in the car."

"I am meeting with a seidkonur."

I shot my boss a glance of pure astonishment, got honked at, and had to concentrate on traffic for several blocks. Then I went back to being shocked.

I'd honestly not expected any explanation from my boss. Like I said, he keeps himself to himself, and I've never gotten out of him so much as whether he had a childhood pet. And if I had expected an answer, if I *had* been angling for one instead of just filling the silence with nonsense—well, this wouldn't have been it.

A seidkonur, by the way, is a woman—nearly always a woman—who practices divination. Seidr,˙ if you want to get technical. They're ... I guess you could call them traditional. Superstition claims they can find hidden things, bring good or bad luck, control the weather, and predict and manipulate the future. If you don't mind the Old Testament injunction against divination, and if you were born yesterday, I guess you might go to one for help.

There is exactly zero chance my boss did not know all this, which made the situation weirder. It explained his behavior, though: respectable, sensible men who wear suits and shine their shoes and get chauffeured around in black luxury cars do not go to see seidkonurs. And my boss was about as respectable and sensible as they got.

"I met a seidkonur once," I commented, dropping into the left lane to let an aggressive tailgater pass. "At a fair when I was a teenager. She offered to tell my fortune and give me hot tips for snagging the boy of my dreams."

"You mean you met a charlatan," my boss corrected.

"Well ... yes."

"I would not go to a charlatan."

I didn't answer. I didn't want to punish my boss's compulsive confidence, but I couldn't agree with him. Here's the thing: my boss is brilliant. I mean, really, seriously brilliant. I hadn't been lying to Avior about that. My boss is the best cryptanalyst we have—I've heard some of the others admit it, my own judgment aside. He absorbs knowledge like no one's business, and I've never caught him forgetting anything. His brain is basically a supercomputer, except that none of our supercomputers have anywhere near his flexibility nor, when it comes to ciphers, his creative problem solving ability. His brain is amazing, and I esteem it more than I can say.

But he can also be an absolute idiot when it comes to people. I mean, he fell for my doe-eyed vulnerability routine. He honestly believes the persona I present to him of a sweet, eager, butter-wouldn't-melt admirer. (Which is exactly my preference. I don't think he'd like me much, if he knew the sorts of things that actually go on

---

˙ Translator's Note: This term is consistently written not in Plishan but in Old Norse, and should be pronounced /SAY-der/.

inside my head.)

"You disapprove?" he asked, and I realized this was the reason he'd told me where we were going: he wanted reassurance.

"I'm definitely surprised," I said, "but you know I trust your judgment."

He didn't answer. I wondered if I'd offended him, but I couldn't think of what else to say. Being supportive is all well and good, but I wouldn't be doing him any favors by encouraging him to make a fool of himself. So we rode in silence for another ten minutes until he said, "On your left. Park here."

I pulled into the auction house parking lot and slid my boss's sleek car into the spot I judged safest. For the car, I mean. It was a nice car.

"Handsome building," I said, leaning on the wheel to get a good look. The auction house was two stories of alternating crimson brick and dark, reflective windows. A glass dome topped the building. It must've sent their heating bill through the roof, but I'd bet it was a great place to stargaze. "I haven't seen it before, though I've definitely been in this part of town. Is it new?"

"Thank you for driving me," my boss said, withdrawn and stiff. I'd definitely foot-in-mouthed. "You may take the car."

"Sort of misses the point of me driving you," I pointed out. "I said I didn't mind waiting. Talk shows—"

"Mercedes," my boss said, making eye contact for the first time that evening. "This is non-negotiable. Go home."

Well, drat. "Yes, sir," I said. "Have a pleasant evening."

Silvertip's street pattern is about as simple as a polyalphabetic substitution cipher with three levels of transposition. There's constantly road construction at the taxpayers' expense to "improve" the maze, which just goes to show that politicians use a different dictionary from the rest of us.

Luc and I moved to Silvertip three years ago, at Francis's behest. I'd completed my degree and was hunting for a job that didn't involve teaching or flipping crêpes, and Luc's home business had taken off enough that he could afford to move out of our parents' house. Funny how, for all of us, our primary goal had been to get away from Batata Prefecture.

After moving, one of the very first things I learned about life in Silvertip City was the necessity of a GPS. My pride rebelled, but constantly getting lost and being late for job interviews is terrific for quashing pride. It's not like I was even driving most places: after Francis got tired of my borrowing his truck, I was taking the bus most of the way and then getting lost walking the last few blocks. We're talking pathetic here.

Or not so much, considering Silvertip. You see, Silvertip has straight roads that you think ought to be curved and curved roads that ought to be straight. One-way streets abruptly go one way the opposite direction or become two way and then end at concrete pillars. Beyond anything, Silvertip is in love with circles. They call themselves boulevards, lanes, streets, drives, and roads, but they're lying. They're circles. Except when a circle would be particularly convenient.

I'm explaining all this to make it perfectly clear that what happened next was not my fault. I did everything right. I set the car's GPS, and I obeyed it. I noted familiar landmarks. I glimpsed Al's newsstand and knew that I was one block from the parking garage. The parking garage itself was actually within eyeshot when my two-way street turned one way, the wrong way, and forced me into a detour.

The GPS did not yell at me, but I detected snideness in its suggestion to turn around when possible.

I didn't lose my temper at it. That was another thing Silvertip had taught me: the GPS doesn't care.

"Recalculating," it announced. "In five-point-three miles, take your second right."

Good thing I'd started out with a full tank of gas. I turned right after five-point-three miles, took my third left, and circled three roundabouts.

"Arriving in fifty yards," the GPS informed me. "Destination on the left."

No way was I fifty yards from the parking garage. We weren't anywhere near the right part of town—this seemed to be a warehouse district near the docks. I expected that if I rolled down the window, I'd be able to smell the Gyllan River.

"You have reached your destination," the GPS informed me.

I slowed and pulled over... across the street from the bricks and mirrored windows of the auction house. "Don't tempt me," I muttered at the glass dome glinting mysteriously in the streaks of red and gold sky.

Had my boss really gone to consult a seidkonur? The more I thought about it, the more unlikely it sounded. But he *had* been uncomfortable, so the story he told me fit. Besides—what would he find so embarrassing that he'd think a seidkonur the less shameful story? And why had he felt compelled to tell me anything instead of maintaining his usual closed lips?

I grabbed the GPS and poked at it to stop myself from giving in to my desire to march inside the auction house and find out what was going on. I figured the GPS had gotten confused when I'd missed my original destination—*thank* you, Silvertip—and so had redirected me back here. "Dear confused, sorry GPS," I said to it, "we're going to attempt a different route. *Try* not to bring me back here, or you're going to be demoted."

As it calculated, I pulled back out. Traffic had vanished at some point—I guess everyone who worked around here had already headed home—so I had enough concentration to do as I had threatened and search the radio for a talk show.

"—honey, if you know your boyfriend's unfaithful—"

"—God's unending love in your life—"

"—have to make an example of them. If Vela believes—"

This street . . . wasn't right. I pulled over again and took a good look at the GPS map, but it still said the correct destination. I had asked it for a detour, I supposed, and if it was compensating for traffic, this might really be the fastest route. Certainly, the roads were abandoned enough.

Suspicious but willing to play along, I kept following the GPS's directions. Left, right, ahead, keep—

"Oh, come *on*," I complained as we arrived back in front of the auction house. "I warned you!"

Once again, what happened next was not my fault. I did everything right. I used my phone's GPS app and set the address for the parking garage. But once again, I ended up back at the auction house.

By this point, I was far too frustrated for talk shows and had turned to Japanese metal and then given up on the radio entirely—and things only got worse. They went like this:

I set the address for my home, in case the parking garage was just too tricky, and ended up back at the auction house. I set the car and phone GPSes simultaneously for Tey Prefecture, and ended up back at the auction house. I decided to rely on my imperfect memory of how we'd arrived, and ended up back at the auction house. I employed maze theory and tried taking every right turn (and ended up on a one-way street dead end, which caused some illegal maneuvering to escape), every left turn (and ended up in an endless series of concentric circles leading nowhere), and every other left-right turn (and nearly drove into the river). I tried taking the opposite turn of whatever the GPSes, in extremely improbable and unnerving synchrony, told me to do.

"Turn around when possible," they insisted. "Destination ahead. Turn around when possible. Destination on your right."

In the end, I pulled back into the auction house parking lot. It was nearly seven-thirty by that point, and the sun touched the horizon, sending brilliant rays across the sky in its swan song. All around, the streets were barren and the warehouses dark, but this parking lot was as I'd left it: half full of cars, motorcycles, and bicycles ranging from the ridiculously overpriced to the disgustingly rusted.

"I," I said aloud, "am calm, collected, and professional." I repeated the phrase once or twice more until I almost believed it, and then rang my boss.

The call went directly to voicemail.

Long meeting? Or had he just forgotten to turn his phone back on? Had he already left? Regardless, the only help I was going to get was inside that auction house.

"So you see, I have to go in," I told the dash, listening to the words to make sure they sounded convincing. "It's not nosiness: it's desperation. I need to ask for directions . . . or better yet, drive him back."

Yes, I had a cast-iron excuse for butting in. So that was one good thing to come out of this whole mess. And maybe—morning dawned on the new idea—maybe he'd be pleased about not having to take a taxi home.

Real pleasure in my boss is a joy to witness, and a rare one. Anyone who meets him can see his obviously impressive points: his cryptologic brilliance, his breadth of knowledge, his impeccable grooming. But it's the subtler, rarer aspects of him I most appreciate: the delight in his eyes when he hits upon a solution; the arid slice of his humor, too often mistaken for seriousness; the warmth of his honest praise. I'd worked for him for five months before beginning to understand him—and before beginning to perceive that most people never did.

Attempting to explain this to my brothers had been a mistake.

Just in case he turned on his phone, and to bolster my case for disobeying him, I shot him a text explaining the situation before hopping out of the car.

It really is amazing what a difference perspective can make. I practically skipped up the stairs to the dark double doors. I grabbed one heavy metal bar, and tugged.

Noise, smell, and color rushed out at me from a hot mass of humanity. The interior of the auction house was absolutely packed with people, talking or yelling and stinking of sweat, perfume, cigarettes, and a hundred other aromas rendered intolerable by thick atmosphere and overcrowding.

The people were as varied as their odors: rich and poor, young and old, pretty and plain. I heard accents from each of Carina's nine prefectures as well as from Akter and Vela and perhaps even further afield. Here was as diverse a collection of people as I'd ever encountered, and none of them paid me the least attention. So I stuck out my elbows, planted an unassailable expression across my face, and dug in.

Body heat enveloped me immediately, and I heard snippets of a dozen conversations, most of them about the weather. I elbowed my way further in, and the crowd parted enough for me to get a good look around.

The auction house's interior designer, with more extravagance than taste, had decked out the lobby in red velvet and gilt. It looked like an opera house: gaudiness and cheapness masquerading as style.

In the dead center of the lobby was a central island desk—a circular structure enclosed by ceiling-high glass and hosting four of what I assumed to be information clerks. All four were handsome, male, black-haired, and wearing a starched white uniform, gold choker, and secretive eyes.

There wasn't any furniture about, but there were doors: the exterior double doors through which I'd come, double auction-hall doors, bathrooms, and three others with plaques I couldn't read from this distance and certainly not through the crowd.

I checked around twice for my boss and didn't see him—not that I expected he'd hang about in a crowd like this. Even under ordinary circumstances, he hates crowds, but this crowd struck me as having a particularly unhealthy atmosphere. Why was everyone out here anyway, instead of in the auction hall?

I shook my head and elbowed my way past a sequined woman and a pajamaed teen to the nearest information clerk. Like most men, this one was a head taller than me despite my power heels. "Hello!" I shouted, pitching my voice to cut through crowd and glass. "I'm looking for someone! He had a meeting!"

The clerk tapped the glass, where someone had taped a schedule of the day's auctions. Dubious, I read the schedule. It was distinctly lacking in useful information, such as "Jon Nordfeld is behind Door 3," but it did tell me exactly when I'd need to bid if I wanted an eighteenth-century distressed mirror (the schedule didn't say what had upset it) or a bottle of wine older than my Akterian grandfather.

"No!" I shouted through the glass. "I'm looking for the meeting room. Meeting room!"

It was no good. The clerk should have worked for the Carinan Security Service, he was so good at not changing his expression. I needed a different tactic—and someone who could actually hear me.

In an instant, I'd dumped my businesslike pose. I curled inward, and looked around with wide eyes, vulnerable and helpless.

It took approximately 1.8 seconds for a man in a tux to come to my rescue. He had gelled silver-fox hair, manicured nails, and the air of an aging film star. "Are you lost?" he asked—or that's how I read his lips. He bent toward me, all concern and slightly closer than the crowd justified.

"I'm supposed to go to the meeting room," I explained, neck exposed, eyes blinking through the shadow of my lashes. "But I've never been here before."

"Come with me," he said, taking my arm. He led me through the crowd, free arm held before us to protect me as I shrank in close. This method was distinctly less effective than my elbows, but I wanted to let him feel useful. We arrived at the door labeled UPPER ROOMS, which he propelled me through and then shut behind us.

The noise cut off. Not a hundred percent, but close. That was some serious soundproofing there.

"Phew," I said, smiling up at him. "The fire department would have a fit if it knew about that."

"It's not usually this crowded," he apologized. "They'll be back in the auction hall soon enough—once the private items have been sold."

I continued oozing charm. "Then thank you even more for taking the time to help me out. I hope it won't make you late—but I guess we'd better hurry. The meeting room must be . . . this way?"

I was playing my role, but, aging-actor look or not, the man failed the chivalrous part I'd assigned him. He didn't budge. His face took on a sly look more suited for a villain as he said, "I'd be happy to take you the rest of the way. I'm sure we can come to an arrangement."

I processed this in a blink. Being creepily propositioned by strange men isn't that unusual for me—it's just one of the reasons I'm not big on public transport—but the men who try it immediately upon meeting me usually have worse teeth. I'd have to reevaluate my damsel-in-distress signal. "No," I said.

"Nothing comes without a price," he informed me, "and I am a reasonable man."

My fingers crept into my handbag. "Tell you what," I said, "I'll find my own way. That reasonable enough for you?"

He reached out to pat my shoulder, and I stepped back sharply, exchanging my scrunched shoulders and tilted head for square-on alpha posing, vulnerability erased. He twitched, but he didn't give up. "I led you this far," he said. "You owe me for that, even if you go the rest of the way alone . . . and I wouldn't advise going alone."

I removed the pepper spray from my purse, and made sure he saw me thumbing off the safety.

"Hey!" he cried. "Come on, don't—there's no need for *that.* I did you a favor—"

"Out," I ordered, not raising my voice. "Back to the lobby."

The man shrank back, feeling for the doorknob. "You wouldn't really spray me, would you?" he said, attempting a smile.

I stayed where I was, pepper spray in a steady hand. "Out."

It was almost enough to make me feel bad, how much he crumpled. But he had his pride to satisfy, and he rallied. "With that attitude," he warned, "no one will want to make a deal with you. The proprietress doesn't like people who don't keep their bargains."

"Three," I said. "Two."

He whipped the door open in a gust of noise and sweat, and slammed it between us.

I waited a ten count before lowering the pepper spray, heart racing. Funny, how being small and young-looking makes the predators of the world think you're easy prey.

More fool they. Larger women—those who almost never get perved on—are generally far gentler and more naïve than we small ones. They don't have to learn viciousness in the cradle.

I replaced the pepper spray in its easy-access holster and continued inward. The hallway wasn't long—only a couple of dozen steps—and it ended at a steep, well-trod spiral staircase. Up I went, and pushed through the heavy fire door at the top.

The room beyond was windowless but brightly lit with sunny yellow lights. Milling people scrutinized displays, murmuring to themselves and to one another, scrawling numbers on silent-auction forms. Occasionally, a high-pitched laugh edged with hysteria interrupted the dignity of the proceedings, and everyone pretended they hadn't heard it.

Like in the lobby, here was a wide variety of humanity; but here, the offness of the people struck me more, and gave them a certain uniformity. I couldn't identify what, exactly, was bothering me—and I was too distracted to try.

The interior decorator had really outdone himself. Everything was green. Grassy carpet, emerald velvet displays and damask wallpaper, avocado ceiling. The furniture had been painted green and bore green cushions. The items for auction, although admittedly not always green, were nature themed: exotic flowers, gems, and . . . living creatures.

I didn't recognize most of the animals, but I was pretty sure the ones I did recognize were endangered or non-native. Although not behind glass—they were tethered or in fine-mesh wire cages—they made no noise and no attempt to escape.

Forget the fire marshal. I'd be contacting Animal Welfare the moment I got out of here.

I walked on, not caring to ask anyone which way. The sorts of people who came to bid in a place like this weren't ones to whom I'd like to be beholden, even for directions. Besides, there was only one exit. It wasn't like I could get lost.

I turned through a curtained arch and into a room as blue as the first one had been green. Appropriately enough, this one was filled with water-themed merchandise—from shells to fish to miniature ships. The room after that was purple and sold cloth, sewing machines, and (unless I was misunderstanding) seamstresses. Then came a pink room decked out like a child's play area; then a red room like a beauty salon, if beauty salons carried liposuction machines, plastic surgeons, and disturbingly real-looking replacement noses, eyeballs, ears, and fingernails.

That red room was the worst so far, but each of the rooms was horrible. The change was gradual, from green to red, but you couldn't miss it. Room by room, the conversation faded and the faces became more drawn: the skin grayer, the eyes bleaker. If I'd seen anyone from that red room on the street, I'd have thought him a heroin addict. As it was, I suspected the addiction of choice was something else.

And I had not yet found my boss, who had gone this way. Who had not wanted me to tag along. Who had seemed nervous.

Swallowing hard, I wiped my hands on my skirt and passed into the next room.

I expected black or brown to be next, but it was gold: gold as vibrant and oppressive as any of the colors that had come before. There were no bidders currently in this room, although the bidding papers showed there had been. No bidders—but I was not alone.

There were eighteen podiums, and on each stood a human being clothed in gold cloth draped in the ancient Grecian style. They posed, skin painted gold.

There was an ideal for everyone, in this room, a perfect cross-section of Carinan beauty: old, middle-aged, young adult, child; short and tall; male and female. The youngest was maybe eight years old, maybe nine. She looked like she belonged in a commercial, with her cherubic cheeks and glossy locks. The paper at her feet told the story of a bidding war between two numbers. She would not look at me or speak.

The others had no problem looking; their eyes followed me across the room.

I paused again in front of the last display, the one next to the exit. The man who stood on it was about my boss's age but had a considerably more heroic build. One arm extended before him; the other reeled back, as if about to throw a discus.

"Don't you get sore, posing like that?" I asked him.

His head inclined ever so slightly, the better to stare at me. I suppose I was an irregularity in this place, not looking like a strung-out drug addict.

"If I bid on you," I said, "what would I get?"

His voice was ordinary, his accent from Hemmel Prefecture. "Me."

"You mean you'd be my slave?"

"My debt would transfer to you."

"Forever?"

He twitched a finger to indicate the bidding sheet. "Until my debt was paid off."

There was a number on the top right of the sheet that I'd taken for an item code. It was long, and I didn't have the key to decipher it.

The golden man's eyes narrowed thoughtfully. "Unless," he said, "you would like to make a private deal—just between you and me."

That was what the aged-actor type had wanted too. I reevaluated his proposition in light of this information. I still didn't know what he'd been after, but I definitely should have pepper-sprayed him.

"Make a private deal?" I echoed. "But what would the proprietress think?"

I said it to provoke a reaction, and I sure got one. His expression seized up; his eyes resumed their middle-distance stare; and I could not get him or anyone else in that room to speak to me again no matter what I said. So I left them behind.

This room had a door, not a curtained arch, and I found it was the last room on the level. Beyond it lay only a whitewashed stairwell with a whitewashed staircase going up and, at the top, a whitewashed door. The place smelled like whitewash too, and my heels clicked on the wooden floor.

I didn't go up immediately; I prefer not to rush headlong into potentially dangerous situations. So I stopped, leaned against the stair rail, and really thought.

Point one: this place was incredibly bizarre.

Point two: there weren't any guards. Half the displays must be illegal—slavery certainly was—but the auction house didn't even have a doorman to stop curious personal assistants from wandering in after their errant bosses.

Point three: nothing I'd witnessed thus far had any connection to seidr. I could definitely reject any lingering notions about my boss coming here to consult a seidkonur. Which meant whomever he had come to see must be not only much less respectable, but also much less *probable*.

Those three points were bad enough on their own, but the fourth was the worst: I had tried to leave, and I had failed. Silvertip roads are bizarre and twisted, but they don't actively change on you, and they don't mess with what satellites are telling your GPS. I could accept it if the car's GPS went out of date or wonky; things break. But for my independent phone, actively streaming updated information, to go crazy in exactly the same way as the car GPS? And my memory is generally excellent. I should have been able to find my way back on my own. Eventually.

I called my boss's phone again, and again got his voicemail.

My fingers tapped the railing. I've always been a firm believer that seidr is superstitious nonsense because magic isn't *real*. But this—this seemed like magic. The really ugly sort of magic that makes you crave it more and more even as it takes everything you have. The sort of magic that a man with a towering IQ might think that he could turn to his advantage because *he* wouldn't fall into the same mistakes as most people. He would be careful with his words. He wouldn't leave any exploitable loopholes in his bargaining.

Like I said, my boss is by far the most brilliant man I've ever met, but he can be a total idiot when it comes to people. And he doesn't read his fairytales.

With a feeling of coming to the end of things, I climbed the stairs and pushed into the room beyond.

Chapter 4:

EXTORTION

The proprietress, like the room, was dressed in white. The sun had nearly disappeared behind the horizon, leaving the sky above the dome purple dark, and no harsh electric light intruded. Pale moonlight bathed her skin in luminescence, dimming the redness of her hair, brightening the silver of her eyes, softening the razor edges of her skirt suit. She was very tall and very beautiful and very regal. *Be in awe of me*, her aura commanded, and I was in awe.

For about five seconds. That was how long it took me to catch sight of my boss. No, that's not right: I'd been looking at him this whole time; I just hadn't realized it. The proprietress held him folded over one arm, like a waiter holds a hand towel. She held him effortlessly, without wrinkling her perfect suit or bending her spine or tottering in her four-inch heels.

My boss had been folded lengthwise once and then draped evenly, but the proprietress was so tall that neither his hair nor his toes brushed the white wood floor, the same floor as in the stairwell. I kept noticing things around him, like the scrubbed emptiness of the room and the small cracks between floor and wall and dome, because it hurt to look straight at him; my eyes kept sliding off.

He didn't look any thicker than a towel, but nor did he look thinner than usual. The way he was folded, I could see slivers of his face between his meticulously buffed black shoes. His visible eye was closed, which I hoped meant he was unconscious. Magic or not, being folded up like clean laundry with your back bent at a broken-doll angle couldn't be comfortable.

Besides, although I wasn't sure what it would take to release him, I was pretty sure I didn't want him witnessing it.

"Whatever deal you made with him," I told the proprietress, "is invalid."

Her eyebrows went up disdainfully, and I was struck again by the radiance of her skin, the delicate perfection of her nose, the unearthly superiority of her lips.

I was ready for the zinger this time, and returned my most sarcastic look. "You can't have Jon Nordfeld," I said slowly, clearly. "Release him."

The proprietress held on to her glamor whammy as she let the silence stretch, trying to make me feel uncomfortable.

I didn't feel uncomfortable. I felt utterly focused, waiting for her to speak but not needing it, watching her and calculating.

When she finally spoke, her voice matched the rest of her: icy and beautiful as the ringing of silver bells. She asked: "Are you offering yourself in exchange?" She peered more closely at me and laughed— because, yes, it's written all over me. Even my boss has noticed, though he pretends he hasn't. "Do you think that will make him love you?"

Another time, her words would have bothered me. Now, I only thought, *So we aren't playing fair. That's good to know.* To the proprietress, I said, "No, of course not. But that's the point, isn't it? He doesn't love me."

"Not that I'd take you in exchange if you did offer," the proprietress mused.

"He doesn't love me," I pressed on, "but love demands a response. That's part of the nature of love. He owes me a response, but he hasn't given me one. That means he's in my debt, and being in my debt makes him mine. Since he's mine, he has no right to offer himself in exchange to you. Your deal is invalid."

My boss stirred on the proprietress's arm, as if he had heard me. The instant he moved, she snapped back, hissing in pain. He crumpled to the ground, unfolding and expanding to fill his normal space, to bend only in the ways humans are meant to bend. He groaned faintly and rolled to his side. I was by him in an instant, propping him up. He's a head taller than I am and seventy pounds heavier, so no way could I carry him. "Come on, sir," I said. "On your feet. Help me out here."

The proprietress was staring at me, holding her arm with the opposite hand. There was something brittle about her, and I didn't like the expression in those silver eyes. I wanted to get out from under it as soon as possible.

I angled my shoulder under my boss's armpit and stabilized him as he wobbled to his feet. I don't think he was exactly aware of what was going on, but he could clearly understand my murmured instructions. He stumbled where I guided him, and it was only because we were under that silvery gaze that it seemed to take so long to reach the door.

I tried the knob. I didn't make a big deal of it, shaking and pounding and crying to the heavens. I turned it once to the left, once to the right, and gave up. It was locked.

"Would you unlock this door, please?" I asked the proprietress. "I don't want to break anything."

My boss slipped through my fingers like sand. I yelped and scrabbled to grab on to him, but though I felt his jacket, his face and hair, I couldn't get a grip. With the soft sound of flowing cloth, he slid through the floor and was gone.

Fury replaced shock, flooding down my arms and morphing my fingers into claws to scratch out eyes. I clenched them to dam it, and the fury flooded back up, flushing my face and burning down through my sternum. My legs ached to leap at her, to force her, through sudden, overwhelming violence, to *give him back*.

I tamped the anger down, hard. I didn't need to see her amusement to know that she would use strong emotion, any emotion, against me. I thought of the gold room and the red, and I let my limbs relax. Voice level, neutral, I said, "Where did he go?"

The proprietress said: "Our business is not yet concluded."

"You have no further business with him," I said; "we've established that. As for me, I have no interest in making a deal with you. I came only for what is mine—and every second you keep Jon Nordfeld from me, you are stealing my property. If you had released him immediately upon recognizing your mistake, I would not have charged you—but I charge you now. If you hold what is mine, you owe me for it. Would you put yourself in my debt?"

The proprietress regarded me with two eyes like distant stars. She said: "Jon Nordfeld made a deal with me using collateral he did not own. Knowingly or not, he conned me. That puts him in *my* debt—and I always collect on my debts. Since you claim ownership of him, his debt is yours. I am holding him against that debt, to ensure its repayment."

Unlike my boss, I had read my fairytales. And so I knew that one consistent element is that making deals with fairies or demons or your supernatural creature of choice always ends badly. No matter how clever you think you are, no matter how good the deal you think you are making, they are getting the better end of it.

And the proprietress didn't play fair.

She went on: "I don't like the logic you used to free him, and I don't want it used again. Make a deal with me."

"I don't own the logic," I said. "And I'm not about to make a deal that'll prevent other people from thinking it up."

"You can prevent yourself from sharing it. Make a deal with me."

"Is it even possible for me to make a deal?" I wondered. "Do I own that right? My brothers love me, and my parents and friends and those who love their neighbors. I cannot trade myself."

"That is your logic, not theirs—and I do not ask for you, only for your silence. Make a deal with me."

"No."

The proprietress wasn't bothered by my refusal; I might as well have stayed quiet. I wondered how many of the people she'd made deals with had had their arms twisted into it. She said: "I don't like your logic. Invalidate it. Remember that you are in my debt and that I am under no obligation to do anything for you—not even unlock that door. Remember also that I hold Jon Nordfeld as collateral against your debt, and that once you are dead, your ownership reverts to him."

"You are holding me against my will," I said. "Therefore, I am within my rights to break down that door and leave—and I will accrue no debt through property damage."

The proprietress smiled. I didn't like her smile any more than I liked her stare. Less. It made me consider how awfully convenient it was that she'd been in the process of folding up my boss at the moment I'd arrived, although he'd entered the auction house two hours before I had.

She had redirected the streets to bring me here, into her territory. And then she had shown me exactly what I needed to see to engage her in her game—a game I didn't know the rules to. So what made me think I could escape even if I did break down the door?

In stories, fairies and demons *always* get the better end of the deal.

I had argued that it was within my rights to defend myself, and she hadn't contradicted me. She was a lot bigger than I was, but I had pepper spray, and I can move pretty quickly when I set my mind to it. If I attacked her—

Then she would have the right to defend herself against me, by any means at her disposal. In her domain, in power, it wouldn't be possible for me to succeed in such an attack unless it were so sudden, so violent and complete, that she couldn't react.

It might work, if my chain of logic was correct—which I was far from sure about. I could run while she was unconscious, while Silvertip's streets had no commands of hers to follow. I might even be able to escape.

But I wouldn't be able to take my boss with me.

I didn't try to hide my bitterness. "Tell me what you have in mind," I said.

If smugness were an energy source, hers could've powered Argo Navis for a week. She said: "Offer me something, and I'll tell you whether it's acceptable."

How many of those below had been given such an open-ended offer?

"Incidentally," she added, "you might consider that Jon Nordfeld knew the dangers before he came here, probably better than you do. He saw what you saw and, knowing and understanding and without the motivation of rescuing a beloved, he still came and he still made a deal with me."

"What deal?"

The corners of her lips went up. "Information is a commodity."

Guess I should've figured that. I grunted and turned my mind to the deal. Time wasn't exactly of the essence here, and if she really had been waiting for me for two hours in those heels, she could stand to wait a few more minutes. If I was going to have to make a deal in her favor, it was jolly well going to be the least in her favor as possible—and was going to leave absolutely no possibility of outstanding debt.

I went over my words about a hundred times, while the proprietress added "inhuman patience" to her list of annoying traits. Then I spoke slowly, making sure I was saying exactly what I meant to say and leaving nothing out.

"Here is the deal I offer you," I said. "On my side of it, I'll never use the logic I used against you here again; nor will I share it with anyone who does not already know it. On your side, first, you will fulfill your side of your deal with Jon Nordfeld as he would want it fulfilled but without any payment outside this deal; second, you will not seek any form of retribution or recompense, directly or indirectly, for anything either Jon Nordfeld or I have ever said or done, and you will not prevent us from leaving."

"Agreed," snapped the proprietress, almost clipping my last word, and I knew I hadn't asked for nearly enough. "You may depart."

"Not without Sr. Nordfeld," I said. "Where is he?"

She considered me, pale eyes glittering, and for a second I thought she was going to say that information was a commodity. But getting a good deal must have put her in a generous mood, because she said, "Walk directly out of this building, the way you came. Do not look back until you get outside. If you follow my directions exactly, you will see Jon Nordfeld then, in the parking lot with you, unfettered and unharmed."

This struck me as unnecessarily complicated, and was probably another way of her getting one up on me, but it also had a certain mythological ring to it.

I sidled back to the door, unwilling to turn my back to her, and the knob turned easily under my hand. She watched me, head tilted, expressionless, distant and delicate in the moonlight but making no attempt to augment her beauty. I wondered what she was.

My boss would know.

I nodded to her in acknowledgement, because it didn't hurt to be polite, and shut the door after me. It stayed shut as I tiptoed down the whitewashed stairs and into the gold room.

It was empty.

I mean *empty*. The walls and carpet were still there and still gold, but a faded and tawdry gold, the lights dimmed by half. But the golden people had vanished along with the bidding papers, the tables, and the pedestals. It smelled of dust.

I started across, neck hairs bristling, and about jumped out of my skin when a second set of footsteps began behind me, not in time with mine, soft against the carpet.

I didn't look back, but it was a close thing.

The red room was empty too. Dark stains outlined the tile floor where some of the heavier objects had rested, but they were old stains, and this room was as unused as the gold one, with its musty smell tinged with the astringent edge of chemical cleanser. Odd, considering how not-cleaned this place looked, but I wasn't in a mood to be impressed or even particularly interested.

The pink and purple rooms lay likewise: as empty, dull, and dis-used as a childhood dollhouse left in an attic while the decades sloughed by.

I quickened my pace and listened for the footsteps.

After a beat, they sped up also, but their nature changed. Before, the footsteps had been soft, measured—the steady steps of a confident man in expensive leather shoes. Now, they shuffled and limped with effort, and I became aware of another sound: a slithering, swishing, as if the walker were dragging something.

I stopped, and the footsteps stopped with me.

What, exactly, had the proprietress's instructions been? *Go directly out the way I came and don't look back before I get out.* Nothing there about not speaking to my boss.

If it was my boss. "Are you hurt?" I asked.

He didn't answer. The urge to turn around screamed up another whirlwind. I nearly gave in to it there and then, but managed to grab my phone again and call my boss instead.

Voicemail.

"You could turn your phone on," I said. "Send me a text. She never said you couldn't. And part of the deal was that she couldn't prevent us from leaving."

Still no answer. I replayed the footsteps, the slithering back in my mind, and visions of what *might* be following me swirled into the screaming whirlwind. Heat rushed into my forehead and trembled my hands with adrenaline. I shoved my phone back into my pocket before it slipped from sweating fingers.

"Bluebeard." "East of the Sun and West of the Moon." A dozen other half-remembered stories from my childhood cried, *Don't look! Never look. Never indulge your curiosity. Never—*

I started to turn.

"Don't."

The word was barely a whisper, but it was in my boss's voice. He sounded like he was in pain, like that one word had almost been beyond him.

I clenched the strap of my purse to shut myself up. As the proprietress had given me rules for leaving, so too must she have given him, and I would not cause him any unnecessary suffering by demanding answers.

I walked on, slowly, so that he would have no difficulty keeping up. I didn't have a single doubt about him throughout the blue room or the green room or descending the lower set of stairs. I proceeded with confident determination down the short hall and into the lobby. The milling people in that lobby had disappeared with the rest—but the glass-protected desk island had not. The clerks remained there, unmoving. They did not turn as I entered, and the one already facing my way had his eyes closed. He didn't look asleep, because I couldn't see his chest rising or falling. They looked like mannequins, and I had a sudden vision of the proprietress winding them up before guests arrived.

I didn't speak with them; I kept walking. I came to the double front doors and put my hand on the cool metal.

This wasn't part of the deal.

Never in my deal had we specified that I had to leave in a certain way, only that she would not prevent us from leaving. Nor did she have any right to cause my boss pain, as she had no hold over him. What right did she have to dictate to me that I could not turn around—or that he could not speak?

None. She had merely ordered me, and I had obeyed like a good little girl. And once I had left, as she had instructed, what then?

Then I would not be able to get back in. No matter how desperately I tried. I probably wouldn't even be able to find the auction house again.

Oh, I don't think so.

I turned around.

Chapter 5:

ARSON

The thing following me wore my boss's face, if you count holding a printed cardboard oval on a stick as wearing a face. The suit was better: it was the suit my boss had been wearing, although it was far more wrinkled than my boss would've allowed. The shoelaces had been tied incorrectly, and the tie had a standard knot instead of a Windsor. The voice, when it spoke, was his exactly, but it said a word he would never have permitted to sully his lips.

The thing was humanoid, but I wouldn't have called it human. Starvation had withered it to emaciation; its legs were short and spindly as a child's; and its dangling fingers nearly brushed the carpet. A fat, pulsating umbilical cord stretched from its belly back through the door to the upper rooms, glistening sickly white. There was exactly zero probability I could ever have mistaken the thing for my boss, even in the dimness of a nighttime parking lot.

But maybe, outside this building, the illusion would have become convincing. Maybe I would have happily driven this creature to my boss's apartment to live his life.

"I told you not to look," the creature whined in my boss's voice. "Why can't you people follow directions? I didn't want to kill you. This is your fault."

"An external locus of control isn't healthy," my mouth murmured as my brain rearranged itself. The adrenaline was back, but I welcomed it this time. I had a feeling I was going to need it. "You can't hurt me; I made a deal with the proprietress. She isn't allowed to seek revenge on me."

The creature shifted its shoulders, squaring itself at me. It wasn't exactly Herculean, and I didn't see any weapons.

"Who said anything about revenge?" it asked. "It's trespassing I'm concerned with. The sun has set. You had her protection as long as you followed her directions, but you had to go and look around. And you almost made it, too! You still could make it," it added cunningly. "You could open that door and disappear before I finished getting ready."

The creature wriggled as it talked, muscles contorting and bulging. It wasn't growing bigger or sprouting talons, but clearly something was changing. Whatever it was doing to prepare, it'd be done soon. I could act now, or I could turn into a horror movie victim, the really dumb sort who squanders her only chance to run.

Or to attack. I lunged at the thing, arms extended toward it. It reached out automatically, snagging my wrist. I stopped dead, planting my feet. Keeping my body relaxed, I rested my opposite hand over its in a wrist lock and turned under its arm.

Classic self-defense move. It flipped over my arm and thudded to the ground with a satisfying grunt. The cardboard mask went flying.

"Hey!" it protested, voice muffled by carpet. "I wasn't ready!"

I knelt beside it, up on my toes for leverage. In a practiced, controlled movement, I twisted its arm up and back, and locked it into place. No matter how strong the creature was, no way could it get up without dislocating its arm at the shoulder and elbow and probably breaking a bone or two.

That's when I realized I had no idea what to do next. I have a couple of self-defense moves up my sleeve, but I'm not what you'd call a martial artist. In the normal way of things, this'd be a perfect time to a) run away, b) shout for help, or c) ring the reeves. None of those were options here, not if I wanted to find my boss.

As I hesitated, the creature's free arm contorted in ways no human arm could and grabbed at me. I yelped and leaned back, off balance—giving it the space it needed to turn its head and snap, teeth grazing my knee as I flinched away.

I could see now why it had kept its face covered: it didn't *have* a face. Its eyes and nose had gone on vacation or possibly been devoured by the mouth, which stretched over the entire front of the head. A snake tongue flickered out, tasting the air, but the teeth were the semi-translucent needles of a deep-sea fish.

That was bad. What was worse was that I recognized it from the pictures in the red room. This had been among the "after" photos for available procedures. This creature was human, or it had been.

I still had a hold of its hand. It was struggling upright, snapping at me. Instead of scooting further away, I threw myself across its back, hanging on to that hand. The creature's muscles rippled in ways no muscles should ripple, its elbow and shoulder joints popping out and back in like they were on a spring, its bones collapsing and reforming instead of breaking.

Not that I was sticking around to watch. I somersaulted forward and ran for the UPPER ROOMS door.

The creature's hand lashed out and caught my ankle. I tripped, sprawled, and rolled until I hit the umbilical cord.

I almost didn't make it. The creature flung itself at me, chomping wildly. I grabbed hold of the pulsating umbilical cord and shoved it blindly upward, between those needle teeth.

Foul, gelatinous blood gushed out over my face. I squeezed my eyes shut and held my breath. If this worked, I'd rather not contract any diseases. If it didn't work, I'd rather not watch myself be eaten.

The flow of blood slowed to a drizzle, but I didn't yet open my eyes. The creature had fallen over me, its body quivering and twitching as it died. I rocked side to side to dislodge it, then crawled away, taking off my blazer and wiping my face and hands with the back of it. I had to crack an eye to find the bathroom, but otherwise I kept my face closed up until I'd scrubbed it clean. My blouse was beyond salvaging, and I tied the blazer around my waist rather than leave it for the proprietress to find.

I didn't waste a lot of time on primping. I didn't know what else the proprietress had up her sleeve, and I wasn't keen to find out. But more than anything, I didn't want to give myself too much time to think. If I did, I knew I'd run straight for the car and burn rubber to get away, boss or no boss.

On which note—where was he?

I checked the men's bathroom just in case he was there (he wasn't), the office (likewise), and the auction hall (nope).

That left one option, and I didn't particularly want to take it, so I banged on the safety glass surrounding the central island desk. This close up, I could see the clerks were breathing very shallowly, and that they were propped upright by metal poles that might, in the spirit of optimism, be called chairs.

They had not moved when I was in danger of being eaten by Maw-face, and they didn't move now. But it seemed to me that the clerks' eyes weren't quite closed anymore—that I could see a wet gleam behind the lashes.

"Stop it," I told them. "I know you're faking, and I want to talk to you."

Not a tic, twitch, or jerk. I hadn't really thought they'd help me; if anything, they might alert the proprietress that I'd neither left nor been eaten. I was just putting off trying the last door: the basement.

I hate basements. I've always hated basements for the same reason I've always hated subways. The air down there is stale and unnatural, not meant to be trapped below mounds of earth. And you can feel the weight of that earth pressing down upon you, ready to collapse. Crushing, suffocating. Trapped.

I opened the door labeled BASEMENT, and looked down.

Stairs fell away from me, sharp edges outfitted in plush cerulean. A switch by my hand illuminated everything in a warm glow: satin-swirled cream wallpaper, clean and crisp and new, without a hint of dust. A step in the ceiling blocked my view of the basement itself, but the smell wafted up nice and strong: lavender and more lavender.

Behind me, the creature was already shriveling, its umbilical cord flaccid, its blood dyeing the red carpet darker.

How long before the proprietress came downstairs and saw her pet leaking and a black Mercedes-Benz still in the parking lot?

I stepped onto the top stair and closed the door behind me.

It got much warmer as I descended, and the lavender smell kept growing stronger. I'm not against lavender, but I couldn't help wondering what it was trying to cover up. Beyond that, I was so done having expectations about this place that I wasn't surprised when the lavishly carpeted stairs led down into an equally lavish hotel lobby—

complete with marble floor, overpriced and overstuffed armchairs, hideous statuary, and gold foil inlays. Wide vents in the white ceiling pumped in hot, lavender-heavy gusts, in case we hadn't enough of that. The heating system also provided a rhythmic thumping and thudding to put the worst plumbing to shame.

I walked around and craned my neck at black-and-white striped armchairs and over the reception desk. There was a door beyond that desk, presumably leading to an administrative room, but the other exit struck me as more promising: out the left end of the lobby stretched a wide corridor carpeted in a thinner version of the cerulean on the stairs. This too looked either brand new or properly kept up. It wasn't any more tasteful than the faux-opera-house aesthetic upstairs, mind, just cleaner.

Sticking with the hotel theme, the corridor showcased a door every fifteen feet and always on the left. I tried the first door and found a generically decorated bedroom: double bed with pale green carpet and dark green coverlet. No windows or curtains, obviously. No other doors, not even for a bathroom or closet. Empty, unused. Move along.

I opened the next door upon an identical setup, except that the carpet was powder blue and the coverlet navy. The room after that was lilac and violet.

"I'm sensing a theme here," I muttered. Maybe there was a legitimate reason for the heavy-handed color coding; who knew? But nothing otherwise coordinated with the rooms above, that I could see.

The pink room was the last before I turned the corner. Red came after that, but it showcased nothing more gruesome than poor taste, and I'd seen plenty of that already in this building.

I blinked sharply as I shut the door. The lavender was dizzyingly strong back here, as far from the hotel entrance—and fresh air—as one could get. It had lost its pure floral essence in favor of a chemical undertone. There was some other smell as well, buried under the eye-watering lavender, but I couldn't identify it. If only it weren't so *hot*. The combination was stringing my nerves and plucking them one by one.

Gold room next. White-gold carpet and brown-gold coverlet. Clean and pressed and empty.

I rubbed my hands together and rolled my head. Thick umbilical blood stuck my starched shirt to my skin, and rivulets of sweat crawled down my neck.

This is an evil place.

I don't know where the thought came from, but it clung to my temples like claustrophobia. I tried to swat it away, but the heat made me slow, the smell stupid.

I opened the next door. White carpet, white walls, and there—lying on a bobbly white coverlet, head sunk in a white pillow—was my boss. He wore nothing but undershirt and briefs, his limbs splayed and his feet bare. None of his carefully cultivated dignity modified the pose; none of his intelligence lit his face. I hardly recognized him.

Averting my eyes from the hair on his legs, I rushed to his side, calling him. He looked ghastly, feverish. He did not awaken. I shook him and slapped his face and called him, daringly, by his Christian name.

Not a flutter. Not a sigh.

Luckily for my boss, if not for my brother Luc, I'm proficient at dragging unconscious and/or recalcitrant men from bed. I bunched the four corners of the coverlet, checked to make sure my boss's head was cradled, and ducked under the covers, corners hoisted over my shoulder.

Back turned to the bed, preparing to haul one hundred eighty pounds of deadweight boss, I noticed the entrance side of the room for the first time.

Scratches covered the door and surrounding wall. Long, chalky scratches that tore away white paper to reveal concrete beneath. Hundreds, thousands of scratches overlapping and intersecting, vertical and diagonal. Some stretched nearly to the ceiling; others picked at the carpet. And I knew—I *knew*—that although most had been made by adult hands and adult fingernails, they hadn't all been. Some of the scratches were smaller, the fingers closer together, the marks weaker.

My eyes went to the doorknob. Except there was no doorknob on this side, only a thin veneer of wood torn away from scratched steel. The door had swung nearly shut, balanced against its frame only by the metal latch. If I gave the door a gentle push, it'd click flush with the wall beside it.

The lavender air hung heavy in my throat. I dropped the coverlet and stumbled for the door. My stomach heaved, and my hands trembled so hard that I barely dared move them to the door, lest they betray me and push it closed.

Carefully, *carefully*, blinking away sweat, I pressed my fingertips against the edge of the door and pulled it toward me, then wrapped my fingers around the steel and swung it further inward so I could wedge my toes in the crack.

I stood there for a minute, hugging the door open, knuckles yellow, gasping, tying down panic. Then I remembered my boss, and my spine straightened. I pushed the door fully open, took off my shoe, and wedged it under the door—the carpet was thin enough for that, just. I arranged my blood-soaked blazer around the door frame, to stop the door if it tried to swing shut.

That was as safe as I could make it, but I would never feel safe in this room.

I unbent myself and looked down the corridor, back the way I had walked here.

It was the same corridor. It had the same wallpaper, the same carpet, the same support beams, the same doors in the same frames. But what a difference angle makes. From this direction, I could see marks where fingers had gripped support beams until they'd been torn away. I could see carpet frayed from dragging feet, the warped edges of ceiling vents.

Some part of my brain said: Odd, that the scratches were created by people dragged in that direction. Wouldn't people want to go that way, toward the exit?

Or had the proprietress switched the direction of the hallway, as she had manipulated the streets to bring me back here? What a perfect trap that would be: one that ushered the unwary and herded the wary further in, to whatever lay beyond.

Whatever was beyond? One more turn, and we'd be back at the lobby. There was space for two, maybe three more bedrooms, but we'd run out of colors.

Assuming the halls traced a loop, and not an impossible maze.

Vents sighed and electricity hummed and lavender strangled the air.

I toed off my remaining shoe and hooked the heel around the

doorframe as an extra precaution before returning to my boss. I looked back to double-check the door remained wedged open. It did.

My boss was as I'd left him, limp and unresponsive. He didn't protest when I dragged the coverlet after me, or when it—and he—thumped from bed to floor. But the moment we were through the door, he stirred.

I wasn't gentle. I shook, slapped, and bullied him awake and upright. It didn't take long, only about a decade, and he grumbled incomprehensibly the whole while.

I hooked my boss's arm over my shoulder and prodded him onward, pinching his neck when he tried to stagger away and collapse against the wall. "Just a little further," I coaxed him, and led him with pretty words around the final corner, away from the entrance.

I wasn't done here.

There weren't any more bedroom doors in this direction, only an archway leading to an enormous commercial kitchen, beyond which a windowed swinging door led to the small employee area I'd theorized existed behind the reception desk. The lavender receded slightly, overwhelmed by the chemical astringency.

I hadn't been in a lot of commercial kitchens, but I'd seen enough that this was exactly what I would've expected of a hotel resort: a forest of stainless-steel implements hung from the ceiling in one area and pans from another. More stainless steel lined the left wall in the form of ovens, stoves, sink, and a truly gigantic standing mixer. On the right wall, the stainless steel came in the form of doors: a walk-in fridge/freezer and a pantry. In the center, four cutting boards had been laid out on a long island prep table.

I got my boss to the solid end of the prep table. He slid down it to the smooth gray tiles and slumped over his knees, wheezing, barely aware of me. I crouched beside him, hands steadying him until I was sure he wouldn't keel over. Then, arms prickling, I stood and looked back the way we'd come.

From this direction, the gleaming, spotless kitchen looked . . . exactly the same. There were no nail marks, no scuffs. Even the ceiling had been scrubbed free of dust, stains, and spider webs.

I didn't understand. Everywhere else in the auction house had been different out than in, and I felt so sure this was the heart of it.

What had I missed?

My eyes settled on the doors next to me—first on the walk-in fridge/freezer and then on the pantry.

My knees creaked as I stood. I didn't want to see what was in there. I pulled the door open.

The pantry interior was concrete also, but all the bleach in the world couldn't have erased its bloodstains. Dark brown smears and spatters coated the walls, floor, and ceiling, layers deep. The room itself was half full of stainless steel shelving on which rested the larger bones: femurs, ribs, skulls. Smaller bones were in piles on the floor or in yellow bins. Fingers especially. Messy, incompletely stripped of flesh. And the smell—

It was the smell that got me. Metallic, sickly sweet, sour. It overwhelmed my brain, slammed the door shut between us even as I fell to my knees, retching.

My boss tried to say something to me, but I ignored him. I had to know. I didn't want to know, but I couldn't stop myself. I lurched upright, teeth bared, and unlatched the door of the walk-in fridge.

The interior was spacious, the organization as meticulous here as it had been slapdash in the pantry. Everything was labeled: eyes, noses, livers, hearts. You could find any fleshy part you liked. The variety in the red room upstairs was nothing in comparison to the choices down here.

I closed the fridge door. I didn't need to see the freezer; I had become frozen enough.

My hands no longer trembled. I had been right: this was an evil place. And I would not allow it to stand.

The stove was modern, heavy duty, and fully functional. I turned a burner on high and dropped an oven mitt halfway across it. In twenty seconds, the thick cloth was smoking; in twenty more, the end burst into flame.

My boss blinked and tried to focus on what I was doing. "Stay here," I told him—as if he could walk on his own. "I'll be back."

The white coverlet was some sort of cotton mix. I dropped the oven mitt on it and dragged it down the hall and around the corner, back to the green room. By the time I got there, the coverlet burned with a sputtering but fierce fire, gray-and-white smoke choking out the lavender. I waited for the carpet to smolder and then began dragging the burning coverlet back the way I'd come, opening bedroom doors as I went.

There was varnish on the support beams. It went up like anything.

I dropped the burning coverlet on the carpet outside the white room and went back for my boss. He was on his feet when I reentered the kitchen, supporting himself on the prep table. "Mercedes," he said, "what's going on?"

"We're getting out of here."

"There is smoke—"

"There's a fire," I said. "Let's go."

The air was already thick and acrid in the hotel lobby when we arrived. We coughed our way up the stairs and into the main auction house lobby. I propped my boss against the stair door long enough to lock the hinge open, to let all that lovely oxygen down. Then I shoved him toward the front entrance.

The clerks were still behind their protective barrier, but their eyes were open, and they watched me. "You'd better get out of here," I said. "There's a fire."

They didn't move. They didn't blink. I shoved my boss out the front door and went to tap their barrier. "Come on," I said. "Get out."

Smoke gusted up the stairs, charcoal black. Not enough of it to be harmful, not yet, but I didn't want to stick around.

"Tell you what," I said. "I'll make you a deal: you leave this auction house, and in return, you won't burn to death."

As one, the clerks sagged and then came alive. I held the door open for them and pushed them ahead of me, out the glass doors to the parking lot. They stared at me, dull and confused, awaiting further instruction. "Go home," I told them. "There's nothing more for you here."

My boss had made it to the car while I'd dithered, and waited for me to unlock it. As we drove away, flames burst from the auction house's foundation. They devoured the building so eagerly, I thought they must've waited a long time for the chance.

INTERLUDE

Prefect Lindo demonstrated her usual flair for competent efficiency by arriving the precisely proper eighteen minutes early. Neither the guards outside nor her escort to the reception room saw any spark of her famous temper. Then again, they did nothing to incite it—and it wouldn't have been tolerated at court.

A page brought King Emil news of Lindo's arrival, but it was not in his power to join her before the allotted time. He was closeted with his councilors, enduring exaggerated complaints about the problems of their individual prefectures and dire warnings about the neighboring countries of Vela and Akter. The councilors kept *pushing* him, making demands, stabbing fingers of iron, wood, and obsidian against the table. He flinched whenever one of them did this too close, and wished he could leave to consult his seidkonur in private. Her seidr would reveal what was true and when it was time to act. He would speak with her again this evening, preferably when his chaplain wasn't around to disapprove.

It was a relief when the hour struck and Emil felt able to call on the chancellor to gather any remaining complaints and make a report for him. He hurried away before his councilors could insist on anything further and headed for the reception room. In his mind, Prefect Lindo most closely resembled a dull gray hedgehog: soft or prickly, depending on which way you stroked her. Her dead sister's temperament had, naturally, been perfect.

"Prefect Lindo," he said, entering. "Welcome."

Lindo rose and bowed, prickles tucked in tight. "Your Majesty." She had dressed neatly and properly in her prefecture's turquoise and charcoal, and someone had provided her with lemonade. Emil traced out her features, searching for those that reminded him of her sister. Lindo had none of Zita's raving beauty, and age had deepened the angry lines on her forehead. However, she remained fit and upright, and the intelligence he recalled brightening her eyes brightened them still.

Emil shifted under those eyes, deeply aware of the delicacy of glass. He knew he would not survive a serious attack despite the cushioning velvet of his suit, which had only last week been sewn from his finest purple velvet curtains. Maybe it had been a mistake, insisting on meeting Lindo informally and alone.

"Walk with me," he said, joining his hands behind his back so that she could not perceive this as offering his arm. "You have not—I believe you have not seen the rose garden."

The date was late in March, which in Carina meant autumn, and in the capital meant rain. Rain gushed in great sloshing buckets that day, translating the world into colorblind shades. Outside, bus wipers swished on their highest settings, unlucky walkers dashed across the streets with newspapers over their heads and got drenched despite their slickers, and great whirlpools swirled around insufficient drains.

In the outer ring of the royal palace, one could see the rain through the many-paneled reinforced windows, but an overhang guarded the glass from any but the most determined gusts. Inside the rose greenhouse, with its glass exposed on two sides and above, the rain gave Emil and Lindo a world of their own, guarded from eavesdroppers by the constant noise, and from spies by the distortion of running water.

Emil led her through the paths of the greenhouse, keeping up a running commentary on the minutiae of roses, which were his specialty. Only when he found himself for the third time explaining how he'd had this-and-this thornless rose specially imported did he stop, reset, and switch to, "But you did not come to hear me talk about flowers."

"I came because Your Majesty desired it," Lindo pointed out. "If that is to talk about flowers, then so be it."

"You must have been surprised at the summons."

"I haven't had a chance to sit down all week. Everything is constantly going wrong, and I'm the only one who can deal with any of it. Why should I be surprised to have even more suddenly on my plate?"

Emil regarded her placidly, noting the irritation in her voice. He had never heard it before, though he had certainly heard her temper described often enough. He wondered that she dared express it in front of him. Conscious of how hedgehogs could scratch glass, he said, "Does your prefecture weigh heavily upon you?"

"Not my prefecture—the conference. It's been one thing after another for weeks. I haven't been able to take a breath or a break, and I won't be able to until it's over. Not that I expect I'll get a break then— the conference always just causes me more and more trouble!" She cut herself off with a sharp breath, killing her momentum. When she spoke again, her tone was restrained. "So you can understand that I am a little stressed."

Emil accepted this with a nod. "Is the conference so difficult to host? I always assumed it was simple: having your servants change sheets and wash towels and so on—the sort of things they do daily anyway."

He had offended her. The emotion was suppressed in a flash, but the echo of it remained in her stiff shoulders and tense jaw. "If only my fellow prefects were as reasonable as Your Majesty." She dusted flat palms on the turquoise skirt of her suit. "Actually," she said, her tone abruptly cheerful, "my manor needed repairs anyway, and this is a great excuse for them. Whichever of my predecessors decided to build along the coast had a great eye for a view but no sense whatsoever. The sea air is brutal when it comes to wear and tear—as I'm sure Your Majesty knows."

It had been many years since Emil's stint in the navy, and looking back now, he was horrified at the risk he had taken. He felt a rush of gratitude toward Lindo for reinforcing her manor to protect him from those winds—and was glad he had not before known what danger her manor posed.

That gratitude opened before him, and he knew it was time. He brushed his fingers over the petals of a yellow rose. "Prefect," he said. "Graça. It has been nearly four years, and we have never discussed

Zita."

Lindo's nostrils flared. "My sister—"

"My fiancée," he reminded her.

"You barely knew her," she retorted. "I loved her. If you had—"

"Yes, I know," Emil interrupted. "But do not for a moment believe that you are the only one who mourns her untimely death."

"Her *suicide*," Lindo corrected, though saying the word hurt her far more than it hurt her companion.

"I could not have known of her previous attachment."

A sarcastic muscle pulled at one side of Lindo's mouth. "And if you had known? Would you have given her up? Shamed yourself by losing your fiancée to a lesser man? Put aside a beautiful, charming wife? Found another with such flawless family connections? And let's not forget that your first wife was as fair as snow and ice, and the king must keep his children mixed."

Emil inclined his head, acknowledging this point as one acknowledged the weather. This was one of the duties of Carina's monarch: to marry as would best support his nation. In times of conflict, this meant joining his house to a powerful ally or erstwhile enemy. In times of peace, it meant mixing his blood—which had the dual benefits of preventing inbreeding and of setting a good example for his people.

"Are you angry at me?" he asked Lindo.

Ever stable as a seesaw, Lindo replied staidly, "You are the king. You may do as you wish."

"As I am the king," said Emil, "I may seldom do as I wish but only as I must."

"I stand corrected," said Lindo, with no more emotion than before.

Emil glanced quickly at her and then away. He could not reproach the correctness of her response, but it did not satisfy him. He reached out again to stroke the rose, but stopped his hand short, fingers curling. Nervous habits had been worn out of him from a young age. He stared at Lindo's square-toed shoes, and could not help hearing the fragility in his voice when he asked, "Is Graça angry with Emil?"

Lindo took so long to respond that Emil nearly raised his eyes. When she did respond, her words were quiet, measured. "For a long time, I was," she said. "Hardly anyone understood why. Hardly anyone understands me or why I get so upset. My emotions are so much stronger than other people's, you see, and others don't understand what it's like to really *feel* things."

Emil smiled slightly, thinking of how clearly he saw the world through his eyes and mind of glass. Yes, he knew what it was to be more—more present, more real than those around him.

"If you're asking whether I ever let the anger get the better of me," Lindo went on, "the answer is no. You are my king, and I am and ever have been your loyal subject."

"I am glad to hear it," Emil said. He was glad, fervently glad, if this would get the chancellor off his back. "You once made a formal oath, when you became prefect. Will you make one again, before the chaplain and witnesses of my choice?"

"Of course, Your Majesty," Lindo said, bowing. "It would be my honor."

Chapter 6:

BREACHING THE PEACE

The next morning, I slid the 'Benz into the pickup indent of my boss's apartment building. Almost before I had shifted to park, he was coming down, impeccably ironed and starched.

"Good morning," I said, pretending I wasn't scrutinizing him. He looked considerably better than last night—although by the time I'd dropped him off, he'd been well enough to walk into his apartment building on his own. He hadn't had a key, of course, but someone had opened the door for him, and after that—I don't know. His apartment building is nice enough that it might have a manager there twenty-four seven. Or he could have a keypad lock.

"Good morning," he said, nostrils flaring as he inhaled the stale lavender burnt into the seats. I'd wiped them down and stuck a musky air freshener in the vent, but the smell remained. In the end, I'd decided that rolling down the windows to revel in rush-hour exhaust fumes would be considerably less toxic than breathing in lavender.

I handed my boss his newspaper, and we drove to work without another word. To be fair, that part was pretty ordinary.

I exercised patience through that drive and while parking in the CSS garage (the building's labeled "Carinan Social Services," to deceive the general public, my brothers, and other simpletons). I said not a word on the topic while greeting Tom and Marta and before making coffee. I kept my lips buttoned as my boss sipped and concentrated and got himself properly caffeinated. Then I made my one and only foray.

I cleared my throat and tapped on his desk until he focused on me with polite, pointed incomprehension.

"Look," I said. "Your deal with the proprietress. It's not going to be a problem, is it?"

His voice flat, his mouth likewise, he said, "That has nothing to do with you."

I hadn't expected gratitude, so I was surprised at how much his brusqueness hurt. I knew my boss well enough to know that his dignity was his shield, his intellectual acuity his greatest—perhaps his only— point of pride. To lose so thoroughly when I had (as far as he had seen) won, to be stripped of his good suit and even of his conscious mind, to have me witness this degradation, must be more than he could bear.

And the thing was, I knew he was grateful, deep down—or he knew he ought to be, and was ashamed that he wasn't. Because otherwise, he would have liked nothing more than to fire me, so that he wouldn't have to look at me and remember and know that I remembered.

More than once, my boss had honored my dignity by pretending not to see, not to know. It was only right that I return the favor. He was giving me a chance to withdraw.

I would withdraw, but I had to make sure of something, first. "You said you went there to talk to her—and, I presume, to ask for her assistance with the prefect situation."

"That does not concern you."

"Sr. Nordfeld," I said, "I do not want that woman anywhere near the king."

He restrained himself from answering immediately; that was another way I knew he was grateful. And when he spoke again, he actually softened his tone and gave me an answer. "My deal," he said, "was personal and did not mention you or the prefects or the king. I appreciate your reinforcing it—but please do not ask me about it further."

The sky must've wanted to cheer me up, because it wiped away its cloudy expression and smiled forth the sun. For a few days, summer had come again.

The grass steamed dry and brightened, filling the air with fresh green fragrance. Flowers poked their heads out of buds, spreading white and yellow petals to dress even the cracks of the sidewalk in their finest colors. Sundresses dotted the throngs of gray and black suits, and bare arms caught warmth. Wednesday was so fine that my boss consented to eat outside and hardly laughed at me when I, plant-like, turned my face to the sun.

I got Luc's text during lunch, with instructions, and so I forced my boss to leave work on time for once. I dropped him off at home, tucked in the 'Benz for the night, and headed for my apartment complex.

Housing in Silvertip isn't cheap, but outside the city center it isn't atrocious either. My apartment complex lies along the border of where commercial meets residential: only a block from the nearest drugstore and half a mile from a grocery store. The apartment complex itself is a sprawling affair of three irregular loops of two-story apartment build-ings, clover lobes surrounding a central park.

That park is one of the complex's selling points, along with a pool and tennis court I'm always too busy or too tired to use. I often hear other people using the park, though, and I can see them from the bal-cony. Most days, it's full of happily screaming children, and most eve-nings of teenagers who've come out to play crab ball. There are picnic tables, grills, a swing set, and a jungle gym. On fine evenings like this, the neighbors are out in force—and today Luc was among them.

He waved me over, and I skirted fifteen children, a basset hound, and two groups of picnickers to get to him.

"Fish or beef burger?" he asked.

"What happened to the chicken?"

"I'm out."

"You're—are you *selling* them?"

Luc flashed me a 150-watt smile. He'd better be selling them, I amended, taking in the number of meat hunks on the grill, or he and Francis were binging again. Francis can get away with binges, with the amount of exercise he gets hauling around giant piles of wood and whatever else it takes to build a mansion, but Luc's a sedentary twig.

"It's a good way to meet people," he said. "And someone let Francis do the grocery shopping again."

"You didn't *stop* him?"

Twig or not, no one could mistake Luc for anyone but my brother. He's a couple of years older than I am, a couple of inches taller, and my coloring exactly. He's even near-sighted like I am, although he wears contacts, which I can't tolerate. Women don't flock to him like they do to Francis, whose muscles are out of control. But I've been gravely informed—by four of Francis's girlfriends, no less—that Luc's nerdy charm is irresistible. The Francises of the world are fun to date, but you marry a Luc.

I listened and nodded at these girlfriends and told them about some of the times Luc and Francis had locked me in the closet or put spiders in my bed or made me believe my parents had found me in a garbage heap or engaged in any of the other activities caring brothers perform to improve their baby sister's character. Since one or the other of my brothers generally came in during my epic retelling, these stories were followed up by renditions of my amazingly clever and fully justified responses to the wrongs perpetrated against me.

Although admittedly, that's not how my brothers described them.

The truth is, we Cartier siblings inherited excellent genes for personal beauty, although heaven only knows where Luc and I got our capacity for abstract thinking; I've yet to meet another relative with anything of the kind. My father still speaks with amazement that Luc went off to college instead of a trade school, and he actually fainted when I announced I'd gotten a scholarship to study history at the University of Avior. Why, asked our mother plaintively, couldn't we stay in Batata and follow in the potato-farming trade? Or mimic Francis, who had had the decency to pursue good, honest construction work?

The newspaper recently ran an article about the shortage of skilled construction workers. There's no shortage of people with history degrees. I'm sure I satisfied my parents' ambitions for me when I became a glorified secretary. I never told them that I only took the job because it paid well, and I was saving up to get my eyes fixed for the military. Fainting was bad enough; I didn't want to give my father a heart attack until absolutely necessary.

"Speaking of tasty dishes, by the way," Luc said, "—I'm giving you fish, incidentally—Francis promised to bring his girlfriend by. They should be here any moment."

I groaned. "If I have to listen to Number 44 again, I might shoot myself. Or her. Preferably her. Where are grenade launchers when you need them?"

"Give me some credit," said Luc. "You think I'd be out here, in plain view, if Number 44 were coming? I have some sense of self-preservation. It's a new one. She's—"

"Hot, dim, and insubstantial," I filled in. "Like steam."

"Strangely enough, no. Only one out of the three."

"Dim?"

"Hot."

"She has a brain and she's dating *Francis?*"

Luc shrugged and served up a fish burger on a paper plate and handed it over. "I know, I know, but there's no accounting for taste. Her name's Theodora Banks. You might like her."

Pigs might start wielding machetes while chanting in time to the national anthem.

"See for yourself." Luc pointed his spatula, and I saw. I think I dropped my paper plate. I know I was suddenly on my feet, blood rushing in my ears.

Francis was at the opposite end of the park, coming our way, hand in hand with a woman his age or slightly older. She wore a floaty robin's-egg blue dress and tall strappy sandals of exactly the same shade. Thick ginger curls cascaded loosely over her shoulders, which were level with my brother's eyes. People gaped as she passed, staggered by her beauty. One man whistled. She was too far away for me to see her eyes, but I knew they'd be cold and silver as distant stars.

Francis said something, and she laughed and leaned against him. I couldn't hear her laugh. I couldn't hear anything but the blood thumping in my ears. The sun turned to ice, and the hairs on my arm and neck formed up in ranks and columns.

I like to think of myself as calm and collected. For the most part, I am calm and collected. But Francis is *family*.

They approached, too absorbed in each other to look at us. Then the proprietress broke off, met my eyes, smiled—and I lost it. I think I roared. I know I launched myself at her, because by the time Francis dragged me off, blood dripped from long scratches down her cheeks.

I thrashed and kicked, but Francis simply yelled at me to shut up as he looped his arms under my shoulders and hooked them behind my neck.

There was a gap there, a moment of red and black where I'm not quite sure what happened. But then I heard Francis saying to the proprietress, "I'm so sorry. She's not usually like this—I don't know what— Mercedes, cut it *out*—are you all right? Luc, take her to the apartment, put something on that—I'm so *sorry*. Mercedes, STOP."

The proprietress picked herself up from the grass. She didn't put a hand to her cheek or otherwise acknowledge the scratches, but she had stopped smiling. "I'm glad to see you again too, Mercedes," she said.

My response was brief and to the point.

"Mercedes!" Luc exclaimed. He had moved beside the proprietress, ready to take her up to our apartment and tend to her out of our jointly purchased medical supplies, but the proprietress didn't even look at him.

"Get off, Francis!" I snarled. "Let me go!"

"Will you control yourself?"

"Get off!"

"So . . ." Luc said. "You two have met before?"

"Leave," I choked at the proprietress, unable to scream at her with my neck all bent over. "Go away! You have no right to be here, you—" I devolved into the sort of language that shocked Luc, though I don't know why it should, the amount of time he spends online. Forming a coherent and compelling argument while your brain is swathed in red mist is harder than it looks.

The proprietress—Theodora—standing there with blood running down her face and dripping on her expensive dress, said, "She's mad because of Jon."

That name meant nothing to my brothers, though I stopped struggling under it, listening tensely.

"Don't you know?" she asked, amazed. "Your sister's employer— Jon Erlend Nordfeld. I'd have thought . . ."

"We know about him," Luc said curiously, and it struck me how ridiculous and surreal the situation was. That we should be standing here, in a crowded park, with no one paying attention to us. That no one seemed to particularly care that I'd just publicly assaulted the woman they'd all been drooling over a moment earlier. That I should be mad with protective terror, and my brothers were treating my reaction as irrelevant. That my brothers seemed more interested in hearing gossip about my boss than anything else.

She's doing something, I thought, and didn't know what or how to stop it.

"It's true," Francis said, holding me almost casually now. "Mercedes has never told us his name for some reason. Jon, huh? I expected something more exotic."

"Have you met him, then?" Luc asked, awed. "What's he like?"

"Luc, Francis," I said, "listen to me. Please."

"He was a client of mine," Theodora explained. She came up to us and laid a hand on Francis's shoulder, out of my biting range. "Your sister came in after him, to spy on him. I'm sure she's a fine woman, Francis, but she has a bad jealous streak."

I think she said this to drive me crazy again, but it had the opposite effect. She didn't know I'd spent years building emotional walls around my boss. Very little can get through on me there; it's one of my strongest fronts. The rest of the red mist dissipated, and I let my muscles relax. "You are breaking our contract," I said, reverting to the detached impersonality of our earlier interview. "You agreed not to seek revenge upon me."

The proprietress said: "Your memory is faulty. I agreed not to seek any form of retribution, directly or indirectly, for anything you or Jon Nordfeld said or did during or prior to our deal."

"Exactly," I said. "I'm starting to get a pretty poor view of how you uphold your contracts. First, you set a monster on me—"

"On the contrary," she replied. "I provided you with the key to safe passage out of my home, and you not only willfully contravened my instructions, you attacked my night guard and refused to leave."

"You were holding my boss prisoner!"

The smile was back. "He could have left at any time. No one was stopping him. It's not my fault he preferred my bed to yours."

That was a mistake on her part, which is the problem with not playing fair: other people notice, and they don't like it.

It also showed how little she knew Francis. His head shot up and his voice roughened. "Take that back," he ordered.

Theodora seemed astonished he'd interfered. "What?"

"I will not have you slandering my sister in order to win an argu-ment," he growled, "or yourself by falling into false accusation. Take it back."

I could see Theodora knew he meant it, but that she was confused. "I don't live at my auction house," she clarified. "I keep beds there because I serve alcohol, and sometimes guests overindulge and have to sleep it off. I'm not in a relationship with anyone—except you."

Francis remained unmoved. "Take back what you implied about my sister," he said, "or we're over."

That gave me a second of hope. Unfortunately, Theodora saw it and calculated the correct response. Her expression and voice in-stantly morphed into an apologetic version of the vulnerability that I so often use. She shouldn't have been able to pull it off, tall as she is, but she shouldn't have been able to pull off four-inch heels either. "I'm sorry," she said to him. She repeated it to me: "I'm sorry. I shouldn't have said that."

"Yeah," I said. "It sucks when you say something that makes you look bad."

"Be gracious, Mercedes," Francis told me. "She's apologized. If I let you go, will you control yourself?"

"Yes." I would, too. Now that my reasoning capacity had returned full force, I wasn't about to let it go. I knew attacking her like I had had been stupid—going after a powerful enemy with unknown abilities is dumb at the best of times. It's only when you have the element of sur-prise that overwhelming violence is effective against an opponent who outclasses and outguns you.

That sort of tactic wouldn't work against the proprietress right now; her level of unfazed told me I was hardly the first prospective victim who'd tried fighting back. I needed more information.

In the meantime, let her think I was making a concession by not immediately attacking her again. The more she deluded herself, the better.

Francis unwound his arms and stepped in between Theodora and me. I rolled my shoulders and cranked my neck from side to side. There was blood under my fingernails.

"That was fun," Luc said. "But you distracted me, and the burgers burned."

"Listen to me, Francis," I said. "You know my character. You know I don't randomly go around attacking people. That woman is a dangerous psychopath. You need to stay away from her."

Francis sighed wearily and rubbed the heels of his hands up his forehead. "I know you don't like her, Mercedes," he said. "You never like my girlfriends. But try not to crow."

I could have screamed. "This isn't about her being your girlfriend! I have a very good reason for saying that that woman belongs in a hospital for the criminally insane, and if I had any proof, she *would* be." I grabbed his wrists and pulled them down so I could look him in the eye. "Reach past whatever illusion she's foisting on you, Francis! It's not real. With strength of will—"

"This is no longer funny, Mercedes. It never was."

"Listen to me! Has she gotten her claws into you? Have you made any deals with her? Francis, have you? This is important!"

"Stop it, Mercedes. Being my sister doesn't give you a free pass for false accusations."

Sun played merrily over green grass and picnic tables. Children laughed and shrieked. Burgers charred black. I told my brothers of streets, of rooms full of addicts and slavery, of a deal in an attic, of the monster in the lobby and the scratches in the basement and the contents of the kitchen.

The proprietress listened calmly, eyebrows bent in incredulity, voice making no attempt to stop or correct me. She was the first to speak when I finished, but she didn't say what I expected. She said, "Isn't there an Edgar Allan Poe story like that?"

"What?" I said.

Luc snapped his fingers. "That's it!" he cried. "That's what I was trying to think of. 'The Masque of the Red Death'! Palace full of rooms of progressive colors, oblivious and debauched partiers, a grisly end. I knew I'd read it somewhere!"

"Give her credit," Theodora said; "the story's not exactly universally known. I'd have been insulted if she'd used a blockbuster."

"And Francis isn't much of a reader. No way would he get the reference."

"She's missed some pretty big plot points, though," Theodora mused. "For one thing, my auction house doesn't have a basement. Didn't have one, I should say, since it mysteriously caught fire as Mercedes was leaving. There's practically nothing left of it, but I'm sure a construction expert could take one look at it and verify that it doesn't and never did have a basement." She stroked Francis's bicep. "We could go there now, if you wanted to see."

I had no doubt that Francis would see whatever she wanted him to. "What do you want?" I asked drearily. "Why are you doing this?"

"Doing what?" Theodora shot back. "Dating your brother? Because I like him. How was I to know his sister was the crazy who'd attacked my night guard and burned down my place of business? Try to get past your rampant jealousy, Mercedes. Yes, I do business with your boss. Yes, I date your brother. Deal with it!"

"Leave my family alone."

"Don't be stupid, Mercedes," Francis said, drawing Theodora closer. She flowed into his arms and clung to him, lay her head on his shoulder.

I stepped back. She was trying to provoke me again. I knew what she wanted, but I wasn't going to make another deal with her. I mustn't. I'd seen the results of that game, and I had no desire to join her garden of golden statues.

Theodora met my gaze over Francis's head. She rubbed strands of black hair between her fingers, but no expression save calculation shone from her silver eyes. Maybe she had made a deal with Francis, maybe she hadn't, but it was clear there was nothing I could say that she would not twist against me.

I backed up further, picked up my handbag, and walked away.

Chapter 7:

PERVERTING THE COURSE OF JUSTICE

I didn't go far. I wasn't walking for my health, only to get away enough that they couldn't see or hear me. Then I pulled out my phone and scrolled through my contacts.

My boss has never explicitly forbidden me to call him outside of work hours, but it was understood all the same. I could text him if I was going to be particularly late picking him up, but otherwise I had his number only in case of minor emergencies, such as if the bakery had neglected to make its usual selection of muffins or if he needed to take a call to get out of a meeting. Not even in our plans regarding the prefects had there been any question of my calling him.

Boundaries and barriers: my boss's preference and my self-defense. Break down enough of them, and I'd no longer have a job.

I didn't hesitate for a second.

Ring. Ring. Click. My boss's voice, displeased: "Mercedes—"

"Theodora Banks," I said.

There was a pause on the line. When he spoke again, his tone was one of caution. "How do you know that name?"

"She's my eldest brother's new girlfriend."

The pause was longer this time, long enough that I checked whether the call had dropped. I had to bite my lip to keep from explaining more. He had plenty of information to go on; he just needed to process it, and my interrupting wouldn't help.

His tone was different again when he spoke, grim and hard. "Number three-fifteen," he said. "I'll buzz you in."

He hung up before I could answer. I was too busy staring at the phone to say anything anyway. Three . . . fifteen?

I didn't know what I'd expected. Advice over the phone, maybe. For him to tell me to pick him up and drive him—somewhere. Or to wait until tomorrow morning. Or—or anything, really, other than his apartment number.

Oh, Francis.

My boss's apartment is far enough from downtown to be affordable but not far enough to be inconvenient. It's in a distinctly upper-middle-class area, suitable for someone living on a higher government pay grade than mine. My brothers and I had looked at places like it when apartment hunting. They'd struck me as comfortable and quiet, if sterile. Between the three of us, we'd have been able to afford one, but Luc had put his foot down. "I work from home," he'd said. "You couldn't pay me to spend my days staring at those walls. Besides, you know the kind of people who live there?"

"Professionals," I'd replied. "Which we are."

"I want to live somewhere with a park in the middle. Somewhere I can hear children playing and see actual women, ones who'll look me in the eye instead of down their noses. And I want a balcony."

"To lounge on or to watch women lounge on?"

"Both," Luc and Francis had chorused.

I'd rolled my eyes. "Pigs. I'm related to a couple of pigs." But Luc had won, and I'd eventually become glad of it. Although I'd never admit it to them, those apartments weren't for the likes of us—and they were dull and colorless besides.

I found parking half a block from my destination. My boss's apartment complex had a parking garage of its own not much further on, but I didn't have a pass. I didn't have a pass to get into the apartment building either, but I rang 315, and my boss buzzed me in without comment.

Though I'd never before seen the entrance hall of this particular apartment building, it was designed almost identically to others I'd scoped out: slate carpet, ivory walls, and all the personality of a dishwasher. I saw no one on my way in, heard nothing but a distant vacuum cleaner. The elevator was sterile, modern, and smelled faintly of pine.

My boss met me at his door. He swept his eyes over me but didn't share his findings. "Come in," he said, and took my coat. I was clumsy letting him have it, I was so surprised. He'd never done that sort of thing before. But then, I'd always been his employee before, not his guest.

My boss's apartment was a model of glossy modernity, its personality a twin to the building at large. The main room contained a partially segregated sitting room, dining room, and kitchen, and it carried almost no imprint from its owner. The only splash of color came from the spines of books covering the right wall between two doors.

The place didn't suit him. He was a man who valued old things. I couldn't believe he'd been the one to decorate it.

My boss hung up my coat and ushered me further in, indicating one of the stools on the dining-room side of the kitchen's wrap-around counter. I tucked my heels over the stool rung and propped my elbows on the counter, chin in hands to stop me from rubbernecking too much.

In silence, my boss began the preparations for tea. I guessed it made sense he knew how to make tea, though I'd never seen him do it any more than I'd ever seen him drive. His hands moved with his habitual decision and precision: kettle (stainless steel) on stove (black); teapot and matching cup and saucers (white) on counter (black); milk poured; sugar readied.

Tea cozy (pink). It fit the teapot like they had been designed for each other, and had clearly been knitted by an amateur, judging by the lumps and uneven stitches. The panels alternated between baby and hot pink yarns of different weights and textures. Atop this monstrous creation bobbled a pom-pom, two inches in diameter, alternating the two pinks until near the top, where the maker had apparently run out of pink yarn and substituted in cherry red.

At their best, tea cozies are informal and not the sort of decoration I would have expected him to pull out for a guest. But he wasn't acting like it was anything to excuse or be ashamed of. I wondered who had made it.

Once the hot water was poured, we migrated to the dining table. I could see my boss was readying himself, and I waited patiently. Again, here my mental barriers helped me, and I stayed calm. I knew it was no good being frantic or rushing him. That he had invited me here was proof that he was ready to talk to me; trying to force him would do nothing but make him clam up.

After he had let both the tea and his thoughts steep for several minutes, he poured one and spoke the other. "Have you worked it out yet?"

Had I—?

Clearly, my brain had been somewhere very different than his. "About ... Theodora?"

He spooned sugar into his tea, not displeased. "Mercedes," he said, "what do you think I am?"

It wasn't a rhetorical question or an offended exclamation. He waited for me to respond, genuinely interested in what I had to say.

Which didn't help me in the least. "Would you please be more specific?"

He inclined his head. "You must think it strange that I knew about the auction house and its owner. You saw the sorts of people who made deals there—and what their deals did to them. Why do you think I went?"

"You said it was personal," I said slowly, as if I hadn't been mad with curiosity for days. "You wouldn't have gone without good reason."

"The proprietress did not tell you?"

I shook my head. "She'd have made me pay for the information—and the deal I made was bad enough."

"I ... see." Words stuck on his tongue, and he wriggled them loose. "I admit, I ... miscalculated. I am not in the habit of explaining myself, but you deserve ... especially since ..."

He trailed off. Maybe he wanted me to jump in and say the deal I made wasn't so bad, that he didn't have to worry about it.

I kept my mouth shut. If this leverage was the only thing I had to make him explain what was going on, to protect Francis, then I wasn't about to alleviate it.

"What am I, Mercedes?" he asked. "What do you think I am?"

Back to this. I didn't object; he usually told me things round-about. Like I'd understand them better if I worked them out for myself. Very Socratic, if only I had a clue where to begin. "You're Jon Nordfeld," I said. "Jon Erlend Nordfeld, if the proprietress—if Theodora—knew what she was talking about." A subtle nod confirmed that she had, and encouraged me to continue. "You're my employer," I said. "A crypt-analyst and occasional cryptographer. A Carinan. A civil servant. A doctor in—various academic disciplines. Do I need to name them?"

"No. What else? Human?"

Something about the way he said it stoppered my response. Before I'd met the proprietress, I'd have laughed—or I'd have said *no* and expected him to laugh. Now, I took an opportunity to study him.

The first thing I noticed, which I always forget, was that he was not handsome. His features were too uneven for the aesthetic ideal and had the softness of one who spends his life eating muffins behind a desk. His hands were blunt and large and looked too clumsy to trace his flawless penmanship.

He was dressed, as always, conservatively and suitably. His taste was not so much excellent as discrete—the latter determining the for-mer. Not urbane, merely neat: neat fingernails, neat suit, neat hair. He hadn't dressed down in the comfort of his own home or even ex-changed his work shoes for house slippers.

What these observations added up to, objectively, was that my boss looked ordinary but not suspiciously forgettable. Neither fair nor foul.

The proprietress's most alien feature had been her eyes. But though his were stormy-sea blue and effulgent with brilliance, they had none of her inhuman gleam.

"Yes?" I hazarded.

Those eyes gazed steadily at me.

"No?"

Same.

"Maybe? Partially? Metaphorically?"

"All but metaphorically."

"I need a hint, here."

My boss tilted his head, his fingers tapping a tattoo on the table: one-two, four-three, five-four, two-three, one. I didn't recognize it. He said, "Cipher."

"You are a cipher or you want me to find a cipher?"

"I am Cipher."

"And I'm confused."

One-five, four-five, three-four, two-three, one. A piano exercise? Ciphers usually go for randomization, not pattern.

I tried again. "Are you a cipher puzzle, cipher solution, cipher number, or cipher computation?"

"The first two," my boss said. "I am puzzle and solution—or puzzler and solver. I am human, but I bear the mantle of Cipher. You might say that I am the personification of ciphers, puzzles, and mazes. Have you figured it out?"

"Figured *what* out?"

"Why you've never been in my apartment before."

Apparently, not for the reason I'd always assumed. Wondering what else I'd taken for granted and was completely wrong about, and feeling like an unprepared pupil being quizzed by a particularly intimidating teacher, I sipped my tea and looked around.

I'm not a cryptanalyst. The extent of my expertise is significantly beyond the daily newspaper, which only has a simple monoalphabetic substitution cipher. I can understand the theory of how to solve a certain type of cipher, once it's explained to me, and follow the necessary steps to a solution. But I can't crack ciphers if I don't know the type, and I can't untangle misenciphered messages without direction or invent new ciphers. It's not that I haven't tried; it's that my brain simply doesn't work that way.

But my boss knew that.

Depending on the expert you ask, ciphers exist in two or three general categories: transposition, substitution, and (debatably) concealment. The first two require a ciphertext, and I'd seen nothing of the sort since entering the apartment. That left concealment: a cipher that didn't look like a cipher. Strictly speaking, concealment is a branch of stenography, not cryptography, but it fit under the heading *ciphers, puzzles, and mazes*. Invisible ink, text hidden in a hat band, a null cipher—a block of text in which one read every fifth (or second or ninth) word and discarded the rest. One voice speaking in a chorus . . .

A cipher that didn't look like a cipher. Something hiding in plain sight. The simplest things are often the easiest to overlook, and the most humiliating to admit you've missed. But what did he think I'd seen? What could I have seen? What—

Spikes of headache formed. I closed my eyes, willed my forehead to relax, and released the tension. I was making this too difficult. This was something my boss had expected me to notice immediately, had so feared I'd notice that he'd always kept me out. That he presumed I'd have seen automatically when I so deliberately *hadn't* snooped around.

I examined the room again, this time in full snoop mode.

The apartment was a study in grayscale. The carpet was steely, the walls pearly, the furniture inky. Most of the designs, when there were any, were geometric—overlapping circles, mainly. Even the books had the impersonal feel of a bookstore. Everything was spotlessly clean and looked unused.

He had lived here for as long as I'd known him and likely longer, and yet nothing struck me as to his taste—or having any taste beyond a generic template.

My boss refilled my teacup. He hadn't removed the leaves from the pot, and this cup was strong, dark, and aromatic. The milk swirled through, sending out pale tendrils that mingled beneath the surface and turned the liquid golden brown.

Concealment cipher: a cipher designed not to look like a cipher.

"Do you actually live here?" I asked.

He beamed at me. "You might say that my living area has been transposed. Come." He rose in one smooth movement, and I scurried after him.

"I hope you don't think this means I understand," I said. "Are you the concealment cipher or the concealed cipher or is the apartment the cipher or the concealer or—or something else?"

"All of the above." He pushed open the door furthest from the entrance and stepped into his bedroom.

"Um," I said.

It was as modern and bland as the main room. A gray duvet covered the double bed, along with a matching throw and pillow shams.

Side tables and dresser were black. The lamps were spiraled black pillars with white shades—very Modern Art. Everything looked clean, tidy, and unused.

My boss didn't pause, tramping directly through to the opposite door—the bathroom.

It was nicer than my bathroom—but then, my apartment actually had two bathrooms: one for me, and one that Luc and Francis shared and that I avoided like the plague, which it likely contained.

Again, my boss kept going: straight through and out the opposite door.

Basic spatial awareness informed me that this door led back into the main room, and it did. We arrived a couple of feet down from my boss's bedroom door, which was closed again. Had I closed it? Something felt different. Disassociating.

Back we went to the table, where our tea waited. I moved to sit at my cup and stopped, confused. Which was mine? I'd thought my back was to the front door, but I'd also thought I'd been on his left.

My boss took the right-hand seat.

Of course, he was correct. He didn't take milk in his tea, so this one had to be mine. I sat, swiveled my teacup, and drank. Prince of Wales tea, getting tepid, no discernible variance in flavor.

My boss had an expression on, one he usually reserved for ciphers—like his attention was a magnifying glass for his brain. He was waiting for me to *get it*, and I hadn't gotten it yet.

Holding my teacup to my lips, a barrier of china and infused water against that expression, I took in the room once more.

It *was* different. Backward. The light switch was on the door's left, but most people are right handed. I'd had to swivel my teacup to grip the handle. This couldn't be the same room as before . . . but then, what about the tea?

I downed the last gulps and flipped my cup over. The words were small, smudged, and printed in mirror image:

smmiS & ydraH

Since my boss seemed content to watch and wait, I got up and crossed to the bookcases. The titles on the covers were all backward, but when I opened the books, their contents read forward. Closer inspection showed that someone had painstakingly removed and replaced each cover.

There were more changes; they cropped up everywhere I looked, now that I'd opened my eyes to them. The modern colors of the room were less stark, as if they had been run through a washing machine too many times. There was wear, too, and numerous small signs of habitation. One of the armchairs was pulled closer to the fireplace, its seat dipping to accommodate a particular occupant; the other held a green tartan throw folded over its back. The fireplace set was crooked and marked with soot. Rings marred the coffee table. Nothing was decrepit, but nothing was brand spanking new either.

Perhaps I'd been too hasty about drinking that tea.

"It is perfectly safe," my boss assured me. "Things transfer better from that side. I believe it is because that side is the original."

"And this side is what, an echo?"

"The wrong side."

"Perverted, depraved, and dangerous?"

"As in the wrong side of fabric," my boss explained patiently. "The right side bears the print, a muted version of which can be seen on the wrong side. If you mark the wrong side with a light hand, the mark will not show through."

The image of my boss sewing printed fabric struck me as so bizarre that I had to reconstitute my brain around it. He'd been surprising me a lot lately, and I didn't like it. "If I wanted to get out," I asked, "how would I go about it?"

That was the right question. "Not through the front door," he said; "it does not go anywhere. Continuing on through the bedroom would be fastest. You could also go back, but I have found the transition unpleasant in that direction. Technically, we are upside down here, of course, but since gravity is as well, we don't notice." He abruptly grinned, transforming his face from dignified gentleman to mischievous schoolboy. "Look out the window." He indicated the one over the sink.

I got up, hesitated, and asked, "Why did you turn your apartment into a Möbius strip? Added security?"

I was rewarded for my deduction by another of his rare grins. I hadn't seen him this delighted, this relaxed, in a long time. It must have been a relief, showing someone. "The design is not purposeful," he said. "Things alter their forms in my presence. The longer I am around a place, the more it changes. It is as much as I can do to keep this place as normal as it is. Go on."

"By 'place,' do you mean this apartment, or—?"

"I have lived in Silvertip City for five years. Have you ever been anywhere more absurd?"

I hadn't, and another piece of the puzzle clicked into place. I had assumed the proprietress had been responsible for drawing me back to the auction house, but why would she? She hadn't been interested in me—hadn't known I existed, probably—until I'd made a nuisance of myself. On the other hand, my boss had had every reason to call for help. And if he had been unable to do so, perhaps his unconscious mind had done it for him.

I looked through the kitchen window. Beyond lay a dark expanse, lit by neither moon nor stars. The only light anywhere poured from a window across from me and to the side. I leaned in until my nose pressed against oddly warm glass and squinted. There was a room beyond that window, with the indistinct shadows of furniture. Movement. Someone in the room. Approaching the window.

My boss waved.

I reared back and swung around. He was not in the main room, but the bedroom door stood slightly ajar. I ran for it, flung it open, and found him sitting on his bed, waiting for me.

His real bed this time; that was obvious. The bedroom was designed the same way, except in reverse, but this one had personal touches: a bathrobe hanging from the door, a book on the bedside table, a painting on the wall. There may have been other details, but I was too busy pretending not to look to notice them.

"You see?" my boss asked excitedly, leading me to the window. "We are inside the Möbius strip. This window is nearly opposite the kitchen window. I have often thought I should make use of the connection, but have never had much opportunity to do so. The children use it in some sort of game, I believe. They think it is marvelous."

"The . . . children?"

"It is interesting the extent to which my personification prefers forms related to circles," my boss mused. "I have been meaning to test how far the pattern extends and whether anyone else can identify it. Can you imagine what would happen if my presence were deciphered by some dangerous personification? What would Terrorism or Espionage do if they got their hands on Cipher?"

I cleared my throat. "What children?"

"But then, more likely only Cipher could decipher Cipher. Recursion resides partly in my domain."

"Not *your* children?"

My boss frowned at me, as if he were only now remembering I was there. The cloak of dignity fell back into place, stiffening his back and wiping his face as clean as the right side of his apartment. "Well," he said, "I will let you sleep on it." With stilted politeness, he escorted me through the bathroom (the real bathroom, complete with red toothbrush) and into the main room, where he held out my coat.

Chapter 8

HARASSMENT

That was my cue to leave. I wasn't offended; my boss shuts down like that sometimes. It means he's passed his threshold and has no intention of continuing the discussion—or any form of human interaction. That's the reason I'm usually so circumspect about getting things out of him. Once he shuts down, it can take days, weeks, even months to coax him back. When I first knew him, I kept trying to squeeze more out anyway, which just made him shut down more. I'd never managed to wring a single extra drop from him, once he'd banished me.

But then, I've always been hampered by common decency.

There was plenty of tea left in the pot, kept hot by the childish pink cozy, so I sat and poured myself a cup. That put my back to my boss, and prickles on my neck as he tried to drill sense back into me with his stare.

Only once that didn't work did he try saying my name: "Mercedes ..."

Uncertain. Off-balance.

I sipped my tea and thought of the things I could say. *Would you give up this easily if it were your brother on the line?* Heavy handed and obvious, but not necessarily ineffective. *Or if it were "the children"? Incidentally, what children?*

I indicated his chair without looking around. "Please, have a seat. More tea?"

You'd think I'd hooked and reeled and dragged, the show he made of shuffling forward. He leaned on the back of his chair, fingers making dents in the padding. "Mercedes . . ."

I filled his cup and added two sugar cubes. "I'm beginning to understand the basics," I said. "I get that Theodora is some sort of personification and not a fairy or troll or demon, but I'll need more specifics in order to deal with her."

"You must not make another deal with her!" he cried, voice cracking on the words. "Whatever you do, you must not! Mercedes, you cannot win. You will only make things worse."

I blinked at him, taken aback. "I meant the word rhetorically."

He was going to do some serious damage, if he didn't let go of that chair. He stared at me, and as I watched, the cracks in his mask smoothed over and vanished. His shoulders relaxed, took on a parody of their normal pose. "Of course," he said, and his voice too had been smoothed over. "Mercedes, I am very tired."

"You work hard."

"Yes."

I put a third sugar cube in his tea, stirred it, and motioned for him to sit beside me.

He gave up on tact. "Mercedes," he said, "please leave."

"Sr. Nordfeld," I said, "please sit down and answer my questions. The whole reason you invited me here was so that we could talk about the proprietress and how to stop her—and we've barely begun."

His eyebrows lifted. "What more is there?"

"How to make her leave my family alone, for a start."

He slid into his chair, shaking his head wearily. "I thought you understood. Theodora Banks is the personification of Deals & Bargains. There is no way to make her do anything. That was my miscalculation—I thought I could make a deal with her and get away with it. I was wrong. There is no deal you can make with her that she will not twist to her advantage. No deal that will not give her a firmer grip on you."

"So what do you advise?" I asked. "That I give up and cut my losses?"

"Before it is too late, yes."

"Keeping in mind that 'my losses' refers to my eldest brother?"

He didn't answer.

"And after Francis, then who?" I asked. "Luc? My parents? How far will Theodora go to get back at me?"

His brow crinkled. "She may not want to 'get back' at you. There is no reason for the personification of Deals & Bargains to seek revenge."

"You mean, apart from me" *(killing her night guard)* "burning down her place of business?"

By his reaction, I suspected he hadn't realized that had been me. He *had* been out of it.

"But regardless of her motivation," I said, "I will not abandon Francis to her."

My boss rubbed the bridge of his nose, defeated. "I am sorry, Mercedes. There is nothing I can do to stop her if she is determined to go after your brother. Only he can help himself—by absolutely refusing to make any deals with her."

"He won't listen to me. He's . . . highly susceptible to beauty. I tried to get him to resist, but he wasn't interested."

"Ah." My boss closed his eyes and hardened his jaw. I could see him coming to a decision, and not one he liked. I could see the effort it took for him to meet my gaze and say, "If you bring your brothers here, I will show them what I have shown you. Then they will believe."

I could guess what it cost him, to expose himself not only to me but to two strangers whom I'd admittedly not always spoken of in glowing terms. I stuttered out the best thanks I could manage.

"You will try to convince them again before going to that extremity," he said. "But if you cannot, bring them tonight. There is no benefit in putting it off."

"I'll do my best," I promised. "Thank you. *Thank you.*"

He nodded, but his eyes trailed off my face and fixed on a point behind me. "I do have one other request," he said.

"Yes—of course."

"When your brothers are safe from Deals & Bargains," he said slowly, precisely, addressing the wall, "you will account our ledger closed."

I didn't understand.

"I would rather not be in your debt, Mercedes."

The bottom dropped out of my stomach. I opened my mouth and closed it again. I'd almost convinced myself he hadn't heard my conversation with the proprietress, the logic I'd used to free him. I could feel myself reddening, and I fought the urge to burst out explanations, excuses. *You do know I wasn't referring to* romantic *love, right?*

That would make it so much worse.

You aren't supposed to pay me back. It's not possible to pay me back for what I did freely, only to be grateful to me—to be grateful that there's someone in your life who will freely give when no recompense is possible.

Was it so awful for him, to be in debt to me?

I stood stiffly. The room swayed, distant and surreal. I wasn't sure if I was going to cry or simply shatter into a million jagged pieces. "There's no need for that," I rasped. "If it bothers you so much, then I release you from your debt now. Freely, immediately, and without condition."

I slammed the door on my way out.

My brothers' lives were cheap at the price. I'd driven half an hour before I was cool enough to acknowledge that. Where was my honor— in avoiding the utter humiliation of facing my boss again or in protecting Francis's life and freedom—and likely Luc's, too?

I had no doubt that my boss's scheme would work. My brothers might have disbelieved me, but they would not deny the evidence of their own eyes . . . especially when Theodora was absent. Nor would they refuse to come and meet my boss, no matter how angry they were at me. They'd come, they'd see, they'd listen—and next time Theodora came around, all the smiles in the world would not be able to seduce them.

And in the morning, I'd give two weeks' notice. That'd be plenty of time to deal with the prefects and prepare instructions for my boss's new assistant.

Not that there'd be many instructions to write. What did he need me for except to make him coffee? I'd been hired for my barista experience, not my brain. What did my boss care if—

It didn't matter. In fact, this was probably for the best. I'd get that eye surgery and put in my military application and move on with my life. Past time for it.

I turned the car toward home. There was no benefit in putting it off.

My brothers' lives weren't the only ones at stake.

I was a few blocks from home when that realization broke out of the shadows, and once it had, I couldn't shove it back. Theodora was only what, thirty-four, thirty-five years old? My boss's age. And she had already enslaved and murdered dozens if not hundreds of people. If she lived a normal lifespan (and wasn't it optimistic to think she wouldn't find a way to extend it?), she could easily continue for another fifty years.

Fifty years of victims. Taking my brothers to see my boss would save them, but it wouldn't save anyone else.

They say the only way to stop a serial killer is to lock them up or kill them.

I had to pull over. My hands were shaking.

There's no deal that she will not twist to her advantage. No deal that will not give her a firmer grip on you.

"Help your brothers first," I whispered to myself. "Then—"

Then, one way or another, I would have warned her against me and thus put her beyond my reach forever. Then I would not be able to do anything against her, and it would not be my problem anymore. Then I would be safe.

This is an evil place. And I will not allow it to stand.

I must not.

Chapter 9:

THEFT

I ran a few errands before returning to the parking garage. On my short hike home, I sent my boss a text, thanking him for his kind offer and saying that I'd managed to convince my brothers without his assistance.

In fact, I knew how futile—and ultimately undermining—any such confrontation would be. If I hadn't known it before stepping into my apartment, I sure knew it thirty seconds later, when Francis started yelling.

"It's high time you came crawling home," he said, as glad to see me as snowmen are to see spring. "Are you ready to apologize?"

Luc scurried away to bury himself under four inches of headphone. Lucky him; Francis would destroy my headphones if I tried that. "Excuse me," I said, "you're in my way." When he grabbed my arm to stop me, I turned my most world-weary look up at him. "Really, Francis, why would I apologize for my brother being such an idiot that he'll believe anything a woman tells him, as long as her breasts are big enough?"

That's when the yelling started:

Bust size alone wasn't enough to snag Francis. Francis was a connoisseur of every variety of female beauty. I had no right to use beauty against Theodora—I was just jealous, that's it. Jealous, like she'd said. One of my many shortcomings. "You're lucky she isn't pressing charges!" he bellowed more than once. "You're lucky *I* don't report you! Have you any idea how much that auction house will cost to rebuild?"

"A lot," I said, "of sweat and blood. You're making a hurricane in a cup of water."

"I'll have to rebuild at cost!" he bulldozed on, like I hadn't spoken. "What else can I do, when my own sister burned it down?"

According to her, I thought but did not say. Part of it was that, yes, my own account to him had hinted at this. But mostly, I was *not saying* a lot of things. I didn't even point out how improbable it was that I was jealous of Theodora's beauty when I had such a high opinion of my own (and *mine* was honestly come by). Francis gave me dozens of openings to feed his flame, but it all felt so very petty and enervating. So I mostly ignored him as he followed me around and showed off his chewing-out stamina.

"The worst of it is that you made me doubt her," he informed me through my bathroom door, which I'd barely managed to close before he could follow me in. "I went and looked at the auction house, you know that? I told her that I needed to appraise it. I did, but that wasn't the reason. I went to see if it had a basement, if I could find any basis for your accusations. Guess what I found?"

Whatever she wanted you to find, I thought, and stuffed my toothbrush between my teeth to keep from speaking it aloud.

"Nothing! Not—a—thing! Not a single remnant of weirdly colored paint; not a bone; not a hint of a basement."

I turned the shower on. I'm a morning shower person, normally, but I wanted the white noise and the hot water. Francis must've heard me turn it on, but it didn't stop him yelling through the door. Nothing stops Francis, when he gets like this. Our mother used to joke that it was her berserker blood infecting him, which is nonsense, because she can trace her lineage back four centuries to Brazil, and there never was a berserker in the family. So Francis had no excuse, but he kept yelling anyway. He yelled as I dried off and yelled when I came out in a towel to grab a nightgown. He yelled as I moisturized and yelled as I clipped my toenails. He'd probably have kept yelling all night if his voice hadn't given out.

"This is your fault," he rasped at me. "You know I need my voice for work!"

I said nothing and waited for the obvious to seep through his thick skull. His voice must honestly have been hurting him, because he huffed off a mere five minutes later, slamming my door behind him and then his own.

Half a minute ticked by, and then Luc's knuckles rapped on the wood. "Our brother has a temper problem," he observed, sticking his head in. Nice of him to join me, now it was safe. "Not that you didn't deserve it."

"Don't you start," I said tiredly, and pushed him out before locking my door.

Despite my attempts to ignore Francis, I felt like a wrung-out washcloth. I sank heavily onto my bed and set my alarm for one a.m. It wouldn't be safe to go out before then, and maybe I could catch some sleep.

⌐ ～ ᑲ

I could not catch some sleep. It was a relief when my alarm finally went off. Relying on a penlight, I got up and changed into sturdy, dark clothes. I put my hiking boots and thick socks by my door, but stayed barefoot for the moment to minimize the chances of Francis catching me.

Francis is no stranger to insomnia. He honestly suffers from it but is too pigheaded to book an appointment with a sleep doctor. Half the time, if I get up in the night for a glass of water, there he is: sitting at the dining table, eating junk food, and staring miserably into midair.

Tonight, however, the apartment was dark and sleepy. Moonlight pooled through balcony doors. The faint foody smell reminded me that I never had eaten that fish sandwich.

My stomach twisted at the thought. I could eat something now—

But that would only be putting it off, wouldn't it?

I listened at Francis's door, then eased it open and peered inside. Francis lay on his stomach, hugging his pillow, face turned my way. No glimmer emerged from his eyes, and his back rose and fell regularly with sleep and oinking snores.

I dropped my jaw to breathe silently and deeply through my mouth as I pulled his door shut.

He'd left his phone by his bedside table, close enough that he could grab it with one arm without shifting. I noted its exact position, unplugged it, and took it around the foot of the bed. Shielding the light with body and footboard, I scrolled through his contacts and wrote down the number I wanted. Then back it went, precisely as before.

That was the part it'd be easy to talk my way out of, if Francis awoke. Considerably trickier would be explaining why I was opening his safe.

It was a big safe and had probably been ridiculously expensive, but Francis believes in being safety conscious about his manliness complex. Or maybe it wasn't a complex, the way that he drove a giant red truck, had a collection of guns, and worked on construction sites; in Batata, that sort of thing is the norm, and women do it as much as men. Maybe it had nothing to do with him being a hair under five-foot-five.

I got the combination wrong the first time, and had to try a second. It's not like I got an opportunity to use it much, for all that Francis insisted Luc and I memorize it.

The safe clicked open, and I plucked out his smallest revolver: a .357 Magnum with a walnut grip and a 5.5" barrel. Petite enough to fit my hands, but with a long enough barrel not to kick like crazy. I'd shot it before, although not in a couple of years.

A box of ammo and a holster completed the picture, and then I pressed the safe shut, twirled the lock, and padded out. Francis's lids didn't so much as flutter when I passed him and slipped out his door.

"What are you doing?" Luc asked.

I gasped and whirled. He hadn't turned on the light for the short trek between his room and his bathroom, but the nightlight gave him an excellent view of my armful. His eyes yo-yoed between my arms and my face and widened. "Mercedes," he said, "what—"

"Quiet!" I whispered. "Don't wake him. In my room."

Eyes round as a dead man's coins, Luc followed me. I switched on the light, and let him watch as I threaded the bulging holster onto a thick leather belt and pulled on my hiking socks and boots. I was positively ostentatious about it, to keep him occupied while I thought up a really, really good lie that'd hold up no matter what he learned.

That's one of the problems with working for the Carinan Security

Service: lying becomes so automatic that you forget that, sometimes, it's better to tell the truth.

Could I tell him? He wasn't the one who might've made a deal with Deals & Bargains; he couldn't warn her. And if I did tell him—if I took him with me—then I wouldn't be alone.

"Should I interpret your hesitation as a sign you're going to lie to me?" Luc asked. No warmth tinged his voice; it was too busy being ironic. He folded his arms and leaned against my door, and it struck me how much he must trust me, to see me outfitting myself like this and not try to stop me.

Luc and I have always been more similar to each other than to anyone else in the family. If there was anyone who might understand, it was Luc.

I wanted him to understand, wanted it desperately.

"I wouldn't lie to you," I lied; "I just wasn't sure how to tell you. I'm going to see Theodora."

"With *that.*"

The tricky part was, Luc doesn't like weapons. It's like he doesn't believe in them. In video games, sure—you won't find anyone more knowledgeable about weaponry modern and archaic. In real life, he'd been forced to go hunting with Francis and our father back in Batata, but I don't think he'd ever shot anything. Luc was what I only pretended to be: someone who pored over violence in theory and then went damp and weak at the sight of actual blood.

But.

But he wasn't a fool, Luc. If I could make him understand—if I could prove—

"This? Self-defense," I assured him. "Look, Luc, I wasn't kidding when I said she was dangerous. I'm going to go have a chat with her, but I'm not going to go unprotected."

Luc threw up his hands. "What's wrong with your pepper spray? Or meeting her in a public place in broad daylight? Or, I don't know, crazy idea—*contacting the reeves?*"

"I can't go to law enforcement until I have proof," I said primly. "Such as a recorded admission of guilt. Don't give me that look, Luc. If you'd seen what I'd seen, you'd be the first one insisting I go armed."

Hah. More lies. He'd be the first one insisting I hide under my bed until the bogeyman passed by.

Luc scrubbed the heel of his hand over his forehead, lids squeezed shut. "Mercedes, you need to let this go. You don't honestly believe what you're saying about her. I know you. You'd go to the reeves if she were really dangerous, not head out to meet her in the middle of the night. Face it. You don't like her because your boss—"

"This has nothing to do with my boss," I said coldly. And that was true. He had made a mistake, and Theodora had used that against him, but that was over—and I have never known him to make the same mistake twice. He was safe, and I have never been motivated by revenge. The past was in the past; it was what Theodora was doing in the present and might do in the future that concerned me.

Not that Francis could ever understand that, but Luc—"You say you know me," I said, "but you clearly don't know when I'm telling the truth. You clearly don't trust me enough to believe me about Theodora."

"Because that's not how the world *works*," Luc burst out. "Mercedes, I met Theodora. You can't tell me a woman like that is a magical bargaining psychopath!"

"Why not?"

He threw up his hands. "Because she's nice! Because she eats hamburgers and wears cute dresses and flirts with Francis! Because things like that don't happen in real life!"

I rubbed my thumb over the thin cardboard of the ammo box. I could almost smell the gunpowder. I thought of the things I'd bought before coming home, of fluorescent-lit stores and bored clerks and twisted streets and foolish brothers. "Tell you what," I said, as if the idea were only just occurring to me. "Why don't you come with me? You hide and listen while I talk to her. She'll speak freely in front of me, and we'll see which one of us is right."

"And if I'm right," said Luc, "you'll admit it. You'll stop harassing her, apologize to Francis, and drop your grudge forever."

"Gladly," I said, since it didn't matter what I promised. "You'll come?"

"I guess I have to," he sighed.

Chapter 10:

ASSAULT

We took Francis's truck. Neither Luc nor I owned a car, it was too far to bike, and I wasn't about to borrow my boss's car. Not because it was too recognizable or because I didn't have permission to use it outside of work or because it might implicate my boss, although those things were true. But their truth paled in comparison to the sheer stupidity of starting your criminal activities by retrieving a car from a manned parking garage where you were well known and sure to be recorded by security cameras.

Seriously. Don't do that nonsense.

"I wasn't suggesting we take your boss's car," said Luc, to whom I hadn't explained my logic. "I only meant that Francis might wake up, notice his truck was gone, and wonder where it went."

Yes, well. Every plan has flaws.

I drove us north through Silvertip and kept going when the city ended. Luc made noises about this, but I reminded him that Theodora would only speak freely if she met me privately.

"Privacy is good," he said. "Finding a creepy shack in the middle of nowhere is overkill. I think it's going to rain."

"Not according to the weather report—or not until tomorrow morning."

"It *is* tomorrow morning. Technically."

I didn't reply. I was half regretting inviting Luc along. The night felt unreal—abandoned by human life, soft and unfathomable, thick with cool air. This far from my boss's routine, the streets stayed sensibly straight and right angled. I turned from the main road to a smaller one that paralleled the Gyllan River. I'd already turned off the GPS—had only used it to get as far as the edge of town. I hadn't wanted even that much of a record; but then, I hadn't had much choice.

The Gyllan is powerful, swift, and deep. It flows north through the whole of Silvertip Prefecture until it meets the Bay of Uror, which joins the Atlantic Ocean. Late though it was in the year, the river foamed like a rabid dog. Every year, the *Post* features articles about strong young man (it was young men) who'd decided to show off their swimming skills by diving into the engorged river. The bodies hadn't been found, and the reeves interviewed stated that they probably never would be. People should learn from this and be responsible about the dangers of turgid water, use their common sense in potentially dangerous situations, always wear life jackets, et cetera, et cetera, don't be an idiot.

This was as far as I had planned my route. I hadn't chosen the exact location ahead of time, because I hadn't had to; there are literally dozens of scenic pullouts in this area, all of them deeply overgrown, invisible from the road, and forgotten by everyone but the occasional lost tourist. I picked a particularly sketchy one, and veered onto the winding turnoff. We bumped over potholes, seasick headlights bouncing between dense foliage and heavily mossed trees.

"You arranged to meet her here?" Luc asked as we got out, looking around in amazement at the flora and out across the Gyllan. He inhaled the fresh damp aromas of leaf and twig and rubbed his neck. Silvertip is far lusher than Edenfield; instead of widely spaced beeches, we have dense forest. "How's she going to find the right turnoff?"

I shrugged. "Magic."

"I'm serious, Mercedes. Did you have exact coordinates, or something? Give her the precise mileage? No way this place shows up on a map. I don't want to be hanging around all night, while she's one turnoff over."

"Then consider this another test," I said shortly.

The moon had swelled nearly full and, this far from the source of light pollution, the stars poked out their heads. It wasn't bright by day standards, but there was plenty of light to walk by. Our way was made easier because some gallant group had crafted rocky stairs down to the water, and they were mostly intact. My sturdy hiking boots had no trouble finding traction.

I left Luc halfway down the cliff, right before the tree line gave way to orange-gray rocks. The air tasted of mud and wet vegetation. Moss crept down from above, and the tiny corpses of river-dwelling creatures gritted the dry rocks and slicked the wet ones. A moist breeze ruffled my hair and infiltrated my coat.

I positioned myself a couple of yards downstream of the stairs, feet planted hip-width apart, shoulders rolled back. The .357 Magnum weighed heavily on my belt. I felt around the light-headedness in my mind and banished it, banished anything that might interfere.

There was no benefit in putting it off. I pulled out the disposable phone I'd purchased earlier and dialed the number I'd found in Francis's contacts.

Theodora picked up on the first ring. "Mercedes."

"Would you like to make a deal?" I asked.

"Would you?"

Her voice hadn't come from the phone: it had rung bell-like through the night air, and I followed it up and over.

She stood at the top of the stairs, looking down at me, framed against the night sky, luminous in the moonlight. Once she was sure she had my attention, she began to gracefully descend. Her hands were empty, and she was dressed in a simple white robe with ragged sleeves and hem. Soft boots shod her feet, and a wreath of white flowers crowned her long loose curls. Between her pale skin and that getup, she looked like a human-sized version of a children's-book fairy—which I took to be a joke at my expense.

I noted this clinically, distantly, and it didn't bother me.

She took her sweet time coming down. Business as usual; summons in the middle of the night nothing special. Never did she look away from me, left or right, and I kept my eyes on her. She could not have seen Luc.

"I've been waiting for your call," she said when she stood on the narrow bank with me. She wasn't gloating, just stating a fact. "If privacy was what you wanted, you could have asked."

"Special accommodation is a commodity."

"Not," she said, "always. I owned a many-roomed auction house for a reason."

"But not now."

"I have other places."

That was ominous, but it only reinforced how dangerous she was, how desperately she needed to be stopped. How impossible it would be to stop her by mundane means.

I thought this, filed it, and moved on. "I called you here to make a deal," I said.

"I know. To save your brother."

"No—to save you."

She frowned at me, pulling her head back to get a better view. I wasn't following her script.

"I know the concept is alien to you," I said, "but not everyone is evil. I understand what you are. I understand that you may not have full control over your influence. I do not understand why you are working with the trappings of your personification instead of against them, but I can help you. I can free you."

Her eyes narrowed. "That is certainly a unique analysis of the situation. You must have been talking with Jon; the term 'personification' is pretentious enough for him. What is it he calls himself? Cipher? I suppose he has invented a name for me as well."

I filed this too, and didn't let it distract me. I ground on: "Here's the deal: you agree never to use your personification, to never make another deal with anyone. You forgive all debts and release everyone who owes you. You put aside the mantle of Deals & Bargains for the rest of your life and dedicate yourself to making amends for the evil you have wrought. You perform this in the spirit of my words without trying to trick me or otherwise exploit loopholes."

She laughed. "You can't be serious."

"You arrived here by the power of your personification," I went on, "which means that this deal will prevent you from easily getting home. Therefore, for my side of the deal, I will escort you home."

I didn't expect her to accept; I expected her to laugh again. Maybe Theodora would have laughed, but my phrasing had brought out Deals & Bargains—her eyes silver and bright as distant stars, her voice smooth and cool, her expression immovable as a glacier. She said:

"Your deal does not fall within bargainable parameters," and Theodora added, "as you must have known it wouldn't. Don't waste my time, Mercedes, and don't try to trick me. We both know you're here to save Francis, and that the only thing you think I'll accept in exchange is you."

I had wondered about that.

"Or perhaps I'm mistaken and you have another trade in mind. Do you want me to take Lucas instead of Francisco? Would you sacrifice one brother for another? Would you sacrifice Jon? Whom do you love best in this world?"

Healthy individuals don't quantify love and human worth that way, I thought but did not say. We were bargaining, and I didn't know what would count as part of that.

Theodora raised an eyebrow at my silence. Deals & Bargains said: "Offer me a deal."

"I have."

"That deal was not within bargainable parameters. Offer me a different deal."

I restrained my twitching fingers. Soon, but not yet. Not yet. One more chance. "Tell me what deal will prevent you from continuing as Deals & Bargains," I said. "Tell me what deal will stop you from causing the sort of damage to people that I witnessed in the auction house. Tell me what deal will effectively neuter you. Tell me what deal will save all those who are enthralled to you."

Theodora tilted her head at me. "No deal that would so restrain my power is within bargainable parameters," she said. "Or . . . no remaining deal. But if you are clever and persuasive, you might save your brother. Offer me a deal."

There. I'd made her say it. I'd suspected it, but there had been a chance—no. I clawed my thoughts back into place. One more. Once more. "It seems to me," I said, "that when you know someone is evil, the *last* thing you should do is give them what they want. No matter how bad the thing is that they threaten you with, it isn't as bad as what they're after."

Her eyes flicked sarcastically at me. "I didn't make your brother ask me out, if that's what you're getting at. I was looking through the phone book for a construction company to rebuild my auction house, and I recognized the name. He was one of several I interviewed. It's not my fault he falls at the feet of any woman with a pretty face."

That was uncomfortably close to my own analysis. "I'm primarily talking about the dead people in your larder," I said, projecting extra loudly for Luc's sake. "I suppose that was their idea too. I'm sure they came to you and begged you to saw off their limbs and tear out their hearts."

That got her. Theodora, I mean; I don't think anything could've gotten Deals & Bargains. She tossed her hair and shook her arms irritably, like a woman who has to kill yet another pesky spider. White petals fluttered from her hair into the dark water. "You think I *like* that?" she cried. "I can't stop them! 'I'd trade my eyes to be able to sing like that.' 'I'd give an arm and a leg for a decent sandwich.' 'A horse! A horse! My kingdom for a horse!' They insist on making ridiculous, thoughtless deals and are satisfied by what I provide for my part, but the racket they make when I come to collect! As if it were *my* fault!"

"And so you kill them."

She scoffed. "Some of them die in the process, of course, as if they didn't know what would happen when they gave their hearts or minds away. Some insist on it. 'You can take my life, but you'll never take my freedom!' Sounds heroic, but they're not the ones who have to clean blood out of the carpet. And even that's not as bad as the ones who bring me sacrifices. What am I supposed to do with twenty goats? Or the heads of their enemies on plates? Fortunately, people will buy practically anything, under the name of 'art,' if the starting bid is high enough."

She fixed a glare on me. "And then you come and make more of a mess than the rest combined."

"You kidnapped Sr. Nordfeld!"

"He would have been fine. My night guard, on the other hand, will not."

"Then he shouldn't have attacked me."

"No: then you shouldn't have disobeyed my instructions."

"You're telling me that you were justified in attacking me with a half-human monstrosity for looking backward? That wasn't part of our deal. Nor was you holding on to my boss when you had no right to him."

"Jon is an adult. He can make his own decisions."

"While unconscious?"

She smiled and inclined her head.

So there we had it: an admission of guilt. Even Luc could not deny it.

I took a deep breath. "I guess we won't be making a deal. We clearly can't agree on anything."

Her eyes tightened inquiringly, as if I'd said something peculiar. "Didn't Jon warn you? You summoned me here. You must make a deal. If not willingly now, then unwillingly later."

I didn't answer. Blood rushed in my ears. *No benefit—*

Theodora clucked in disgust. "Later it is. Until then, Mercedes." She turned to go.

She must not leave.

I cleared my throat and heard myself say, as if from a great distance, "There is one thing Sr. Nordfeld told me."

"And what's—" Her eyes caught the glint of metal in my hand.

"He told me you were human."

I shot her three times: twice through the chest, once through the head. I couldn't have missed, she was so close. She fell before I could fire the last round, but I followed her. Standing over her face, I aimed between her eyes and pulled the trigger.

Chapter 11:

BATTERY

My arms hurt. The gun was heavy. How long had I been standing here?

Blood swirled black in the moonlight.

Rocks bounced and crumbled down the hill and gravel skittered as Luc scrambled out of his hiding place. I turned my face his way and waited for him to—what? Come down and tell me off? Try to resuscitate her? Tell me he had heard everything, and that we'd better get her body into the river?

None of the above: he went up the trail, not down. The truck was unlocked, but he wouldn't get far without a key.

I had put a lot of thought into what would come next, in a cold, distant way. I had everything I needed in the back of that truck, wrapped inside plastic garbage bags. There wouldn't be much cleanup to do here: Luc was right about the rain; it was expected in torrents before dawn broke. That would take care of the blood, and I'd used a revolver so I wouldn't have to worry about tracking down spent brass. By the time Francis awoke, the evidence of our presence would be washed clean.

But I'd get Francis's high-powered flashlight from the truck to check anyway. It wouldn't do to overlook a dropped phone, a scrap of cloth, or some other sliver of evidence.

I touched my face. My skin felt disgustingly rubbery, and my mouth was stretched side to side in something like a grin. There hadn't been a joke, so I pushed my lips back to where they belonged. There also seemed to be something wrong with my thinking.

This is what shock feels like, I thought dully. What was I meant to be doing? Ah, yes.

Swapping my gun to my left hand, I crouched by Theodora's body and reached for her neck. I don't know why I felt the need to check for a pulse before I dragged her into the river, but I did. Maybe it was part of the strangeness in my brain, which felt like a swirl of treacle bogged it down.

Her silver eyes were open, but the only light that shone off them was reflected from the stars above. Powder burns blackened her pale skin. I couldn't see the details in the dark, but I didn't need to. I could've told you she was dead even if I were blind. If I live to be ninety-nine, I shall never forget that smell.

Her neck beneath my fingers was warm and smooth. No pulse. I waited, to make sure. Felt nothing. Nothing. Nothing.

And that was when Theodora woke up and started trying to kill me.

$$\mathcal{E} \times \cap 6;$$

I was armed, held the high ground, and had years of scrapping experience with my brothers—and none of that did me a lick of good.

Theodora's leg scythed around as I cried out in surprise. She whacked my ankle, and I sloshed forward, turning my body at the last moment so I didn't land on her. One hand grabbed onto encrusted river rocks. The other held the gun, and metal banged against stone.

Thin, chilly fingers wrapped around my supporting wrist and squeezed. I remembered the gun in my left hand and swung it at her, but Theodora was ready for me. She twisted my wrist hard, stabbing lightning bolts up my arm. My body flipped after my wrist, and I sprawled on top of her—except that she wasn't there anymore. She'd let go of me to spring to her feet. Her boots were too soft to kick properly, but she sure tried, aiming for my face and belly.

I instinctively curled up to protect myself, and heard the gun skitter away. I didn't remember letting go of it. *Oh no, you don't*, I snarled in my mind. I rolled for it, over pointed rocks and smooth, slapping the ground and grabbing at air, hunting for cold metal. There—a glint. I lunged for it.

A booted sole contacted my head. The world blinked out, and then I returned. My lungs took a couple of seconds longer to come back online. Rocks dug into my back. The night sky disappeared beyond a dark shadow with two bright silver eyes.

That was her knee, on which she rested her entire weight over my sternum. I thrashed, but she caught my wrists and pressed them to the ground next to my head. She leaned in, digging that knee deeper, teeth bared.

I bared my teeth right back, and abruptly relaxed. As she fell forward, I snapped at her face and neck. My teeth caught the skin of her cheek before she howled and whipped back. I pushed further up, snapping, but her hands slapped down over my throat. Two thick bolts ground into my windpipe, squeezing out hacking coughs.

I ripped at her face with my fingernails, but Theodora only squeezed harder, leaning her weight into her thumbs. Weak slaps pattered her wrists and shoulders, but she ignored them.

The bones seemed to have vanished from my arms. The moon and stars fuzzed and faded. Hot coals filled my brain.

"Do you think," Theodora demanded thickly, her voice wrapped in the cotton balls plugging my ears, "that I was not protected? Did you think you were the first person to attack me? I've been doing this for *years.*"

Think? How did she expect me to think while she was choking the life out of me? Adrenaline exploded over my thoughts while my body turned to jelly. My only *thought*, if you could call it that, was getting rid of the terrible pressure on my neck, the terrible searing in my head. And if that wasn't bad enough, Theodora had apparently chosen the sharpest rock in Carina to choke me on top of, so I was getting impaled at the same time. What a way to die.

Not that I was prepared to make that trip quite yet. My hands groped for the award-winning rock and smashed it down on Theodora's pretty little head.

The pressure released. Her weight rocked backward, and I followed her momentum, toppling her.

That'd have been a great opportunity to keep pummeling her, but I was a bit busy hacking and gasping and coughing on cool, damp air. I swallowed it down and vomited it up, and it hurt, and the hurt didn't matter. I could *breathe*. I was alive. I'd be bruised black and blacker come morning, but I could breathe and nothing felt broken.

An expert would've been able to kill me in the time she'd had her hands around my neck. Maybe Theodora had never tried to strangle anyone before. Maybe it was harder than it looked.

Maybe less time had passed than it had felt like.

I hacked harder, and the air tasted of blood and bile. Hers—mine—who knew?

Where was she?

I raised my head and spotted her not far away, crouched over her own knees, head cradled in her hands. I scrabbled upright, swaying, and my feet stumbled and staggered crabwise—away, away. She made no move to attack. She looked like she was hurting. Was she faking or genuine?

I put ten feet between us, twenty. That rock seemed to be bothering her more than getting her brains blown out. She was getting up, but slowly, rubbing her head and moaning.

I didn't understand, but I wasn't about to stick around and ask. I hightailed it up the cliff, only pausing to gulp down yet more precious air. Dirt slipped and slid under my sturdy boots. I must've made it up in record time, the way I was going, but it seemed to take forever. When I reached the ridge and looked back, I was amazed to see that Theodora still stood on the river rocks, though her face was turned my way.

I couldn't make out her expression.

The truck cab light was on, covering Luc in its warm glow. He sat in the driver's seat, forehead leaning on the steering wheel. For one horrified moment, I thought he was dead, but his shoulders were quivering, and I smelled sick on him as I ripped open the door.

"Move over!" I shouted, shoving his shoulder. "Luc, move!"

He rolled his head on the wheel, so I could see his blank, unfocused eyes and tear-stained face. What a lump he was! What a useless sack of amaranth! Had he always been this slothful, or was my sense of time skewed? "Move!" I screamed at him.

Had Theodora reached the ridge yet? No—she'd be silhouetted

plainly. We could get away.

"Hurry! Luc, move over! We have to go!"

"You killed her." The tone was dull, hollow.

I slapped him. "Just move!"

He took the blow without flinching—without reacting at all. I swear, there might as well have been nothing but Play-Doh behind his eyes.

Had she reached the ridge? Not yet. What was taking her so long?

I shoved the keys at my brother. "You drive, then. Here, take them. Luc, we need to go!"

He didn't take the keys, didn't move his eyes even when I jingled them against his cheek. I shrieked in frustration and ran at him, shoved him, tried to force him into the passenger's seat.

He took the shove with all the resistance of a 130-pound sack of sand. "You murdered her," he said.

"This isn't the time—"

Instinct screamed at me, and I swung around as Theodora crested the hill. Blood streamed from the scratches on her face and stained the pristine white of her robe, but she moved easily. The powder burns had vanished, returning her skin to its former glory.

And oh, she was beautiful. She was so beautiful it whipped my breath away and staggered my mind. I could hardly rip my eyes from her.

Especially from the revolver in her hands. That had my full attention. It wasn't pointed at me, though. She wasn't even holding it correctly. Did she think she didn't need it, that I would be bamboozled by her bedazzling beauty? I'm not Francis. "Mercedes," she fluted, in her voice like the tinkling of silver bells. The name was a command. It weakened my knees and ordered me to bow before her, to grovel, to accept her punishment and thank her for it.

But I'm just not into that sort of thing. I dove into the trees before she could repeat the command, crushing ferns and bushes beneath my feet. Spider webs wrapped around my face, and branches snagged at my coat. I'd never before realized how unbelievably noisy forests were. Every move was a crash, crackle, and crunch. I broke twigs and strewed leaves behind me, but the forest closed right in as soon as I'd gone. Within ten feet, I was moving nearly blindly. Within thirty, I couldn't see the truck light when I looked back, and the moonlight had shrunk to nearly nothing.

The forest didn't cut out sound the same way; I heard Luc say something amazed, rejoicing.

Theodora didn't respond, but a second later, I heard her moving behind me: she made just as many crashes, crackles, and crunches.

I looked for her, but couldn't see a thing. If she hadn't been so loud, if I hadn't been able to hear the river, I could easily have gotten completely turned around in there.

I began to move again, but stopped almost instantly. If I could hear her, she could hear me. But I couldn't stay here.

I dropped to my knees and crawled, feeling my way around sticks and avoiding most of the foliage. I was leaving behind a trail, but less of one—and Theodora didn't strike me as much of a woodswoman.

Mushy, cool earth gave way beneath my fingertips, and ferns tickled my face. The leaves smelled of incipient rain, and the river rushed off to my right. Hand over hand I went, sliding each carefully over the other. My back creaked, and my own breath sounded loud in my ears.

I was getting farther and farther away from the truck and from Luc. Leading her away was one thing, but what next? I couldn't keep this up forever. I needed to get back, get away.

Quiet though I was being, I couldn't be absolutely silent as long as I kept moving, so I stopped. I curled up where I was, slowing my breathing and concentrating on listening. Soon, everything but the sounds of her movements faded away, and I knew exactly where she was relative to me. She was bumbling, stumbling, and I began to hope. A gun wouldn't do her a spoonful of good without a target.

She must have figured the same thing, because the crashes stopped soon after.

I wished they'd kept on; now I had no idea what she was doing. Creeping closer? It hardly seemed possible; if she could move silently, she would've done so from the start. She couldn't even be sure where I was anymore. No, she was trying to frighten me into giving myself away. I was safe as long as I didn't let her flush me out.

I didn't move a muscle.

She *was* where I thought she was, wasn't she? And as blind as I was? If she had somehow arranged it that bullets wouldn't kill her, had she also arranged for night vision or stealth or—

No. She couldn't have—although she might, after this. In the meantime, I needed to not psych myself out. I needed a plan.

I knew I could disable her, at least temporarily, if I could find a weapon. What was available?

Dirt. Fronds. Keys. A disposable mobile phone with my fingerprints all over it.

A turned-on mobile phone. One that would light up and ring if she called.

I eased it out and pressed its face into the dirt to power it down and wipe it off. Then I had a better thought and threw it away to my left, as hard and far as I could.

It made less of a crunking crickling than I'd expected, but she must've heard it fall. I listened, holding my breath, but she didn't make a sound. Not a *sound.*

What else? Keys could be a weapon, but the painful and inconvenient sort rather than the incapacitating sort—and if I lost them in a scrap, I was in real trouble.

Something sturdier, then. A rock, maybe, since rocks were apparently her kryptonite. Or, better yet, a sturdy branch, if I could find one without making noise.

Ferns rustled under my questing hands and I froze, straining for sounds of approach. The muted passage of the river, the gentle sigh of wind, the flutter of bird or whine of insect. No broken twigs. There— that sound of rustling leaves. Was that her passing or only the wind?

Keep your head down. I could outwait her. She didn't know where I was.

Movement. Definite movement this time: snaps and crackles retreating toward the truck. She was leaving. Had she given up?

Not a chance of it. I bet she was going back to wait next to my only plausible means of escape. As if I wouldn't rather hitch a ride with a stranger than waltz into that trap. As if I wouldn't rather walk. I'd go downhill to the river. There must be a place shallow enough to ford. I couldn't go home, but I could go to my boss. He'd know what to do. He could help me.

Except . . . what about Luc?

What about him? He was nothing to her. She had no reason to

focus on him or harm him. Just like she'd had no reason to go after Francis, except to get to me.

I unwound myself, bullying recalcitrant muscles into submission. I used a mossy trunk to pull myself upright.

Light slashed into the forest, the eye-meltingly intense beam of the super flashlight Francis kept in his truck. I melted into the tree. Theodora crunched back into the forest, flashlight swaying to and fro, not hurrying. "Come out, Mercedes," she called.

Kind offer, but I thought I'd pass.

"I will find you," she informed me. "I find everyone who tries to hide from me. No one has honor anymore," she reflected. "They always run. They always tell me I can have my payment *over their dead bodies.*"

I sure hoped Luc was hearing this, as I clung to my new bestie, the moss-covered tree. Its silhouette melded with mine, camouflaging me. She wouldn't be able to see me from a distance unless I moved.

Twenty feet away. Fifteen. And she was still talking.

"I was perfectly ready to make a deal with you," she said, "but *no*. You summoned me and refused to make a deal, and now there's a vacuum."

Closer. Closer. I could see her clearly now, just uphill of me. She'd braced the flashlight atop the gun, like you see on cop shows. Her bad: she was showing me exactly where she was looking and aiming.

Ten feet. The light swung wide. I waited until it hit its zenith and then launched myself—kicked off the tree, leaped a fallen log, crushed bushes. A shot boomed wildly, and then I was tackling her.

Theodora oofed as she went down. I pinned her between my legs, grabbed the gun with both hands, and wrenched it away. She screamed as her finger snapped in the trigger guard, but that didn't even slow me down. I whipped the gun at her head, snarling. Her hands went up instinctively, and I hit the broken finger. She screamed again and tried to wriggle away, but I kept beating her.

It was like my blows were doing nothing, like I was weaker than a child. I hit her and hit her, but her skull was too hard or I was hitting her wrong. I whimpered with desperate effort and missed my next hit. She used the opportunity to thrash suddenly, throwing me off.

I was a lightweight compared to her: I went right up into the air and landed on my feet. She tried to scrabble up after me, but I was already moving in, swinging the gun like a bat at the base of her nose. The newly healed cartilage shattered.

I've read that shoving cartilage spikes into the brain is fatal, but I guess it doesn't always work that way. Anyway, she didn't die. She screamed again, and blood gushed into her mouth.

I didn't give her time to recover. I kept bashing her with the gun, again and again, harder than I've ever hit anything in my life. I broke the rest of her fingers and her collarbone. I hit her until her skull finally, finally broke and brains spilled out and she fell to the ground, unmoving but not quiet—not while her bones snapped and crackled like fallen twigs and black haze gripped my vision.

I blinked and gasped, coming abruptly back to myself, black fading to red fading to real color in the beam of the fallen flashlight. She was dead, injured beyond recovery, her face unrecognizable.

But we'd been here before.

I left her there—holstered my gun and ran for the truck.

Chapter 12:

HOMICIDE

Luc stood by the truck, dwarfed by his canary-yellow puffer jacket, staring at the forest. His bulging eyes focused on me as I emerged, and he made a brief, abortive movement toward me. "Mercedes?" he asked, and I couldn't have said whether horror or befuddlement reigned stronger in his voice. Then I came nearer, and horror overwhelmed its opponent. "What happened to you?"

Nothing deadly, yet, and if I wanted to keep it that way, I'd better stay focused. I passed him without speaking and headed for the ammo. The gun was slimy, and I had to scrape it off on my split skirt before emptying out the used brass into one of my plastic bags and reloading. Glancing up every few seconds to make sure Theodora hadn't reappeared, I filled my jacket pockets with enough fresh rounds to reload the gun more than seven times over—though I couldn't think of any scenario in which forty-six rounds would be necessary without them also being *not enough.*

Luc had followed me around to the back of the truck, every inch of him pleading. "Tell me what's going on," he begged. "Where's Theodora? Why are you doing this? Mercy, stop and talk to me. You promised that if I came along—"

There wasn't a rustle from the forest, not a shadow of movement. I kept a wary eye on the road and cliff too, in case Theodora got clever. I didn't trust her not to come running out of the forest at me, regardless of the gun. She could survive being shot. She was probably up already, waiting for her chance.

It was too much to hope that she'd gotten turned around.

"Get back in the truck, Luc," I said. "We're leaving."

Luc's jaw worked. He was gathering himself up for something, and there wasn't time.

"Get. In. The. Truck." I jerked my head at the passenger's side. "I'll explain as we drive."

He ground in his feet and went even heavier at me. "I want to know what's going on. Where is she? Is she dead?"

"I wish," I snarled. I shoved the gun back in its holster, grabbed him by the ear, and dragged.

He dug his heels in, although tears of pain spilled down his face. "THEODORA!" he bellowed. "Theodora, are you all ri—"

"Shut *up.*"

"No. Get off me, Mercedes. She could be hurt! We're not leaving her." He thrashed and ducked, and I found my hand abruptly empty. I snatched at him again, but he'd already run out of reach, toward the tree line. "Theodora, if you can hear—"

I didn't see where she came from. I blinked, and she stood behind Luc, one arm encircling his neck, the other pressed to his stomach. I shouted, drawing the gun and sighting before I knew what I was doing.

Theodora turned so Luc faced me, showing him to me. Something gleamed in the moonlight, and I realized the flashlight hadn't been the only thing Theodora had stolen from Francis's truck. She'd taken his hunting knife also.

The blood had bleached from Luc's face, and he squeaked as he gasped, "Theo—Theodora? Is that—Theodora?"

"Put the gun down, Mercedes," Theodora said, gravelly with anger.

I was aiming it at her face, which was peering around Luc's in a cloud of curly red hair. I said, "No."

"Put it down. You can't kill me, but you might miss and kill Lucas."

I wouldn't miss.

"This knife," said Theodora, "is long and sharp, and I *will* make sure it pierces your brother's heart if you try to shoot me."

Her face had healed. Even the scratches from our scuffle down by the river were gone. No blood clotted her hair, and her clothing was clean and fresh as a detergent commercial. The flowers in her hair were back too. I could smell them from here.

"If I can't kill you," I said, "then why do you care whether I put the gun down? Why bother to threaten Luc?"

Theodora's arms tightened, and Luc yelped in pain. "Please," he gasped, "don't. Please don't."

Theodora tucked her head against his, lips kissing his hair. He looked like a child, enveloped in her arms. Next to her, Francis hadn't looked so shrunken, but what Francis lacks in height he makes up for in muscle. Luc's a weed, and he cringed and withered.

With steady hands and time to aim—and I had both—I could shoot her off him. Even if she stabbed him, he'd probably survive. Humans are tougher than people think. Besides, if I shot her in the t-zone—the area where eyes and nose meet—death would be instantaneous. She wouldn't have time to thrust the knife in as she fell. Then I could bundle Luc into the truck and get out of there before she respawned.

I wonder how differently things would have gone if I hadn't hesitated. If things would have been better or worse.

"Fair is fair," Theodora murmured into Luc's ear. "Your sister tried to kill me, so I will kill you as payment."

"Don't, don't," Luc whispered, voice cracking, flinching into her—and away from the knife. "I didn't know. I tried to help you. I didn't do anything."

"No. You didn't do anything."

"P-please," Luc said, choking on the words. He was quivering, sweat staining his temples. "Please don't hurt me. I didn't know."

Theodora nuzzled near his ear, but she made sure I could hear every word. She said: "I'm not interested in what you knew or didn't know. Why shouldn't I kill you? Give me a reason."

Something about the way she said it broke through my paralysis. "Luc!"

He didn't recognize the cadence. How could he? "I—I'll help you!" he cried. "I can—computers! Anything. Please, I'll do anything, just—"

"LUC!" I screamed, finger tightening. "Luc, don't!"

"—just don't hurt me."

Theodora dropped him and stepped away. He crumbled to the dirt instantly, sobbing, heedless. "I accept," she said. She raised her eyebrows contemptuously at me. "How proud you must be of him."

No blood stained the hunting knife. She'd never pierced the skin. Maybe she hadn't been able to, before he'd made a deal. And now—

My hands weren't so steady now. My breath hiccupped. But I could still hit her. Might take two shots instead of one but I could do it.

"You won't hurt us, will you?" Luc whined, crawling away from Theodora, hand clasped to his stomach. I looked away from him. "You'll leave us alone?"

Theodora snorted. "Babies shouldn't leave their cribs," she said. "Go back to the truck and cover your head with a blanket." Almost before she finished speaking, he was forced to obey: scrambling inside and curling up in the back seat, pulling the blanket there over his head.

As Theodora half turned to watch him, I stopped hesitating. My first shot slammed her backward, stumbling toward the tree line.

I didn't shoot her a second time. I wasn't interested in killing her at the moment, though it wouldn't lose me any sleep—or, I suspected, be effective for more than a minute. I just wanted to give myself a head start.

I plunged around the truck and into the undergrowth beyond, leaping over the first ferns to avoid leaving an obvious entry angle. It was as dark as ever, but I didn't care. I crashed forward, relying on my boots to stabilize my ankles, one hand warding off obstacles and the other clutching the revolver. I made so much noise that I wasn't sure if I'd hear her following, but I didn't think she'd follow. I thought she'd wait by the truck for me to return.

She had Luc, and she had the power to do whatever she wanted with him. She assumed that everything I'd done so far had been personal. She assumed that my brothers were my highest priority, that I'd sacrifice anyone and everyone to protect them. She assumed that leaving wasn't an option for me.

She was right on one out of three, anyway. Leaving had never been an option. I just hadn't known it.

I ran and ran and ran, giving myself space to think.

How do you kill someone who won't stay dead? Who heals from fatal injuries in under a minute?

Who heals from *fatal* injuries—but not, I realized, from nonfatal injuries. Those scratches on her face hadn't healed until after she'd died. And that second time, she'd been able to appear out of nowhere—

Not the first time, though. Only after Luc had called her name.

I stumbled through shrubbery, bounced off a tree, and plowed on. No sounds pursued me; I was positive she'd stayed by the truck. I was less positive about where I was, but as long as I could hear the river, I could orient myself.

Theodora was the personification of Deals & Bargains, not the personification of super healing powers or doctoring or endlessly reappearing. She'd clearly arranged it so she could come back from the dead, but maybe not so she could recover from ordinary injuries. The way I'd shot her most recently probably hadn't killed her, but she'd had a knife. She could force a reset. But what if she hadn't had a knife? What if she was so badly injured or so trapped that she could never kill herself? What if all four of her limbs were amputated so she couldn't move, and her tongue removed so that she couldn't make any deal?

We all have lines we will not cross. I had come to stop her, not torture her. To kill her. To commit homicide. To mur—

No, it wasn't murder. Not when it was in defense of those who could not defend themselves.

Those who had chosen their fates?

Ah, but she didn't play fair. And even if she had, that didn't justify—

I tripped again, and this time I went down. The hill disappeared beneath me, and I was falling. I automatically curled around the gun to keep it safe—keeping my finger outside the trigger guard to keep *me* safe. Scrubs ripped at my hair and snagged at my coat, but it was a tree trunk that stopped me. Right in the tailbone.

I spent a minute moaning and clutching. There wasn't any desperate hurry, not now. Only when I found my limbs stiffening did I force myself to move, unwinding my legs and using the mossy trunk to lever myself upright. Prickles exploded in my thighs, and a stitch scolded me for not exercising more often. I cleaned off my glasses with the underside of my shirt, pushed them back over my nose, and looked around.

I'd been running close enough to the ridge that I'd been able to see approximately where I'd been going, as long as I didn't need to do any fancy footwork. Rolling had taken me right to the edge. I could see the river not far beyond, sparkling darkly and smelling of cold. It was wider here, but it remained deep, swift, and dangerous.

I slipped and slid down the last few feet to the edge and then followed the river downstream, hunting for a calmer place—what we as children had called a sink or swimming pool. As I walked, I replaced my spent round, scrubbed off my used brass, and hurled it deep into the river. Maybe someone would find it someday, but it wouldn't mean a thing to them. Anyone could have littered it.

After about ten minutes, I found what I was looking for. A couple of boulders stood sentinel along the river's edge, diverting the water's flow and damming off an area maybe ten feet by eight. Some water trickled between the rocks or splashed onto their sides, but most of it cascaded away from the shore in spitting rapids. Near the shore, the water swirled in lazy ripples and soporific back currents. It looked innocuous, but I knew from experience how suddenly deep sinks like this could be: first step, up to the ankles; third step, up to the waist.

And about as warm as Antarctica in winter.

I rubbed my hands vigorously over my arms and legs, and then set to collecting the slick rocks and arranging them in loose, unstable piles right at the edge of the sink. I tried stepping on a pile and nearly careened into the river, which was the goal.

Taking great care to stand just in front of the piles, and not on them, I turned my back to the river and planted my feet about eighteen inches from the edge of the water. Then I drew my gun and crossed my arms, so that I was aiming under my own armpit and bracing my gun-holding right arm with my left.

This was my only chance. I couldn't screw it up.

I was as ready as I was going to get. I took a breath, curled my finger around the trigger, and called, "Theodora! Theo—"

I'd been expecting her. That was the only thing that saved me. One white-clad sinewy arm was already snaking around my neck when my finger squeezed compulsively and the gun roared. Theodora fell back, knife dropping as she screamed and clutched her hip. Loose rocks skittered beneath her feet. Her arms wind-milled as she crashed back into the water.

I followed her in, pushing her neck down with my free hand, knee pressing her abdomen until she submerged completely. She thrashed, fighting to get to the surface, and I kept firing. I shot her through one shoulder, and her arm went limp. Then the other shoulder. Then the uninjured hip. Nothing that would kill her instantly. Shock didn't knock her out either; she stayed conscious. I think she was trying to struggle, but she was running out of air and blood.

Kneeling on top of her, I dumped my brass and reloaded. It doesn't take that long to drown, and I couldn't let her die until I was ready.

Six fresh rounds. I shot them all through her neck. Any one alone would've been fatal; after six, nothing but her spinal cord sheath and threads of skin remained.

The hunting knife was right behind me, at the edge of the water. Keeping her head submerged, I holstered the gun, snatched up the knife, and hacked through the last shreds of skin and sinew. Then I grabbed the head by the hair and swung it into the jaws of the hungry river.

The Gyllan River feeds the Bay of Uror, right on the edge of the ocean. Salt water decays bodies more rapidly than fresh. Before long, there'd be nothing left of her but bone.

But I had to make sure. I stayed with the body for ages, before I pushed it beyond the sentinel rocks. My feet went numb and my legs screamed at me. I shivered in great shuddering gasps. Clouds closed around the stars and wept, but the bullet wounds did not heal, and the body did not move.

Chapter 13:

SPOILATION OF EVIDENCE

Most murderers who get caught are arrested within twenty-four hours of committing their crime. The twenty-four-hour mark for me was two-thirty Friday morning. I would be able to breathe a little more easily after that. Even if someone came knocking—well, you can't be convicted of murder without a body . . . and the sea around Argo Navis is friendly to no one.

"Mercedes." My boss cleared his throat. "*Mercedes.*"

I focused on him. He leaned one hand on the desk and doodled with the other. He didn't look excessively annoyed with me, considering that I suspected he'd been trying to get my attention for several minutes. This wasn't the first time I'd been distracted today. There was the sick fear, of course, that I'd be arrested or that she'd miraculously return and revenge herself upon me or that Francis would find out, but that wasn't all of it. Memories kept jumping out at me from around corners.

But she had had to be stopped. And if I felt bad about it—so be it. That, too, was a price I was willing to pay.

"*Mercedes!*"

"I'm listening," I said agreeably, fake-bright.

A stack of papers weighed down my arms. I'd been in the middle of—something. Recycling? Bringing them to the computer lab?

My boss's gaze was uncomfortably incisive. I'd promised myself

I'd act normally, not like someone who—

Don't even think it.

I was wearing about five pounds of makeup to cover the bruises and scratches and had to keep sitting down from lightheadedness. If not for the blankets Francis keeps in his truck, and its ridiculously powerful heater, I'd probably be down with pneumonia right now. Luc hadn't said a word to me on the drive back—

I smiled brightly at my boss. "Wool gathering," I said. "I have almost enough for a complete sheep."

"Do you have your costume ready?"

That took me a second. Lack of sleep was getting to me, if I thought he was asking me whether I was dressing up as a sheep. Then my brain connected cloven hooves and horns to demons to prefects, and I thought, *Of course he's asking. The prefects' conference begins on Monday, and today's Thursday.* Wondering how I'd forgotten, and knowing the answer full well, I said, "I was thinking a white skirt suit."

"Not something more . . . compelling?"

"It was compelling enough for Theodora, and she's as close to a demon as I've ever met. But if you don't like the idea, I could dig out my old school uniform. I hear the jailbait look is *in* for hellspawn this season."

Lines of disapproval strained his jaw, but he satisfied himself with, "Use your best judgment."

He was being kind again. I could hardly bear that. It seemed to me that everything I said or did today was somehow vastly inappropriate, that I never opened my mouth but to shove my foot in it—and I had no idea how accurate that perception was. I fought for something neutral to say or something to fix the situation, and found nothing. But I couldn't leave it like that, and so, not knowing if I was making it better or worse, I said, "I'm sorry. I didn't sleep well last night, and I think I overdid the caffeine this morning."

"Then it is well we have no essential tasks for today," he replied, being kind again. "Is there any of the chamomile-lavender tea left, or has it gone stale?"

Neither of my brothers was home when I got back that evening. Francis often works late, and I hadn't seen Luc since a quarter past three that morning, when he'd jumped out of the truck and run up the stairs to our apartment.

I'd trudged up a considerable time after him; I was doing everything on autopilot. It was a good thing I'd worked out and drilled into my brain what to do ahead of time, since I wasn't functioning too well by that point.

Before leaving the riverside pullout, I'd stripped off my boots and outer layers and dressed in the fresh clothes I'd brought with me. My filthy clothes and boots went into a plastic bag. They might be salvageable, but I wasn't about to bet my life and freedom on them.

My first stop on my roundabout way home was at an impoverished apartment complex, where I found an unlocked dumpster half full of detritus. I poured a gallon of bleach in the plastic bag after dumping it in. Undiluted bleach can eat through clothing within a couple of hours, and it would erase all evidence and blood long before that. I dumped the bleach bottle, lid off, over the bag, like it had just spilled that way. I had a second gallon of bleach for my used brass, and disposed of that behind a closed greasy spoon.

My third and final stop was at an unmanned and un-security-cameraed carwash. Theodora had slammed against the truck when I'd shot her, and mud from the pullout caked the tires. Even apart from the physical evidence, Francis keeps his car sparklingly clean. I would've added a couple of gallons of gas if I'd thought I could find a station without cameras, but I didn't think he tracked either gas or mileage that closely. I hoped not.

Luc didn't comment on any of this.

Once home, I wiped the unused rounds and replaced them in their box, then cleaned the revolver. I stuck a rattail file up the gun's barrel to change the rifling, though I didn't know how effective that'd be, and snuck gun and ammo back into Francis's room.

Everything took three times longer than it should have, as it does when you are extremely tired, and I kept remembering more things. After I scrubbed down my hands, arms, and face with oil, white vinegar, and rubbing alcohol to get rid of gunpowder residue, I remembered that I'd better do the same with the steering wheel. Then I

realized that I'd better scrub down and return the flashlight and hunting knife, because Francis would definitely notice if they were gone. By
the time I'd finished that and taken a long, thorough shower, I barely
had time for ninety minutes of sleep.

I woke up with the certainty that I'd forgotten something, and I
probably had. It's never possible to account for every possible scrap of
evidence.

The trick is to make sure they never come looking.

Work ended. I went home again. Luc left the living room as I entered.

Night settled its cloak comfortably over the earth, darkening as I
neared my twenty-four-hour mark. Francis had returned at half-past
eight and chatted with me over nothings, a surreal normality that could
not have held true had I taken him with me to the river instead of Luc.
One or two stars pressed their faces through the haze of light pollution,
no match for the toxic glow of my alarm clock.

1:49, it said. 1:50.

I rolled away from it and shut my eyes. I must have slept, because
when I looked again, the clock read 3:16. Three-quarters of an hour
past the 24-hour deadline, and I supposed I should feel relieved about
that. Instead, I shoved a tissue box in front of the clock and got back to
sleeping.

No one knew what I had done. No one came to arrest me.

Not until the next evening, anyway.

That afternoon, my boss was ready to leave work before the clock had
even struck five, which said more to me about his nerves than he'd
ever express aloud. He hadn't said a word about the prefects' conference all day, but it colored his every gesture, his every request for
coffee.

I wasn't quite so circumspect. When I dropped him off at home, I
said, "Your plan is good. It *will* work."

"Thank you, Mercedes," he replied, and closed the car door between us.

It *was* a good plan. It was a simple plan, which helped. Tomorrow morning, we'd separate: he'd go to Avior, and I'd go to Edenfield, to scout things out and wait for him. He, impersonating an arrogant, mysterious demonologist, would convince Avior that the only way to make the ritual work was to move the conference to Edenfield. When they came up, I'd join them as my boss's browbeaten personal assistant. The more slavishly meek I appeared, the more dramatic my eventual demonic reveal.

And yes, I was massively looking forward to that.

We were a good team, my boss and I. Once the conference was moved to Edenfield, the rest would take care of itself: the spying devices would record evidence of infamy, and we'd warn the king in plenty of time. A little prodding might be necessary, true, but spreading dissension and raising doubts are well within my capacities. And if Avior demanded a demon summoning by way of yours truly executing a one-eighty personality shift, so be it. Avior would believe it, the rest of the prefects would continue to consider him a complete lunatic, and voilà.

It would work. Chess might not be my preferred form of strategizing, but I trusted my boss. And then we would be heroes.

My mind was resting so fixedly on Edenfield that when I got home, I didn't immediately process the significance of the strangers filling the sofa; or why they stood when I entered; or why Luc's face hung bloodless and strained.

"Oh," I said wittily. "Hi."

These were not local reeves; they were knights. Silvertip knights, by their green-and-silver uniforms. I couldn't imagine what they were doing in my living room.

"Mercedes Cartier?" asked the knight on the left, his pointed chin set in professional blandness.

I returned the greeting with a side helping of mild curiosity. "Yes. What's going on?" My response came out admirably innocent and bewildered, and only afterward did the obvious answer slam into my brain.

I wasn't just being stupid. Silvertip knights are concerned with matters of prefecture-wide security, not ordinary law enforcement.

There was zero reason they would be investigating Theodora's disappearance . . . unless she had made a deal with someone very high up the food chain.

Luc looked like he wanted to throw up. I let myself stare at him, horror creeping into my eyes, mouth dropping. "Where's Francis?" I whispered, and jerked into frantic action, looking around wildly, the picture of an anxious sibling. "Where's Francis? Has something happened to him? Luc—"

"Miss Cartier," the knight said, "you are under arrest."

The breath slammed out of me, and I had to fight to make it look like shock rather than fear. The room spun. "Arrest?" I said stupidly. "What do you—what for?"

"I suspect," said the knight, "that you already know the answer to that."

INTERLUDE

Lord Chancellor Rodrigue Thomas was not aware of His Majesty's aversion to gray tweed, but at this point very little from that quarter could have shocked him. If he *had* known, he would have abandoned his tweed, though reluctantly. It was one of the few materials that could effectively cut the chill of the palace, and he found velvet tasteless. But tasteless or not, he knew his duty, and he would have worn velvet if it meant the king listened to him. He would have dressed as a clown or a ghost or gone stark naked, if it meant the king listened to him.

Thomas brooded over Prefect Lindo's visit. He was not as well pleased with her visit or subsequent renewal of vows as King Emil clearly expected him to be; nor did he rejoice over the king's retelling of the conversation in the rose garden. Nor did he have any intention of allowing the matter to rest, as the king had so pointedly indicated he ought. If he had his own way—if he were king—Thomas would simply arrest and try all the prefects and have done with it. He understood why this was diplomatically dangerous, but as sick and disgusted as he was by the reports of the prefects' behavior, and as inclined as he was to think treacherous prefects worse than replaced prefects, he was willing to take the risk.

He played with this fantasy briefly and then released it. Unless the arrests were performed in perfect unison and complete secrecy, the prefects could retreat behind their hordes of knights—or worse, team together against the capital. What would come next? Civil war?

Only if any prefects remained to support the king. Otherwise, it'd be a plain old deposing.

How had things come to this?

This question frustrated Thomas in more ways than one, because although in name and rank King Emil ruled the country, in practice that onus had increasingly fallen to the chancellor—and since the chancellor's official power was limited, Thomas found his hands tied. Sometimes, he resorted to more creative measures, uncomfortable though they made him, but there were things simply beyond his power.

He could not act against the prefects. He could not ignore or disobey the king's orders. He could not make more than paltry diplomatic motions toward Vela and Akter. He certainly could not declare war, if it came to that—as it surely must, if a stronger hand did not take the wheel. If only he could gain the king's approval and carte blanche! Yet he felt utterly helpless to gain that approval or even to understand what might be necessary to gain it.

Frustrated and desperate, he expressed these sentiments to the chaplain, his long-time friend and confidant and (since cancer had eaten Thomas's wife to a husk before finally and mercifully releasing her into death) the only person in the world whom he absolutely trusted.

"I have spoken to the king as well," the chaplain admitted. His name was Abraham Beck, and though time and age—he had half again Thomas's years—had bent his spine and stiffened his fingers, passionate energy brightened his eyes and brought a smile to his withered lips with gentle frequency. There was no smile there now, however; only a pained hope. "It did not go well. I fear Emil has abandoned his faith for good—although, God willing, the Holy Spirit will drag him back kicking and screaming, and our faltering nation with him."

Thomas sighed, not rejecting his friend's hope but weary for its fruition. "He trusts no one but that *woman* and her magic. Whenever I think we've finally convinced him, that he might be willing to listen to reason, he falls back to saying no, no, we can't do anything until the seidkonur reads the birds, or whatever it is she does. If only—" He paused uncomfortably. "I don't suppose—is there any way—"

Abraham turned such bristling eyebrows on him that Thomas let the rest of the thought fall silent. "Do you know," the chaplain asked frostily, "why all forms of divination—including seidr—are banned in the Bible? Why only true prophets can tell the future? Why telling the future accurately is considered absolute evidence of a true prophet?"

Thomas nodded slightly, but Abraham's eyes burned. The curve in his spine seemed to unwind when he got like this, and he seemed to grow taller, larger, and brighter. "The clue is in the name," he said: "divination. The power of the Divine. For Ebba Lundquist to claim she or her tree or her birds can tell the future is for her to claim that they have the power of God. And that is vile blasphemy. It is also," he added, in case Thomas got any ideas, "ineffective blasphemy. She cannot and does not have any real power."

"I never thought her anything but a charlatan," Thomas assured him. "I only thought, perhaps, that evil might be turned to good."

Abraham passed a hand over his brow and apologized for his heated tone. The chancellor wasn't the only one worn out by King Emil's stubborn peculiarities—or the only one considering extreme responses. "You may be right that the only way to motivate the king to action may be to create a false response to that woman's seidr," Abraham admitted, "but I don't know if I can be a party to that. Is giving credence to divination sinful? I think it must be—unless it is the Lord Himself turning it to His advantage. And yet so too is it sinful to stand uselessly by as a man runs toward his death and the ruination of his country."

"Let's say we can justify it," Thomas said. "How would we go about it? I don't know what the king and the seidkonur expect will result from her magic or how they'd interpret such a result—but whatever it is, it must be something so unusual that it has not occurred in these many months of her attempts." He threaded both hands through his hair and then regarded them unhappily. "I cannot pull a coin from my great nephew's ear without him catching me out."

Abraham ran his tongue along his back teeth. He had an idea, but not one Thomas was likely to jump on. As he was considering how to phrase it, Thomas's attention fixed on him, and he knew he had to try. "This isn't the first time I've thought about this," he hazarded, "but the problem remains that neither of us has the abilities necessary to act. We need help."

"Someone we can trust with our suspicions, with a plan this—precarious?" Thomas said doubtfully. "Is there such a person?"

"I believe so. As I said, I've thought about this before—long and hard. I believe we should confide in Keir Skuli."

"The skald!" Thomas exclaimed in horror. "Why not confide in the seidkonur herself and be done with it?"

Abraham smiled grimly. Once, he would have reacted much the same way. On the surface of it, the skald—the court bard—was not an individual to inspire awe. Young and gangly, he was friendly with everyone, liked by nearly everyone, confided in by many, and respected by few. The joke around the palace was that Keir was better suited to the role of court jester than bard.

To his credit, Keir seemed to be in on the joke. On one occasion, Abraham had seen him dressed in the colorful diamonds and innumerable bells of a jester—which he must surely have dug out of some dusty attic, for Carina had kept no jester for two hundred years. Keir had run about the palace, apparently immune to embarrassment, turning cartwheels to make people laugh and putting on a truly spectacular juggling show in plain view of everyone. There had been no apparent reason for this abrupt show, except that a little girl with a broken leg had been depressed because she had been unable to play outside with her friends, and had needed cheering.

He was like that: ridiculous and generous and shameless, and most people who knew him left it at that. But then, most people weren't in a chaplain's privileged position. They hadn't been summoned to deathbeds only to, invariably, find the skald there before them, soothing the patient until the chaplain's arrival if the chaplain arrived in time . . . or waiting solemnly, unwilling to abandon the corpse, if the chaplain arrived too late.

No one but Abraham had ever seen him like that, with the glisten of tears upon his cheeks, with his face the proper age in absence of the perpetual smile. But Abraham had seen, and that seeing had led him to see other things.

He saw that people who confided in the skald found things inexplicably going better for them.

He saw how seeming coincidences regularly made the servants' lives easier.

He saw how arguments sparked in Keir's presence sizzled out in a few carefully placed words.

"I do not understand it," he told Thomas, "but Keir gets things done—and he does them for good."

"And it doesn't hurt," said Thomas, "that he attends chapel on Sunday *and* Wednesday."

"No, it doesn't hurt."

"Even though he spends twice as much time with the seidkonur as in chapel? Or do you suppose he's trying to convert her?"

Abraham spread his hands. "You now know as much about him as I do. What do you say? Shall we consult him?"

"I trust your discernment," said Thomas. "If you trust him, then so shall I."

Chapter 14:

PERJURY

I'd been waiting for ages. I couldn't tell how many ages, because the only clock in view had said 6:31 when I'd come in and had continued to say 6:31 ever since. I could've dealt with that, if it had meant a completely dead battery, but oh no. The battery had just enough juice left to keep the clock ticking, the hands shuddering but lacking the strength to win the battle against gravity.

None of the knights or lower prefectsmen acted bothered by the clock. Maybe they kept it that way on purpose to torment prisoners. It sure added to the décor of the place, heightened the atmosphere. They were big on atmosphere, in here: ugly lighting, bars covered in layers and layers of flaking diseased frog green paint, a metal slab for a bed, and the overwhelming stench of chemical cleansers. Admirable, the way they'd managed to attack all five senses. Masterful work with dinner, honestly. And the toilet arrangement—genius.

I unstuck my thighs from the metal bed and hobbled around in my cursedly impractical work shoes, for the variety of it.

"Is anyone going to charge me?" I asked the prefectsman who came for my empty plate. "Interview me? Get me a lawyer? Or a pillow? I'd settle for a pillow."

The prefectsman avoided eye contact.

"Clean underwear? That's just uncivilized."

The clock ticked without progress, the paint flaked, and the prefectsman left without answering.

No one had told me where I was. I guess they meant that as an extra level of intimidation, carting me here in a windowless van and not pulling me out until we'd reached a windowless garage. No one had informed me of the charges against me either, so I was left to guess and imagine the worst.

Why was I here? Had Luc betrayed me? Had Theodora told someone where she was going, with whom she was meeting? Did she have other safeguards in place of which I knew nothing?

Those were the sorts of thoughts they probably wanted me to have, and I absolutely refused to entertain them no matter how they pushed in, because they weren't the thoughts an innocent woman would be having. An innocent woman wouldn't be guessing how she'd been caught; she'd be guessing what had happened. She'd be wondering how such a mistake had been made. She'd be worrying about Francis and her boss.

And so I thought, over and over: *There must have been a mistake. I know my rights. I did nothing wrong. I'm so confused. I want to see my family. I want to go home.*

That was the truth. It had to be, and I had to believe it. You see, you can always tell when someone is lying, if you know what to look for. Always. No matter how slight, lying creates dissonance between words and body language. You can try to distract an interviewer from your body language, but you can't make your body lie along with your mouth—and distractions won't work, if they pay attention to the recording of your interview. There's only one way you can't be caught if you tell falsehoods:

Don't lie. Oh, say whatever untruths you need to, but believe them. Believe them totally, absolutely. Don't let your mind acknowledge other truths even for a moment, or dissonance will creep in.

I lay down, settling my body on the metal slab. An outsider might have thought I was preparing for sleep, but I wasn't, not for hours yet. I was working on my mind, going over my day beat by beat. Wednesday had been a perfectly ordinary day, nothing special. Not pleasant, but not special. I had gotten up, eaten breakfast, met my brothers in the park, argued with them, stormed off, come home, listened to Francis harangue me, and finally collapsed in bed.

Did I argue with my brothers a lot?

Sometimes. Mostly about silly things.

You argued in the park, though. What about?

I don't like my brother's new girlfriend; she's vicious and manipulative. Yes, Theodora Banks—wait, is this about her? Yes, I hit her; lots of people must've witnessed that. No, I haven't seen her since then. I drove around to calm down, got home around eight, maybe nine. The parking garage attendant and cameras can verify that. So can my brothers. So can the neighbors, the way Francis was yelling. No, I didn't go out again. I went to bed. I was upset. I hadn't handled the situation well, and I wasn't sure how to make up with Francis.

He's all right, isn't he? The knights who arrested me wouldn't say. . . .

No, I slept that night. Had breakfast in the morning, went to work. I came directly back after dropping my boss off. It was an ordinary day. Nothing special.

Nothing to see here.

Jour / 14

Oatmeal heralded morning with currant eyes and a cream smile. The prefectsman who'd brought me breakfast was less fresh-faced than acned, and with an eager set to his round cheeks. "Coffee?" he asked me, and brought me a plastic cup of stuff that was hottish and brownish.

"This," I said, sniffing it dubiously, "cannot be coffee."

"It is too," the prefectsman said, laughing. I gazed up at him through my lashes and replied something guileless and innocent, and his lips loosened plenty enough to admit that it was nine o'clock. "I can't tell you anything else," he said, leaning against a flaking bar like maybe he could be persuaded. "It's not up to me—and it's not like anyone ever tells me anything."

I looked terribly sympathetic and he kept going, warming to his topic. My concerned attention was rewarded by an insight into the day-to-day life of a junior prefectsman. I was genuinely interested—I might apply to be a prefectsman or knight someday, although it wasn't my initial plan. For one thing, if I ever wanted to be head knight, I'd have to apply in Batata, and I'd no desire to live there again. But if I did, this information would be desperately useful, because it gave me an insight into the complaints of the lower ranks: knights were a snooty lot who thought they were better than ordinary prefectsmen. It was incredibly irritating, being treated like a lackey; the lack of respect was demeaning. Someone should do something about it.

On a more immediate level, I was putting together fragments of information that fluttered down to me along with the occasional chip of green paint: I was being held in one of the knighthouses surrounding Silvertip Manor—a structure far grander than its Edenfield counterpart. Eight other knighthouses of various sizes dotted the manor grounds.

That was as far as he got before another prefectsman pulled him away, but it was enough for now. The logical conclusion for someone in my position (i.e., complete innocence) was that this arrest had to do with my job: there had been a leak in the Carinan Security Service, and I'd been fingered. The crown had ordered my arrest, and I was being kept in the most secure location possible until I could be transferred to the capital. Kingsmen would arrive soon to move me.

That explanation struck me as remarkably plausible, and I began to wonder if it might not be correct after all. If it was, my boss might have been arrested also. *Definitely* not ideal. I'd vouch for him, but it struck me as improbable that we'd be able to get free before the conference was over and the king dead.

If only I had more accurate information!

I returned to my cozy metal slab to keep kneading my brain into the appropriate shape, but I jumped up again when two new people stomped up to my cell. They were knights, square-chested men with hard chins and harder eyes. Hostility, but impersonal hostility. Sometimes men like this could be won over by delicacy and repressed tears, but sometimes they were the sort who enjoyed distress.

"Good morning," I said, clutching my hands hopefully. "Am I being released? I want to go home."

"Stand against the wall," the leader barked at me. "Hands up."

They'd disappointed me severely, and I let them see it, but I didn't hesitate to obey. My compliance was rewarded by no new bruises as one of them held me while the other gave me a professional pat-down.

My suit was far too formal to have anything as practical as pockets, but they took the blazer away anyway, the better to cuff me.

I know how to break out of the ordinary sort of cuffs, in theory, but these were nasty: they held my hands in front of me, palms turned out and thumbs down, wrists kept four inches apart by a solid metal shaft. The sort of cuffs that can be attached to neck and ankle shackles for condemned prisoners.

"Are we going somewhere?" I asked timidly, eyes doe-wide.

No wonder the chatty prefectsman hadn't been happy in his position; apparently, Silvertip liked the strong, silent types. They frog-marched me out of my cell, out of the knighthouse, and into radiant sunlight.

I squinted through streaming eyes. Sure enough, we were outside Silvertip Manor. I had seen it before in person only once and on the news plenty of times. It wasn't the sort of place you forgot, once you saw it.

The building was smooth eggshell-white concrete, its lines irregular and curved. The best way I can describe it is as if the architect had taken an unevenly squashed hardboiled egg and sliced it shortwise four times, then pulled it apart and rotated the layers to show not yolk but floor-to-ceiling green-framed windows. Each layer of white fluctuated unevenly around the smooth interior. Francis had called it dynamic.

I had called it excessive. What had been wrong with the old manor other than its being old?

"A prefect's manor needs to be impressive, not just functional," an exasperated Francis had told me during our visit. "This is Silvertip's seat of power, his base of operations, the face he shows to visiting dignitaries. A prefect's manor must reflect the state of his prefecture, and the old building was shoddy. Is that what you want the other prefectures to think of us?"

"He's been reading the brochure," Luc had told me, *sotto voce.* "Do you think he believes his own propaganda?"

Francis had huffed but neither yelled nor stomped off: we'd paid a stiff C15 each for this tour, and it had been Francis who'd insisted we go. He'd said it was because it was important we see the capital and that the architecture was something-something-pretentious-I-tuned-out. His real aim was to show off the most impressive building project he'd ever been part of, and he made sure to comment on this loudly enough that the rest of our tour group heard him.

The tour guide had led us through the grand front entrance, but prisoners weren't afforded that honor. The knights marched me to a nearly plain side door, up stairs of slate-gray Saxony carpet, and into a spacious sitting room.

I'd give Silvertip this: he hadn't sacrificed style for ostentation. Genteel wall clocks chimed the quarter hour; the faint aromas of gunpowder green tea and lilac clung to the walls; polished oak supported patterned sage-green seat cushions, table runners, and curtains. Most of one wall comprised windows, lightly tinted and designed to display the landscape to maximum advantage: a vista of intimidation and aesthetics. Concrete, knighthouses, and ornamental fountains stretched into the distance.

Here was a room to please the senses, to relax, to entertain sophisticated guests. To make me extremely aware of the difference between Silvertip's lifestyle and the lifestyle his prisoners lived. To make my unwashed back itch in its unwashed blouse. To make me feel how desperately I needed to brush my hair and wipe away the smeared remains of day-old mascara.

If I hadn't been aware of how purposeful the effect must be, I would have squirmed. As it was, I made myself annoyed over how frankly insulting such blatant manipulation was. This would work for my innocent persona; the innocent have as much pride as the guilty.

I subtly rolled my wrists as far as the cuffs would allow, which wasn't far. I was chilly, since they'd taken away my blazer, and that had made my wrists shrink—but not by enough. No way could I slip my wrist out of its cuff without losing a significant amount of skin and possibly a chunk of my thumb.

Picking the lock was out of the question, with my hands faced outward like this, unless I held the pick in my mouth. Were rigid cuffs as easy to pick as the ordinary sort?

I chose a chair and sat, wrenching my thoughts back to the practiced innocent sort: the confusion, the desperation over my brother, the horrified suspicion that this might be work-related. I arranged those thoughts right before my eyes, and held them there as the door opened and two new men entered.

The first new man was a weathered fifty with the granite expression of a career military man and the stars of Silvertip's head knight. His quick eyes gave me a once-over as thorough as it was disdainful.

The second man wore no uniform, but I knew him immediately. He too was a man of middle years, the sort who keeps himself in excellent shape and boasts about it. His hair had been gelled into a politician's helmet, its brown gracefully bowing to the inevitability of age. His eyes were light blue, his skin golden with tan, his suit ruthlessly ironed. He wasn't smiling as he entered, but I'd seen enough photographs to know that his teeth were an orthodontist's finest achievement—for this was Lord Otto Ostberg, the current Prefect Silvertip.

"Wait outside the door," Silvertip told his knights. I'd heard his rich baritone a hundred times over the television set, knew the politician's lilt of his accent. "Dinez will stay with me."

Speech therapist, I thought. *Voice trainer, personal trainer, and tailor. Velvet furniture and solid silver tea set.*

"Yes, my lord," my escort said, and retreated outside.

Silvertip locked the door behind them and pocketed the key. Every movement was improbably casual, the motions of a man who cannot be fazed because he holds the power, because he does not for a minute doubt that what he says will be done, and all who come before him will lick his feet.

I'd sometimes been guilty of thinking of my boss as vain, with his insistence on an expensive car and fine clothing and not a hair out of place, but he wasn't. He dressed and acted and purchased like that because he thought doing so was proper for a man in his position. His manners were habitual, trained from childhood and as natural to him as breathing. He hadn't made a big deal about taking my coat when I'd visited his home; he'd have been surprised if anyone had mentioned it. What was there to mention about common decency?

Silvertip had inherited his prefecture from his uncle, not his father, and in preference to two elder siblings. That had been twenty years ago, but he had already been the consummate politician. Up until last night, I'd considered his ascension to prefectship perfectly natural for a man of his talents and proclivities. Now, I wondered if Theodora had had a hand in it. If so, she'd either been about fourteen at the time, or she had already extended her life by some devil's bargain.

"Good morning, prefect," I said, standing but ducking my head. If they'd been free, I would've wrung my hands nervously to show how shy I was at meeting this rich and powerful celebrity.

"Good morning," Silvertip replied urbanely. He glided over to a chair near—but not too near—mine and hiked up the thighs of his trousers before sitting down. His head knight hovered beside him, glaring at me like I was going to do something. To make him feel better, I sat again.

"What's going on?" I burst out. Once started, I figured I might as well keep on going. "Please—I'm sorry, but I don't understand why I'm here. Knights came to my house yesterday and—and they arrested me! Without telling me why! I didn't realize they were from you—of course, they must have been, since they were knights—and I know you have the right to arrest anyone you want, I just don't—I'm so *confused*. And no one will tell me if my brother or my boss—" I gulped, visibly restraining the flood of words. My eyes flickered to Silvertip but were too bashful to settle on him for long and made do with his shoes instead.

Silvertip nodded understandingly. "Ah, yes, your boss. The code-breaker."

I bit back my response. Codes and ciphers are *not* the same thing. Codes replace words or phrases with other words or phrases. Ciphers replace and scramble letters. My boss is capable of working with codes, but he practically never actually does.

"You need have no concern for Dinez's ears," Silvertip reassured me, motioning to his head knight. "He has my complete confidence."

"Respectfully, my lord," I mumbled at his shoes, scrunching my shoulders further in as if afraid of being hit, "I can't talk to you about that." I squeezed my eyes tight to make them water, and got up my bravery to look him in the face. "Am I in trouble?" I whispered. "Did something happen?"

When cryptanalysts make mistakes or turn traitor, people die. Brutally. We weren't at war, but that didn't mean Akter and Vela threw parties for our spies.

I'd heard stories. Not many, but enough.

I let my horror shine through. "Has there been . . . a security leak?"

Silvertip tilted his head, watching me with scientific interest. "You tell me."

I blinked rapidly at him, genuinely unsure what he was getting at. This hadn't been how I would've figured a conversation about Theodora would go, but if it was about ciphers, you'd think he'd manage to get the word right. Or sound more interested in my job.

Still, I could be wrong. "You think I'm the leak," I acknowledged, regaining my strength of character and streaming it at him. "Well, I'm not. I would *never* betray Carina."

Silvertip and Dinez exchanged a glance full of private information, and then Silvertip braced his elbows on the arms of his chair and leaned in, fingers pressed together. "Tell me," he said, "about your relationship with Lucio Winter."

"Prefect *Avior?*" I exclaimed, more flatfooted than ever.

"You don't deny that you know who he is."

"Doesn't everyone?"

Silvertip raised his fingers to his lips. I've seen men who can make that sort of thing look natural; he looked like a coach had told him it made him look clever. "Do you deny that you spoke with him the Tuesday before last?"

"No, I—no, of course not. Why? I don't understand. Have I done something wrong?" I swung between Silvertip and Dinez in bewilderment. "Was I supposed to ask you first? I didn't know."

Silvertip glanced again at Dinez, so swiftly I almost missed it. "And what did you two talk about?"

"Just about—um." I stopped, more bewildered than ever, *letting* myself be bewildered rather than trying to work out what was going on. Honest bewilderment rang true—and besides, I wasn't liking where this was going. Not one bit. "He, um. He asked me not to repeat it."

"And I'm asking you to tell me." Silvertip's tone remained pleasant and level, but I heard the threat loud and clear.

I dropped my chin and picked at my skirt, thinking hard, letting my brow scrunch and my teeth bite my lower lip. "Could you, um, order me, please? Only, if you don't, I don't think . . . I don't think I can . . . am I allowed?"

Another glance between them.

"I order you to tell me everything you and Prefect Avior talked about," Silvertip said.

"Well," I hedged, "I don't have a photographic memory"—I re-membered the conversation perfectly—"but it wasn't anything suspicious. He asked about our work, and I said I couldn't tell him, and he didn't mind that. He mainly wanted to know about my boss." I lifted my cuffed wrists apologetically. "In general terms, you know. If he was a good employer. I said he was, and asked if he—that is, Lord Winter—wanted to hire him, and he said yes. And that was about it, I guess. Um. He asked me about myself too, but not anything personal." I looked at them earnestly. "That's all right, isn't it?"

Silvertip angled his face up to Dinez. "What do you think?" he asked.

"I think," the head knight replied, "that Miss Cartier is possibly the most accomplished liar I have ever met."

Chapter 15:

PRISON BREAK

One of the most essential skills of the truly accomplished liar is the ability to successfully respond to accusations of falsehood. It's appalling, how easy it is to fall apart when you get your beard caught in the mailbox. Even if you manage not to blurt out a full confession in the style of detective stories, your expression gives you away.

This is another problem with not fully building and maintaining your internal belief that you are telling the absolute truth; this is where the buried dissonance comes out fully. In such cases, it isn't enough to believe what you're saying; you must believe that you are an honest person. You have great pride in your integrity, but you are not irrationally angry, and you certainly aren't calm and rehearsed.

"No, I'm not!" I said, shocked and bewildered. "Why would you even say that?" Anger crept into my body language. If someone didn't answer me soon, I was going to find a high horse and climb on it.

"Let's lay our cards on the table," Silvertip proposed.

I nodded eagerly, as curious as I was offended. Silvertip was such a great man that he wouldn't accuse me without some funny business going on, and I was sure that once he explained what it was, I could clear the air and my name. Then he'd apologize, and everything would be all right.

"I'll tell you what we know," Silvertip went on, "and you'll tell us what you know. I'll start:

"We know that you're a spy. We guess that Avior recruited you while you were at university—you did, I believe, attend the University of Avior? Dinez has suggested that Batata might have sent you, but he doesn't know Batata like I do; man wouldn't have the stomach for it. So it was Avior.

"Like many spies, you found a job where you would be invisible but would have access to information of national importance and to influential and knowledgeable individuals. How am I doing so far?"

"You're completely mad," I said, awed.

"A spy working among spies," Silvertip mused. "Brilliant. Lucio's mind may be twisted, but one cannot deny his incredible foresight."

"Lord Winter only became prefect two weeks ago," I pointed out. "I've been out of university for three years."

"Impressive, isn't it?"

Silvertip's delusional capacity? Astounding. And here I'd thought I'd have to act innocent. "I'm not a spy," I said. "I've never been a spy, and I've never worked for Avior."

Silvertip shook his head pityingly. "There's no point in denying what we both know is true. Miss Cartier, I am not a patient man. It's a failing of mine, I know. I've tried to remedy it, read self-help books on the subject, but it's no good. I'm built to be a man who gets what he wants without waiting for it, and I recommend you remember that."

He crossed his legs and leaned back, comfortably amused. I'd seen him do this before, in news casts. I appreciated it even less in person.

"No, I'm not patient," he said, vastly misinterpreting my disbelief, "but I am reasonable. I understand your hesitation, and I'm not asking you to work for free. I'll pay your normal rate twice over, starting your time log from when I had you arrested—which I did for verisimilitude, you understand, and to make sure you didn't run off before I was ready for you.

"Now that that's settled, it's your turn. Tell me what Avior is planning. Tell me everything about the conference and its repercussions. Tell me especially what he thinks of and plans for me. Give me both theories as well as facts—I respect your opinion—but tell me which is which."

If I were in his position, I'd sure want to know whether Avior planned to turn on me once the king was dead, so I could turn on him first.

I debated, unsure of the best response. Really, it depended on what sort of man Silvertip was. Having an ally could be a great benefit, but Silvertip wasn't exactly honorable, and I didn't trust him not to reveal to Avior what he'd found out from me.

Besides, ultimately what I wanted was for Silvertip to release me. If I told him I was a spy and told him what he expected to hear, would he really just let me go and call it good? He'd already demonstrated a willingness to imprison me.

As I deliberated, Silvertip moved to the chair next to me. Captain Dinez stiffened and postured and made a noise of protest, but Silvertip ignored him. He gripped my wrist, none too gently. "Tell me everything you've learned about the other prefects," he insisted. "What is Avior planning? Is Lindo on the level? Why is Edenfield nervous?"

Edenfield was nervous? I cursed silently. If he'd found the spy equipment, we were in trouble. My boss could be walking directly into a trap.

I had to warn him—which meant I had to get out of here immediately.

"My lord, kindly release me," I ordered Silvertip icily.

He let go of my wrist stiffly, honestly astonished.

I drew myself upright, the image of offended virtue. "Your behavior is appalling and inappropriate," I informed him, "and I will not play along. How dare you arrest me on false charges, drag me here, touch me without my permission. For shame. You are a prefect, my lord, and your people look to you. You need to stop this now. Stop tormenting me! Let me go!"

I turned pleadingly to Captain Dinez. "I just want to go *home.*" My voice cracked on the last word, and I buried my head in my arms in an unsuccessful attempt to hide tears of exhaustion and hysteria. I could work myself up to a full panic attack if I had to, but that was a thoroughly unpleasant experience and left me shaky and useless for hours afterward, so I'd leave it as a last resort.

Through watery eyes, I saw Silvertip sit back, chin wrinkled in a frown, eyebrows furrowed. He didn't seem put out or affronted by my accusation—that would take actual conscience—just baffled. "Are you *sure* she's acting?" he asked Captain Dinez.

"At this point," Dinez returned, "it doesn't matter. Either she's telling the truth, in which case she can't help us, or she's lying, in which case she won't help us."

"Please," I said miserably, "just let me go home."

Silvertip nodded with the same paternal warmth he granted small children and potentially generous donors. "If you are innocent, then I apologize for this," he said, standing and returning to his original chair. "Dinez, disable her."

"Wait, what?" I exclaimed. But while my brain was stalling, my body took over. In the time it took Dinez to draw a gun, suppressor already in place, I'd thrown myself into a somersault ending at his toes. I carried through my momentum by kicking both legs out as hard as I could at his right knee.

Dinez flinched away at the last moment, but not anywhere near enough. The kneecap gave away with a horrifying crack. The shot Dinez had been readying banged at the same moment, loud as a clap, and drilled a hole into the carpet.

As I sprang to my feet, Dinez collapsed. Though gasping in agony, he managed to hold on to the gun. So I stomped one pointy, impractical heel down into the back of his hand and ground it in. He howled, and my heel broke off, nailing his hand down. I stumbled back, snagging his gun as I went. I had to hold it upside down—I was starting to really hate these cuffs—but I could hold it.

As I backed up, Dinez swung his foot at me, but he had no leverage, so I let it connect and kicked his dislocated kneecap.

The blood drained from his face, and he didn't try that again.

I got out of range, kicking off my broken shoes as I went.

The doorknob rattled. "My lord?" one of the knights in the hall cried. "My lord, are you all right?"

I trained the gun on Silvertip. He hadn't moved an inch, but he had gone rigid as a crane, and he dug his fingers into his chair arms until fingertips and knuckles turned bone-bleached white. "You know what to say," I told him softly.

Silvertip swallowed. He did know. "Maintain your post, Bento," he called back to the knight. "I'll yell if I need you."

"Yes, my lord."

Sweat beaded Dinez's forehead, but he was tough. He ripped out my shoe heel and stuffed his hand under his jacket to staunch the bleeding. Or that's what it looked like; he'd gone tense in a way I didn't like. Could he have a weapon in his jacket?

I took another step back, seeing the cold combat madness in his eyes. Captain Dinez, I thought, was the sort of man who'd spring at me with a knife even if I'd blown his leg off instead of merely wrecking the knee. Head knights play for keeps. I needed a definitive action.

The problem was, I had no idea *what*. I mean, yes, I could have shot them both then and there and then shot the knights in the hallway and anyone else in my way—at a guess, this semi-automatic held fourteen more rounds—but that's not what I'd call a great plan. Even aside from the fact that within twenty-four hours I'd be hunted down, convicted of treason, and executed, my opponents were (for the moment) defenseless.

I can justify killing in defense of myself or of others. Not so much an unarmed politician, no matter how smarmy; nor a disabled knight. Not when there is any other option.

Guess I was back to gambling.

Silvertip shifted in his chair, and I snarled at him, "Hands up!"

He showed me his palms, but a smile curved his lips. "Amazing what stress can do, isn't it?" he said, and I wondered at him having retained so much of his confidence. "It always makes people revert to type. Still going to deny you're a spy, after taking out a highly trained head knight?"

"It wasn't a fair fight," I said. I shook my head, not taking my eyes off them for a moment. "Look, I have you both at gunpoint. I could hardly miss you from this distance, and despite his sneaky movements, your head knight isn't in any condition to tackle me.

"Do you understand? I could kill you both, kill your guards, and walk away. That's what a spy would do: kill you and run for safety. But I'm *not* a spy, I'm just not. I'm a personal assistant. I make great coffee, run errands, and tidy up after my boss. I've taken self-defense classes, like any sensible woman; and I've tussled with my brothers, because they're older than me, and there's a pecking order to maintain. But I am *not* a spy."

Silvertip's palms remained extended and empty, and his smile remained smug and disbelieving.

"I believe in the rule of law," I told him, earnest but not weak; they wouldn't believe "weak" anymore. "I believe that you're a good man at heart and a good prefect. I understand that you got some misleading information at some point, that there's been a terrible mistake somewhere. But I believe it was an honest mistake, and that we can figure out how to undo it. And I'm sorry I had to hurt you," I told Captain Dinez. "I know you were just doing your job—but I didn't want to be shot."

I stepped back further, next to a side table, and took my finger out of the trigger guard. "I'm afraid," I said, "but I don't want to hurt anyone else. Please believe me. I just want to go home." I ejected the magazine, tilted it onto the side table, and laid the gun beside it. "Please," I said. "Please believe me. Please let me go home."

Silvertip's expression smoothed out and he nodded, coming to a decision. Continuing to show me that he wasn't going for a weapon, he stood and went to the door.

I relaxed fractionally as the door clicked open, and the knights in the hallway came to attention. More witnesses was exactly what I wanted. "My lord?" Bento asked promptly.

"Help!" Silvertip cried, flinging a finger my way. "She's trying to assassinate me!"

His delivery was weak, and if the knights had stopped for two seconds to look at my handcuffs and the emptied gun on the table, maybe they'd have wondered. But instead they spotted Captain Dinez, their fearless leader white-faced and agonized, blood staining the carpet, and their body language turned murderous.

That was my cue to scarper. I scooped up gun and magazine and bolted for the window. As I ran, I fired the shot I'd left in the gun's chamber.

Ducking between shards of glass and skipping panty-hose-clad toes around anything shiny, I leapt through the window and onto the skewed boiled-egg ledge beyond, then flung myself to the right. Fire seared along my left arm. I instinctively tried to clutch it, but the cuffs wouldn't let me. I kept glancing at it, amazed that such a slight graze could burn so badly.

It doesn't matter, I told myself. It only mattered that I ran and that, as I ran, I worked out the curious puzzle of how to shove a magazine into a gun while rigid cuffs held my palms apart.

I rounded a corner and paused long enough to do what I needed: pin the magazine between my knees, shove the gun down over it, and whack the gun butt into the wall to lock the magazine in. Two seconds, three, and I went on running, thumbing the slide release as I went.

The ledge had been barely over a foot wide where I'd first stepped onto it, and the ground was a very, very long way down. Sunlight glared off the eggshell concrete of the ledge and the white concrete of the ground far below, and it turned the tinted windows into mirrors. Wind buffeted me, pushing and pulling toward the building, toward the edge.

The ledge widened until it was at its widest point—four feet—and then narrowed again to its skinniest as I rounded another curve.

A flash of movement, and I dropped onto my backside. Thunder broke the air a moment later, but the shot didn't even come close. I rocked forward and fired between my legs, but the knight had already ducked away, and the only thing I managed to destroy was a chunk of concrete.

Without looking, I swung the gun above my head and fired behind me. I was rewarded by a cry of alarm. The knight who'd been chasing me must've not been hurt too badly, though; I could hear him mumbling into his radio.

I scooted up to my feet, facing the window. The room beyond was another sitting room of some variety, though it specialized in loveseats rather than armchairs, and I could see a collection of bookshelves. Unfortunately, Silvertip had apparently built his manor not thinking that anyone would run around the outside rings, because he'd neglected to put a window-opening latch on the outside.

Here was hoping the carpet padded any broken glass.

I fired right and left again, to stave off the knights, and then aimed for the window.

The door in the room beyond opened, and Silvertip stepped through. He made eye contact through tinted glass as he entered, and I was astonished to see the change in him. Stripped of the smugness, the smarminess, the politician's façade, the look in his eyes was one of rodent fear. He froze like a rat in the light and then moved suddenly, raising his arm—

Hot metal pierced my scalp, and I was falling, falling backward over the edge, cuffed hands slapping helplessly.

For an instant, my fingertips caught on the ledge. I slung inward, smacked into solid concrete, and dropped again. My stomach flipped and then I landed hard on the ledge below, legs crumpling beneath me.

I rolled against the window, hugging it as I gaped like a beached fish. I could feel the cold glass, but my vision had turned black. Then oxygen flooded into my lungs and stars flashed. I wiped blood from my eyes and blinked down at the vivid scarlet smear staining the white concrete.

My gun was, of course, gone.

Dizziness crowded in on me. I didn't trust myself to stand, so I crawled, shredding the remains of my pantyhose into bloody threads. My knees didn't much like it either.

Alarms blared to life, and red lights swirled. Had they lost track of me? It hardly seemed possible. But knighthouse doors slammed open and knights jogged out with military precision, some of them adjusting their green-and-silver uniforms or listening seriously to radios. It struck me then, as it never had before, the extent to which Silvertip kept a small army on his grounds. I knew he had to keep men, to protect his prefecture and lend support to the king in times of war, but despite technically *knowing* how many there were at the manor, I'd never processed it. I'd assumed that most of them patrolled the border, where Silvertip met the bay separating Carina from Akter. What did he do with so many knights here?

In another moment, they were going to think to look up, and then they'd spot me. I stopped crawling and lay on my stomach. I'd again reached a narrow part of the ledge, and the ledge below me was two, three feet wider. I could try a controlled drop.

Of course, if I missed, they'd be scraping my remains off the concrete ground with a spatula—and if I didn't miss, it was still a fifteen-foot drop. Even if I didn't break my ankle, I'd probably be spotted. But what choice did I have? Staying here, I'd definitely be spotted.

If I thought about it, I'd chicken out. So I didn't think about it. I rolled to face the building and prepared to fall.

Chapter 16:

HUMAN HUNTING

In retrospect, it was obvious, but it honestly never occurred to me to check. It was sheer luck that I glanced up and over before dropping, and that up and over was exactly the location of the open window.

Too relieved to feel stupid, I scooted toward it on my backside, ending the blood trail where I'd intended to jump. I'd probably dribbled blood over the side, too, and with luck down onto the ledge below. I'd rather them be hunting me the floor above than the floor below, but as long as they weren't hunting on the same floor, I'd take it.

Three yards later, I pressed my nose against the glass long enough to make sure there was no one—or no one with an obvious gun—in the room beyond. There wasn't, so I got in in a jiffy, latching the window behind me.

The room was rather musty—hence the open window—from the traces of cigar smoke. Akterian cigars, like the sort my grandmother used to smoke. Her husband would bring them for her, whenever he'd gone back to visit his family. That's how they met, those cigars. She hadn't smoked a single one since he'd died.

I'd never particularly liked any of my grandparents, but something of the safety of childhood lingered in the smell, and I inhaled greedily as I wiped my feet on a corner of savoy-blue carpet and spied out the room.

The lights were off, of course, and the tinted windows more tinted than usual. That and the general décor said to me that this might be the prefects' conference room, which gave me a funny feeling.

It was a large room but not enormous, and dominated by a shiny walnut table. Chandeliers hung heavy, and various green drapes over everything provided an extra layer of soundproofing and insulation. It was, in short, the sort of place Francis describes as masculine. Curly designs are manly when dark colored.

More importantly, it looked like the sort of place with drawers containing pens, notepads—and paperclips.

Keeping to the edges of the room, and frequently checking the window, I went through drawers and cupboards. I found plenty of pens, which might do but probably wouldn't, a few scraps of paper, a tissue box, and—wonder upon wonders, something far better than any paperclip. I smelled it before I saw it: subtle, waxy, hint of lemon, lots of oil. Wood polish.

By dint of a variety of uncomfortable contortions and a tremendous mess, I soaked my wrists and hands until they glistened and stank. Then I dropped the bottle, squeezed the fingers and thumb of my left hand together . . . and slipped it right out of the cuff. My other hand came out a moment later, and then I shoved cuffs and polish back in the cupboard, along with the tissues I used to clean up my hands. The clues were there for anyone who looked, but no need to make them more obvious than necessary.

Rubbing my chafed wrists, I crept to the door and stuck my head out to check up and down the hallway. Maybe five minutes had passed since I'd dropped off the ledge above, and I wasn't going to fool myself into thinking they weren't putting two and two together. I needed to get out, and I wasn't going to be able to do it looking like a blood-stained madwoman. Cliché though it sounded, my best bet was to steal a uniform and simply walk out. That meant I needed to locate a bedroom, laundry, or changing room. And then—then I'd figure something out.

This hallway was as stupidly overpriced as the rest of the building. Portraits of former prefects hung on its walls, smugly observing the lesser beings scurrying back and forth, their features enhanced by a flatterer's brushstrokes.

Their eyes didn't bother me. I was far more concerned with the eyes of the security cameras. I straightened my back, pretended to walk casually, and hoped they were in black and white and wouldn't pick up on the blood.

The alarms shut off.

That ... couldn't be a good sign. I froze, skin prickling, feeling like a hare abruptly aware of a beagle. And then, like the hare, I went to ground. I sprinted to the end of the hall, swung through a door, and thundered down the stairwell. I made it past the first landing no problem, but a group of knights stood in conference outside the ground floor exit. I heard a shout as they spotted me, but I kept going—down one more flight and through the basement door.

This door had no lock, but the basement was stuffed full of filing cabinets. It was the work of a moment to shove the nearest cabinet over in front of the door. It crashed down with satisfying solidity, landing diagonally and creating a wedge between door and wall. With a bit of effort, someone could push the door open an inch or three, but not nearly far enough to squeeze through. No one would be getting in that way. If I could find a different exit—

Then so could they. *Use your brain, Mercedes. They know this building better than you do. If you try to escape, you will be caught. If you hide, you will be found. And Silvertip's told these knights you're a dangerous criminal. Face it: you're going to be caught. So get caught on your own terms. Have an open radio connection.* Would a radio work in this basement? What was in here, anyway?

The room's other entrance was an arch, and beyond that a veritable maze of storage shelves loaded with cardboard boxes, plastic tubs, and crates. I might be able to find a weapon in there or a communication device or a white flag or *something* useful. But I'd have to move pretty quickly, or I'd be caught red-handed and probably shot before I could open my mouth.

I paced, hitting my forehead with open palms, trying to *think.* If I were a crazy, paranoid prefect with a brand-new manor and delusions of kinghood, what would convince me to stop? What would convince my knights not to shoot first and interrogate never? Would I accept any form of negotiation? How would I trap her?

I lowered my hands slowly, staring at nothing, an idea forming. It was ludicrous unless I'd read Silvertip correctly—in which case it was inevitable.

If I were building myself a prefect's manor, the first thing I'd do would be design an exit strategy, one with plenty of redundancies. Entrances to my super-secret, not-known-even-by-my-knights secret passage on every floor.

Knights outside the basement door rattled the knob. I stepped against the wall, out of sight as they got it open an inch and banged against the cabinet. They'd be able to see me if I went for the arch, but if I were fast, no way could they shoot me from that angle.

When they found they couldn't get through, they closed the door again, and I heard the murmur of voices.

"But where?" I wondered.

The secret passage would have to be somewhere Silvertip could reach quickly, but which wouldn't be within eyeshot of either door or arch. Preferably, it'd also be in a natural space—somewhere it made sense to have an extra-wide wall. Somewhere that wouldn't draw attention or look weird.

Such as the wall blocking off the underside of the stairs.

Bangs made me jump. The knights were throwing themselves at the door, trying to push the filing cabinet out of the way, not able to see how it was wedged. Let them. There were more futile endeavors in the world, but not many, and I couldn't be bothered to pay much attention. I moved as one hypnotized, hardly believing I could be right.

I traced my hands over the most likely spot, in the corner where the back wall met the stair wall. There were more filing cabinets here, lining both walls, dull industrial green with shining silver handles. Except—except the drawers of this cabinet were fused together.

The cabinet lying in front of the door rocked and slammed back against the wall. Knights cursed themselves, one another, doors in general, filing cabinets, and me. It occurred to me briefly that if I did want to try to convince them of anything, I had a captive audience—but no, better not let them know I hadn't fled through the arch, to lose myself in the maze beyond.

I ran my fingers along the fake cabinet, trying each false drawer. Not one budged. I couldn't see a keyhole or anything, so I tried kicking it. That didn't work any better for me than it had for the knights.

A man's voice rapped orders, and the swearing knights exchanged violence for listening. More orders were spat into a radio. They contained the words "back entrance."

I tapped the false cabinet. Come to think of it, it'd make an awfully small door. Not too small for me, but Silvertip was tall and broad-shouldered. Besides, he might want to bring others with him—his wife or Dinez. And all three of them were considerably larger than I.

It couldn't be in the wall behind the cabinets, but—yes, of course; the next cabinet over. The connection to this one was set back, but they were connected. I tried the handles, and, with a silent laugh, caught the middle latch.

The cabinets swung toward me as a single unit, revealing a dark space beyond, wood paneled on the sides and above, dirt below, smelling of dry earth and stale air. I stepped through and relatched the secret door behind me. As the light cut out, I spied a pile of glow sticks by my left hand and grabbed one.

Silvertip had been bright enough to forgo even minimal luxuries here; neither interior decorators nor electricians had ever been inside this passage. It was wide enough for me to stick out my arms, but no more than that. The dirt floor dulled my footsteps, and I walked quickly—glow stick in one hand, opposite hand trailing along the low ceiling above to support it in case the weight of the building decided to collapse on me.

The passage wasn't straight, but it didn't wind madly either. It turned along the edges of walls and then shot straight ahead. It must have come out somewhere beyond the manor grounds, in a shrouded area where he could emerge secretly and escape. If Silvertip was too paranoid (or not paranoid enough) to alert his knights to wait at the end of this passage—and thus ruin his secret exit—then I was free. I could run to my boss, if he hadn't left without me—or to a newspaper office, or to my Akterian cousins. True, it was possible that Silvertip had the foresight to plant himself or Dinez at the end of this passage, but he'd no reason to believe I'd found—

I stopped. My fingers had run over a wide crack in the wood ceiling and then, yes, metal hinges.

I backed up and lifted the glow stick near the ceiling.

A trapdoor stared down at me, exactly square, two feet on a side. It wasn't locked, didn't have a lock—there was a pull rope that'd allow me to open it. No doubt, this was where the escape routes from the upper levels converged with this one.

Wasn't that interesting.

My lips curled upward. Not like a smile, except maybe the Grinch's version.

As long as I kept running, kept hiding, kept letting Silvertip decide the plays and set the rules, I would keep losing. Maybe it was time for a change of strategy.

I pulled the trapdoor open and started climbing.

Chapter 17

INTIMIDATION

Whoever had designed Silvertip's secret passage system had done a solid job of it—and I say that even if it was the prefect who did it himself. Its brilliance was in its comfort and simplicity: the vertical metal ladder was roomy enough that one could wear a backpack or carry a child. On each floor, a passage led off the vertical shaft.

I followed the ground floor passage—it wasn't long—to the door, and found a peephole, the wide-angle sort. Blobs of green obscured part of my view in the form of wide fronds. This entrance was from a greenhouse of some sort. In fact—yes, there was a peephole in the wall several feet earlier. From there, I could see directly out to the sunshine-lit glass walls and, beyond them, to the manor grounds. Apparently, prefectsmen had been recruited as backups, because they patrolled regularly, eyes peeled for a bedraggled personal assistant.

I again wondered why Silvertip felt he needed such excessive staff. What did they *do* all day?

On the second floor, I got peepholes along a hallway, and then an exit into a dark-wooded library bisected with double-sided bookshelves to obscure the view from the door. The third floor was Silvertip's private office. For all his flaws, I've never heard a word about him neglecting his prefect duties. He might live in luxury, but he paid for it in hard work.

Then again, keeping your prefect in line is one of the primary jobs of the head knight. We've had executions before, by head knights who feel their prefect isn't doing his job. It's definitely not encouraged, but it is considered honorable on the head knight's part—as long as he executes himself directly afterward, to show that the reason behind his action was necessity rather than ambition. Yet another reason choosing your head knight wisely is so important—especially nowadays, as the popular virtues are shifting away from honor and courage and toward diplomacy and circumspection.

The fourth floor exit opened into a bathroom; the fifth onto a roof. Silvertip's private helicopter waited on that roof. He could fly it himself—a point of pride for the prefecture—and probably kept it ready to go at all times.

I have no more idea of how to fly a helicopter than of how to fly without one. I returned to the fourth floor.

The bathroom was luxurious, even beyond what I'd come to expect of this manor. It was dressed in pearly marbled beige tile and gold fixtures. Gold curtains hung in the windows like Christmas lights, and the bathtub could've doubled as a Jacuzzi. Light from outside gleamed off the curved mirror above the sink. The mirror had, not accidentally, two flaps that together gave anyone peering through the peephole an excellent view of the entire bathroom and a large portion of the room beyond—a bedroom sporting another mirror that reflected a reduced version of the otherwise hidden side of the bedroom.

In short, this exit was exactly as I might have wished, which I'm sure wasn't the prefect's intention in arranging it.

I released the handle and stepped out onto smooth tile. From inside the bathroom, this door was part of the rest of the wall, complete with a row of hooks supporting two spa-style white bathrobes. The nearest hook would let me back into the secret passage.

Blood and dust crumbled off my filthy feet and onto the spotless tile. Wrinkling my nose, I dampened a wad of toilet paper and retreated to the secret passage to wipe myself off. Then I dumped the wad into the toilet and flushed.

The toilet was admirably quiet, the plumbing good-natured. No one came to investigate, so I ventured onward.

The bedroom matched its bathroom, except that it was carpeted and didn't take it so easy on the gold damask hangings. The bedroom door was closed, the walk-in closet full of bespoke suits and dresses, the vanity aptly named, the chaise lounge more elegant than comfortable. As hiding spaces went, none of these appealed to me, but I didn't want to stay in the secret passage. Sooner or later, checking it would occur to Silvertip.

That left the bed.

I lay on the carpet and scooted under the giant bed until I was completely concealed, taking care to keep my ripped knees out of staining range. Then I probed until I found the edge of the gauzy material protecting the base of the box springs.

There are three types of box springs commonly available in Carina. The type with actual springs is hopeless unless you have wire cutters, which I didn't. The type with regular metal bars every ten or twelve inches, running horizontally, would do in a pinch, and would pinch a great deal. But though it'd be horribly uncomfortable, I was small enough to make it work.

Silvertip's box spring was the type I'd been expecting and hoping for: a foundation. More box than springs, it was basically a frame with a couple of crossbeams underneath and a great many wooden slats on top. Like most expensive foundations, it was extra tall to allow the bed to tower.

I grinned through the hole I'd torn. I've played a lot of games of hide-and-seek in my life, and no one ever checks inside of box springs.

I left the underside of the bed only once, to use Silvertip's golden toilet and drink from his golden faucet. Aside from that, I slept and dreamed of black beans, burgers, and coffee.

Morning brightened into afternoon and faded into evening. The last dregs of sunlight had long been washed down the drain when the bedroom door swung open and Silvertip said, "Be thorough. I don't want to be gutted in my sleep."

"Oh, Otto," sighed a deep female voice, "do you have to say such things?"

"You didn't see what she did to Dinez. It'll be months before he can walk again."

"Yes," said the woman, whom I tentatively identified as Silvertip's wife, Signe, "but I have to be able to sleep tonight. And you *said* she found the—"

Silvertip cleared his throat loudly. "We can rely on Pius here. He'll check in the closet and under the bed for monsters."

Signe sniffed. "You don't have to make fun of me. You're the one who said she was dangerous. I was willing to believe she'd escaped, but now you've made me think she might be hiding in the bathroom or outside the window."

"Don't worry, my lady," Pius said. "If she is, I'll find her."

There was a significant pause, and then Silvertip said gallantly, "You stick to the bedroom, Pius. I'll check the bathroom myself. Can't be too careful!"

I heard the bathroom door click closed, and could guess what Silvertip was checking. I was sure I hadn't left any traces—I'd double- and triple-checked—but I held my breath anyway.

Just as well: material shushed as Pius lifted the bed skirt. I'd pinched the torn corner of the box spring gauze and run it taut over a nail head, but it didn't look exactly the same as before.

"Clear," Pius announced, standing. "Do you need any help in there, my lord?"

"Thank you, no," Silvertip said, emerging from the bathroom. "No one under the sink; no one in the tub. I locked the window."

"Lock these too," Signe urged. "Ooh, I hate the thought of that woman creeping about while we're asleep. Tell me again that she's long gone, that you're only being paranoid."

"She's long gone, and I'm only taking reasonable precautions," Silvertip assured her.

"Please make sure you lock the door after me," Pius said, once the windows were double-checked and locked and the closet cleared. "I'll have someone stationed outside it all night and knights patrolling the rings. No one will get past us."

"Thank you," Silvertip said. "Dinez will be pleased with your diligence. You may go."

"Yes, my lord."

A few more seconds, a few more soft sounds, and the door clicked closed. Keys jangled, a drawer opened, and then a set of unpleasantly familiar sounds: a gun slide pulled back far enough to check for a chambered round, a magazine dropped and then slammed back.

"Is that necessary?" Silvertip asked quietly. "I told you—"

"Do shut up, Otto. Or try being a man for once in your life."

"What do you call what I've been doing?" Silvertip protested. "Give me that." Scuffing sounds, then a gun clacked down on the bedside table. "I'll deal with her if she comes. I almost shot her once already today. I thought I had shot her."

"But you missed. You wouldn't have missed if you'd practiced."

"I do practice! And there was blood. So I must have shot her, see?"

"I see that if you really cared about my safety," Signe said precisely, "you would practice every day instead of whining out endless excuses."

"They aren't excuses! I have real work to do, you know."

"What I want to know," Signe replied silkily, "is how she knew about your escape route."

"How does anyone know about anything? Lucio must have told her."

"And who told him? You promised me we could trust those builders, but you can't trust anyone these days. Avior snaps his fingers and flutters money at them, and they can't spill our secrets quickly enough."

"Let's not argue about this again," Silvertip groaned. "You got your manor—"

"Yes," said Signe, television's perfect wife, always in the background, always smiling and supporting her husband, "I got a building. A *manor.* And in the meantime, the king sits fat and complacent on his throne and you neglect your target practice."

The conversation paused as water ran, teeth and hair were brushed, and the Ostbergs generally engaged in their nightly routines. They exchanged habitual comments, mostly neutral and all mundane.

"There is one other option," Signe said, once she and her husband had settled into bed.

"No," Silvertip said. "No, Signe. We've discussed this."

"He will turn on you."

"Yes, but until then, we need him. We need to be united."

"He'll know about you by now. His spy will have seen to that. You need to be ready to make the first strike."

"Yes," Silvertip sighed. "I know."

"I only nag because I'm worried about you. You know how much I love you."

The Ostbergs clicked off their bedside lamps and snuggled down in the middle of the bed.

"Yes," Silvertip breathed. "I know."

Signe fell asleep quickly; her husband took longer. They shifted and grunted their way through the light stages of sleep and into the paralysis of deep sleep.

I could have emerged then, but I didn't. Maybe some instinct stopped me, or maybe I was only so stiff and aching and hungry and nervous that I chickened out. In any case, while I was vacillating, Signe cycled into lighter levels of sleep, which was no good.

The next time they entered deep sleep, I was ready for it. I slithered out from beneath the bed, my limbs like rubber hoses, my back screeching at me, my shins as bruised as the rest of me. I'd never spent hours upon hours in box springs as a child, and I'd been more limber then. It took real strength of will not to go through stretching contortions right there in the middle of the floor and instead get to work.

The curtains were drawn, but a sliver of moonlight slicing between them and reflecting off the mirror gave me enough light to maneuver. I couldn't see any matching light from outside the bedroom door—the carpet was too thick—and the guard was quiet, but I had no doubt he was there.

I brushed my fingers over the doorknob to ensure it was locked. It was. Which meant the door could've stopped a particularly determined four-year-old, but definitely not a trained knight. In his construction efforts, Silvertip had apparently not invested in a reinforced bedroom door.

The thick carpet would provide some soundproofing, but I'd better also make sure they couldn't call out—or wouldn't.

I flitted to Signe's well-stocked vanity and spent several Jenga-intensive minutes identifying and excavating hairbrush, powder brush, and powder foundation. Presentation, as they say, is everything.

I retreated to the bathroom with my bounty and got to work.

Signe's skin was pink to my brown, and caking her powder on gave me a ghostly, chronically ill sheen. I blended the color down my neck and dabbed it on my hands but avoided the area around my eye sockets and outer jaw to achieve that stylish I-haven't-slept-in-days look.

My hair came next. It's naturally straight and goes straighter under the influence of water. After some initial trouble getting the brush through the mats, and a lot of bloody water running down my neck and arms, I succeeded in styling it: part in the dead middle, curtains on either side of my face, a few strands falling over my eyes.

The blood helped. I looked like something out of a Japanese horror film.

The Ostbergs were where I'd left them, snuggled up in their extravagant bed, sleeping the sleep of the unjust. Neither one shifted when I went through the jewelry atop Signe's dresser. For all she'd put on a show in Pius's presence, she obviously hadn't been worried enough to lock it up. And she had some heavy, expensive loot. The necklace I used to tie her ankle to her husband's must've cost more than I make in a year. It had plenty of sharp, fat jewels and square platinum settings to dig into her skin when she struggled.

I left her other leg free as I tucked her in nice and tight and went for some glue. Lash glue? No; it wasn't strong enough. Ah—nail glue. I couldn't read the lettering in the dark, but the bed of fake nails gave it away. If it was any good, she'd need a proper solvent to get it off. I dabbed it liberally on her lips and let time do its work.

With some regret, I left Silvertip's lips alone. He had to be able to talk, and he didn't strike me as a screamer.

Maybe five minutes had elapsed. In another two, I'd finished my preparations. I perched on a chair on Signe's side of the bed—feet on the seat, hunched over my knees, watching them through my hair, head cranked to the side, near arm dangling, far arm supporting.

I aimed Signe's bedside lamp at her eyes and clicked it on.

She'd been sleeping deeply, but the light was bright and intruded no matter how she shifted. She grunted and would've mumbled if she could've opened her mouth. She rolled to face her husband, and the necklace around her ankle restricted her from rolling further. She flopped back to face the ceiling. Her eyelids fluttered, opened, squinted. Her hand shaded her eyes as she looked toward the light—and toward my shadowed presence. She didn't understand. She frowned and squinted harder. I saw the exact moment she panicked.

Her thrashes and desperate hums didn't take long to wake Silvertip, but it must've felt like ages to her. When he did wake, he couldn't understand why she wouldn't open her mouth and tell him what was wrong, and that made her panic harder. She stabbed a finger at the chair where I'd been sitting, only to find it empty.

"I could kill you," I said.

I'd been right about Silvertip: he wasn't a screamer. His voice disappeared entirely, and if he hadn't been in bed, he would've fainted. His hands scrabbled for the gun on his bedside table, and then he was aiming it at me and squeezing the trigger wildly. The gun clicked empty every time.

I lifted my fist so that he could see it clearly and then opened my fingers. Bullets tumbled to the carpet. "I could kill you," I said again. My back was to the door, my head tilted to the side, my arms loose. Not the parody pose I'd put on for Signe, not now they were awake enough to discern and, perhaps, find it ridiculous.

Signe's clawing fingers tore at her lips as she pushed herself upright and back, as she flattened against the headboard, but she stopped trying to scream. She was recovering quickly, despite everything, and if she could've spoken, I might've been in trouble.

"What do you want?" Silvertip had meant to demand it, but the words emerged in a harsh croak. "What did you do to my wife?"

"Your men are incompetent," I said, "your methods infantile. Fourteen hours, you've searched for me; fourteen hours, you've failed to catch me. I watched you run around and I watched you sleep, and you never knew I was here."

Silvertip licked dry lips, eyes flitting from me to the door and back again.

"I could kill you," I said a third time, "but I've been ordered not to."

Silvertip stilled and Signe grasped his arm. Finally, I was behaving like they expected me to, admitting what they believed to be true. I had them, if ever I would.

Running a hand nonchalantly through my hair to normalize it as I went, I stepped toward the door and flicked on the main light. Then I went and perched again, this time at the foot of their bed. I even tried a clipped, professional smile to go with my clipped, professional tone. "Your treatment of me has been unacceptable," I said, "but I like to think of myself as merciful—and obedient." I quirked my eyebrows, and let the smile become faintly humorous although no less hard. "Consider this a learning experience, Otto. My employer does not appreciate your games, and neither do I. If it weren't too late in the day to change our plans—but as you yourself pointed out as you were climbing into bed, unity is important."

Unhurried, I removed my glasses, polished them, and hooked them back over my ears. There's nothing quite like glasses for peering at people. "My employer," I informed Silvertip, "is especially interested in any information you might have regarding Prefect Edenfield."

Silvertip swallowed, but he'd spent decades as a politician, and he wasn't about to let a little thing like midnight assault ruin his recovery time. "You've spoken to him?" he asked. "To your employer, I mean?"

"I've made a full report." I smiled again, not like I meant it. "Now, about Edenfield."

Chapter 18:

FALSE ACCUSATION

Francis was awake when I got home. He looked at me, I looked at him, and then I went and piled leftovers on a plate. I didn't bother with the microwave. It had been a good twenty hours since my last meal, and I was *hungry*.

I wasn't the only one who'd been craving food. Evidence of unhealthy living littered the table: chips, cookies, doughnuts, and soda cans. For the past thirty-three years, Francis has managed to convert lack of sleep and poor eating habits into muscle, but I'd lectured him more than once on what would happen if he didn't reform. He'd smiled, nodded, agreed, and regressed every time insomnia struck.

By the cavelike quality of his face and the mechanical movements of his arms, he hadn't slept a wink this night and possibly not the previous one either. Red rimmed his eyes like puckered lips.

I stuffed two chocolate-covered doughnuts into my mouth and dug into cold soba and fish.

"You have blood in your hair," Francis said.

I nodded. "I hurt my head."

He kept watching me as I shoved noodles in my mouth. I'm pretty good at putting up with uncomfortable stares, but he's even better at giving them. He kept this one up all through the fish, and I'd barely begun on the noodles before I gave up and said, "Let me take a shower, and then you can disinfect me."

"Hmm," Francis said.

I'd seen myself in the mirror by daylight in Silvertip's bathroom and again by moonlight. It hadn't mattered, then; what had mattered was first that I stay hidden and later that I frighten. Only after I left Francis to take that shower did I really stop and process my appearance.

I was filthy from head to foot, thick with dust and cobwebs. The makeup I'd applied to hide my adventures in the forest was gone, save for the black gathered under my eyes, leaving plenty of little slashes and big bruises perfectly visible. Silvertip's bullet had grazed the left top of my skull and taken away a strip of hair on either side of it. The graze itself looked remarkably shallow, considering how much blood it had produced and how much it had hurt. Faint blood trails decorated my forehead, cheeks, neck, and arms. I must've been dripping blood-filled water over Silvertip's coverlet and carpet the whole time I'd been chatting with him.

Blood stained my shirt too, especially the collar and the left sleeve, which was soaked down to the wrist. I looked like I was going to a Halloween party, only too ghastly.

I stripped off my ruined clothes and took a closer look at the damage. And oh my, how I hurt, and in what creative variety. None of my injuries was severe, but each contributed its own brand of vindictiveness, from my lacerated knees to my finger-bruised neck. And these were the wages of *victory!*

Not for the first time, I wished those magical med packs in videogames existed in real life. I wouldn't have minded an Undo button, either.

"You look awful!" Luc burst out, when I returned to the kitchen after my shower—freshly scrubbed, dressed in loose clothing, and feeling infinitely refreshed.

"She looks better than she did before," Francis commented. He'd cleared and sanitized the table to make room for the first-aid kit. Not his little one, either: the giant one he brings to construction sites in case he has to staunch a stump or impalement.

I guess I could've felt touched or honored or something, but I mostly felt weary. I pulled up a chair next to him and slumped into it. Though it was my softest, my sweatshirt scratched various fine cuts on my arms and rubbed against the giant bruise that extended down one side of my body, where I'd slammed into the concrete ledge.

"Your wrists too?" Francis asked.

I nodded. The cuffs had done a real number on me.

"What'd you do, wrestle a bear?" Luc asked unsympathetically.

"Yes, that's right," I said.

"Bear scratches don't look like this," Francis said, examining my scalp. He's not squeamish about blood unless it's his own. "This is ugly. You should get stitches."

"You do it."

"Are you sure?"

I was sure that hospitals were required to report gunshot wounds, and that I really didn't want to deal with reeves right now—and that I didn't have time anyway. "I'm sure."

Francis shrugged and dug through his supplies. He's competent, if no artist: he went in for a basic medical training course a couple of years back, and I know he's had to deal with various emergencies since then. Of course, that didn't mean he had access to anesthetics. . . .

"Luc said you were arrested," he commented as he readied a surgical needle.

I forced my eyes away from it. "Did he."

Luc tensed, but I didn't start in on him. It had occurred to me more than once, during my long night in the cell, that he had betrayed me; but I hadn't thought he had. That would've taken moral fiber.

"Weren't you?" Francis asked.

"Arrested? No. A couple of knights showed up here and brought me in for questioning, but I was never charged. They kept me overnight to soften me up before interrogating me. Turns out that I'm a master criminal—or the woman who stole my identity is. Turns out—"

Francis started in on my head. I'd done my best to wash the graze in the shower, but the water had hurt like crazy. Despite this, I had managed to get my hair clean on the rest of my head. As for the grazed area itself—well, the hair had been blown clear away. I felt the tickle of scissors against hair, and knew Francis was delicately cutting off more. I was going to do some artistic coiffing until it grew back.

As Francis dabbed on cooling antibiotic cream, I heroically went on with my story.

"Anyway, she's a total psycho, and they thought I was her," I said. "But Prefect Silvertip had met her in person, so he knew they'd arrested the wrong woman the moment he saw me."

"The *prefect* was there?" Francis breathed, in awe of my brush with celebrity.

"He sure was," I said ruefully. "Which was great—he was very kind about the mix-up—until my namesake showed up, guns blazing."

I broke off as Francis started suturing, because I wanted his full concentration on that, and because I was busy whimpering. Only after he tied the last knot did I go on.

"Thanks," I gasped. "How bad was it?"

"Bad enough," he said. "So what happened?"

I made a face. "It was horrible. I didn't know what was going on most of the time, and I kept thinking—this is the worst part of it—I kept thinking about how I was late for picking up my boss and he wouldn't know what had happened. Isn't that stupid? I spent hours hiding in a dusty old closet and more hours in the foundation of a bed, hoping I wouldn't get shot. It took hours and hours for the knights to—ow!"

"Sorry," Francis said. He was examining my wrists again. "This happened at the reeve station?"

"At Silvertip Manor. That's why—"

"Don't touch that. Let me."

"It itches!"

"I said *don't*."

"What were you doing at Silvertip Manor?" Luc wanted to know.

I rolled my eyes up at him and he flushed but didn't recant. "I told you," I said, "they brought me to the prefect. There was a lot of the knights accusing me and me being really confused, and then once the prefect verified I was who I said I was—or I wasn't who they thought I was—they were going to send me away without explaining anything. The prefect had to intervene, or I wouldn't know even the little bit I've told you ... which I wasn't supposed to tell you, by the way, so don't spread it around."

Naturally, being my brothers, they weren't satisfied with this summary of a story. They dug in, demanding details, wringing every last minute of my adventure out of me.

I didn't mind. I had a good story ready, plenty of embellishments to spread like pâté over store-bought wheat bread, and time to kill as I packed.

"There's one good thing to come out of this," I said cheerfully as I zipped up my suitcase. "The prefect felt so bad about dragging me into the whole mess that he loaned me an official government van. I can drive it instead of taking the bus—and I can even use the official lanes, if I want." I glanced at the clock. "I'll call my boss at eight to let him know I'm coming—I figure better late than never. Don't let the apartment burn up while I'm gone."

"You're not going," Francis said.

My mouth widened derisively. "Excuse me?"

Francis didn't laugh and he didn't tell me he was joking. His brow lowered, and he straightened. At some point, he had planted himself in my doorway. He wasn't bulky enough to fill it, but he sure tried. "You're in no condition to work," he said. "You've been through a highly traumatic experience, and you're obviously in shock."

"I am *not*." I might be, at that.

"He can't possibly expect you to work after what you've been through. And on a Sunday! Call him up, or I'll do it for you—but you need to rest, Mercedes. He'll understand, if he's anything like half as decent as you say he is."

"This isn't about him," I retorted. "This is about me. *I* expect me to work. *I* choose to work. Don't bother arguing with me—you won't win."

Francis argued with me. He didn't win. "Fine," he snapped, "but you aren't going alone."

"I won't be alone; my boss will be there."

"You'll take Luc."

"I will *not*."

"I'm not going with her!" Luc cried. "You go with her!"

"You've slept," Francis told him, "and I have work today. It needs to be you."

"Why should it be? She can go alone, for all I care. And I have work too."

"You can work anywhere. Bring a laptop with you."

"No! I have had it up to *here* with you assuming that because I work from home I don't have a real job. It is real, and it can't be carted off to the side whenever convenient. I need my desktop. I need time and space and quiet, not a sister to babysit. Just because you seem to think—"

It's easy to make Francis angry; happens at the drop of a screw, and stops about as quickly, most times. Luc's another story, and this argument had been boiling beneath the surface for years. If it was going to pick right now to erupt, the least I could do was take advantage of it and slip away as they bickered.

If only Francis weren't blocking the doorway. I tried to squeeze past him anyway, and he held up a hand to stop me.

"I am not taking Luc with me," I informed him furiously. "Fob him off on someone else."

"You're in no condition—"

"That's my decision!"

My brothers stared, their argument evaporating like morning dew. My pitch doesn't usually reach such exalted heights.

"I am in a hurry," I stated. I aimed at a cold tone, to restore my equilibrium. The result left much to be desired. A gust of dizziness swirled around me, and tears crawled along my cheeks. What was the matter with me? I was fine. *Fine.*

"Francis is right," Luc said, a strange twinge in his voice.

"Frankly, I can't believe the prefect let you go in this condition," Francis said, bolstered by Luc's turnaround support. "He should have had someone drive you to the hospital and then call us. He's a busy man, but this is plain irresponsible."

The wave of fatigue and useless, interrupting emotion had left me weak. I did not want to deal with this, or with anything. I just needed to keep going, get done what I'd meant to, get to Edenfield. I wished people would stop interfering. "Would you move?" I asked. "Please, move. I'm hideously late."

"A few more minutes won't matter," Francis said, although that'd never been his attitude when *he* was the late one. But he wasn't reflecting on his hypocrisy; his eyes unfocused to other thoughts. "Maybe it would be good for me to get away," he mused. "Deodato can take care of things for a few days, and I haven't had time off in months."

"You aren't invited," I said. "Please move."

"Better you than me," Luc said, and I recoiled from the intense dislike in his voice. I tried to catch his eye, but he turned away from me.

Fine. Let him be like that. What did I care?

"I can be ready in fifteen minutes," Francis said. "Don't let her leave without me."

Luc folded his arms and watched Francis retreat down the hall and into his room. He left his door wide open, so he could keep an eye on the hall.

I guessed Luc would leave then, or maybe just stare at me and rat me out when I snuck away, but instead he stepped fully inside my room and closed the door. Whatever he was going to say or do, he didn't want Francis to hear.

"I don't appreciate your highhandedness," I said. Not quietly; this extended to Francis. "Get out of my room."

"Did you steal the car?" Luc asked.

That was about the last thing I'd expected him to say. It took me a good few seconds to figure out *what* car. My mind went immediately to my boss's car, which made no sense, before cycling around to the official van I'd driven home. "No," I said, like he was a complete idiot— because at the moment, he was. "Of course not. I told you—"

"Yes, and I didn't believe you. You and I know the actual reason you were arrested. So what I really want to know is what level of stupid you were to come back here after escaping. Why didn't you drive straight for the border? You can't imagine they wouldn't look for you here."

"*I didn't steal the van.*" Silvertip had offered it, actually, without any prompting from me. Funny, how some people will do anything you want once you show them you're not cowed. Or once you start acting the way they expect you to. I'd had the feeling I probably could've wrangled a few prefectsmen out of him too, to play chauffeur and minion. Naturally, they would've been minions who would've turned on me the moment he changed his mind, if he changed it, so I hadn't asked. But I could have. . . .

Luc clearly didn't believe me, but he didn't pursue that line. Instead, he asked, "What happened? I didn't turn you in, if that's what you're wondering, so you don't need to look at me like that."

I hadn't been. This was dull frustration, not accusation.

"They must've found the body," he concluded. "Seems your preparations weren't as clever as you thought they were."

"I have no idea what you're talking about."

"What would our parents say, Mercedes? They raised you better than this."

Because they were such bastions of virtue, a pair of uneducated potato farmers groveling in the dirt for a few cowries. Truly, I should strive to be like them!

"If there is any decency left in you," Luc pressed on, "you'll turn yourself in."

I sneered. "I guess it's true what they say. There are none so blind as those who will not see."

"And even the Devil can quote Scripture."

If he'd struck me with his fist, it would've been easier, simpler. I could've hit him back. But words are an uglier weapon, and I couldn't make him understand. I kept seeing the carefully catalogued, shrink-wrapped human lungs, the surgical steel of the kitchen; kept smelling the tang of iron, the echo of blood from the pantry, from the riverside, hovering around the slices in my wrists and the gash in my scalp. Gushing heat and bleached lavender and the sickly sweet of brain.

"That's what you think I am," I said. "The Devil. Then you'd better run back to your room, or you might get infected. By all means, let yourself out."

Luc slashed the air awkwardly, partly in exasperation, partly in anger, and partly to take back his words. "Just tell me the truth," he said. "I just want the truth from you, for once in your life. Don't you have any feelings at all?"

I think I hated him, in that moment. Hated him for demanding I pour out my feelings to him and make myself vulnerable when he was actively attacking me. Hated him for demanding the truth when he had repeatedly refused to listen to it, refused to see it when it was before his eyes. Hated him for his words, which were a far greater betrayal than all that had come before, because they denied our long friendship, his supposed intimate knowledge of me—and because they denied, more than anything else, my basic humanity.

If he had been kind, if he had listened, I could have shown him as great a display of emotion as even he could desire. But instead he had attacked me, and so I retreated and froze my expression into scorn. "What an ugly little fool you are," I sneered. "You think I should care more about my feelings than about Francis's life, than the lives of hundreds of others. But oh, yes, that's exactly what you would have done: let anyone and everyone die rather than offend your pathetic bleeding heart. Because heaven forbid anyone not enslave herself to the gluttony of her own sentiment. How dare I do what is right over what is pleasant. How dare I?"

"If you had feelings," said Luc, "you couldn't have done what you did."

"That's true," I said. "People with feelings never protect those they love, and they certainly don't protect total strangers."

"They don't commit murder!"

There: it had been spoken aloud, and it couldn't be unspoken.

I turned my back on him and fussed with my suitcase, though there was nothing more to be done with it. I told myself that this, too, was a price I had been willing to pay. I told myself that if Luc knew me so little, trusted me so little, then it wasn't that much of a price. I told myself that I didn't need his good opinion anyway. I told myself anything and everything that might stop me from sobbing, because Luc had no right to see me cry, and I *would not let him.*

Luc still wouldn't leave. He sighed and said, "At least tell me if they really let you go."

That helped; it let me retreat from hurt to coldness again. "I will give you no further information," I told him.

"Tell me," he ground out, "if I can expect reeves banging down my door, wanting to know where my sister is—or if you somehow convinced them you were innocent."

"Get out of my room, Luc."

He didn't move. He was trying for hardness of his own, and failing pathetically. "Did you murder anyone else to escape? Where are you headed now—the border? Should I return unopened any Christmas cards I get from Akter and Vela?"

I slapped him as hard as I could. I didn't mean to; I meant to stare icily at him. But I wasn't sorry, and I didn't apologize. I pushed up my window and dropped my suitcase through. I was shaking. I wanted to hurt him. "You won't get any cards from me," I spat. "You're no brother of mine. *Coward.*"

I didn't wait for his response. I climbed out of my window and into the early morning and away, away, away from him.

Chapter 19:

CONSPIRACY

Francis anticipated me. He couldn't get into the van without a key, but he could prevent me from getting in. He lounged against the driver's door, quite neatly dressed in one of his visiting-clients outfits: tartan flannel shirt and jeans, so they'd know he was a tough man, but cleaner and better fitting than the clothes he actually worked in. A duffel bag slouched by his feet, half-covered by a shearling jacket.

He couldn't have had more than ten minutes to prepare, and less if he'd wanted to be sure to beat me. I was impressed, although I suspected he'd find himself in dire need of toothpaste and underwear once we reached our destination. No doubt he planned to buy them in Gjerde.

And he *would* be coming with me to Gjerde. I had spent my fight . . . and to tell the truth, I'd be glad of the company. So I tossed my keys at him, slid into the passenger seat, and set the GPS.

I didn't expect to sleep, but I did. I woke up after we crossed the border into Tey Prefecture, when Francis stopped at a gas station. The store was closed, but the vending machine worked, which was all we needed. While Francis bought coffee and breakfast, I called my boss and left a message. "Sorry about flaking and not calling earlier," I informed the voicemail cheerfully. "Things have been a real mess on my end, and I just had to get away. Francis and I are going on vacation in the south for a few days. Hope you enjoy your trip!"

"Was that your boss?" Francis asked curiously, balancing drinks, mini-muffins, and a parfait on the dashboard as he climbed in. "Did he tell you to go home and rest?"

"I left a voicemail," I said, starting up the van.

Truth be told, I'd have liked my boss's input on what to do with Francis—mostly because my boss dislikes random factors messing with his plans. Francis was a random factor . . . but he didn't have to be. In fact, managed properly, Francis could be an extremely useful asset. Since he had made it clear that he was sticking to me during this trip, I might as well deputize, minionize, and utilize him. Then he could function as a subset of me, and no plans would be messed with.

I turned this over in my mind as Francis woke himself up with muffins and coffee. "This," I said, "is no ordinary business trip. I didn't tell you what it was about before because—well, you'll soon understand why. But I'm telling you now because I think you can help . . . and because I know that once you hear what I have to say, you'll want to help."

That sure got his attention. He forgot to finish chewing, which was distracting as anything. I told him this and he got his jaw going again as I drove on. At least I didn't have to worry about traffic, between the Sabbath and the government lane.

"My boss," I explained, "is very, very good with numbers. In fact, most of his work involves manipulating numbers: looking for patterns and discrepancies and then tracing them back to their source."

Francis nodded his understanding. "Fraud-detection expert," he said. "You never told us what kind of accountant he was."

I'd never used the word "accountant" at all, but I wasn't surprised that that was the conclusion he'd come to.

"Over the past year or so," I said, "he started noticing . . . not fraud, but unusual patterns in the distribution of money across Carina. It wasn't anything definite, anything illegal or reportable, but it niggled at him. He started digging in, hunting for the source of the pattern, for the fly in the ointment. He didn't neglect his other work, but he—you might say he layered it in.

"It took me a while to catch on to what he was doing, but he has very strict habits, and they shifted during that time. I eventually asked him about it, and he confided in me, showed me his evidence. He was right that most people wouldn't believe him about it: it was a delicate shift in many different factors over time. Such things can usually be explained by economics, but he demonstrated—I can't go into his proofs; I don't remember them well enough—but he demonstrated that the economic explanation didn't make sense, that in some ways the numbers were acting in the exact opposite fashion to how they should. It was clear that the shift was occurring in every prefecture, but was focused on Avior, Lindo, and Canopus.

"We got stuck then; there didn't seem to be anywhere else to go. Were Akter and Vela to blame? There was movement there, but it didn't correspond. Some underground group? The prefects themselves?

"We researched the prefects exhaustively. You'd be amazed what I could tell you about them. Did you know that Lindo blames the king for her sister's suicide? And that Hemmel's proposed to her at least six times? And that although Fjordland's doctors say he's not mentally competent to remain prefect, he won't step down?"

"I don't read tabloids."

"I'm not talking empty gossip, Francis; I'm talking motives. Fjordland and Batata are under Avior's thumb; Tey will believe anything he's told; Canopus is power hungry; Silvertip is greedy *and* power hungry; and Edenfield is in desperate need of resources."

"Back then," said Francis, who isn't the fool he sometimes acts, "Avior had a different prefect. I can't imagine Lord Gil Winter getting in on a conspiracy."

"No," I agreed, "Gil had no motive; they conspired with his brother. And for the record, we *didn't* know Lucio planned to kill him."

"Are you sure Lucio *was* the one who killed him?"

"He practically admitted it to my face—no, Francis, not yet. Let me tell this thing in order. Anyway, Lucio did have a motive. You've probably guessed at it. Twenty years ago, Lucio was passed over for Avior's prefectship. The official reason was that his mother thought Gil more suitable, but the real reason is that Lucio is and always has been mentally unstable. Even as a child, he was interested in what the locals called black magic, and demonology is his pet project."

"You believe he sold his soul to Hell."

"He certainly tried. Or—or maybe not. My boss is the one who traced him down on various demonology forums, and Lucio seemed to be obsessed with reality. He posited that the people around him weren't quite real and that, since unreal people worshiped God, the way for him to be real was to contact the enemy of God—the Devil. At one point, it even looked like he was looking for a way to summon the Devil, but he gave it up years ago and started asking about demons instead. Yes, I know," I said, in response to Francis's expression. "He needed a psychiatrist, not a demon."

"He needed a minister," Francis replied, and I saw how disturbed he was.

"Yes, well," I said, "I didn't get a chance to chat theology with him. My boss might've, only he was trying to ingratiate himself, find out what the prefects were after. He posed as an expert in demonology and began making wise comments on forums until Lucio contacted him. Long story short, Lucio thought that the reason he hadn't managed to summon a demon was that he wasn't important enough for demons to bother with. What he needed was a really juicy evil, something that would put him on the demons' radar."

"So he killed his brother," said Francis, "and became prefect."

"As a stepping stone," I said, "to killing the king."

Tey Prefecture really is exceedingly picturesque. The Star Ridge Mountains start up to the east almost as soon as you enter the prefecture, and follow you all the way up into Edenfield. They keep away the bay weather, which means the thick, wet forests of Silvertip give way to the drier woods of Edenfield. Unlike Edenfield, however, Tey is quite populated. It has the best universities in Carina, and has the reputation of being a haven for artists and musicians, poets and academics. It also has the reputation of being the most expensive prefecture to live in, and it looked it: beneath the Star Ridge Mountains and among the groomed forests and flowering parks rose elegant buildings of creamy stone, two or three stories high, flat-faced, each story complete with fenced wrap-around balcony and constant towering windows.

I had a lot of time to admire it all, while I was waiting for Francis to stop swearing. I kept thinking he was about to stop, only for him to remember something else I'd said and rev back up again. Only once did he ask for my input, when he asked whether we'd reported Lord Winter to the palace.

"How can we?" I asked. "We don't have proof. He may be crazy, but he's not stupid. He hasn't given us any absolute evidence—and he's prefect now."

That set Francis off some more, but I admired the scenery until it was my turn again, and didn't mind him. "It's just as well we couldn't pin him down," I pointed out, "because if they arrested Avior, they'd be missing the others. *All* the prefects are in on it. Not the demonology part, obviously. The others plan to kill the king the old-fashioned way. And the only time they can do that, when no one but the prefects and the king is present—"

"Is at the prefects' conference," Francis realized. "But—Mercedes, the conference this year is in Lindo, not Edenfield."

"I know," I said, "but Lindo is the most dangerous prefect. She's out for revenge, and she's spent the past year turning her manor into a death trap for the king. If he steps in there, he's never stepping out."

Francis's comment was unprintable but beautifully elegant. It lasted only a single breath, but it did justice to both the aesthetic of the tough working man and the rules of flyting. At the end of it, he asked, "Why Edenfield?"

"Aside from the fact that it's at the opposite end of the country from both Avior and Lindo," I replied, "because A) it has minimal security, which means we could plant the spy equipment needed to listen in on and record what the prefects are saying—"

"Which is highly illegal."

"—and B) because Prefect Edenfield is our most likely ally, if we need to recruit one of the prefects. Batata is well-meaning but useless; Fjordland is old and confused; Hemmel is hopelessly besotted; and Tey is young and impressionable. The others are simply nasty people.

"Edenfield, as we understand it, agreed to regicide because he thinks it's the only way he can protect his prefecture and his nation from spies and invaders. He says Akter and Vela are getting more aggressive. I don't know how much truth there is in that, but I believe he believes it."

"Nothing can excuse treason—or murder."

I paused. "By 'murder,'" I said, "do you mean *all* killing? I mean, if we went to war, would you join up?"

Francis flared. "Of course I would! What do you take me for?"

"No, it's not like that. Luc—"

"Oh," Francis said darkly. *"Luc."*

I opened my mouth automatically, to defend Luc against that tone, and then shut it again. This wasn't the time to get distracted—and opening the floodgate guarding that topic was not something I wanted to do in front of Francis. Not until I knew where I stood.

I cleared my throat. "Anyway," I said. "As far as we can tell, Edenfield was the last and most hesitant to agree to treason. My boss thinks that if Edenfield feels he has any other option, he'll jump on it . . . which makes it worrying that Silvertip is suspicious of Edenfield. We can't have any prefects backing out—because if they do, they become unpredictable, and we might not be able to stop them."

I summarized my earlier trip to Edenfield and my encounters with Prefects Avior and Silvertip, and let Francis digest. He didn't swear when I'd finished. He didn't say anything. He stared out the window and went thoughtful and quiet.

I let him stew until we'd crossed the border into Edenfield and the buildings had gotten steadily poorer and sparser. Then I asked, "Are you in? Will you help us?"

He remained a studious scholar of the scenery, but he wasn't ignoring me. After a few seconds, he said, "It's weird how things work out."

"It . . . is?"

Francis abandoned the scenery in favor of a sidelong glance. "Yes, Mercy, I'll help you. That's obvious." He sank back to the window. "I mean this whole situation. My whole situation. Things never go like you plan, you know?"

"They sometimes do."

He went on like he hadn't heard me. Maybe he hadn't. "I won't say you were right about her. You acted way out of line. But if you hadn't, maybe I wouldn't have found out."

So we were talking about Theodora. I adjusted my hands on the steering wheel and kept alert for street signs.

He took a breath. "We got into a fight. I called her after you came back, you see. I thought—but that doesn't matter. What matters is that she brought you up again. Asked me if I wanted to hear what had happened with your boss. If I wanted information on him. It was weird how she phrased it, like she wanted me to pay for the information. And I remembered what you said about making deals with her—"

Francis had listened to me? And remembered what I'd said?

"—And besides, it wasn't right. She was acting as if friendship, as if dating, were an exchange. As if you only did something nice for someone or only told them something because you owed them or wanted them to owe you, and not because you loved them or because it was right.

"I couldn't believe she thought in a way that wrongheaded. I didn't understand. Not at first. But she—it was—"

He rubbed his face as if in pain.

"Like I said, we got into a fight. She couldn't understand what my problem was. She got angry, and that made me angry, and I said things I wish I could—that I shouldn't have said. But you would have understood, Mercedes." He spread his hands appealingly. "You know not to take things personally. When I'm angry, I say things, but I don't mean them."

"I know you don't," I said, and did not add, *Usually* or *But sometimes they hurt anyway.*

"I would've apologized if she'd let me," Francis complained. "She said plenty of things that were as bad or worse! She could call me to apologize—she should—but she hasn't.

"We'd agreed to meet again, but she didn't show. I waited for hours, and I called her, but nothing. I've called again and again, but she never answers. She's completely blocked me out."

I cleared my throat. "Sounds like it was for the best. If she was like that, better to find out early on."

"You don't understand, Mercedes."

I didn't want to understand. I didn't want to hear this. But like a good little sister, I said, "Then explain it to me."

He scrubbed his hands through his hair, trying to find the words. "She's not meant to be like that," he attempted. "She's clever and funny, and she knows so much. More than anyone else I've ever met. She can talk about practically anything and make it interesting. And she's fun. It's like she glows, and I want to bask in that glow forever. I want to be a part of it. She's far too good for me, too smart for me in so many ways. I could hardly believe it when she agreed to go out with me. You don't know what it's like, Mercedes, being with someone like that."

He didn't mean that comment in a nasty way, I assumed; it was the classic condition of believing your own pain the center of the universe. But it sure didn't make me feel more sympathetic.

"I could've happily spent the rest of my life with her," Francis went on. "Admiring her." He shook his head and thumped his wrist against his thigh. *"She shouldn't be that wrongheaded.* She should know better, but something broke somewhere. Maybe it was the way she was brought up. Maybe it was some other bad influence. Maybe she never had anyone to teach her Christian values. I know that if someone explained them to her properly, she'd see in an instant what's wrong with her thinking, and she'd fix it. She's like that. But I didn't have the words."

He fell silent again, and I thought he was done. I could see his reflection in the window. I searched for another topic, any other topic.

"I think," he said slowly, "that I would've married her, if I could've."

This was too much, even for Francis. "You barely knew her a week!"

"Three days. I knew her for three glorious days before our argument. And I will treasure every moment of them until the day I die."

He made no effort to wipe away the fat, rolling tears. He leaned his forehead against the window and sobbed as if there were nothing else in the world.

Chapter 20:

MANIPULATION

We arrived in Gjerde around ten in the morning. Under the chipper sun, I could see what had not been apparent at night: that every one of the houses was a different shade of orange, yellow, or red. Gjerde may have been poor, but it had civic pride: the houses were old, but the paint was fresh and crisp.

My boss's plan had been that I stay in a bed-and-breakfast in town and not let Prefect Edenfield know I was there. A spy is much more effective if the other side doesn't know she exists. But thanks to Silvertip, that was no longer an option.

I called my boss again, and again got voicemail. That was disturbing, but I could come up with reasons for it. I left him a cheerful nonsense message and asked him to call me.

What was going on? Had something gone wrong on my boss's end? Had he succeeded in moving the conference, or should I be collecting the spy equipment and rushing down to Lindo Prefecture?

Somehow, I didn't think I'd get it through their security nearly as easily—unless I attached myself to Edenfield's retinue, which would mean getting him on my side . . .

Which went with what my boss had wanted anyway, so there couldn't be any harm in that.

Mind made up, I directed Francis, who was back at the wheel, to drive through the brief town and up the single lane to the manor.

By daylight, when one could dismiss the hill behind it, Edenfield Manor was nowhere near the same scale of impressiveness as Silvertip Manor. The roof was simple and brown, the windows narrow upright triangles, and the wooden walls white-and-chocolate zigzags and reverse zigzags.

"Mock Tudor," Francis commented. "A fancy one. Those've been less popular in the last fifty years."

I hummed. "Look at how the pure white reflects sunlight; it's clearly meant to blind enemies—and then drive them mad."

"The style was originally medieval, so you could be right."

"Could be?"

"My dear sister," Francis said, in true flyting cadence, "your head is already as swollen as a week-old cow carcass. I don't want it to explode. Then again," he mused as we approached the front door, "maybe I'm wrong. Maybe instead of exploding, it would inflate like a balloon, and you could float instead of walking."

"On the superheated hydrogen of my own ego."

"Not so different from what you do anyway, then." He knocked on the manor door, and we waited. After a minute, he tried the knob. Locked. He banged harder. "Doesn't anyone answer doors around here?"

"The servant couple is pretty old, judging by their snores," I said. Francis gave me an odd look, so I clarified: "I mean they might not have great hearing."

Francis grunted and hunted around for a doorbell. I thought again of Silvertip Manor, and the idea that Edenfield might have already left for Lindo, and shifted from foot to foot. I needed information. If I couldn't get it from Edenfield, I could get it from his office—which would also allow me to recollect the spy equipment.

"No one's coming," I said. "Let's do this the hard way. Over here."

"There's a back door?"

"There's a window that's easy to jimmy."

"Mercedes!" Francis cried, more with affectionate exasperation than actual rebuke. Clearly, I wasn't the only one who remembered our childhood hijinks.

I crooked a finger at him, and he followed me around to the east side of the manor. I was halfway through the children's window when a voice behind me commanded, "Stop right there!"

I stopped right there, knee over the sill, and laid my eyes on my first Edenfield knight.

He was barely more than a boy: thin haired and knobbly cheek-boned, but with excellent posture and one hand on his sidearm. Edenfield knights wear midnight-purple uniforms with ice-blue trim. Although he was young, this knight's uniform had clearly been well worn. It looked warm, sensible, and intimidating.

I withdrew my leg and wrestled down the instinctive *This isn't what it looks like!* in favor of a smooth, confident, "Oh, good! Finally, someone who can let us in. Why isn't anyone answering the door?"

The knight wasn't impressed. "I'm going to need you to step inside the knighthouse," he said.

I tossed my head airily, already moving his way, mildly surprised but utterly unbothered. "It's no secret why we're here," I said. "We've come on urgent prefect business. You must've noticed the Silvertip van. We need to see Prefect Edenfield immediately. Ah—he hasn't left for Lindo, has he? That *would* be a mistake."

The knight treated me to a slow, steady, law-enforcement-approved expression that gave away nothing. "Come into the knight-house," he drawled, "and we'll discuss the situation."

"We'd be happy to," Francis said.

I frowned. "We really don't have time for this."

"We don't have time to get arrested over a misunderstanding," Francis countered. "Or shot."

I sniffed, which didn't stop him from rubbing it in.

"I should've known better than to go along with one of your hare-brained schemes. Through the window! If you weren't so good at pretending to know what you're doing—"

"I did know what I was doing!"

"You've broken into places before?" the knight asked.

I threw up my hands. "No one was answering the door! We needed to get in. What were we supposed to do?"

The knight didn't bat a lash. "I'd gladly believe you," he said. "But under the circumstances, I'll need to check out your story before allowing you near the prefect."

"So he hasn't left—good. We're in time. Don't let him leave before

I've a chance to talk to him."

"If you are who you say you are," the knight told me, "you'll have my apologies and my assistance. But you understand that we can't let people run around breaking into the manor."

"Of course," I said. "Lead on, Sir Knight."

The knight led on, around the corner of the knighthouse. I saw the moment he spotted the Silvertip van, and the impression it made on him. For an instant, I thought he'd change his mind there and then, but he checked himself and led us inside the knighthouse instead.

The bulk of the interior was taken up by the main room we stepped into, but there were two doors beyond—at a guess, one led to a bathroom and the other to a storage area/holding tank. It was clean and well cared for, but age had degraded it to shabbiness. To be fair to it, I thought it honest shabbiness, not the pointed sham inside the holding area of the Silvertip knighthouse. It reminded me of Batata of all places: poor but honest.

The knight—whose name, according to the picture award on the wall, was Olaf Olafsson—took our driving licenses and tapped away at his computer. Francis definitely had his share of driving violations, but I doubted that anything else would show up. As for me, no ordinary knight would know what "CSS" really stood for—only head knights and prefects had access to that sort of information—if it was listed at all.

Whatever Olaf found, it didn't raise his eyebrows, but it did raise a landline to his ear. He didn't bother to lower his voice or go into another room or make us go into another room as he talked; but then, he wasn't saying anything secret. He told his head knight what was going on, along with reasonably flattering descriptions of us, and asked for instructions.

I waited, listening to his tone, and thought he wouldn't need much of a push to give me what I wanted.

"It occurs to me," I said ruefully, shamefacedly, when Olaf hung up, "what us trying to break in must have looked like. You've already seen proof of legitimacy, but I still owe you an apology. You have to act superior and snooty in Silvertip or no one will give you the time of day, but here . . . I recognize that Edenfield knights have to be suspicious of strangers, official van or no. Please forgive me."

"I forgive you," Olaf said mildly, shuffling the papers on his desk. "And I believe you. I know city folks don't act like us out here."

"That's the worst of it," I said. "I wasn't city folk until I moved to Silvertip three years ago; I grew up in Batata." I offered him my hand and smiled shyly and sweetly. "Shall we start over? My name is Mercedes."

"Not this," Francis muttered, but he had the decency to mutter it low enough that Olaf didn't hear.

I kept smiling.

Olaf's ears went red, and he shook his head. "Sure," he said. "Only, I mean . . ." The red spread from his ears down his jawline and across his cheeks. He cleared his throat. "Unfortunately, it seems the prefect is in lockdown until the conference ends and isn't accepting visitors."

"Oh, dear," I said. "But surely that doesn't apply to official messengers. Perhaps if you called Prefect Silvertip—"

He ducked his chin apologetically. "Prefect Silvertip isn't in charge of this prefecture; Lord Holst and Torben Nass are—and Captain Nass requests that you remain here with me until the prefect departs. In the meantime, I hope I can count on your honor that you will respect this and not attempt to leave prematurely. Edenfield wishes to maintain a good relationship with Silvertip."

Those were surely the head knight's phrases, not his. I groaned and rubbed my eyes, then stopped before I scraped off my makeup. It'd taken me the last hour of the drive to hide the effects of the past few days, but no amount of makeup or hair styling stopped me from hurting. I must've been tired still, because I wanted to cry. Again. I'd been doing more crying in the past couple of weeks than in the previous year.

"I am sorry," Olaf said. "I know this must be frustrating. How about something to eat? You must have been driving for hours."

"Your head knight made his decision without all the information," Francis said. "This is a matter of life and death."

"Francis," I whispered warningly, "what are you doing?"

His jaw tightened. "In an emergency, secrecy can be broken, Mercedes. This is too important."

"That's not your decision to make!"

Olaf was watching us curiously. Of course he was.

"Then whose decision is it?" Francis asked. "Yours?"

Well . . . yes.

And what decision would I make? Francis had a point. Was the habit of secrecy so deeply ingrained in me that I could not break it if necessary? Clearly not, since I'd told Francis what was going on. Was I only relying on my boss's advice and not thinking for myself? Again, clearly not.

See, Francis had been a safe person to tell; I knew him, and knew where his loyalties lay. A strange knight was another issue—especially because knights owed their loyalty to their prefects, and only through their prefects to the king.

I hissed icily in Francis's ear, too low for Olaf to catch: "Do you want him to arrest us for treason? Because that's what sharing government secrets amounts to."

Francis's eyes bulged. "What are you talking about? We're trying to stop—"

I slammed my hand over his mouth, wrapped my free arm around his neck and drew his ear close to my lips. "You fool," I breathed. "You cannot accuse a prefect of treason without evidence, especially not to his personal knight! It'll be your word against his, and the only proof you have is your sister's boss's theory. What do you *think* would happen?"

My hand was shaking when I released him, and the blood had drained from his face. He really *hadn't* understood. Score one for Mercedes's vehicular expositional skills. It should've occurred to me that he wouldn't automatically keep his mouth shut. He hadn't had to sign a twenty-seven-page document before being hired to a top-secret job. He hadn't read the consequences of flapping your lips in public. He hadn't been taught to mistrust knights.

I think Olaf was embarrassed by our argument, or maybe he understood part of what was going on. He was on his computer again, clicking away.

I drew Francis further back into the corner. He was looking at me helplessly, deflated. "Then what can I do?" he asked piteously. "I came here to help you, but I don't know how to help. Tell me what to do."

It seemed obvious to me: I needed to talk to Edenfield, and Olaf wasn't going to let me. My eyes traveled between Olaf and Francis, sizing them up.

"Oh, no," Francis said. "No, Mercedes. He's a knight."

Olaf was taller, younger, and lighter. He'd certainly been trained in hand-to-hand combat against bigger opponents, and he was armed. But Francis could punch like a sledgehammer.

"Buy me five minutes," I murmured.

"Are you crazy? I can't attack a knight."

"You can and you will. You know what's at stake—and I'll make sure you don't get in trouble. If I can't talk Edenfield around, the king can always pardon you. You want to help, Francis—and this is something that you can do but I can't. Ready?"

"No! I'm not—"

I turned, brushed myself off, and walked out of the knighthouse. The moment the door clicked shut behind me, I took off at a sprint—but I wasn't fast enough to miss the sound of Olaf's shout or the meaty thump of a punch.

I rounded the knighthouse and vaulted through the children's window. It was too late for him to be sleeping and too early for lunch, so I made a beeline for Edenfield's office.

Right on the first try. Prefect Edenfield sat behind his desk in a massive chair that looked like it had been made for him. Not the chair I had hidden behind—or I didn't think so. It always amazes me how different rooms feel in daylight. Now that I could see it properly, I observed that the whole room had been decorated in a comfortable, masculine, faintly old-fashioned style: with layers of dark, richly woven rugs; wide armchairs; a broad, dark desk; and solid bookcases covering every available wall.

The prefect matched his room perfectly. Lord Holst was tall and corpulent, with a magnificent crop of auburn hair unstreaked with white despite his nearly sixty years. His expression was benign and academic. There was no hostility in the set of his double chins, no suspicion in his pale blue eyes, nothing but politeness in the lift of his bushy eyebrows when I sauntered in uninvited.

"Good afternoon," he said, his voice suitably plummy and well-mannered. "I don't believe we've met."

He spoke with such obvious and genuine good humor that I was momentarily taken aback. It struck me incongruously that *this* was how Prefect Avior had meant me to perceive him. He had come off as creepy. Prefect Edenfield was the sort of man I immediately and instinctively liked and wanted to please.

That first glance at Edenfield decided my tactic. I had twenty schemes lined up for getting him to do what I wanted. At least half of them would have worked, but only one would reflect my automatic respect for him.

"My name is Mercedes Cartier," I said. "Here is my identification." I handed him not my driving license, which Olaf had returned, but my work ID.

Edenfield's eyes widened when he saw the *CSS*. Unlike Olaf, he'd know exactly what that meant: Carinan Security Service. The department in charge of not just cryptology, but also special investigations, spying, and doing whatever else needed to be done secretively to ensure national security.

For obvious reasons, my card doesn't have my job title printed on it, and my security level is embedded in a hidden chip, innocuous to casual eyes but clear to those who already know what they're looking for to find.

Edenfield swallowed hard. "I see," he said. He focused his small blue eyes on me, inquisitive but shuttered against other emotion. "What may I do for the king's agent this afternoon?"

I took back my card and tucked it in my wallet. "May I sit?"

"Yes, yes of course. Perhaps a cup of tea or coffee?"

"No, thank you." I sat on the other side of his desk. The chair spread its lap wide, and only by bracing my arms on the sides did I manage not to slide off. I think the tension from holding my body in that position impressed Edenfield, because he had to press his palms against the desk to prevent trembling.

"I imagine," I said, "that you plan to leave for Lindo soon."

Edenfield began shuffling his desk, then controlled the movement. "In a few hours," he said. "I'll be flying."

So my boss hadn't managed to change the conference location. And he hadn't contacted me about it. Had he heard that Silvertip had picked me up? Or had Avior proven less tractable than he'd assumed? Maybe I should have headed north to back him up instead of coming here—but no, this was where he'd expect me to come.

And if he wasn't having any luck with Avior, maybe I could help him from this end.

"You won't arrive until evening, at that rate," I told Edenfield. "Wouldn't you prefer an extra half day of Lindo's hospitality to settle in?"

He shook his head. "She doesn't want us early."

"No," I said. "I didn't think she would. She has preparations to finalize. She is a woman with a long memory and a thirst for revenge. Her sister, wasn't it?"

"Her younger sister," Edenfield said, eyes going distant. "Zita Silveira. I met her on several occasions. Charming girl. Graça was so happy about the engagement, went around boasting about what a wonderful queen her sister would make. No doubt she would have been, if not for—" Prefect Edenfield stopped himself, blinking back to the present. "Of course, that's only rumor."

"Rumors can be true," I said, "though there are many versions of this one. Which version does Prefect Lindo believe?"

He fluttered a hand. "I prefer not to indulge in idle gossip."

"And I," I said tartly, "did not drive two hundred miles to ask idle questions, prefect. Tell me what Lindo thinks happened. She's told you."

Edenfield looked away. "She thinks her sister didn't want to marry King Emil. That Zita was already engaged to someone else. That she and her fiancé made a suicide pact and walked into the ocean together. She saw that part," he clarified, meeting my eyes again. "Graça did. She followed her sister to the ocean. She thinks that, at the last moment, Zita changed her mind and tried to swim, but her fiancé pulled her under."

"And she blames the king for her sister's death," I said. Edenfield nodded. I gripped the edge of the desk with both hands and leaned in, lowering the tenor of my voice. "So you can see," I said, "why it would be unwise to have her host the prefects' conference this year. You understand the danger in which it would put the king."

Edenfield was too honest a man. He tried to bluster, but I read guilt in every line, and I let him see that I read it. "If he's worried," he said, "why doesn't he move the conference? Any of us would be willing to host."

"I'm sure you would," I agreed. "But that wouldn't look very good for him, would it? No one wants a coward for a king. Besides, on the off chance that Lindo *isn't* planning something, a show of weakness might give her ideas. No, that wouldn't do. The change of location must come from someone else—and it must come at the last moment, so that Prefect Lindo doesn't have time to adjust her plans."

I leaned back and folded my hands, face solemnly set. "Edenfield is on the opposite end of Carina from Lindo, and you have a reputation for honesty and fidelity. There is no one we would rather have host the conference. If you are loyal to Carina, if you are as dutiful and wise and forthright as your reputation would have you, call the others. Move the conference here."

Edenfield searched my face for excuses, for alternatives, but he'd have been better off looking to the door; it burst open behind me. I could tell by the pained panting that it wasn't Francis. He wheezes in a lower tone.

I kept my hands gravely folded, kept my gaze on Edenfield.

"My lord, are you all right?" Olaf gasped.

Edenfield tilted his head and jerked up his chin. "Certainly. Is there some difficulty?"

"There's an intruder! A woman—twenties, dark, short. She claims Prefect Silvertip sent her, and she came in a government van, but she disobeyed Captain Nass's direct order. I was holding her, but she made her assistant attack me, and she escaped!"

Edenfield looked at me. I looked back at him, unemotional but expectant. The chair was so big and so tall it was no wonder Olaf hadn't spotted me.

Olaf did, however, see the exchanged look. He arrived at my side in a trice, handcuffs rattling, prepared to arrest me but glancing to the prefect for approval.

I never moved my gaze from Edenfield. I sat as one waiting patiently for my host to dismiss the pesky servant, as one who respected Edenfield as master of his own prefecture, and as one who would judge him before the king for his actions now.

It was an eloquent gaze, and an effective one. "Leave her," Edenfield told Olaf. "Ms. Cartier is my guest."

I breathed again. My pulse was going crazy, but he couldn't see that.

"But—my lord!" Olaf cried. "Captain Nass ordered—"

"I hope," said Edenfield, "that Captain Nass's orders don't super-sede mine."

Olaf snapped his posture straighter. "No, my lord! I only meant that he was relaying your orders."

"My orders are to treat Ms. Cartier and her assistant as my honored guests. You will provide Ms. Cartier with anything she requires and obey her orders as you would mine."

"But—my lord—"

Edenfield could do pretty good gazes himself. Olaf stuttered to a halt, and corrected himself to, "Yes, my lord."

I'd won and so, for the first time since his arrival, I moved my gaze to Olaf. He looked down at me, youth shining through his training. It was too early for the bruising to come out, but a slight puffiness promised a fine black eye. "Thank you for being so concerned," I told him in my most gracious tones. "I am sorry for the trouble we've caused, necessary though it was. Would you please brief my assistant on the current situation and then bring him here?"

Olaf went red, then white, and finally a delightful greenish shade. He bowed to me and said, "Yes, ma'am." He also gave Edenfield a bow before leaving, stiff as a tin soldier.

I'd not made a friend there, and I'd have to make time to sweet talk him later lest he become an enemy. *He'll understand when everything is over,* I assured myself, hoping it was true.

On the other hand, I reflected, maybe it'd be easier to have Francis sweet talk him. His charm was usually aimed at potential girlfriends, but he got along well with his underlings, and businessmen tended to be impressed by the flannel tartan.

"Is it true that Silvertip sent you?" Edenfield asked, recapturing my attention.

"He inconvenienced me," I said, "and loaned me the van to make up for it. He also told me that he was concerned about you. He seemed to believe you'd been acting strangely."

Edenfield shifted uncomfortably in his chair, resettling his bulk and laughing unconvincingly. "You know how it goes," he said. "I'm under a lot of stress. Leaving my prefecture for a week—who's to take over for me? I have to make so many arrangements ahead of time, and what if something goes wrong and I'm not here to deal with it? Terribly awkward. I suppose I must have said one or two frustrated things over the phone and Otto misinterpreted them."

"No," I said. "That's not it." *Come on, tell me!* I thought at him, beaming trustworthiness. *Turn king's evidence and convict the others. I can help you.*

Edenfield shook his head and resettled himself again. "It's not important, just a few death threats—normal stuff, when you're prefect. We all get them. Unpleasant, but part of the job. Like being a weatherman. Shouldn't have let it get to me. Forget it. The real question is: how do I go about convincing the other prefects to move the conference?"

Chapter 21:

FRAUD

The prefects' conference is something of a modern development. When the diverse factions of Carina agreed to unite under a single king, they did so on the understanding that the king would regularly tour the country. For hundreds of years, he did: he spent one month of every year in each prefecture, dealing with the issues of that prefecture and staying on top of current events. For the remaining three months, he lived in the capital (which, although located within Canopus Prefecture, is not part of it), dealt with national issues not fixable from within the prefectures, and rested.

From what I've read of that time period, the system was highly satisfactory to everyone except the king, who found it exhausting. Each prefecture felt equally represented and knew that the king understood and empathized with the problems unique to that prefecture. Nothing much slipped past the radar; and as long as the king chose his court with care, everything ran smoothly.

Then, a few of generations back, there came a period during which the king—that was Emil I—couldn't tour. Queen Flavia of Vela had gone mad and was doing her best to conquer Akter and Carina while indiscriminately slaughtering her own citizens. She couldn't possibly have succeeded against both her neighbors, which was why she got further than anyone expected.

For Carina, the long-term effect of her invasion was a strengthened national military. Whereas previously, the king had no substantial military of his own and had to rely entirely on the prefects' combined might, now he was as strong as any two prefects put together. As with most consolidations of power, the more the king grasped to his hand, the more he lost touch with local issues.

King Emil I died, and Queen Éliane took the throne young enough that she barely remembered the tours except that they had been unpleasantly full of strangers bending over her and patting her head when she had been dragged along, and unpleasantly lonely and fatherless when she had been left at home. The older and more modish she grew, the more the tours struck her as old-fashioned, absurd, and unnecessary. During the fifteen years her father had been unable to tour, he had held semi-yearly conferences in which the prefects came to wherever he was. That, she thought, was a much better system than constant touring—except that twice a year was excessive when once would do.

The prefects objected strenuously, but Queen Éliane would not listen to reason. Revolt threatened until Éliane gained Prefect Silvertip's support by marrying Silvertip's son and Fjordland's support by marrying him to her younger sister. The other prefectures caved in turn, save for two amendments: first, that each retain a representative on the queen's council; and second, that the conference take place in the prefectures, not the capital, and in a different prefecture each year.

Éliane conceded. The debate had been going on for nearly two years by that point, and she had other problems to deal with, including the birth of twins, one stillborn. The official Carinan history glides over the next bit, but I've read Akterian history that suggests Éliane suffered from post-partum psychosis, a condition from which she never fully recovered. In any case, the other twin died soon after, and Éliane was eventually succeeded by her nephew, King Enéas.

Enéas saw even less point to the conference than Éliane had, and the prefects had become too accustomed to their diminished positions to protest overmuch when he shrank the conference from two weeks to ten days. It stayed that way until our current king, Emil II, shrank it again to a single five-day work week: four days for the prefects to discuss among themselves what was most important and the fifth day to present, in simplified form, the most essential points to the king. This,

Emil II reasoned, would separate the wheat from the chaff; anything more was a useless time-sink. Urgent issues didn't need to wait for a conference; these were modern times, with modern cars, phones, and computers. The conference was less of a necessity and more of a bow to the past, a state-of-the-nation summation recorded for posterity.

King Emil's redefinition of the purpose of the conference and its inception during Emil I's time was the extent of what we learned in high school. I learned more in college, when I discovered how watered down (i.e., blatantly false) much of high school history and government classes are.

The remainder of the information, I'd learned in the past few months, when I'd really dug in. Turns out that college classes can be pretty watered down too.

The purpose of this historical research, however, was not to disparage either biased schooling or the current conference system, but to discover if there was any precedent for the conference being held somewhere aside from the prescribed prefecture. The answer was yes: twice, the conference had been moved due to natural disasters; four times for murky political situations; and once because of a bomb threat. So it could be done.

"True," Edenfield said, "but in most of those cases, the impetus for moving the conference came from the host prefecture. The flood of '77 in Fjordland, for example. And in that case, the conference was moved after it had begun and to the nearest available prefecture. This is more like the bomb threat against Tey. But how am I to convince the other prefects of the danger? Or that the answer is to come here? I'm not," he said with self-conscious humor, "the most respected of my peers."

My boss had sworn up and down that there must be a set procedure for moving the conference, one that any prefect could initiate, because this sort of thing always had a set procedure. But then, like I've said, my boss's genius does not extend to an understanding of people and especially not to laziness.

"You could tell them there was something essential the king see in Edenfield," I offered. *"Is* there something essential he see?"

A shadow passed over Edenfield's brow. "Yes," he said shortly. "But no doubt the others feel the same—and, you understand, there'd be no point in him seeing it if (as you say) Lindo seeks revenge and believes she will succeed."

That was as close as he'd come to admitting that he knew the score. I nodded to acknowledge but not push, and kept laying out options.

I was on option number four (Edenfield had shot down numbers two and three also) when a knock interrupted us.

"That'll be my assistant, my brother Francis," I told Edenfield, springing to my feet. But when I swung open the door, I found myself looking up at a complete stranger.

I recoiled before I knew what I was seeing. It wasn't so much that something was wrong with his face as that everything was wrong with his face. It might have been sculpted by a man who'd seen a human face only once, distantly, and was working from memory. The effect was utterly repugnant, made the more so because there could be nothing clearer than that its appearance was natural.

I have no doubt whatsoever that the man saw my reaction and judged me for it, even as he swept past me.

"Torben," Edenfield said guiltily, pushing himself to his feet. So this was Edenfield's head knight. I had seen his name many times but had never been able to find a satisfactory picture of him. No wonder. "I thought you were checking out the patrols. Don't you have a lot of work to get done before the conference?"

"Olaf called me," Captain Nass replied, in a voice like the rustling of dry leaves. "He believed that you might be in danger."

From behind, away from that face, the rest of the man came into focus. He wore Edenfield midnight purple and ice blue, with a head knight's stars. His boots were soiled with forest mud. He had tightly curled ash-blond hair, a runner's build, and casually perfect balance. For all that he had passed me and turned his back to me, I sensed that he was exactly aware of my presence and location and every move I made.

He had also not come alone. Sitting alertly at his feet waited a small fluffy white dog, its curly tail vibrating against its back, its black nose twitching. It gazed adoringly at its master, hoping for permission to explore.

He wants something beautiful to love him, I thought, and was immediately ashamed of myself. But it might have been true, all the same.

"That was a misunderstanding," Edenfield said, annoyed, but holding out his hand for the dog to snuffle. After looking to Captain Nass for permission, which he gave with a quick motion, it trotted forward, wriggling delightedly. Edenfield scratched behind the upright triangle ears as he explained, "This lady was on an important mission, and Olaf wouldn't let her pass. I'll vouch for her."

"He wasn't meant to let her pass," Captain Nass said. "You were on absolute lockdown, as we agreed."

"As *you* agreed."

Captain Nass pressed his hand downward, conciliatory. "For your own good. We discussed this."

"And what a lot of good it's done me! I might have missed Ms. Cartier's message, and that would have been disastrous. Tell him," he urged me.

Captain Nass turned pale eyes on me, their greenish-white the color of Spanish moss. I let my gaze unfocus from the rest of his face and tucked my hands behind my back, acutely uncomfortable and pretending I wasn't. "That information was for your ears only," I told the prefect.

Edenfield tsked. "Torben Nass is my head knight. My ears are his. Anything you can tell me, you can tell him."

No doubt. Silvertip and Avior had certainly managed to get their head knights in on their schemes, and it was impossible for Lindo to have gotten as far as she had without her head knight at her side. I licked my lips and deliberated on what to say.

"She works for the CSS," Edenfield told Captain Nass. "You know what that means."

"I do," Captain Nass said noncommittally. "Your identification, please."

There didn't seem to be any way around it. I dug my work ID back out and handed it over, careful not to touch Captain Nass's long, thin fingers—though they were perfectly ordinary, as fingers go.

Captain Nass received the card with exaggerated care. I knew he despised me for my reaction, but I couldn't help it. Besides, who was he to judge me? He must have known the effect he had on people. He must have been used to it. It wouldn't have killed him to try to put me at my ease.

"Well?" Edenfield prompted, with an eagerness I didn't understand.

"It's either genuine or an expert fake," Captain Nass admitted. "These cards are designed not to give much information to the casual viewer, however; I'll have to run it to learn more. Unless Ms. Cartier would care to enlighten us?"

If he wouldn't smile, then I would, a professional smile tied with wide-eyed innocence. "Certainly," I said. "You'll find the card is genuine. Go ahead and run it. Every record will show the same thing: I'm no one and nothing special. A mere personal assistant to a cryptanalyst—not that cryptanalysts are allowed to have assistants, normally speaking. But I'm no one interesting. No one to look at twice or raise a single eyebrow."

Captain Nass's hand clenched around the card.

Edenfield laughed. "Of course you are," he said, winking broadly. "Of course you are. Well done, madam."

"Have you gone mad?" Captain Nass asked coldly. "She's playing you."

"What," I said, hand fluttering to my heart. "You're not saying you think I'm *not* a lowly personal assistant, surely."

"Surely," said Captain Nass, "I think you are a fake. I *will* run this." He tucked my card in his jacket pocket.

"Really, Torben," Edenfield said reproachfully. "So suspicious."

Captain Nass was about as bothered by that as an ancient oak is by nightfall. He didn't twitch a leaf. "What has she been trying to get you to agree to?"

Edenfield shrugged. The guilty look was back, like a young child confronted by his parents. "Nothing bad," he said. "Nothing you wouldn't approve of. Apparently, the king's also nervous about holding the conference in Lindo. Agrees with you that Graça's unstable. He's sent Ms. Cartier to get me to move the conference to Edenfield."

"You want to move it here."

"It makes sense! I was sure you wouldn't object."

"If you were so sure," said Captain Nass, "then why were you sneaking about, trying to change it without asking me?"

"I'm the prefect here, not you," Edenfield snapped, flushing. He straightened abruptly, banishing the dog. "I don't sneak, and I don't need your permission."

"Security is *my* responsibility."

"We're perfectly secure!"

"I see," Captain Nass said sarcastically. "And you don't see any possible security risk in changing long-standing plans involving the prefects and the king on the say-so of a complete stranger? One who might easily be, for example, a spy from Vela or Akter? Or even, since we're on the topic, from Lindo?"

Edenfield pressed his clenched fist to his stomach. "You haven't a chivalrous bone in your body."

"Chivalrous," said Captain Nass, tasting the word and spitting it back out. "Is that what we're calling being emotionally compromised by beautiful women nowadays?"

It was hard to tell how old Torben Nass was, but I guessed somewhere between twenty-five and thirty-five—about half Edenfield's age. "Do you feel emotionally compromised by my beauty, Captain Nass?" I asked him sweetly.

He sneered. "What trait of yours am I supposed to consider beauty—your lies, your blatant manipulation, or your pathetic attempt at impersonation?"

"Enough, Torben!" Edenfield shouted, purple with fury. "I will not have you speaking to my guest that way!"

Spanish moss eyes turned slowly from one of us to the other, and I saw the face behind them tucking away the anger, closing itself off from emotion.

So that's where Olaf had learned it.

"You have been looking for an excuse to defy me," Captain Nass told Edenfield, "and she's provided one. It won't do you any good."

And I thought Edenfield had been outraged before. "Are you threatening me, sir?"

"I'm the one protecting you against threats—or trying to. But you seem determined on getting yourself killed. How am I supposed to guarantee your safety when you won't obey the simplest instruction, when you hide your activities from me?"

Some of the high color faded from Edenfield's face, to be replaced by fatigue. "I've kept my bedroom door and window locked, like you suggested. Doesn't that make you happy?"

Personally, I doubted that anything could make Captain Nass happy. But this did give me a clue, one that would explain both Edenfield's and Captain Nass's behavior, and one that didn't involve them finding the spy equipment: the intruder who'd crept into Edenfield's bedroom while I'd watched.

I stepped forward. "Your head knight's concern is valid; the security here is minimal, especially for the conference. My assistant and I will therefore stay on as an extra line of defense. I believe this manor has a spare room that will accommodate us?"

"What an excellent idea," Edenfield said. "You see, Torben? Nothing to worry about. Now get off and run that card to soothe your conscience. No need to return if it checks out; you can send it with Ms. Cartier's assistant. Send your apologies with him too, if you can bear to make them. We," he said, smiling at me, "have work to do."

No head knight can disobey a direct order from his prefect unless the imminent destruction of the prefecture is at stake. Captain Nass bowed and went, his puppy bounding after him.

The instant the door closed, Edenfield turned to me. "Tell me what to do," he said, all hesitation gone from his voice, "and I'll do it."

INTERLUDE

It was not, King Emil reflected, entirely bad, being made of glass. The many facets of his skull acted as a focus for thought, allowing him much greater clarity than anyone else in the world. It often amazed him how befuddled ordinary people became over the simplest issues. The sand inside him no doubt helped as well, sand being pre-glass and therefore a worthy part of his royal person.

"Your Majesty," said his high marshal, briefly dropping to one knee, "forgive the intrusion, but I have urgent news. The prefects have moved their conference to Edenfield!"

King Emil lowered his spoon. Although it appeared to be made of metal, close inspection revealed it to be only cleverly disguised plastic, and therefore no danger to him. Emil had also taken to having his food precut for him (and his bread pre-buttered) to eliminate the dangers associated with sharp edges, serration, and fork tines. It had never occurred to him to wonder why a man made of glass might need to consume buttered toast or lemon-baked cod, and he would not understand the dilemma if anyone did point it out.

"Moved it to Edenfield! That is good news," the king said, glancing up briefly from his lunch. "Whose idea was it? Our lord chancellor's?"

"No, sire. I mean the prefects themselves chose to move the conference, without reference to your royal self. I only just received the message from one of my spies. You see—"

The high marshal began his story, and persevered despite the fact that the king wasn't paying attention. He restarted it when the royal secretary arrived halfway through, and then again when the chancellor burst in.

"Edenfield!" cried the chancellor, when the high marshal had finished. "That is strange—and suspicious."

"You think so?" inquired the royal secretary. "I find it the most predictable thing in the world. What other response did you expect from His Majesty's treating with Prefect Lindo? She must have realized what was behind it, and chose Edenfield to assure us of her good intentions. Where is more innocuous than Edenfield? Where more distant from Lindo?"

The chancellor shook his head. "Then why did the prefects not ask us instead of informing us? Why not make the changes sooner, and through the proper channels? Why not tell us of their reason for the change instead of staying tight-lipped? No," the chancellor concluded. "This bodes ill."

"Only if you aren't familiar with the concept of diplomacy," the royal secretary said. "Their silence implies respect; an explanation would imply they believed the king, ah, *weak*."

"And making changes to the king's protocol without his permission is how one reacts to strength?"

"I know the reason for their move," King Emil put in mildly, secretly chuckling at how densely and opaquely his advisors saw the world. "It's clear as day. Prefect Lindo was unable to complete the repairs to her manor in time, and so she wanted the conference moved to a more fitting location."

"Then why not say so?" the chancellor argued.

"Come, come," said the royal secretary. "If the prefects were going to be treacherous, they wouldn't make such a large and obvious change; they would be subtle. You see conspiracy everywhere."

Emil did his best to tune the argument out. His fish was getting cold, and the nagging guilt that invariably accompanied any reference to Prefect Lindo was not helping him get his food down. He wished his chancellor and royal secretary would relax. People were always pushing him, wanting him to decide in one way or another, before the time was right. It was utterly wearying.

The king's advisors eventually realized they had lost their audience, and the chancellor sat down across from the king, where Emil could not ignore him.

"We must act," the chancellor insisted. "We must mobilize this minute, before the prefects have finalized their plans, before they have arrived in Edenfield. Allow the high marshal to collect his kingsmen, alert his knights. We can arrest them as they travel and before evening. We can put an end to this."

The royal secretary crossed his arms and scowled, then straightened as the king looked to him. "It's nonsense, of course," the royal secretary said, "but if it gives Your Majesty peace of mind—if Your Majesty thinks such excess necessary and wise—then I cannot argue with it. If only we knew what would befall our nation after such a melodramatic move! We would not want to cause division between your royal self and the prefectures."

King Emil brightened at this hint. "But we can know what will befall," he said. "The Tree could tell us. Where is the seidkonur?"

"The skald would know," the chancellor put in quickly. "I'll call him."

The king blinked in surprise. The chancellor was seldom helpful about anything, when it came to the Tree.

The Tree stood in the innermost courtyard of the innermost ring of the palace, quite alone. No benches, no shrubs, and certainly no other trees inhabited that courtyard. No grass sprouted around the Tree's roots, and no sunlight ever reached it—for the once-open ceiling had long been covered over, to make way for an upper level.

The Tree itself was a massive thing of uncertain origin, with a vast spread of black branches clawing the air with twig fingers. It was quite dead and had been dead for decades, but death had not weakened it. If there was any rot in its heart, it had not spread; and even the most fragile twig had petrified as hard and rigid as quartz.

In the soul of Emil's childhood, that Tree loomed impossibly large. He had been able to forget it for a time in his manhood, when he'd been distracted first by the navy and later by a wife and newborn. But in recent years, the Tree had drawn him to it again and again, as if its claw twigs had embedded themselves in his chest and would not release him.

The Tree had terrified Emil, but whenever it had called, he'd come. And then one day, the seidkonur had walked in on him as he'd stood staring, awestruck and trembling before the Tree. He had looked around to her and found himself struck by the recognition of what he ought to have known all along. She was its key, the conduit by which the Tree would speak to him. Instead of banishing her, he therefore invited her forward, to be his interpreter and his guide.

That moment also ended his terror of the Tree. He revered it still, but he triumphed that it should have chosen him. That it alone, of black quartz and rotten heart, had recognized the glass within him.

"But where is the seidkonur?" he wondered aloud. "Has she not gotten my message?"

"She has," said a pleasant voice from beyond the Tree, "but she was in town. She'll be here shortly." A gangly young man emerged, grinning toothily at the king and his advisors, hands casually stuffed in pockets. Everything about him was casual, for that matter, from the unruliness of his hair to the suede of his jacket to the slouch of his shoulders.

King Emil had seen him around the palace many times, often in the company of the prince or at formal events—for this was the skald, and the memories of epic poems from the past resided in his head; and the creation of new poems for the future resided in his hands.

Emil rumpled his brow. "Did the seidkonur send you here to tell me? Why not send a servant?"

The skald sketched a bow. "I am your servant always, Your Majesty."

"But why did you wait in here?" Emil asked, knowing he was being petty but unable to resist. "Don't you know this place is private?"

"Is it?" The skald's grin tightened, and he shrugged one shoulder. "Then I apologize. Ebba wanted me to tell you where she'd gone, and I thought this as good a place to wait as any. I'm working on a poem, and what better inspiration?" The skald motioned expansively at the black trunk and branches.

"Your poem is about the Tree?" the king asked eagerly. "Recite it for me."

"Gladly," the skald said. "I never mind an audience." He struck a pose and lowered his voice, replacing the jerking, jocular tone with a beautifully accented baritone:

"Terrible, terrible hanging tree,
Auger and prophet of misery,
Your tempting vision a broken vow.

"Nine are your branches on every bough;
Nine are the boughs that your trunk endow.
Nine men are hanging by your decree.

"Terrible, terrible hanging tree,
I won't believe in what you foresee.
You might have them, but you won't have me."

The skald beamed around at them, apparently delighted with his performance and oblivious to the king's reaction.

Emil was not pleased. He didn't fully understand the poem, but he did understand that the skald was not flattering the Tree. Calling it terrible—well, yes, it certainly could evoke terror. But what was this nonsense about broken vows and denying the Tree one's allegiance? No, it wasn't right. And who was this—this boy to criticize the Tree? This boy with the clothing rough enough to scratch glass, with the irrepressible grin, the improperly casual attitude toward royalty?

Emil did not remember any of the skald's other songs and poems being as offensive as this one, but he had never before paid attention to their words: the skald's voice had been background music at banquets and such, but it had never been important. If the presence of a skald at court hadn't been such a tradition, Emil would never have allowed one in the first place. Truth be told, he could not recall hiring this one—the skald had simply appeared one day, and Emil had assumed either the chancellor or the seneschal was to blame.

"Is that all?" the king asked coldly, not bothering to hide his sour displeasure.

"It's not going to be any longer than that," the skald said. "Did you notice? Nine lines, nine syllables per line, an increasingly broken meter. I was quite pleased by that, but now that I've heard it aloud, I think it needs to be chanted, not spoken. I admit, some of the words could use tweaking."

"They certainly could," said the royal secretary.

"It's a way to pass the time," said the chancellor. "I thought it was rather good; we don't make enough use of you, Skuli."

"Want to lose yourself in the traditions of the past, my lord?" suggested the royal secretary.

Things might have grown heated then, had not the seidkonur herself arrived, red faced and panting. She was a not-unhandsome woman of nearly seventy, with loose, pure-white hair down to her narrow hips. Age had wrinkled and spotted her olive complexion and clouded her eyes with cataracts, but she moved with the uninhibited grace of a dancer half her age, and her bare feet were delicate and perfectly formed. She carried a long stick, and her clothes swirled with her every movement. "Forgive me, Your Majesty," she said, forcing her breathing into a more regular pattern. "I came as quickly as I could. Keir no doubt gave you the details."

"He did," Emil acknowledged. He cast a cold eye over the skald, and his annoyance flared once more when the boy bowed in reply, formal but loose-limbed. Emil's lips compressed, but he restrained himself enough to say merely, "You have delivered your message, skald. You may depart."

"I'll stay, if you don't mind," the skald offered, bouncing up on his toes. "I'm quite interested in seidr. Not to perform myself, naturally, but I've often thought there's a certain symbiosis between the masculinity of poetry and the femininity of magic—yin and yang, you might say."

"You may depart," the king repeated emphatically, and in such a way that there could be no misinterpretation.

Emotions flickered across the skald's face, and he glanced at the chancellor—whose expression, Emil was baffled to see, was one of sick disappointment. By the time Emil looked back to the skald, however, the man's smile had reappeared, and he was bowing and grinning himself out the door.

Chapter 22:

ESPIONAGE

Acrid wood smoke smuggled tendrils past the edges of the double glass doors of the fireplace. The tendrils brushed the burgundy carpet, crept up the legs of wingback chairs, caressed the mighty painting above the mantelpiece. Black soot marred the underside of the heavy gold frame, but it did not obscure the regal figure depicted within.

Every chair angled toward the portrait, their empty seats in awe of the artist's skill—or of his subject. For there in paint and brushstrokes reigned King Emil II in all his glory, at the height of his power, covered in military honors from his youth, more alive than life, gaze piercing. Every chair bared its sinful soul before that gaze and submitted to its judgment.

Every chair but one. The final chair was not empty—although of its occupant, only one arm could be seen; and the sleeve and hand melded in with the chair so well, in the shadows of the corner, that no casual glance would uncover it.

That arm was my insurance, proof that I wasn't exactly hiding. I couldn't be hiding, not when my arm was visible. Not when I was sitting here alone, only wanting a little peace to contemplate the fire and think. And it wasn't like I was in disguise. It wasn't my fault that my red blouse and neat brown skirt blended in with the colors of the room. It wasn't my fault if the prefects chose to invade the room I'd happened to be sitting in. The fact that I stayed hidden after their arrival, that I didn't stand up and announce myself and let them know that I would overhear whatever they said... well, why should I? I'd come here for quiet, not to be bombarded with questions and company. And as for the mirrors cleverly positioned to show me the room without showing the room me? Coincidence. Didn't even notice them. Certainly didn't spend two hours setting them up myself.

I adjusted my position—I wouldn't have a chance, once the prefects began arriving—curled my legs beside me, and sank into thought.

Earlier that afternoon, Edenfield had arranged for the other prefects to arrive in good time for a seven-o'clock dinner. Once he'd stopped fussing about it and started listening, it'd taken us five minutes to throw out any attempt at underhandedness. Edenfield would tell the truth as he knew it, and we'd go from there.

He'd phoned Canopus first. "I wasn't supposed to share that information with you," he told her, as we'd agreed, "but I needed advice. What should we do?"

"We'll have to do what she says," Canopus had replied. "It'd be too suspicious otherwise. You were right to call me first." And she coached him on his strategy for talking to the others.

Edenfield listened and nodded and replied, and since he was engaging with the situation as he believed it to be, he was utterly in character and flawlessly convincing. What gaps he could not fill in, the other prefects filled in themselves. By the time he got to the last couple of calls, those prefects had already heard the information from other prefects, and I got a fascinating glimpse into the progression of information and gossip.

While Edenfield was on the phone with Fjordland's assistant, Francis showed up, looking bruised, battered, and ridiculously pleased with himself. I put my finger to my lips and shooed my brother back into the hallway, closing the door so we could whisper without disturbing Edenfield.

"Success?" Francis asked.

"Success," I confirmed. "They'll be arriving in time for dinner. We're staying in the spare family room—the children's room we tried to crawl into. There's not much time, and I'm worried about how much there is to do; Edenfield Manor isn't exactly overburdened with staff."

"I'll take care of that," Francis said. "I could use some exercise—

and I can't always be beating up knights. What do I do after the prefects arrive? Play bodyguard?"

"Play servant, if the Gulbransens—they're the help—need you to. I know you didn't come here to do dishes—"

"I'll do whatever needs to be done," Francis promised.

I blinked at him. You know, for all that I disparage my brother, he can sometimes be pretty awesome.

"By the way," Francis said, "the head knight showed up. Ugly, isn't he? Asked me to give you this."

My CSS card. I noticed Francis wasn't conveying Captain Nass's apologies along with it.

My snore analysis of the Gulbransens proved on the nose: they were both in their seventies and, although reasonably spry, definitely not up for readying the manor for eight prefects and two unexpected guests *and* making lunch and dinner *and* prepping for the king and the king's retinue by the end of the week. To prevent heart attacks, Francis and I spent ten minutes assuring them we were their dogsbodies for the next few hours and getting lists of chores. Even Edenfield did his part. He wasn't the sort to haul chairs around, even if he hadn't been bogged down with his own work, but he set out quite a decent cold lunch for us at one and encouraged us with many jolly words.

The following hours were a flurry of chores. Mrs. Gulbransen drove to town to buy as much food as the car would hold and to order more; Mr. Gulbransen started prepping a dinner suitable for prefects used to fancy chefs and the finest ingredients. Francis and I aired sheets, dusted, vacuumed, and scrubbed. Here again, Francis proved indispensable. He worked like a machine, faster than I could believe, uncomplaining and untiring. I had known that his job involved a lot of manual labor, but somehow I had never connected the ability to hammer nails and maneuver boards into place for eight hours at a stretch with the ability to vacuum a dining room and polish a table.

I had to stop helping him before we were entirely done, to make my own preparations. I arranged the sitting room, gave the Gulbransens and Prefect Edenfield specific instructions, and kept an eye out for approaching vehicles. The moment a shiny car nose pushed up into the parking loop, I zipped over to my armchair in the corner.

Five minutes passed. Ten. Then the door opened and Prefect Tey entered. He wavered in the doorway, eyes adjusting. Dim lamps and firelight glinted off his straight, mousy brown hair and cast shadows in the sockets of his face. The dredges of sunlight that remained outdoors would have flattered him more, but the heavy, drawn curtains hid them as thoroughly as midnight.

Tey was by far the youngest of the prefects and, from what I'd heard, an excellent harpist. My boss had observed that he also appeared to be struck by the same eager fanaticism that made college students everywhere try to change the world by way of handmade signs, rallies, and pickets. He even dressed like a student, rather than in his prefecture's colors. Then again, if my prefecture's colors were cardinal red and sky blue, I might limit them to a pin also.

Tey paced about the room once, absently snooping in drawers and poking decorations, and then flopped into one of the wingback chairs to stare moodily at the king's portrait. He was still in that attitude some minutes later, when the door opened for the next prefect.

Prefect Hemmel had chosen to wear his prefecture's colors, and although their russet and pumpkin orange didn't suit him, they did pretty much sum up my impression of his personality.

"Thank goodness someone's here!" Tey exclaimed, springing to his feet when he saw Hemmel. He didn't add, *Even if it's only you*, though I heard it all the same.

"Tobias," Hemmel stated, in such a tone as to indicate that he didn't think much more of Tey than Tey thought of him. With a nod at the younger prefect, he made directly for the sideboard and poured himself a brandy.

"I was beginning to think I was the only one coming," Tey gushed. "I'd already left when the call came in—I was halfway through Canopus. Too bad we didn't know earlier—I could've saved myself hours of driving! I'm flat out. Why do you think the king chose Edenfield, of all places? Who cares about Edenfield?"

"Who cares about Tey?" Hemmel responded indifferently. "Who cares about Hemmel?"

"Our prefectures are as good as anyone else's," Tey said, so offended that I pegged this as a sore point. "What would they do without my museums, music academies, art schools? Tey's the center of Carinan culture. What's Edenfield? Lumber. Who gives a half cowry about lumber?"

Hemmel shrugged and offered Tey a brandy. When the boy waved it off, he drank it himself. Hemmel's largest export, I remembered, was fish. Not much better than lumber, but it could be worse. In Batata, we'd bragged about our potatoes.

Canopus swept in next, Batata at her heels, glamorous in a wine-red dress suit with gold trim and gold pumps. Hemmel offered her a brandy, which she accepted disdainfully and posed with.

Batata, in his prefecture's dark hickory brown and beige, was more interested in the sidebar than in making an entrance. He downed his first glass with the steadiness of a man preparing to make an evening of it.

I watched him with especial interest. I'd grown up with Joel Pinho as my prefect, though I hadn't lived in his prefecture since I'd hit eighteen and run off to university. The years had done him no favors, but neither had they ruined him: he remained fit and, aside from a few gray hairs, largely unchanged. Batata alone of the prefectures can't afford to pay its prefect a living wage, and Pinho worked the fields alongside the rest of us. It must've hurt his pocketbook considerably to fly on short notice to Edenfield, when he'd thought he only had to drive to Lindo, but I doubted he'd complain of it. That wasn't our way.

"This isn't Canopan brandy," Canopus announced reproachfully. "Typical of Edenfield, cutting corners. Did he think we wouldn't notice? Not," she added, casting her words at Hemmel and Batata, "that he wouldn't be right that some of us couldn't tell the difference."

Hemmel made a rude gesture, but Batata only stared morosely into his drink.

"Your aunt," Canopus informed Tey, "had an excellent palate. I see she has passed it on to you. Normally, I'd commend you for choosing thirst over substandard brandy, but this isn't a normal situation. Hemmel, pour the man a glass."

"No, thank you," Tey said. "I don't drink."

"You'll need it," Canopus warned. "Take it from one who's been in this game a long time: prefects' conferences may sound exciting, but they're dead dull. Consider the company."

Tey perched on the seat next to her, turning his long legs to the side until his knees nearly knocked the carpet, fingers clutching the arm, eyes bright. "I *have* been considering the company," he said. "I've been waiting for this week for a long time—for my whole life. Waiting for a chance to make a difference. Whether we get along personally or not doesn't matter, not to the history books. The thing people will remember of this week is our unity in our common goal: the good of Carina."

Hemmel snorted. "More likely the good of Therese Ferro," he told Batata *sotto voce*

Canopus whirled. *"What* was that?"

"Don't delude yourself, lad," Hemmel told Tey. "Batata's only with us because Avior owns him. And Canopus doesn't care about anyone but herself."

Canopus's eyes narrowed, but she kept her neck extended and her pose superior. "And Hemmel doesn't care about anyone but Lindo, you might as well say," she shot back. "Not that she'd look twice at the fat old goat."

Tey shook his head indulgently. "Don't think you can trick me. You may pretend to bicker, but I know it's really flyting to disguise your humility. You admire each other, and you stand together." He tilted his head to rest it against the chair, lids blissfully closed. "When a country's too far gone for a peaceful revolution, violence must take its place. A timely small violence can prevent an untimely large violence, as a boil must be lanced before it bursts. A king who neglects his duties doesn't deserve to be king. Look at him!" He sprang to his feet, spitting at the royal portrait. "Smug, selfish, pompous pig, sitting fat and greedy in his kingly larder while the country falls apart around him. He deserves to fall with it. No—instead of it!"

"That's enough, lad," Hemmel said.

"Enough? How can you say that? How can it ever be enough when our country suffers? How can—"

"I don't care about your crusade," Hemmel interrupted. "None of us does."

Tey flushed red, eyes flipping from one prefect to the next, and finding support nowhere. "How dare you?" He began in a whisper, but it grew as he spoke. "How dare you be like this? You're as bad as he is! This isn't a time for calming down; this is a time for rage."

"This is a time for keeping your mouth shut," Canopus snapped. "Grow up, Tobias."

"When grown men see evil before them and do nothing—"

"We're here, aren't we?" Batata shot back. "We're in, all of us. And unlike you, some of us have had to make sacrifices to be here."

"I suppose you mean yourself," Canopus sneered. "I'm sure it's such a sacrifice, letting Avior pour money into your economy, not having to support your own prefecture like the rest of us."

Batata slammed his glass down. "Avior loved his brother," he said, "and I love my prefecture. Excuse me." He swept up the half-empty brandy bottle and stormed out, banging the door behind him.

The fire crackled, sending sparks up the chimney. A log crumbled to ash. The room breathed.

"What's eating him?" Tey wondered.

"He's prefect of Batata," Canopus drawled. "Isn't that enough?"

"Ha, yes." Tey braced his palms against the mantle, basking his face in the firelight. He stayed that way when the door swung open and a new prefect entered.

"Here you are," Silvertip said, elegant in tea green and silvery gray, his tone self-amused. "Was that Batata I saw stomping off? Oh, you're here, Canopus. No wonder he couldn't bear to stay in this room."

"It wasn't me, little man. Ask the boy."

Tey pushed off the mantelpiece. "It's hardly my fault that—who in blazes are you?"

He had stopped mid-spin to gawk at me.

If my face showed any change in expression, it wasn't by design. My eyes rested on him as if by mistake, my posture indolent to the point of insult. I had been waiting for him to see me. In our current positions, it had been impossible that he wouldn't.

"What are you doing here?" Tey demanded, voice rising from astonishment to panic. "You've been spying on us!"

My eyebrows made for my hairline.

"Who are you talking to?" Canopus wanted to know, though not badly enough to ruin her elegant pose.

"There's a woman here. She's been spying on us!" Tey seized my upper arms and shook them. "Say something! Who sent you?"

If I projected any more scorn, I might give myself an aneurism.

"What are you going on about?" Canopus demanded. "Hemmel, go see what he's talking about."

"Go and see for yourself, you lazy biddy," Silvertip said. "Pour me one of those, my good man."

Tey's eyes were like pheasant eggs, and you could've pushed another egg through the O of his mouth. "You're the king's agent!" he breathed. "You're the one who made us come here!"

"What?" the others cried, rushing over to see for themselves. Canopus ripped Tey aside only to be herself forced aside by Silvertip.

"You!" Silvertip exclaimed.

"Hello, Lord Ostberg," I said.

"You know her?" pressed Canopus.

"She spoke to him," Tey muttered. "Why would she speak to him and not to me?"

"So what if I know her?" Silvertip said. "It isn't any of your business who I know."

Canopus bristled. "It is if you've been talking to a king's agent!"

"Don't be any more of a fool than you already are, Canopus."

"You're the fool, Silvertip, if you've let a king's agent into our midst! Don't think I'll stand for this."

"Naturally not," said Silvertip. "You prefer to take defeat lying down."

"You—"

"For instance," he cut in with his politician's smoothness, "when I tell you that she isn't the king's agent. She's Avior's."

"What would one of Avior's agents be doing here?" Tey wanted to know.

"To keep junior prefects from spilling secrets, I imagine," said Silvertip. "And to make things run smoothly. Isn't that right, agent?"

"It's always wise to have a backup plan," I acknowledged.

Tey's mouth fell open. "You don't mean *she'll* be the one to—"

Canopus slapped her hand over his mouth and pulled him back, unapologetically rough.

I'd grown up admiring Prefect Canopus. All the girls in my school had. She was so classy, such a perfect example of a powerful woman.

The only other female prefect at the time had been the current Tey's aunt, and she had been *old* to our minds. When I was ten, Canopus was in her early twenties, and I'd desperately wanted to be like her. I'd wanted to dress like her, to be important like her, to be respected like her.

Now, Canopus must've been nearing her fortieth year. She was still a good-looking woman, and she still knew how to dress, but I could no longer admire her.

"Avior should have told us," she said. "I'm going to complain."

"Like you ever do anything else." Silvertip licked his lips, and I got the uncomfortable feeling that the only thing stopping him from taking me outside and devouring me was what the others would think. *"Is* everything running smoothly?" he asked me.

I lifted my shoulders and dropped them again. "No plan survives with any certainty beyond first contact with the main hostile force," I said. "But listen—the clock strikes seven. It's dinnertime. Shall we?" I flowed to my feet, and the prefects parted before me like the Red Sea.

$$L_{\gamma n} - \delta ;$$

Dinner came and dinner passed, and the final three prefects did not arrive. Neither did my boss, whom I expected to come with Avior. It made a certain sense that my boss wouldn't call, text, or otherwise update me beforehand, and that he would not answer my calls. He probably didn't even have his phone on, lest a distraction raise Avior's suspicions.

But it would've been nice.

I didn't have dinner with the prefects; I wanted to give them a chance to gossip about me. So I joined Francis in finagling sandwiches out of the Gulbransens, and we ate in our room, looking out the windows at the darkened woods to the east and the darkened parking lot to the north.

Francis is seldom talkative when exhausted, and this evening, he nodded over his food. I didn't realize how far gone he was until he keeled over between bites and I had to dive to rescue his plate. I gave him a few minutes to fall into a deeper sleep, then arranged him on his bed and wrapped blankets around him. With luck, he'd sleep until morning. Without luck, he'd wake up around midnight and spend the early watch pacing Edenfield Manor—making his third nearly sleepless night in a row and leaving him grumpy and useless.

I pulled my chair right up to the north window so I could close the curtain most of the way without obstructing my view. Pulling my knees to my chest, I rested my chin on them and settled in to while the hours away.

Fjordland arrived at the manor five minutes before midnight. Lindo and Avior didn't arrive at all.

"I expected they'd be with you," Edenfield said. "Is there a problem? Have you spoken with them?"

Fjordland trumpeted his ear. "What's that?"

Edenfield inhaled into his stomach and projected. "Lucio and Graça. Where are they?"

"Not with me."

"Are they coming?"

"What?"

"ARE THEY COMING?"

Fjordland's frown added extra layers of wrinkles. "You don't need to shout; I'm not deaf. Of course they're coming. Don't you know how late it is? Man doesn't know how late it is."

Edenfield smiled politely.

"No need to show me my room," Fjordland cackled, tottering forward. "I've been using the same one for as long as I can remember." He tapped Edenfield's shoulder. "Good man. You can carry my bag for me and tell the prefect I'm here."

Edenfield didn't correct Fjordland; he was too much of a gentleman, and it was a lost cause anyway. He simply picked up Fjordland's bag and followed the elder prefect up the stairs.

He was back a quarter hour later. "You'd better go to bed," he told me. "Cai will answer the door if anyone else comes."

"Maybe you should call Prefects Avior and Lindo," I suggested. "If there's a problem—"

Edenfield shook his head. "I think we both know what the problem is. Graça is not pleased with me and is kicking up a fuss, but Lucio will talk her around. He always does."

"The conference begins in under ten hours."

"Yes," Edenfield agreed, "and Graça wouldn't miss it for the world."

I supposed I knew that.

"Good evening, Agent Cartier."

"Good night, Lord Holst."

Chapter 23:

CRUELTY TO ANIMALS

Before the morning sun had poked his inquisitive head above the horizon, papery hands shook my elbows and patted my cheek; and a voice hoarse and gravelly with years of use whispered my name. "Miss Cartier! Miss Cartier, the prefect needs you!"

I groaned. Without the adrenaline and excitement of the previous evening, my litany of minor injuries ached and burned at me, and the knitted-up graze itched like a colony of ants.

I focused on ungluing my eyes and enunciating. "What time is it?"

"The prefect needs you," she repeated. "Please come. It's urgent."

I hooked on my glasses, and Mrs. Gulbransen snapped into as much detail as the darkened room would allow. She had drawn the curtains all the way back and left the door open. The hall light was on, and my sleep-adjusted eyes could see just fine. I shot a look Francis's way, but he was fast asleep for once.

"I'm coming," I whispered.

Mrs. Gulbransen backed away enough for me to swing my legs over the side of the bed and hunt for socks and robe. Her eyes were opened wide and over-bright, and she moved jerkily, though yesterday she'd been popping spryly about town and the manor. Tight shouldered, she held one palm to her chest, nearly high enough to clutch her neck, and the other cupping her lips and chin.

In thirty seconds, I was ready. In another ten, we were standing outside of Edenfield's bedroom door. I gave Mrs. Gulbransen an incredulous look, but since Edenfield didn't have Gil Winter's reputation, I didn't wrestle my voice to full wakefulness. Mrs. Gulbransen knocked once and turned the knob.

Edenfield's bedspread was striped red wool and tremendous—it had to be, to cover that bed and its typical occupant. It had been pulled half back to reveal dark-chocolate bamboo sheets beneath. The man himself sat on the side of the bed in a knee-length night shirt: deathly pale, skin spongy as if dehydrated. He stared blindly at the thing he held, deaf to our entrance.

I squeezed his shoulder. "Lord Holst."

He raised his face to mine and met my eyes, uncomprehending. I held his gaze for a second; with him seated like this, we were of a height. After holding his shoulder and eyes firm for another breath, I gently pried the bundle of cloth and twine from his hands, which fell limply to his lap. He watched me, a broken man, as I examined the bundle.

It was a doll, made in Edenfield's likeness with tremendous cleverness but limited skill. The face had been drawn on with a black permanent marker, and the hair was real. It was, in fact, Edenfield's hair: auburn and messily glued on. The doll wore a bag of an outfit, badly hand sewn—purposefully badly, I thought—in ice blue and midnight purple.

That alone would've been enough, but the caricaturist had gone a step further and had both inscribed ultra-thin red lines on the nose to mimic broken blood vessels and glued extra fabric to the jowls. Under the too-short outfit, the doll's belly was bloated and round, with a slit down the middle. Into this slit and up around the neck wove a strand of barbed wire. Where the barbs dug into the doll's flesh, flecks of dark reddish brown marred the cloth; and where the ends of the wire dove into the doll's body, the red stain spread thick and moist. I lifted one hand and found blood smeared on the palm.

Edenfield swayed but remained fixated, as if he could not look away.

Gingerly, minding the barbed wire, I used my thumbs to pry open the belly slit. The sides parted easily, blood oozing over my thumbs. Inside the doll lay something solid.

I tipped the doll over Edenfield's bedside table and shook it. A small brown bird flopped out. Its fragile body was mangled and crushed, its wings cracked, its head hanging on by a sliver of skin and feather—but I recognized it.

A faint keening reminded me of Edenfield. I turned to him, amazed at how calm I felt. It wasn't really calm, but I thought at the time that it was.

"In my bed," Edenfield croaked. "I woke, and it was in my bed." He extended unsteady hands, sleeves grubby with blood and sweat. "In my arms, against my chest. Like hugging a baby, its face pressed—" He touched a jowl, broad as extra fabric glued on.

"Are you hurt?" I asked. "The barbed wire."

He heaved a laugh that was not a laugh. "No. Maybe. I could feel it cutting me, but look—no scratches. Its blood, not mine. The smell. I thought it was me. It was in bed with me, in my arms."

The smell. It wafted up to me, hot, sharp, metallic, tanging inside my nose. Blood, yes, but stronger than that were the organs, the beginning of rot. It had been dead for hours.

I dropped the doll next to the bird on the bedside table. I had a sudden, vast desire to wash my hands. Edenfield's bathroom was attached, and I made speedy use of its sink.

Mrs. Gulbransen hadn't left. She tidied the room, running her forefinger disapprovingly through the dust atop the dresser and re-arranging the photos. Edenfield might not have had a wife or children, but there were people he loved—or once had loved.

"Mrs. Gulbransen," I said. She jolted guiltily, snatching her hand to her breast. "Please go to the knighthouse. Bring Captain Nass here if he's available; if not, bring one of the others."

Gladness flushed her face. "Of course! Captain Nass will fix everything; he always does. He'll know what to do."

"Don't tell anyone else what's happened," I warned her. She nodded, and escaped—relieved for a reason to, I thought.

"Torben," Edenfield grumbled. "Always Torben. I don't want Torben; that's why I told her to get you."

"He's your head knight," I pointed out. "He's in charge of your security. I might not like the man, but I thought . . . I was sure . . ."

"That I like him? That I chose him? What choice did I have? I must have a competent head knight, and there's no one else who can do his job—not who will stay in Edenfield, anyway. He runs the border patrol, law enforcement, security . . . and he runs me. He'll tell you this was my fault." Edenfield's eyes closed and his head lolled. "Oh, God, please help me. What have I done?"

"Of course I'll help you," I said, before I realized he hadn't been addressing me. "This is *not* your fault."

A whimper began in the depths of his chest, mutated into a sob, and scuttled out between his lips. "I was warned. He warned me. He knew—he saw . . ."

I stood next to Edenfield again, gripping his shoulder and hand. He squeezed my fingers, but his gaze hit the floor. "Saw what?" I prompted softly.

Edenfield shook his head. "I should have listened. How can he protect me when I never listen? This is my punishment."

"Captain Nass threatened you?"

Edenfield shook his head. "He knew about the threats. He told me to leave until the conference was over, let him go in my place so no one could hurt me. Told me to go fishing, to let one of the knights protect me while he investigated. But instead I've kept the madman here and brought him others to prey on."

"Someone's snuck into your bedroom before," I said. "How many times? What did they do?"

Edenfield moaned and buried his massive head in his equally massive hands, his breathing hacking out in a laugh, a sob. "Last chance. That was my last chance, and now we will get what we deserve. I should have told you. Forgive me." He grabbed my wrists, pulled me closer, on the verge of falling off his bed to his knees before me. "I deluded myself. Pride, Agent Cartier. Beware pride. Pride dragged me down, destroyed the man I was. Torben warned me. . . .

"I have to get out of here!"

Edenfield released me and stood, absolute in his decision although wobbly on his feet and jerky as a marionette. He dragged a suitcase out from under his bed and began throwing clothes into it. He never once glanced at the bedside table, though he avoided it well enough.

"You can't leave," I said blankly. "The conference!"

"What good does a conference do me if I'm dead? What good does it do anyone? I have to get away. He won't come after the others if I'm away. I'll lead him on a merry chase, and if he catches me—"

"Lord Holst, please, calm down. Think clearly. If you keep your bedroom door locked—"

Edenfield rounded on me.

"It was locked. Don't you understand? It *was locked.*"

I didn't understand, but I tried again. "Then what you need is a guard. If you have someone watch over you—and over the other prefects—"

There was that hacking laugh-sob again. "It wouldn't do any good; the madman would find a way. Always listen to Torben Nass, agent. He's always right. He was right about this, and he was right about—"

He shook his head and kept packing. Some instinct made me turn then, though I can't say I heard the door open. But it was open, and Captain Nass stood under the frame: leaning inward, reedlike, having heard Edenfield's rant. Mossy-green eyes took in everything. "You're leaving," he observed. It wasn't a question.

Edenfield jolted. "Torben! You're here!"

The fluffy white dog from before trotted up to Edenfield, tail wagging. But the moment it got a good whiff of the air, it changed direction: snuffled around the bed and then jumped up against the side table. Its nails scrabbled against wood, but its twitching nose didn't come close to the tabletop. It was only a puppy, really. When it realized it couldn't reach the bird, it whined piteously at its master.

Captain Nass stepped around the dog and picked up the doll. He looked at it a long time, and then down at the bird. "Regal sparrow," he said in his dry, rustling voice. He didn't add *our national bird* or interpret the reasoning behind the choice of animal. Again, he said, "You're leaving."

Edenfield gave up trying to get his shirt to fold properly and tossed it on the heap of his suitcase. "You mean I'm running away. Abandoning my duties. The others won't be surprised, not with what they think of me. But you think I should have run away weeks ago."

"You can't leave," I said. "What about the conference? How will it look if you bring everyone here only to disappear?"

"I learned a long time ago not to judge things based on how they look," Edenfield snapped. Captain Nass tilted his head humorously, but didn't comment. "Especially not to *that* group of vipers."

"And here I thought," I said severely, "that you were the prefect most likely to do his duty to his God, his country . . . and his king."

"So did I. So I am." Edenfield threw a handful of underthings into the suitcase and zipped it shut, jamming the zipper and having to redo it three times. Mrs. Gulbransen reappeared as he struggled, and rushed to help him.

"You forgot your toothpaste," Captain Nass said.

"My toothpaste can go where the peppers grow!"

Mrs. Gulbransen gasped, but Captain Nass remained unfazed as he fetched the toothpaste and stuffed it into the suitcase's outer pocket. "Ms. Cartier has a point," he said. "The conference must be able to continue. Without your authority, I can provide only information; I cannot make your requests and decisions official."

Edenfield paused in the act of wrapping a striped navy scarf around his neck to splay his right hand, exhibiting the heavy ring on the pinky finger. The metal was ebony, the face a flat oval disc ringed with white and decorated with Edenfield's crest. The workmanship was handsome, the great ring not too small for Edenfield's hand.

Within that ring lay a prefect's power. Legally, there was more to it than that, but symbols are potent things. For all intents and purposes, whoever wore that ring was Prefect Edenfield.

How long, I wondered, had Captain Nass coveted it? I had assumed that all the prefects were in on this together, but Gil Winter hadn't been; it had been his brother, who had replaced him as prefect only at the last moment. It might not be Lord Holst who was the traitor in this prefecture.

I cleared my throat. "Captain Nass is going to be busy enough keeping the prefects safe without having your duties as well—and, as you said yourself, there's no one competent to take his place. You can't do this to him, my lord. He needs you here."

Edenfield's eyes were distant and his voice was hollow, but his movements remained determined. "You're right." He yanked off the ring. "Hold out your hand."

He seemed to be talking to me. He *was* talking to me. To *me*.

Captain Nass started forward. "My lord, what are you doing?"

"Your hand," Edenfield ordered me. Mrs. Gulbransen's fingers fluttered to her lips. I held out my hand, hardly believing what was going on. He slid the ring onto my thumb. It was too big, but it stayed on. "With this ring—"

"My lord, you can't!" Captain Nass cried.

"With this ring," Edenfield repeated, overriding his head knight, "I, Bo Holst, transfer the power of Edenfield Prefecture to you, Mercedes Cartier, with all the attendant powers and responsibilities—"

Captain Nass shoved himself between us, trying to stop Edenfield; but what Edenfield lacked in muscle, he made up for in bulk. I've no doubt Captain Nass could've stopped him, but not without breaking bones. In any case, Edenfield immobilized him with a glare and a slash of his hand, never breaking off his words:

"—until such a time as I can take up those powers and responsibilities again myself. Now you."

Feeling rather like I was getting married, I said, "I, Mercedes Cartier, take up the powers and responsibilities of Prefect Edenfield until Bo Holst takes them up again."

"Captain Nass?"

Captain Nass ground his teeth, but he said, "I, Torben Nass, head knight of Edenfield, stand witness that Mercedes Cartier is acting Prefect Edenfield, with all attendant powers and responsibilities, until such a time as Bo Holst resumes his position."

Bo dropped my hand. "There," he told Torben. "Happy?"

"Foolishness never makes me happy. Nor does petty vengeance."

Bo snorted. "Don't mind him, prefect. He'll do his duty. He always does." He picked up his suitcase and brushed past us.

There didn't seem any point in following him, and I was staring at my thumb, feeling the weight of the metal, the way it lingered with the warmth of Bo's hand. A minute later, I heard a distant garage door open and the crackle of gravel under tires. He had left. It hardly seemed real.

Torben had stayed with me, examining the crime scene and— what? Waiting for orders? Or was he going to try to bowl me over, to control me as he had Bo?

"I imagine you'll want to take the doll and bird away for forensic analysis," I told him brightly, like everything was normal. "Bo and I touched it, but I don't think anyone else did—aside from the psycho who put it there, obviously."

"You realize," said Torben, "that if the 'psycho' doesn't follow Lord Holst, he will be after you next."

I smiled. "I'm sure you'll keep me safe."

Torben didn't smile back. He stood over me, swaying forward. He'd swayed like that the first time I'd seen him, too. It gave him the impression of looming, although he wasn't much above average height for a man—which put him at eight inches taller than me. He was the same height as Sr. Nordfeld, I reflected. Probably the only thing those two had in common.

"Would you like to know my dog's name?" Torben asked.

I squinted up at him, wondering if I'd misheard. "What?"

"My dog's name," he repeated, as if this were the most ordinary thing in the world to bring up. "It's Shiro."

The dog's ears, ever pointed, perked up further, and it trotted over. Torben obediently squatted to scratch under its chin. It flopped onto its back for a belly rub, and then wriggled ecstatically as he obliged, trying to lick his hands and face at once. It would've been cute, if Torben hadn't been involved.

"Shiro is Japanese for 'white,'" he said.

"And your dog is white," I said. "Well done."

"I didn't name him after his color," Torben said mildly. "I named him after the dog in the Japanese folktale, 'Hanasaka Jiisan'—'The Old Man Who Made Flowers Blossom.' Have you read it?"

"I must've missed it."

Shiro scrabbled to his feet and pawed at Torben, who had paused in his petting. Torben massaged the dog's neck, not bothering to look at me as he spoke. "Once upon a time," he said, in the rhythm of story-telling, "there was a kindly old couple who lived off their tiny plot of land. They were happy, except for one thing: they had never had any children. Instead, they had a dog named Shiro, and on this dog they lavished their love and attention."

"How sad," I said nastily. "Someone with no one to love but a dog."

Torben didn't take the bait. "One day," he said, "Shiro was digging for a long time in the back yard. When the old man went to find him, he discovered to his astonishment that the dog had dug up a heap of gold coins.

"Now, next door to the kindly old couple lived a cross man who hated everyone and never missed an opportunity to torment and strike Shiro. When he saw the treasure Shiro had dug up, he became envious and begged the kindly couple to lend him the dog. The kindly couple agreed, and the cross man took Shiro to his own plot and waited for the dog to dig, expecting Shiro would find him some gold. Instead, Shiro dug up a pile of stinking garbage.

"Furious, the cross man seized a shovel and killed the little dog. Then he threw the body into the hole the dog had dug and covered it up and didn't tell anyone what he had done."

I waited. Torben didn't go on. "Is that it?" I asked.

Torben waved a hand. "Does it matter? The story continues on with your usual folktale elements. The kindly couple ends happily, the cruel man unhappily. The dog remains dead."

"I see," I said. "You named your dog after a folktale dog who got killed by a shovel. Charming."

Torben shrugged and finally looked up at me. He was still crouched to pet the dog. It was strange, having a man's face lower than mine. Disconcerting. He couldn't have known it, but this reversal made me far more uncomfortable than looming ever could.

"At least one Shiro should have a happy ending, don't you think?" he said. He gave the puppy a final pat and stood. "What sort of 'kindly couple' do you think loans their beloved dog to a neighbor they know loves to strike and torment it?"

"The crazy kind."

"I agree," Torben said. "It takes a certain type of crazy to *know* what a person is like and *realize* that person is wicked and *still* entrust what he loves to her. Don't you think?"

Chapter 24:

IMPERSONATION

I may have mentioned something at some point about not taking well to manipulation. That included guilt tripping, threats, insinuations, and, apparently, Japanese folk tales. But there are certain advantages to people trying to manipulate you—such as the fact that they give away their positions.

If Torben could have made me leave, he would have. If he could have arrested me, he would have. But he was, at least at present, unwilling to move openly against his prefect.

I had to make sure I kept that advantage.

"Gina," I said, turning my charm on Mrs. Gulbransen. "I wanted to thank you for the good work you've done here. I know this whole situation must have been incredibly stressful for you, but you've been an absolute champion."

Gina shuffled her feet.

"I promise," I said, pressing her hand, "that we'll get rid of this unpleasantness as soon as possible. In the meantime, we must continue to be strong and make Bo proud. Torben here is right." I released Gina to clap him on the shoulder. He recoiled, so I firmed up the hold and took his forearm in my opposite hand. I smiled up at him, then back around to Gina. "We can't let the madman behind this attack frighten us. Now that Torben is alert to the situation, we can trust him to protect us.

"You will, of course," I told Torben, sickly sweet, "remove the bird and doll immediately, for forensic analysis. Take the sheets too: I'll use fresh ones. Yes," I said at their mutual expression, "I will be sleeping in this room. I will not let some psycho choose how Prefect Edenfield acts. *I* choose my ground, and together, we will stand fast against every trouble. This conference will progress in a calm and timely manner. When Bo returns, he'll find everything exactly as he would have it."

I swept bedding onto the floor and bundled sheets into Torben's arms. The doll and bird, I wrapped in a pillowcase and balanced atop his armload. Torben didn't stop me, and he didn't comment. He watched me closely, calculating—like Sra. Ahlgren watching her opponent across a chessboard.

"Fresh sheets please, Gina," I said, propelling Torben out of the room. "I need to get dressed. There's a lot of work to be done."

I bustled out after them, a fire lit under my brain. In no time I had showered, rearranged my hair to hide the graze, slapped color corrector and concealer over my bruises, and dressed. I would've worn Edenfield colors if I'd brought any, but I hadn't, so I wore Carina's black and white and borrowed an Edenfield pin from Bo's dresser for my lapel. *Sharp*, I told myself, modeling in Bo's full-length mirror, and strode out to the knighthouse to see how Torben was getting on.

I found neither Torben nor Olaf inside the knighthouse's main room. Instead, the knight at the desk was a man of about forty, with a ruddy complexion, broad lips that spread in welcome as I entered, and pouchy sea-blue eyes. Those eyes flew to the ring on my thumb, and the grin broadened. "Prefect Edenfield," the knight said, rising and circling the desk. "The captain told me about your temporary elevation and Lord Holst's departure. I hoped I'd get a chance to meet you." He offered a fleshy hand, and I shook it. There was real strength inside the flab, and I got the impression that, as with Olaf, there was more competence to this knight than his appearance indicated. "Roald Steensen, at your service."

"Mercedes Cartier."

"I hear," Roald said, sounding delighted, "that your brother packs quite the punch. Olaf's face is as black and blue as his ego. Couldn't stop talking about it."

"No hard feelings, I hope."

"Nah. Do him good, knowing he can be surprised. You'll want to see the captain, I guess. He's back there." He jinked his head at the door. "Want me to fetch him for you?"

"In a minute." I smelled opportunity, and I doubted Torben would be as accommodating as Roald. "I didn't get a chance to look around yesterday, and I ought to be familiar with this place." I strolled around the room, examining the various certificates, clippings, and posters on display. Three of the certificates were proofs of knighthood for Olaf, Roald, and Torben. Torben's had his head knight star and was dated this past July. It didn't say what had happened to his predecessor.

"Is it only the three of you in Gjerde?" I asked.

"Olaf and me, mostly. Wouldn't even have that, without the manor here; it's that quiet. The captain comes and goes, too busy to sleep half the time. Man's going to run himself into the ground unless he slows down. Needs a wife to ground him, not just that dog. Not," he said hastily, "that I'm saying anything against him. He's the best head knight we've had in a long time."

I smiled at that, but said only, "How many knights has he recalled to the manor for the duration of the conference?"

Roald's face went blank as printer paper.

"I mean," I clarified, "to keep the prefects safe from the madman who's been threatening Bo."

"Oh," Roald said doubtfully. "I don't know about that. You'll have to ask him."

"I heard."

I jumped and cursed myself for it. This was the second time Torben had overheard me talking without my realizing it. I've never known anyone to move so quietly, and I was going to have to stay on alert lest he overhear something he really oughtn't.

I turned to him with polite friendliness. He leaned against the doorframe behind the desk, backlit by the room beyond. "The answer, Lady Cartier," he said—and I gave a start at the title, though my temporary prefectship necessitated it—"is that there are no knights or prefectsmen of any description available for recall. No Edenfield knight holds a less-than-essential post. Having two knights wrapped up in a low-risk area like the manor is a necessary if wholly unfortunate waste of resources; having me here is worse. Recalling more knights would be criminal."

"Low risk?" I responded. "You see no potential for violence against all nine of Carina's prefects in a single location? Or all nine prefects *and the king?*"

"The king will bring his own protection," Torben said. "Beyond that—Lady Cartier, if that was your concern, you should not have chosen to move the conference here. Not without also providing the resources you considered necessary."

Truly, his diplomacy knew no bounds. And I couldn't exactly explain that the reason I wanted more knights was to have enough around to contain and arrest the prefects if that proved necessary. And, preferably, knights other than Olaf and Roald, knights whose loyalties would tend more toward King Emil (and me) than to Torben and Bo.

"Thank you for your input, Torben," I said, still aiming at warm rather than frosty. "I will take it into account. In the meantime, please alert a dozen nearby knights that they may be needed. Keep them on alert for the duration of the conference."

"A dozen knights?" he echoed. "Let's see. Would you prefer the ones stopping foreign spies from infiltrating the government, the ones preventing bandits from attacking civilians, the ones preventing a buildup of landmines along our borders, or the ones providing essential relief work? It doesn't matter which—any choice will mean that some of your people will die. The only question is, which ones are you most willing to sacrifice?"

Bandits? Landmines? Since when had either of those been issues in Carina? Was Torben testing, teasing, tricking—or telling the truth?

I might as easily have read the answer off a blade of grass as off Torben, so I looked to Roald for confirmation.

Embarrassment was his predominant emotion, I concluded. But embarrassment at what? At an exaggerating superior or an ignorant prefect?

"My dear Torben," I said, "are you implying that your knights are so incompetent that *being on alert* will kill them? I hope not, but just in case, I will permit you to choose which of your men you think least prone to such extreme emotional delicacy."

"The acting prefect is choosing to misunderstand me."

"By no means," I said. "I understand you perfectly, and I understand that the consequences of actually withdrawing knights could be dire. I will therefore not even consider doing so except in the most extreme need. But if *the most extreme need* arises, then I will not be without a contingency plan. Frankly, I'm surprised that, as head knight, you don't already have a contingency plan in place."

A muscle in Torben's jaw twitched. I thought he was going to argue. Part of me hoped he would, because that would give me an excuse to be truly nasty to him, but he didn't. Instead, his eyes closed and his head tilted intently, listening. Then he pushed off the doorframe and passed me to open the front door.

I could hear something too, now that I knew to listen. Heart skipping, I darted around Torben and ran to greet our guests. What would my boss think, when he saw my ring? Except—no, he wasn't my boss at the moment, was he? A prefect can have no employer. By taking on the position, I had quit my job—at least, for the duration. What a strange thought!

So: what would Sr. Nordfeld think, when he recognized my ring? This wasn't what he had planned—it was ten times better. I'd be on the spot, an eye witness.

I couldn't wait to see his face.

A rather misshapen purple car rolled into the parking loop, gravel crinkling away from the tires. It was clearly a rental—I wouldn't have fancied the ten-plus-hour drive from Lindo Prefecture, either—and maybe that's why the driving was so erratic. It stopped and started and jerked around in angry bursts made angrier when an attempt to park in a too-small space between Tey's car and Hemmel's failed. It veered too sharply and took off a strip of purple. The driver held down the horn for a full ten seconds at that, backed up violently, and stopped the car where it was, in everyone's way. The driver apparently thought this was good enough, however, because the engine stopped and the driver's door swung open.

The woman who emerged was in her late thirties, swarthy and stringy, the sort who isn't ugly but has never been called pretty either. Stress lined her face in permanent creases, and strident energy sizzled through every line of her limbs. She sprang from her car, whipped its door shut, homed in on me, and tramped vigorously over.

"You work here?" she trumpeted.

Prefect Lindo sure seemed a lot calmer on television and in newspapers, but I guess no need for pussyfooting when she was in a hurry—or in a temper.

"Get me Edenfield!" she demanded, when I didn't immediately respond. "I want to see him."

No one had been quite that rude to me since my university years, when I'd worked as a barista at a series of increasingly fancy coffee joints. It's amazing, how screamy people can get over a cup of caffeine, especially when one of our more popular seasonal flavors was out of stock.

I slapped on my dealing-with-difficult-customers expression—concerned eyebrows elevated, lips sympathetically upward but without a hint of humor, ears back—and said, "I'm afraid Bo Holst isn't available at the moment, but I can help you."

Someone had trained Prefect Lindo to take deep breaths and count to ten to avert explosion. She did so now, snorting like a flaming ghost horse and grinding out each letter beneath her breath. "Work with me here," she told me. "This is prefect business, and it's important. I don't care if he's asleep or stuffing his face or in bed with your sister. I want him."

I'd been empathizing with her up until that last line. It wasn't so long since I'd been in her position, blocked by a stranger from seeing Bo. And in other circumstances, insults don't faze me, since I can return them. It's a great way to defuse situations, giving the other person increasingly ridiculous (and sometimes obscurely flattering) barbs until they begin flyting back, and we both go away happy.

But a good flyte requires some form of agreement and equality between parties. I could flyte casually with my brothers and equals; and they wouldn't take it personally, because they were free to respond in kind. I would never attempt it with Sr. Nordfeld unless he proposed it and set parameters.

Lindo thought that I was a servant, and that I'd lose my position if I riled her. She was abusing her power for no other reason than that she was annoyed, and that annoyed *me*. She didn't deserve a response, let alone an honorable insult.

My gaze trailed back to the car, to its second occupant. Diagonal stripes of sapphire and ivory decorated Prefect Avior's tie. Otherwise, the only differences in his appearance were a pronounced fatigue, probably from having shared a car with Prefect Lindo, and a glittering excitement as he transferred his gaze from Edenfield Manor to me.

Prefect Avior had been riding in the passenger seat. The rental car's windows were slightly tinted, but not so much that they would hide someone sitting in the back.

Sr. Nordfeld had not come.

Maybe, I told myself, stomach contracting, he had taken a second car. Or maybe he'd opted for train instead of plane and wouldn't be arriving until later.

Regardless, I hadn't realized until this moment how much I'd depended on him arriving with Avior, on him telling me that I was exactly on track, doing an excellent job, well *done*, Mercedes.

"I would appreciate it if you looked at me when I talked to you."

I blinked back at Prefect Lindo. She might know what had happened to Sr. Nordfeld. Prefect Avior would definitely know, but I wasn't keen on another tête-à-tête with him. I prefer to leave skin-crawling experiences to absolute emergencies.

"It's extremely rude to ignore people while they're speaking," Lindo informed me. "I could have your job for this. I don't care how you behave when it's only Edenfield about, but I expect a higher level of respect."

I needed to stay focused. I said, "I'm Prefect—"

"Excuse me? Excuse me?"

I was decreasingly inclined to excuse her.

"Was I speaking?" Lindo demanded. "I think I was. Don't interrupt me while I'm speaking."

She waited. I waited. She bugged her eyes at me.

"I'm Prefect Edenfield," I said.

"Like hell you are."

This must've been how Prefect Avior felt, when I'd done the same thing to him. So I responded in the same way he had: I lifted my right hand and flashed the signet ring at her.

Lindo was less gentle than I'd been. She grabbed my fingers and crushed them close to her face, squinting like I do without my glasses.

It took her a good beat to process what she saw, but in that beat she became a new woman. She might never have been angry, when she released me and stood back. Her face smoothed out, and she assumed a determined and conciliatory dignity. "I'm sorry for yelling," she said, dear as strawberry shortcake, "but you shouldn't have tricked me like that. This week has been extremely stressful for me."

I gestured in gracious sympathy.

"First, there was the conference to set up. My manor's been torn to pieces and back again I don't know how many times, because my workers keep getting it wrong and having to fix their mistakes. I haven't gotten a wink of sleep in weeks, what with the constant noise and no one but me able to think for themselves. They keep coming at me twenty-four seven and bothering me with this and that and the other thing like the incompetents they are. I have to micromanage every single detail, and *never mind* that I have my own work to do."

I think the ring had genuinely surprised her out of her anger. If I'd been a neutral observer, I'd have been fascinated at how she worked herself back up without meaning to, each sentence angrier than the one before. Francis has a temper, but he doesn't have the imagination to yell over nothing, and my coffee customers would've been kicked out by now. So this was a new experience for me.

"—and then Bo calls me and *announces* the conference is moving. He doesn't *care* about anything I've done or my hours and days and weeks of hard labor. He doesn't bother to ask, no 'if you don't mind' or 'I'm so sorry to inconvenience you,' just *orders me*, like I'm one of his *damned knights*. 'You don't have a choice, Graça.' 'There's a king's agent, Graça.' 'Boohoo for you, Graça.' Like I believe any of that.

"I know what he wants, the fat bastard. He can't think of anything but himself, but *I'm* the one who deserves this. *I'm* the one who's done the organization, the work—months and months of hard work, preparing for this, being interrogated, being questioned, having to prove myself to them—and then he *orders me around* and my plane is delayed and I have to wait and wait, and Avior's no help *at all*—and then I get here and Bo's *run off* and you say you're Prefect Edenfield, and who the *hell* are you *anyway?*"

"I'm Prefect Edenfield," I said.

She snapped back to me, accusatory, shrill. "You don't look Edenfieldian."

"She's not. She's Batatan," said Avior, stepping up to join us.

A gentleman, I thought, would've interfered sooner. Maybe, like me, Avior had been staring in horrified fascination—but maybe he just knew Prefect Lindo and didn't want her to turn on him. If so, he should've waited longer, because she turned.

"You know her?" Lindo demanded. "Is she another one of yours?"

"No, and I didn't expect to see her here. She's Jon Nordfeld's personal assistant." He'd been watching me since arriving, with that excited gleam, with an edge of hunger. I was abruptly glad Lindo was here with me—and that the knighthouse was barely fifteen yards distant. "How did you get here?" he asked me.

I opened my mouth to fabricate another cheap knockoff of the truth, but Lindo beat me to the punch. She squawked, "She's *who?* What have you told her? Can't you keep your mouth shut for *two seconds?*"

"I said I didn't know she would be here," Avior said, irritability edging into his voice. "And I didn't tell her anything."

"On which note," I said, "where is Sr. Nordfeld? I expected him to arrive with you."

"He's in prison, where he belongs," Prefect Lindo said, puffing up her chest and smirking at us. "Avior might be too stupid not to spot an obvious plant, but I'm not. A member of the Carinan Security Service, for heaven's sake! And he didn't think to do a background check!"

"I did check. I *told* you—"

"And you're his assistant," Lindo mused, shifting her attention back to me. "That means you work for the CSS too."

"I work for Edenfield Prefecture," I said coolly, glancing over at Torben without meaning to. He stood halfway between us and the knighthouse, watching me. "I told you, I'm Prefect Edenfield."

"You're a king's agent," Lindo said. For the moment, hardness superseded the anger. "You're *the* king's agent, the one who convinced Bo to change the conference location. Bo wasn't lying."

I hate losing control of a conversation. Lindo had taken me by surprise; she hadn't been what I'd expected, and I still wasn't sure what she was.

Politeness hadn't worked, and she definitely wasn't listening to Avior either, so I tried a new tactic.

I lifted my chin and puffed out my chest. "My dear prefect, I assure you that everything will work out for the best." I waved a negligent hand. "That's why I was sent."

Lindo regarded me with empty eyes. Almost conversationally, she said, "You self-satisfied little bitch. You sniveling, conniving—"

The rest of the sentence wasn't printable. Luckily, it was also nearly incoherent, as her voice got louder, shriller, and more distorted with every word, until she was full-on screaming insults at me. I had never seen anyone so angry, or made so ugly through anger. Her face crumpled into a clown's mask of rage, horrible and hideous and strangely comic.

I think my lack of response enraged her further, because she ended in a scream of rage and threw her handbag at me. It missed by a mile and plowed into the gravel, and she screeched, "Now look what you've made me do! You'd better pay for anything that broke, you little—" She lurched at me, closer and closer, arms flailing.

I was so confused. I had no idea how to react. The problem was, I didn't understand her, and I'm not used to not understanding people. Also, pepper spray was not an option.

Lindo's flailing arms began slapping me—aimless, open-handed slaps, heavy enough to hurt but not to bruise. She kept screaming at me, calling me every name in the book and a lot of gobbledygook besides. She accused me of everything from conspiring to kill her to killing her sister to wanting to destroy her prefecture and bring the country to ruin to seducing Avior and Edenfield (and possibly the king as well) to whatever else flew up her throat and down her tongue and out her lips without bothering to check in with her brain along the way.

As she screamed, the blows grew more forceful. She whacked my head hard with the heel of her hand, shooting white-hot shards through the bullet graze, and screamed at me for hurting her hand. She hacked the arm down again, but a midnight-purple uniform interposed itself. That made her scream more, and rain down blows on the new body. I stumbled back, gasping and shaking my ringing, scorching head.

Torben didn't defend himself against Lindo's blows any more than I had, although that wasn't due to shock in his case. A head knight striking a prefect not his own would've been political suicide—if not the outright sort—unless his prefect's life was at stake. It did help him that he was so much taller than I, and Lindo's blows reached only his chest. Shiro barked and danced, and I was afraid he was going to bite someone. Avior had wisely backed up to watch from a distance. I kept shaking my head and blinking against the darkness behind my eyes. I was going to have to get Francis to look at my graze again, the way it was splitting.

Everyone was doing something, but what no one was doing was interfering in any constructive way.

But this was my prefecture, wasn't it? It was up to me to interfere. Not by yanking Lindo back by the hair—a prefect assaulting another prefect was the same as her head knight doing it. Besides, I needed her around for another five days.

Taking Lindo for inspiration, I therefore walked right up beside her, filled my lungs, and screamed in her ear.

Screaming effectively requires proper technique. You want your diaphragm to support you and your throat relaxed, like with singing. Higher is usually better, which gives women an advantage. Practice will let you hold the scream longer.

Even an older brother will have trouble keeping his grip on you with a one-hundred-decibel scream an inch from his ear—and, unlike Lindo, my brothers had practice.

Lindo's screeches fell away into baffled silence. I stopped screaming on the instant, and moved into my third tactic: taking charge.

"The conference will go to plan," I announced. "I understand your frustration, Graça, but we need you. Where are your keys? Ah." I swooped the handbag from the ground and plucked out her keys before returning it to her. Then I marched to the car, got her suitcase from the trunk—I was assuming the flowered turquoise one was hers—and shoved it into her unresisting hands. "The conference begins in a few hours; you need to have breakfast first." I took her right arm in my right hand and placed my left hand on the small of her back, the better to guide her to the front door. "Your room's upstairs—it's the same one as usual: end of the hall on the right. I'll take you to the stairs. Breakfast's on the ground floor, in the dining room next to the stairs. You've been under a lot of stress trying to plan, so I want you to relax. Everything's going to be taken care of from here on out."

I opened the front door and propelled her neatly through. She moved stiffly, tensely, but she moved and she didn't swear at me. "I know it might not mean much, coming from me," I went on, "but I've always admired you. There aren't many women prefects, and you're a force of nature. You put up with so much. I'm only beginning to realize how difficult your job is, and you've dealt with it for years. Well, for today, I want you to relax and let me deal with everything." I took her to the foot of the stairs and released her there, frowning seriously. "We're going to do good work this week, the nine of us. And we can't do it without you."

Lindo's shoulders plumped back and forth, pride battling mollification. I kept my face stern and honest, and she gave in with a sniff. "Place would fall apart without me," she said, hoisting her suitcase. "Save me some toast and marmalade."

"I will," I promised, and stopped by the dining hall to make good on that promise. In fact, Gina hadn't even begun setting out breakfast. It was that early. The sunlight remained cool and distant behind the easterly mountains, and the breeze nipped my face as I stepped back outside.

"I see what you mean about having things under control," Avior commented. He'd gotten his suitcase out and was sitting on it, waiting for me. "You sure controlled her."

Torben was nowhere to be seen, though I trusted him to pop out again like hair in soup—at the most inconvenient moment. In case he popped sooner rather than later, I kept my voice low and my smile sheepish as I approached Avior. "Is she always like that?"

"Only when stressed," Avior said, not like he cared about her, "and she's usually stressed. Although maybe not *this* stressed." He laughed humorlessly. "You talked up Jon so much I didn't realize that his assistant's starry eyes hid a powerhouse. I honestly believed you knew nothing of the conference. I should have remembered—all exceptional men must have exceptional assistants. Tell me, how did he know to send you here in his place—or do I have it backward? Do you control him like you controlled Lindo?"

He was lying to me. Not in any of his words, but in the way he was pretending not to mind being fooled—being handled, as it must seem to him, the way I had handled Lindo.

I cast my gaze to my feet and shook my head. "Don't call it that. I didn't control her. She just wanted someone to listen to her. To understand her. I get that." I raised my eyes to him, pulsing pathos. "You're talking like I tricked you, but I didn't. I knew the conference was happening, but not the rest of it. Sr. Nordfeld doesn't discuss stuff like that. And I wasn't supposed to come to the manor, not like this. But things kept happening—Prefect Silvertip knew you had come to see me, and he wanted to know why." I steadied my mouth, certain and determined. "I don't know what's going on, but I do know that I'm going to do my best to make sure everything runs smoothly. Only ..." I let the vulnerability shine through, the determination slip and shrink inside my voice. "Only, I would like to know where Sr. Nordfeld is. He isn't *really* in prison? You're going to get him out, aren't you? And bring him here?"

"That was the plan, before I knew you were here." Avior tried a winning grin. He should've practiced it more first. "One doesn't need the master when there's a well-trained apprentice available. You *are* well trained?"

"I'm afraid I don't understand."

"Nonsense," Avior said, standing up from his suitcase. "You'll do just fine—or you will if you ever want to see Jon Nordfeld alive again. I'll see you later, prefect."

"Prefect," I half replied, half echoed.

Chapter 25:

MISINFORMATION

If you predict the variables thoroughly enough, Sr. Nordfeld had told me, you can predict every move in advance so completely that you can instruct someone else on what to do when, so that they can win even without you being present—even without that someone understanding what they're doing.

But that's the problem with people: they're only predictable to a point and, unlike a game of chess, random factors *will* intrude. Where factors were stable, Sr. Nordfeld had predicted perfectly: the spy equipment was in place; the prefects were gathered. But his plan had hinged on one or both of us being present to collect the information from the spy equipment. He had not taken into account Silvertip arresting me or Lindo arresting him, and now a pawn was out of place.

If I left things as planned, maybe the game would still be ours. But I don't believe in letting chance choose my fate, when I can stack the deck. And if Sr. Nordfeld wasn't here to read the board, then I was going to change which game we were playing.

I never have been any good at chess.

～ ⋀

Prefect Batata arrived at breakfast first. He exchanged cheerful words with Gina and started the coffee himself: dark and potent as a black hole, and with the same sucking capacity against the light of lassitude. I never get coffee like that except when I visit home, which I do as infrequently as possible. I've spent years spoiling myself with luxury brews and fresh beans and coffee machines more advanced than most sci-fi robots.

"Thank you," I told Batata, accepting a mug and sliding into the chair next to his. "It's nice to see that someone around here gets up at an honest hour. Sometimes I miss it, rising with the dawn to feed the chickens. It's not the same, when I go to visit my parents. They aren't sure whether to treat me as a guest or a farmhand."

Batata looked at me in wonderment. His alcohol-steeped evening hadn't left him much the worse for wear, and the coffee had mostly eradicated the fatigue bags gathering beneath his eyes. It struck me that this conference might be the closest thing he ever got to a vacation. Even on Christmas and the Sabbath, he'd normally be out caring for his animals at this time of morning.

I said, "You probably don't remember it"—darn right he wouldn't, since I'd been fourteen at the time—"but we met once, a few years ago. You came to my school—we won the prefecture flyting award. You shook my hand." I offered my hand now, for a firm, down-to-earth handshake. "My name is Mercedes Cartier, acting Prefect Edenfield. It's a pleasure to see you again."

"You too," Batata said, matching my grip. He didn't seem alarmed or even curious about Bo's absence. That was my home prefecture for you: accepting of what came our way, especially if it was bad, because that was life.

I was not nostalgic; I'd pulled myself out of the mud instead of accepting it, and you couldn't have paid me to move back to Batata. But you wouldn't have known that by the way we jabbered on, Batata telling me about his plantation and I reminiscing about hard summers and harder winters.

Somewhere above and behind me, the stairs creaked. I stood and slapped Batata's shoulder. "It's a relief to know I have one prefect I can trust," I told him. "You're a good man, Joel."

His smile dropped off, but I pretended not to notice as I hurried away.

The creaking was Fjordland; only he descended stairs so slowly.

He wasn't much older than Bo, but he moved like a man on the verge of a century, and a glance at his face could've told anyone that his brain had been deteriorating for years. No wonder Avior was able to prey on him. I doubted he'd recollect any more than his impression of me: whether I had caused him pleasure or agitation.

There were no witnesses, so I threw my arms around Fjordland and squealed, "Uncle Calixto! It's so wonderful to see you again!"

Fjordland shook his head and touched my shoulder, unsure whether to hug me or push me away. "Young lady—"

I drew back, deeply hurt. "Don't you recognize me, uncle?"

He rallied magnificently, "Of course I do, my dear. It's been a while—hasn't it?"

"Too long," I agreed. "But I remember the advice you gave me, and I live by it every day." I pressed my lips together to hold back proud tears. "You're the wisest man I've ever met."

"Coming from you, that's a real compliment." Fjordland patted me, delighted. "I wish my sister could've seen you, all grown up and pretty as a tulip. You are Cruz's girl, aren't you? I can't keep track of you all."

"Don't worry," I said; "you're better at these things than you know. I'll see you later, uncle." I kissed his withered cheek and hurried on, only glancing back once. He tottered off to the dining room, expression bemused but glowing. He might not remember me the next time we met, but he would trust me without knowing why—or I hoped he would.

I paused in the laundry area to call Sr. Nordfeld. He didn't answer, but I hadn't held out much hope that they'd let him keep his phone in prison or even that his warden would answer.

Another point for the king's remembrance.

Canopus's suite was the last one on the left. She hadn't locked the door, so I let myself in. I figured she'd be up—that much hair and makeup took time—and sure enough, I found her in her bathroom. She glanced at me in the mirror but didn't otherwise react. Maybe she's used to people walking in on her primping.

"Therese," I said, "I'm glad you're up. I have something you'll want to hear without the others listening in."

"Avior's spy." Her hand lowered, powder brush dusting product on the counter. She didn't sound too overjoyed at being interrupted, although maybe that was the lack of eye shadow talking. I admired her gold silk pajamas and wondered if she wore the color in tribute to her prefecture or merely because it particularly suited her skin tone. "I thought you'd scampered back to your master. Or hasn't he arrived?"

"If you are referring to Prefect Avior," I said, "he arrived an hour ago, along with Prefect Lindo. No doubt they will soon be at breakfast, if they aren't already. But before we join them, I'd like to chat with you—or, rather, you'd like me to, since my information is to your advantage."

"That seems unlikely."

I watched without speaking as Canopus painted gold shadow on her lids and pitch black mascara on her lashes. She ignored me for a minute longer, but she hadn't gotten where she was by ignoring opportunities. When she saw I meant it, she motioned to the bed. "Have a seat. I'll be right out."

I let her close the bathroom door on me and sat on the rumpled blue duvet. When Francis and I had made up the place, it had felt like an empty motel room: nearly identical to its neighbors, void of personality. Canopus had made it feel more lived in—empty suitcase tucked under the bed, clothes in drawers and closet, rosy perfume pervasive—but it remained Edenfield's room, not hers. That made sitting on her bed less awkward, which I appreciated, since I waited for several minutes while she finalized her face. I defied the temptation to straighten the duvet but not the one to dig through her drawers.

When Canopus finally emerged in a fresh gust of perfume, I was sitting on her dresser. I said, "Our time may be short."

"A spy's time often is," Canopus said, smoothing out the crumpled duvet before settling her derriere. "What do you want?"

"For you to stop referring to me as Avior's spy, for a start. I'm not his minion, and I never was." I raised my right hand to show off the ring. I'd moved it to the forefinger and jammed a bit of wadded tissue under the band to make sure it stayed in place. "Examine it, if you like. It's quite genuine, and should reveal to you my true loyalties."

Canopus bent over the ring and then sprang back, hand clutching her throat, crying, "No!"

I have never seen anything so mawkish and contrived.

"How did he die?" she gasped. "Who—who killed him? Not you."

"Bo is not dead," I said; "merely in hiding. He has been putting up with death threats for weeks now, but last night was the final straw: he woke up in a bed full of blood. He'd locked his door, but somehow the madman threatening him got in and left behind a mutilated animal wrapped in barbed wire inside a voodoo doll. The smell," I said, "permeated."

"And he brought the conference *here?*"

"He had a choice," I said. "He could remain as prefect, endangering the rest of us—or he could lead the madman away. He chose to protect us."

"How very noble," Canopus spat, "after he'd endangered us in the first place."

I shook my head. "Don't blame him for that; he was maneuvered into it, and not by me. Not by a king's agent either—not unless someone crowned Avior while I wasn't looking. I couldn't stop him."

"That rat!" Canopus slammed her open palm on the wall and, when that didn't make her feel better, did it several more times. "That traitor!"

"I don't think Prefect Lindo knows," I said. "I don't think any of them do, except us ... and whichever of the others Avior is working with."

Canopus had a better grasp of her temper than Lindo, but her eyes flashed, and she growled, "Others?"

"It stands to reason," I said. "He'd never succeed without support. That's why I came to you instead of one of the men. I knew you'd never stand for this nonsense, and I needed someone I could count on."

"To throttle him?"

I tilted my head slightly. "Not ... at present. The moment will come when we can catch them both at once. That will be the time to strike."

Canopus sized me up, from my ring to my dangling feet to the blue-and-purple pin on my stylish black-and-white suit dress. One strong woman to another, I vibed at her. She must've liked that, because she seized my hand and shook it until it creaked. "If you betray me," she said, "I will eat you alive."

I smiled graciously. When I betrayed her, she wouldn't have any teeth left.

Lyn _ é;

It took me longer to arrange a meeting with Prefect Silvertip, because the conference got in the way.

Canopus had recommended Tey medicate himself with brandy to get through the conference, but brandy would've only made things worse in my case. It was awful. I have never felt so ignorant in my life. Francis's ex-girlfriends would've come across as intelligent and educated in comparison to the hack job I made of it. My few moments of respite from utter shame were taken over by a vast and marveling awe that I could have grown up and lived all my life in a country and studied its history while being so utterly uninformed on it.

"I'll discuss it with Bo this evening," was one of my stock responses to questions. I meant it, too: I was going to get that man's phone number if I had to ask Torben for it. "I'll consider it," was another. I took copious notes and slowly, agonizingly, built up my knowledge base.

I didn't join the others for lunch. Cai Gulbransen delivered me a sandwich in Bo's office, and I ate while hunting for information in his drawers and on his computer. I needed something, anything useful to say.

After forty-five minutes, I had found hints that Torben's spiel about bandits and landmines and spies hadn't been complete drivel, but without solid details and an action plan, that didn't do me much good. About Edenfield's special needs, imports and exports, agreements, laws, and intentions for the conference, I found nothing. Bo must have kept everything in his head.

Francis joined me with a sandwich of his own, and peered over my shoulder at my notes.

"You were listening?" I asked him.

He tapped his earpiece. He had been trapped in the conference as much as I had, except that his version of trapped had meant lounging on his bed with as many bathroom breaks and snacks as he pleased. The memory card Sr. Nordfeld had provided could record audio for an entire week if it had to, but we didn't want to cut things closer than necessary. The moment we had anything condemning, off to the capital it'd go.

"Maybe we should've dragged Luc along with us," Francis mused. "He could be your research assistant. I could call him up and make him come."

"Was my ignorance that obvious?" I asked plaintively. "Don't say 'yes.' You're my brother. You're supposed to console me that, all things considered, I did exceedingly well."

"You want me to lie?"

I groaned and buried my head in my arms.

Francis patted my shoulder. "If it helps," he said, "the others might have found it less obvious than I did. I *am* your brother."

My grasp of the material I should've already known continued to improve, but not without a cost. By the time dinner rolled around, my brain was pretty nonfunctional for anything not involving crashing. But I couldn't afford to miss the opportunities dinner provided, and so I dragged myself there.

Every moment I spent in the company of my esteemed peers was a moment I learned more about them. I'd already discovered that Tey found me attractive and that Lindo was perfectly reasonable except for when she suddenly was not. Canopus ignored me assiduously while Silvertip kept trying to catch my eye. Hemmel was interested in me only on Lindo's behalf. Once we got to dinner, Batata cared for nothing but the food, although he was quite polite in asking me to pass the salt. Avior spoke only to Fjordland, and then only in murmurs. I'm not sure Fjordland understood more than one word in ten, and I'm positive that Avior didn't care.

Silvertip caught up with me as I left the table, and followed me to Bo's office. He didn't say a word until he had shut and locked the door and sat across from me. Then he said, "You should have told me your plan. I could have helped. I would have helped. If replacing Bo was what Avior wanted—"

"What *Avior* wanted?" I interrupted sharply. "Why would I care what Avior wants? I'm not his agent, and I never have been. I represent Edenfield. This prefecture is my concern, and I will do what's best for it . . . regardless of whether that matches what Avior wants."

Without his head knight there to help his denial stay strong, Silvertip fell into confusion. I held up a hand to forestall his questions.

"You guessed a lot accurately about me, but you didn't have all the information, so I'll give it to you. Let's start with this: what grown man in this day and age believes in demons? Actually believes you can make deals with them, like in folktales? Actually believes that doing so would be a good idea?"

Silvertip shifted and opened his mouth to answer. Then his brow crumpled, and the words died in his throat.

"Exactly," I said. "Avior's playing a game with us, and what that game is is exactly what Bo sent me to find out. Things didn't go to plan—you were alert enough to realize I'd met with Avior. You were also alert enough to realize that something funny was going on in Edenfield. Yes, you were right about that. A madman has been threatening Bo's life, and Bo had to leave to draw him away."

I launched into a full story. It bore about as much resemblance to the truth as chicken nuggets do to actual chickens, but Silvertip seemed to like it. "He must've been planning it for years," he said darkly, when I'd finished. "I remember hearing about how Gil's elder brother was obsessed with demons *ages* ago. It was one of the reasons Lucio was passed over for the prefectship. Talk about your plan backfiring!"

"Be fair," I said, "there is something off about Lucio. He may be genuinely delusional. Or maybe back in his teen years, he went through a phase and never managed to kick the stigma. It makes sense he would play it up now. Or maybe the rumors about his demon obsession were started by Gil—it seems the sort of thing a younger brother would do, doesn't it, if he was determined to be prefect. We can't be sure—but whatever the case, Lucio's certainly run with it."

"I've always known he was mad," Silvertip said. He was the one who looked mad, gripping his knees, eyes hot. "I knew he would betray us, sooner or later, but Signe—well, that doesn't matter. The real question is: is he working alone, or does he have an accomplice?"

"I don't know," I said wearily. "That's why I came to you: you're the only one I could be sure *wasn't* working with him. We'll have to keep our eyes and ears open to spot the traitors. Until then, we'd better not say a word to the others."

"Not a word," Silvertip promised. He might have believed he could keep quiet, too.

I didn't know if I believed it or not, and frankly it didn't matter. The way he was behaving, he'd spread paranoia either way.

Chapter 26:

THREATENING

I woke up.

That's the phrase, and it's as misleading as "the day is long" in winter. It implies that there are two states of being, and that a person is either awake or asleep, without a third liminal state between. The borderlands of sleep, I've heard it called, as if sleep were a country and we foreigners within it.

I have never yet woken up in an instant. Even in my most abrupt, adrenaline-filled moments, there is a lag—jet lag, perhaps, from travel through the borderland.

I woke up.

I traveled between countries too smoothly to pinpoint when the black of sleep slid into the monochrome of the borderlands into the full Technicolor of awake. Cobwebby dreams clung to my mind before giving way to the winds of consciousness. Sensations returned: the unfamiliar texture of Bo's sheets sliding against my bare shins and catching on my nightgown; the hugeness of the bed. No morning light touched my eyelids. What had woken me?

I shifted and began to roll over, and a weight tumbled off my chest. I tried to brush it away, but it was heavier than expected and not the right texture for sheets or blankets. Sleep sand gummed the corners of my eyes as I peeled them open.

I hit the light switch at the far end of the room before I'd processed what I was looking at. My chest heaved and my eyes bulged. My brain, sleep logged, took about a decade to catch up and another decade to decipher the information into plaintext.

It was a rabbit. A tapeti, to be exact, the Brazilian cottontail that, within Carina, is endemic to Batata Prefecture. I knew every line of its tan legs, its white chest and neck ring, the dark fur speckling up its back to the top of its head, the precise oval of its upright ears and the slope of its snout. I knew the way it would move when alive, the quick, scattered movements of a full colony. I knew how impossible it was to see when hunkered against a dirt hill, perfectly motionless except for the quivering of its nose.

I knew what it was like dead, too, as this one most certainly was. Its head had rolled off the bed away from me, toward the door. The rest of its body, neck cleanly hacked through, flopped brokenly on the chocolate-brown sheets.

There was a lot of blood. The front of my nightgown was one spreading blood stain, and further stains sprayed the wool blankets and soaked the sheets.

The tapeti isn't huge, as rabbits go. This one was maybe fourteen inches from nose to tail, not counting its ears. Not huge—but it'd have been difficult, restraining its struggling body with one hand and bringing down a knife with the other. Difficult, but clearly not impossible. There was way too much fresh blood for the animal to have died anywhere else, and the body had been warm.

But I locked my door!

And Silvertip had locked his.

A glimmer of an idea came to me about that, only to be brushed away by anger. I wasn't afraid. Wouldn't be afraid. I'd been more than half expecting something like this anyway, though I admit I'd thought locking the door and wedging books under the window latches would be enough.

Did Torben think I was a complete idiot?

You haven't done much to convince him otherwise.

Oh, please, like he'd looked for evidence before making assumptions. I'd spent my whole life dealing with this drivel: small meant victim. Pretty meant dumb. Female meant hapless. What else did a man like Torben need to judge me?

My fists clenched. Breath heaved through my chest. I clicked my teeth together, considering my next course of action. Then I got cleaned up and dressed.

I put on all white, like the proprietress. It seemed appropriate.

I'd gotten up early but not earlier than the Gulbransens. They were already in the kitchen, chopping boards out, preparing meals fit for prefects. Cai had dough rising in the warm oven, and only grudgingly moved it atop the refrigerator so I could use the broiler. I heard Batata enter the dining room while I worked, but I didn't go out to see him. Bad enough that the Gulbransens saw what I was up to without my giving the prefects any ideas.

When I reached my office, the calm of performance descended. It's always this way with me: I'm only nervous or upset or distressed up until the point. When it comes to it, I settle right down, intent on nothing except the task before me. Calmly, therefore, I cleared off the desk and arranged the platter upon it. Calmly, I picked up the landline and pressed the button for the knighthouse.

I wasn't surprised that Torben was the one to pick up—or that he did so upon the first ring.

"Captain Nass," I said, with the tone of a woman trying desperately to keep herself under control, "would you please come to my office immediately?"

"Are you in danger, prefect?"

How strange it was, hearing that dry-leaf voice divorced from its face.

I swallowed, the sound barely audible over the line, and made sure he could hear the faint smacking of lips. "I require your presence without delay. There is a . . . matter . . . I'd like to discuss with you."

"I'll be there directly," Torben promised, and the line clicked.

I returned the phone to its cradle and settled myself behind the desk to wait. My hair and makeup were flawless, my expression polite expectation, my posture proper but relaxed. I stood, a welcoming smile spreading, when Torben slammed through the door at a run.

My smile faded into gentle confusion at the way the door banged against the wall and Torben skidded to a halt. "Prefect?" he snapped, primed for trouble.

"You are prompt," I congratulated him, "though I didn't mean you had to run. Still, I appreciate your keenness."

Torben's head tilted, and he remained on high alert as he swayed and stalked to the desk. "What is this?"

The covered platter had been designed for a turkey or goose, and really was excessively large for my purposes, but it had been the only one available. "Breakfast," I said. "Please, sit with me."

I sat, and he leaned at me.

"We don't have a lot of free time this week," I chided him, "which makes it all the more important that we take good care of ourselves and eat well. Join me, Torben. You're my head knight and I'm your prefect; we ought to be on good terms."

"I've already eaten," he said.

I shook my head and tsked. "Nonsense; it's barely six-thirty. The sun won't rise for another hour, and you'll be running around until long after it has set. You need the energy of a proper meal. I won't take no for an answer; prefect's prerogative. Sit down, Torben. Time's a-wasting."

Torben sat: rigid, frowning, making no attempt to pretend he believed me.

"I was hoping you'd tell me more about my predecessor, and what he intended for this conference," I said sweetly, handing him plate, fork, and butter knife, and giving myself the same. "For your lap," I told him maternally, passing over a cloth napkin. "Bo hardly had time to give me instructions before he left. I found his phone number, natu-rally, but he isn't answering it. As head knight, you must have some idea—ah."

I lifted the platter lid and inhaled blissfully. "I hope you don't mind spices. Those of us brought up in Batata can't bear our meat plain. I guess I'll have to learn new habits, here in Edenfield."

Torben made a strangled noise, which I took for assent, and I began carving.

This was the first rabbit I'd skinned, gutted, and butterflied in years, but it's not something you forget how to do: just like peeling off a sock and scooping out gourd seeds. It hadn't come out badly, I thought, and the ultra-spicy sauce I'd drizzled over it would hide any rough spots. I'd spooned some leftover boiled potatoes around the rabbit to fill in the platter and hide my cutting job, and sprinkled fresh cilantro over the top. It smelled magnificent and looked like something Luc might have put together—probably because Gina had taken pity on me and helped out.

"Do you have a preference?" I asked politely, carving knife poised. "No? I'll halve it."

His expression flickered like an aspen leaf in the breeze.

I wielded the knife lazily, digging the tip into the rabbit and then smacking the top of it to split the spine. Using fork and knife to balance the meat, I transferred one half of the rabbit to Torben's plate and the other to mine. Then I laid the greasy knife across the remaining potatoes, pointed his way, and set the entire platter to one side—easily in my reach but out of his.

"Try a bite," I encouraged him, and made a show of cutting a piece of meat and rolling it around in my mouth. I don't particularly like rabbit, and I'd gone too heavy on the vinegar, but you'd have thought it the finest food on the planet, the way I savored it. "Go on," I told him. "It's delicious."

Torben didn't touch his plate. He sat, wrists propped on the edge of the desk, observing me. Not speaking, not reacting, just observing with those too-pale green eyes and a shuttered mien.

"There's no need to stand on ceremony," I said, wishing he'd give me something to work with—some momentum I could turn to my advantage.

He didn't. Well, if that's the way he wanted to play it, fine. I could adapt.

With harsh movements, I dropped fork and knife and grabbed the rabbit with bare hands. "Like this," I growled, and tore viciously into the meat, tearing off chunks with my teeth, gorging myself on it. Grease and spicy sauce oozed down my chin and wrists, staining my white cuffs. I grinned ferociously through shreds of meat and chewed with my mouth open.

Torben's expression closed down entirely. He might've been made of olivewood or walnut. He stayed like that as I ripped through the last of my meat: distantly observing.

My throat burned, and my stomach pressed against my waistband, tight and aching. I threw the empty carcass onto his plate to drip my saliva onto his untouched food. "Did you think," I snarled, rising, snatching for the carving knife, "that you could scare me away with recycled tricks?"

I barely saw him move. In a blur, he was on his feet, reaching for me. I ducked back, but he was faster. Cold fingers seized my hair and dragged me over the desk. I clawed at his wrist, swearing at him, tears of pain streaming down my face as flesh ripped apart around stitches and scabs.

But I was ready for it, when I hit the floor on the far side of the desk. The moment my feet touched carpet, I launched off, aiming for his eyes. He twisted his wrist sharply. My knees folded, and I fell stomach-first into his chair.

I howled, and immediately Torben's free arm wrapped around my neck, choking the noise to silence. My body went into panic mode, thrashing, tugging, but he left no gaps between his body and mine that would let me get movement, and his arm was like ironwood around my neck, cutting off not just airflow but also blood. A single second stretched, and my legs went limp beneath me.

If he'd wanted to kill me, he could have done it then: eight, nine more seconds of that hold was all it would take. But instead, he released my neck, twisted his hand in my hair to tighten his hold, and dragged me to the far corner of the room. I thrashed weakly at him, but he held me away from his body, out of fingernail range. I was too busy gasping for air anyway, to start thinking about traction.

Torben shoved my face in the corner of wall and carpet, and the rest of my body followed. I bent my legs to try to get them under me, but he simply rested a knee on my backbone and twisted my hair harder.

That was all right. Between gorging myself on the rabbit and being chaired in the stomach, I really had only one recourse: I began vomiting, emptying my stomach of grease and vinegar and masticated rabbit.

Torben didn't spring back in disgust. He held my head up high enough that I didn't suffocate, but no higher; and when I was done, he pushed my head back down again. Vomit squelched beneath my cheek, its sharp, rancid stench setting me off again. I puked and puked until stomach acid burned up my throat and I sobbed for air.

He didn't have to push me back down after that; I was weak as a newborn kitten mewing helplessly for its mother. But he held me down anyway, waiting until my cries had quieted, until the spasms had shivered themselves into micro quivers.

I don't think I've ever hated anyone the way I hated him, in those moments, and there wasn't a thing I could do about it.

"Let me be clear," Torben said, voice soft as the crinkle of fall leaves on their clinging twigs. "Artifice may work on the prideful, the lascivious, the greedy, and the weak-minded, but it will not work on me. You've had your turn playing dress-up and treason, but this is my prefecture and my country, and I will not allow you to continue."

I made a noise of protest, and he ground my face into carpet and vomit until I stopped.

"Your ego," he went on, "is remarkably swollen for a woman of moderate talent who has achieved nothing more in life than a minor secretarial position for a man as far her superior in intellect and status as the redwood is to the weed."

I croaked, "When the other prefects—"

"You want to see the other prefects?" He sprang off my back, his fistful of hair dragging me toward the door.

I mewed and snatched for his wrist with both hands, desperate to relieve the burning in my scalp. "Stop!"

"Stop?" Torben exclaimed. "What for? We're going to see the other prefects. Right now." He threw the office door open and tried to pull me through, but I was determined not to go no matter how much hair it cost me. My clutching hands found the doorframe and held on for dear life, nails scratching lines in the smooth beech.

"What's the matter?" Torben asked me. "You said you wanted to go. Canopus would be impressed, I'm sure. Or Silvertip. Or Avior." He leaned his weight back, and one of my hands slipped from the frame. The other followed soon after, leaving a sliver of fingernail behind.

I thought Torben was going to drag me into the dining room there and then, to parade me in front of Batata and the mud coffee, but he didn't. He released me instead.

I scrabbled upright and back into the office, before anyone could see me. Torben followed deliberately, unhurried. As I sprinted for the knife and grabbed it with both greasy hands, he closed and locked the door behind him. "You won't hurt me," he said.

People always believe that; he was no better than Theodora. I grinned savagely and sprang at him, thrusting the blade at his stomach.

Torben stepped casually to the side and caught my wrist. Without tensing, he turned underneath my arm, and suddenly I was blinking up at him from the floor, the knife tip an inch from my eye. The hilt remained in one of my hands, but he'd twisted the arm in such a way that I had no strength in it. His hand rested on top of mine, supporting the knife, both guiding it and preventing me from releasing it.

He gave me a solid minute for the situation to sink in, and then he peeled my fingers loose and plucked the knife away.

Never turning his back to me and yet unafraid, he put the knife in a desk drawer and stood back, waiting for me to follow him, to attack again. A clump of hair fell from his hand, soaked with blood.

I didn't bother standing. There didn't seem to be any point, and the hot poker bisecting my scalp made a really good argument for rest. I made just enough effort to sit up and scoot my back against the desk, knees propped so I could stare between them. Blood welled through the white tights I'd worn to disguise the scabs. No doubt blood and vomit had smeared my makeup off, revealing the full extent of my injuries.

I really needed to quit ruining my suits like this. Maybe I should invest in armor.

Torben squatted next to me, face barely eighteen inches from my own. I didn't focus on it; it'd only be uglier than ever. The far wall was much pleasanter, once I'd cleaned off and adjusted my glasses.

"Here's what is going to happen," Torben informed me. He was careful not to touch me, I noticed, now that I wasn't fighting him. Interesting. "You are going to gather your belongings," he said, "and your brother, and you are going to leave. You will not speak to anyone. You will not say any goodbyes. I will deliver your apologies."

"Or?" I prompted tiredly. "There's supposed to be an 'or.'"

"Or I'll arrest you for treason."

I nodded. That was a good "or." The one I'd expected. And I believed that he meant it, both parts of it. I believed that he'd let me go if I did what he wanted. Why not? I was nothing to him. What does it matter whether the wasp is dead, as long as it's no longer at your picnic?

I cast my eyes down on the Edenfield signet ring, the crest of midnight purple and ice blue, the edenbear. Carina doesn't have many native mammals; we're a bird sort of place. Our rats and squirrels and rabbits all came from elsewhere, initially. As I remembered it, the edenbear wasn't technically even a bear, just a supremely enormous rodent of some sort. It was found nowhere north of Edenfield, though some managed to survive south of here, in the wind-swept wasteland that was Plisp.

"I'll need that," Torben said, holding out his hand for the ring. The hand was rough and calloused, and I realized out of nowhere that this was the first time I'd seen him without his dog. The realization struck me as ridiculous, and I laughed. Then I realized that Torben could easily have taken the ring from me and thrown me in prison or out of the manor, but he hadn't. Stealing a prefect's ring is treason, and he couldn't risk anyone discovering what he'd done. Not for *my* sake. That made me laugh even harder, high and hysterical, a trickle of red running down my forehead and into my eye.

If Torben hadn't already thought I belonged in a madhouse, that laugh would've convinced him.

He let the crazy lady calm down again before he said, "Hand over the ring, and you can go."

He hadn't beaten me as I'd feared, or not in the only way that mattered to him. I laughed again and said, "No."

"Stop it!" He grabbed my arms and shook me. I flopped obligingly. "Shut up! This is serious. Give me that ring, or I'll arrest you and drag you to the knighthouse in front of everyone. The other prefects will see you like this and shame Edenfield. Is that what you want?"

I laughed harder, laughed until a fresh torrent of tears cascaded down my face and my gut sloshed and cramped.

"Stop it!" Torben slapped my cheek. Hard. Pain rang up through the graze and gasped my laughter away.

That was fine by me; laughter made it hard to speak. I said, "Does a head knight assault his prefect?"

The voice was hardly mine. I ached. But I knew he could not win, and that was all that mattered.

He snarled. "A treasonous prefect is no—"

"What treason?"

He broke the sentence, eyes narrowing.

"What treason have you witnessed me commit?" I pressed. "Was it when I refused to let the prefect pass on his duties to the head knight who'd threatened his life? Who kills and mutilates animals for pleasure? Was it when I didn't let myself be harassed and bullied into handing over my prefecture to that same man? Or was it when I refused to give up Edenfield's signet ring to the head knight who attacked his own prefect because she wouldn't scare as easily as her predecessor?"

Torben squeezed my wrist, turning his nails in and digging. Wild light lit his mossy-green eyes. He might do anything, like that. He might kill me. The safe thing would be to back down, but I wasn't thinking safe. I was thinking *winning.*

There was pain, but I made no sound of it, and the tears dried from my eyes. "Ugly, cowardly little man," I grated, "there's the knife. Cut the ring off my finger if you want it. If you dare."

The hand squeezed harder and then abruptly released. Torben stood and backed away—paced to the door, stiff and brittle as dead grass, and then spun and paced back, unhooking handcuffs from his belt. The ordinary kind, with a chain linking the cuffs. The rogue danger in his eyes had vanished, replaced with something subtler.

"Mercedes Cartier," he said, kneeling and snapping the cuffs on my wrists, "I'm placing you under arrest for impersonating a king's agent, willfully manipulating a prefect, and attempting to sabotage the prefects' conference."

Chapter 27:

DISORDERLY CONDUCT

One of the most essential skills of the truly accomplished liar is the ability to successfully respond to accusations. The downfall of this skill is that it is utterly useless when the person you're talking to will not under any circumstances believe anything you say—not just because he knows you're a liar; that can be overcome. But because he is personally set against you, and will dismiss your words without ever really hearing them.

My laughter had left me a light-year ago, and my voice rasped when I forced out words. "On what evidence?"

"On my testimony," Torben replied, "and my witness."

I twitched my lips up, closing my eyes and leaning my head back against the desk. "Testimony that directly contradicts mine. One voice against another. Prefect against head knight."

"You're forgetting Lord Holst."

I shook my head, rocked the back of it side to side against the solid desk. "You're right. I should have said *prefects* against head knight. Chivalry isn't dead."

"Once Lord Holst has the situation explained to him—"

I opened my eyes and looked up at him. He was standing again, rising above me. Not so sure of himself as he'd like. "Once Bo has the situation explained," I said, "he'll say three things. First, that his head knight manipulated and threatened him into abandoning his post.

Second, that his head knight did this in order to get the prefectship for himself, and that only my presence prevented this catastrophe. Third, that I never attempted to make him leave—that I encouraged him to stay; you were the one telling him to leave—and that I never asked to be made prefect or in any way acted against either Edenfield or him."

Torben scoffed, but I'd seen him rear back from these accusations. "I notice you don't deny lying about being a king's agent," he said.

I raised my handcuffed wrists and dropped them again. "What's to lie about? You saw what happened. I showed him my identification and told him what it meant. You verified my words. You can check my ID again if you like, but you'll find that it's real. I have plenty of colleagues who'll vouch for me."

"Then why are you *here?*" Torben snarled. "Why would a cryptanalyst's personal assistant appear out of nowhere, assault one of my knights, and break into the manor? Why would you force the prefect to change the conference location?"

I'd gotten him pacing. Not much—a couple of steps as he spoke.

"Would you believe I'm just a concerned citizen?" I asked.

"I would not."

"I am, though—both concerned and a citizen. You can hardly deny there is a lot going on here to be concerned about. But"—he'd opened his mouth to interrupt—"you're right: I was sent. My then-boss, Sr. Jon Nordfeld, was invited by Prefect Avior to be his guest at the conference, and Sr. Nordfeld is a very particular man. He likes things *just so*, and I was to ensure a smooth stay." I blinked broadly up at him. "You saw yourself how surprised I was that Sr. Nordfeld didn't arrive with Prefects Avior and Lindo."

"I have seen you pretend a great many things," Torben said, "surprise being the least of these."

I shrugged, letting this roll off one shoulder.

Torben tried again. "Nordfeld. Another concerned citizen, I suppose?"

"Cryptanalysts are a strange lot," I said, with feeling, thinking of Sr. Basile. "Who knows what he wants and why he wants it? If he were here, you could ask him."

"But as he's in a Lindo prison, he's none of my concern," Torben said, "and he wasn't the one who changed the conference location."

"No," I agreed; "that was Bo. After having met Prefect Lindo, can you dispute his decision?"

"I can dispute your motivation."

"Ah, but let's review the actual situation," I said. "You threatened Prefect Edenfield until he fled, and you tried to do the same to his replacement. It's pretty clear what's going on, isn't it? This is a power grab. You want Edenfield... and perhaps not only Edenfield. How powerful would you be if you could discredit the prefects in front of the king—or in front of Prince Emok, should the king prove unavailable? Any astute king would have grown wise to the con man's pretty face, but who better to take into a royal confidence than Torben Nass, ugly but honest, so loyal that he stuck by the crown even though it meant betraying his prefect. So—"

I gasped and cringed away. I couldn't help it; he was *fast.* I thought he was going to strike me, but no. He stopped short, out of reach, tamped down by staggering self-control. I curled into the desk, words lost.

It felt like we stayed that way for ages, me frozen with my back to the desk and knees hiding my face, not breathing; him on the knife-edge of temptation.

When he spoke again, it was as if from a great distance. "Silvertip is no friend to you."

My face must have indicated the obviousness of this statement, because he added, "Nor Avior."

"Nor Lindo, nor Tey, nor Fjordland," I said. "Nor you, nor any of the others. I didn't come here to make friends."

It took Torben a long time to answer. I'm used to seeing people shut off, from working with Sr. Nordfeld, but never like this—never from one extreme to the other, from vast emotion to cool distance. It's something I'd like to be able to do myself, but I never think of it in the moment. If I plan ahead of time, I can separate myself and prevent strong emotion, but once I'm angry, it's hard for me to remember to stop. To want to remember. It takes a real shock to interrupt me.

I'd had a real shock. I couldn't seem to find any words. I was glad when Torben spoke again, tonelessly, having reanalyzed the situation and come to a decision.

"You may wish you'd let yourself be frightened off," he said. He stepped back and moved to leave. His hand was on the doorknob when he stayed himself, half-turned, and tossed something small and glittering onto the carpet by my feet.

The handcuff key.

Ten minutes, maybe fifteen. That was how long our meeting had lasted. That was also how long it took me, after Torben had left, to pull myself together enough to crawl over, grab the handcuff key, and stand up. When I peeked into the hallway, nothing had changed and no one was visible. As far as anyone else was concerned, the encounter might never have happened.

It took me twice fifteen minutes to get cleaned up and calmed down, and that long again before I'd prepped and primped and perfumed myself to my satisfaction. I wanted to look perfect, too perfect for anyone to imagine me looking otherwise.

Bo's antibiotic ointment was expired, but I used it anyway. He had plenty of aspirin, and I cupped my hands under the tap for water to get it down.

When I emerged from the bathroom, I found Francis lying on my carpet, staring blankly at the ceiling. I lay on the floor next to him to try out the view, but it was only a ceiling, and I was wrinkling my outfit, so I got back up again.

"I keep calling and texting her," he said, "but she won't answer. I know I should give up, let her go, but I keep hoping. Is a 'goodbye' too much to ask?"

No prizes for guessing whom he was talking about. Something clenched in my throat, and I swallowed it back down. I wasn't sorry for killing Theodora; I did my best to be proud of myself. She'd needed to be stopped, and it had been my duty to stop her in the only way I could. If I'd walked away, part of me would have been responsible for all the future deals she made, all the people she mutilated and hacked body parts off and murdered.

But that didn't make it easy to think about, or pleasant, and I could not afford to let the roiling ball of rawness in my stomach catch up with me, not now. I had to concentrate on what was important in the moment, or more people would suffer.

I asked, "Have you slept?"

Francis didn't seem to have heard me. He said, "I can take a hint. I can. I only wanted to hear her say it in her own voice, to give me that closure. Even if she doesn't apologize. I could understand that."

"Francis," I said, "I know this is hard, but you've gone through this before. You'll be fine in a week or two, and there'll be another woman."

"Not like this one." Francis rotated his body my way. He hadn't slept a wink. I idly wondered if, as Prefect Edenfield, I could order him to visit a sleep doctor in such a way that he'd have to obey. Maybe if he resided in this prefecture. Or maybe I could ask the king to order him, as part of my reward. That and nine years' hard labor for Torben sounded about right. Or the cat-o'-nine-tails. Whichever.

"You just don't understand, Mercedes," Francis moaned. "I'm going to be alone forever."

He was looking full at me, but he couldn't see anything wrong. I'd done a good job with my makeup, then, because Francis would notice if anyone would—even through his melodramatics. But the funny thing was that as soon as I assured myself of this, I found that I desperately *wanted* him to notice. I wanted to tell someone what had happened. I wanted someone to take my side.

But pride won—or shame, I guess. "I'm going to head to breakfast," I told him. "I know you're feeling low, but you need to pull yourself together. We're beginning at nine this morning; that gives you nearly an hour to pour some coffee down your throat and get your brain straightened out. Maybe take a shower."

"It won't matter," Francis said. "They're not going to say anything interesting. Besides, we're recording everything. You can just tell me if anything happens."

I shook my head. "That relies on a secondary factor. What if you notice something I don't? Or what if something stops me from getting back to you? Or what if the delay makes an essential difference? No, Francis: you said you'd help, so now you need to help. Besides, I've been working on them."

He groaned.

"On which note," I added, "watch out for Torben."

Francis raised his head. "The head knight? Is he still around?"

I nodded. I hadn't meant to bring up Torben; it'd just slipped out, and now it required explanation. "He's the one who made the voodoo doll for Bo."

Francis perked up. I'd told him about the doll yesterday when I'd showed him the ring, but there hadn't been time for details.

The topic was safe enough, so I curled up on a chair and went over the incident again, including Torben's folktale threat, and that led naturally to the cottontail in my bed this morning—

"That's where the blood came from?" Francis exclaimed.

I frowned at him. "What did you think it was? No, never mind. I can guess."

In my flurry of activity, I had never dealt with my bedding. There simply hadn't been an opportunity, though each time I'd passed my bed, I'd seen the mess of blood-encrusted sheets and made a mental note to hand them to Gina. Then again, I didn't want to freak her out. Maybe, I thought as I unwound myself from the chair and set about stripping the bed, I could get Francis to deal with it. Or do it myself, in my copious free time.

"Francis," I said, "most of this blood is at chest level or above. Do we need to have a chat about basic anatomy?"

"I didn't look closely. I was respecting your privacy."

The sheets were resisting my efforts to peel them off. I tugged at them, increasingly exasperated. Why wasn't this *working?* Tears of helpless frustration beaded in my eyes, but the joke was on them: I was wearing waterproof mascara.

I tugged harder, helpless against the fitted sheet. What was I doing wrong? Why wouldn't it come off? Why was this so difficult? Why—

"Mercedes, sit down," Francis ordered me, alarmed. "I'll do it."

"I can strip my own bed!"

"Sit *down.*" He pushed me toward a chair, and I slapped him. He stepped away but didn't back down. "Fine. Sit down on your own. But stop screaming at the sheets."

I hadn't been screaming. Had I?

I sat down and watched Francis, in two easy movements, strip off the dirty sheets and the mattress cover beneath. The mattress itself had survived its second ordeal in a row.

I didn't move when Francis left or when he returned with fresh sheets and blankets—blue ones, to match the furnishings upstairs, and blessedly clean. He remade the bed while I watched, and I found myself talking again, to fill the silence.

Once I had started, I couldn't stop. I disgorged my morning from beginning to end, leaning rigidly over folded legs, gripping the chair. At some point, I found I'd begun striding, gesticulating. Story time had long ended in favor of theorizing, threatening, ranting, working myself up even as Lindo had.

I clamped my mouth shut. The comparison was too appalling.

"I'm going to beat him to a pulp," Francis announced, flexing his hands. He was flushed dark and breathing hard. I must have been working him up at the same time as myself, without realizing it. Well, why shouldn't he be worked up? He was my brother. "You can stay here," he told me, "or you can come watch. But he's going to wish he was never born."

About time someone stood up for me, I thought. Then my better sense surged back, bringing with it the red dye of alarm. "Francis, you can't. He's a head knight."

Francis's growl was eloquent.

"Francis," I said. "Francis!"

Francis was not listening to me. He was lunging away, out of the bedroom, down the wood-paneled hall.

"Francis, calm down!" I ordered, jogging after him. "Francis, he's Edenfield's head knight. *My* head knight. You can't—"

Francis stopped at the front door and swung on me. "Shut up, Mercedes."

I stepped back and folded my arms. "Don't I have a say in this?"

"No."

"Ex*cuse* me?" I demanded, but Francis was already throwing open the front door and thundering outside. I ran after him, yelling at him to *stop*, and that he was going to get in *trouble* and that it wasn't *worth* it, and that as prefect I *ordered* him—

I caught up and grabbed him, and he brushed me off like a fly, not looking back when I hit the ground, not even when I yelped in pain.

"Mr. Cartier," Torben said when Francis flung open the knight-house door and pounded in. I knew it was Torben speaking: no one else has a voice like wind rustling through dry grass. I verified that a second later, when I flung myself in after Francis and saw him. He stood behind his desk, reed thin, four inches taller than my brother but a hundred pounds of muscle lighter. "I can see that you're upset."

Francis's response was more battle cry than coherence, and he charged.

My brother was fast, but Torben was faster. He waited until the last moment and then slid to the side. Francis's right hook went wide, and I thought the left would too, but the desk hampered Torben, and the follow-up clipped his chin.

Torben backed around the desk, wary, graceful and light to Francis's sheer power. Shiro went wild, barking and barking, lunging at Francis's ankles. Francis kicked at the dog, and Shiro squealed and scurried away.

"Grab him," Torben told me, eyes barely brushing mine.

I grabbed the thrashing dog, who rewarded me by barking madly in my ear and then licking it apologetically. The back door opened and Olaf appeared, baffled and alarmed. Torben cut a silent hand at him, and Olaf stayed put.

"Stop it," I said, and didn't know if I was talking to Francis or Torben or the dog. "Stop it!"

Francis moved in, tight and low, first jabbing and then windmilling into a baffling whirl of motion: punching, kicking, kneeing, snapping his teeth. Most men would've gone down under that, but Torben stood his ground, utterly focused. It felt like he was hardly moving, fast though he was, the eye of the whirlwind: ducking, blocking, avoiding hits, but not attacking. It was utterly breathtaking, watching these two—until I realized that Torben wasn't fighting my brother; he was playing with him.

Any inclination I might've had for fairness vanished. I put the struggling Shiro on the floor and let him go. The little dog immediately ran for its master, interrupting the careful footwork, the ease of the game, and Torben had to stumble aside or step on his pet.

Francis pressed his advantage, landing a sledgehammer punch on Torben's stomach and, when Torben doubled over, smashing a second one against his cheekbone.

Torben lurched back with the blow, and Francis grabbed his shirt to punch him again.

That was what Torben had been waiting for. He put a hand over Francis's, fingers wrapping around the base of the thumb, thumb pressed between the middle and ring knuckles. Then he dropped his weight and leaned in.

Francis blenched and crumpled instantly. All the rage in the world couldn't keep him upright, and muscles don't do you any good when they're working against you.

I'd seen the move before, in my self-defense classes, though I couldn't have replicated it. Using techniques in an actual fight is a lot different than in practice, and I'd used the only aikido move I knew well on the creature in the auction house. Like that one, this move, done properly, stopped your opponent instantaneously without doing any permanent damage. Aikido is a purely defensive martial art.

Of course, part of the reason aikido's purely defensive is that when done aggressively, you don't just disable your opponent so you can escape—you break their bones, dislocate their joints, and even kill them. Such as, to take a random example, when your opponent shoves a broiled rabbit at you and then attacks you with a knife and you maneuver that knife around so that they're shoving it at their own eye. Lean your weight in and, with barely any effort, you've made them stab themselves through the brain—and who could blame you for defending yourself?

Francis gasped in agony, unable to wriggle away without shattering his wrist. Torben reached back with his free hand, unhooked a fresh pair of handcuffs from his belt, and casually shook them out. He snapped one bracelet around Francis's torqued wrist, then switched hands so he could bring up the other wrist. Only once Francis was secured did Torben relax the wrist lock at all, and then it was only to twist it another way so that, with an agonized yelp, Francis was forced to his feet.

Olaf, eyes shining, held the door open as Torben guided my brother forward with one hand on the back of his neck. Then Olaf followed Torben in, to attach the cuffs to a ring on the wall above a bench, presumably installed for exactly that purpose.

Francis recovered enough to start swearing at them, and he kept swearing even after Torben and Olaf had returned to the main room and closed the door behind them.

Torben looked at me. I looked at him. Shiro whined and rubbed long white hairs onto his master's uniform.

"Such violence," I said. I crouched and clicked my fingers at Shiro, who obligingly trotted over to have his chin scratched. I smiled prettily up at the men, both of them. I really poured it on, and kept pouring it. To Olaf, I said, "He told me the Japanese folktale, the one about his dog. What I want to know is: has he banned all shovels from the prefecture, like the spinning wheels in 'Sleeping Beauty'?"

Olaf laughed. "I hope not! If he has, we're breaking the law—along with everyone else in Edenfield!"

"In that case," I said, "you'd better keep an extra close eye on Shiro here until we can find the madman who's been killing animals. Have you run any tests yet? DNA? Blood analysis?"

With a pained glance at Torben, Olaf sobered up. "Sure, we've started, but we didn't find anything helpful. We didn't find anything the previous times either, with the notes. I'm sorry, prefect. I wish I had better news for you. Um." He shot another look at Torben and then back at me. I kept my gaze steady and polite, as if his boss and my brother hadn't just been brawling all over the knighthouse, as if papers hadn't fluttered to the floor and pens rolled and chairs overturned.

Torben didn't stir. He wasn't breathing heavily, but I consoled myself that he probably didn't have concealer, which meant I could look forward to seeing some lovely new bruising on his jaw.

"I appreciate you looking after my brother," I said, sweet as sucrose. I gave Shiro one last scratch and stood to brush myself off. White fluff clung to the sweat on my hands. "He's an insomniac and hasn't slept more than one night in the last five. Twenty-four hours in the drunk tank is exactly what he needs. I hope it isn't too inconvenient, watching over him. You understand that I can't have him around the other prefects when he's like this."

"Of course," Olaf said, hugely relieved to have this explanation.

Torben watched me inscrutably. What'd he expect, that I'd start accusing him to his subordinate? That I'd try to bull my way past to free my brother? Francis was worse than useless when he was out of control, and unless he got some sleep, he'd only escalate.

In all honesty, I think I'd found Francis more alarming than the knights had.

My oh-so-pretty smile took on a sharpish edge. I said to Torben, "You will contact me if there are any developments?"

"Of course, my lady," Olaf assured me. "Happily."

Torben moved abruptly. I tensed, but he was only going to his desk and reaching for a slim sheaf of stapled papers. He picked them up and carried them to me, offering them at arm's length.

I took the sheaf and flipped through. It was maybe twenty pages long and single spaced, with bold headers and bullet-pointed lists. The words "lumber," "border," and "fiscal" jumped out at me; they were repeated often enough. Even at a glance, I could see multiple mistakes in the typing, as if the document had been written in a tremendous hurry. Not just written this morning, either: he must've begun preparing this almost as soon as I'd become acting prefect.

"Study it," said Torben, "and ask me if you have any questions; that is only the bare minimum. Pay close attention to the checklist on the first page: I've included everything that must be discussed in the conference." He gave me a little bow. For the sake of Olaf's eyes, he made it look genuine. "I advise you to use your time wisely."

Chapter 28:

SEDITION

I used my time wisely, although my first act had nothing to do with the manuscript Torben had given me and everything to do with scooping and scrubbing vomit out of the office carpet, returning the dirty dishes to the kitchen, and cleaning them. I drank down a tall glass of water and hesitantly ate a few salted crackers to settle my stomach.

Barely twenty minutes remained after that, before the day's meetings began. Not nearly enough for me to read the entire sheaf of papers, let alone fully digest it, so I didn't try. Instead, I cross-compared sections to my notes from the day before, and managed to answer two of the questions I'd promised to ask Bo about before the other prefects joined me. I managed a lot more by skipping lunch, and quite competently put in my grains of salt at several points during the afternoon segment. Then back I went to studying.

Since it was blatantly impossible for me to come across as omniscient regarding Edenfield matters to the other prefects, I let them see exactly what I was doing. I kept my notes and Torben's in front of me on the table and consulted them whenever anyone asked me a question—or said I would answer tomorrow. I listened attentively when the others were speaking and remained humble, eager, polite, and devastatingly sweet. The only one who ever made a snide comment was Lindo, when Silvertip had set her off, and the others looked quite embarrassed for her. Poor Prefect Edenfield had been dumped in this position at the last second; terribly bad form to make fun of her when she's doing her best. And a jolly good job she's doing of it, too.

That was the easy part, and it gave me strength to return to the knighthouse that evening around nine, after I'd stuffed as much of the manuscript as possible into my brain. Torben wasn't there, but Roald had him summoned in no time, and I kept him up until midnight, asking questions and clarifying details.

He did not bring up our encounter in the office or, indeed, anything not directly related to the subject at hand. He had the courtesy not to express any surprise that I was grown up enough not to betray my prefecture because I was displeased with its head knight. Indeed, it wouldn't have shocked me if he thought me what I thought Silvertip: someone who just needs to be beaten to be your best friend.

Frustrating though it can be to be misestimated, it sure can be useful—and I made awfully sure that neither Torben nor Roald saw a hint of what festered beneath my professional veneer.

That was Tuesday. On Wednesday, we discussed Tey Prefecture for most of the morning . . . and then it was my turn, Edenfield's turn, to present.

I was ready, or as ready as I'd ever be. With Torben's assistance, I'd outlined my exact speech, full of bullet points, essential questions that needed answering, deals that needed brokering, and little boxes to check off when I'd finished each point.

I began with the mundane items, the things that wouldn't cause anyone an unduly high heart rate—lumber featured heavily—and only in the mid-afternoon moved into issues of national security.

"Unfortunately," I said, tapping my notes, "we simply don't have the manpower to ensure the border's security, let alone patrol Plisp." I did not give exact statistics; far be it from me to reveal Edenfield's military secrets to the other prefectures—even if I knew them. "Both Vela and Akter have planted landmines along their borders, causing the accidental deaths of several Carinan citizens. We have evidence that one or both of them may be moving their landmines further inland. I have records of two injuries and one fatality resulting from a mine fewer than five miles from our border."

"Has it been reported to the crown?" Canopus asked.

"There have been multiple reports," I said. "None has been met by any response."

"Typical."

"Typical?!" Tey slammed the table, flushing hot. "Is that what we're saying now? That it's typical for acts of war to be met by silence?"

"Tobias—"

"No, prefect, I will not be quiet. Not while that man is sitting at the table with us." He stabbed a finger at Avior. "How can you let this continue? How could you betray us? Knights dying, our borders flooded with spies, and nothing but silence from the man whose duty it is to protect us!"

Avior looked from one of us to the next, utterly baffled. "Why are you yelling at me?" he asked. "What have I done? I'm not the king."

"Don't pretend you don't know!"

Avior clearly didn't know. "Are you accusing me of something?"

"Too right I am. I'm accusing you of—" Tey's eyes caught on my face, and his teeth clicked shut.

I didn't smile or do anything but look on with mild, neutral interest. I hadn't spoken personally to either Tey or Lindo; they'd struck me as too volatile. But clearly, someone had done my job for me.

"He's accusing you of conspiring to betray us to the king, Avior," Silvertip drawled. "Don't look at me like that, Canopus; Edenfield obviously knows."

Every eye was on me in an instant. I kept my shoulders and jaw relaxed, confident, unsurprised, intelligent.

"What does she know?" Lindo asked dangerously. "What have you been telling her?"

"Nothing!" Silvertip snapped. "She already knew! She knows everything! Isn't that obvious?"

No one answered him, although plenty of the prefects shifted uncomfortably.

"What do you know?" Lindo shot at me.

Hemmel cleared his throat. "Surely, it isn't necessary to—"

"Shut up."

"It's true that I never heard her say it outright," Avior observed. "The rest of us said it, even Bo, but never her."

"True," I agreed. "I have been circumspect—but then, each of you has been likewise."

"We don't have anything to prove," Canopus said. "We're real prefects."

"And I am Bo's representative," I said, keeping my tone steady and unbothered, politely neutral. "I act as he has instructed."

"I don't trust Bo," Lindo growled. "He ran away and left us in this mess. None of us knows you; you appeared out of nowhere."

"Come now," Silvertip interjected, "you aren't implying this has all been a bluff. She knows far too much. It's obvious."

"You're only saying that to cover your backside," Canopus said.

"Whereas you prefer to keep yours uncovered."

Classic flyte, but Canopus didn't take it up. She'd turned back to me, thoughtfully adjusting her gold-edged cuffs. "Come to think of it," she said, "when I spoke with her, she was very careful, very exact. Said a lot, but nothing that could be taken the wrong way, if reported to the palace."

I'd been hoping she wouldn't notice that. Classic rule of lying: when possible, don't say anything actually untrue.

Silvertip rolled his eyes. "You're paranoid, Canopus."

"And you're overconfident. I want to hear her say it outright."

Lindo nodded. "I agree."

"Me too," Hemmel said quickly.

Tey bounced in his seat. "We should make it official! Record it for posterity! Write out a statement of intent and sign it!"

"No!" cried every other prefect there, me included.

"We don't want to leave a trail," Hemmel said scathingly, with one eye on Lindo. "Right?"

"If she doesn't say it," Canopus said, "we should lock her up until afterward. We don't want any possibility of her interfering—or blabbing."

"Or we could otherwise silence her," Avior murmured.

"You're being excessive and melodramatic," Silvertip complained.

"I wasn't saying we should *show* anyone the document," Tey grumbled. "Why do *my* ideas always get shot down?"

"Let's take a vote," Canopus proposed. "Everyone who wants acting Prefect Edenfield to make a statement regarding you-know-what, hand on the table." She laid her right palm flat on the table, left hand tucked on her lap. The others followed suit, including the reluctant Tey and Silvertip. Sheep.

Clever sheep. Sheep who could well turn into foxes at the first sign of wriggling from me. I had to be very, very careful here and give them exactly what they wanted. But if I had to be recorded speaking treason, I was going to make darn sure I wasn't the only one.

I put my right hand on the table. "A reasonable and sensible precaution," I said, "and one I'm surprised we haven't taken before. You want to be secure that I am who I say I am and am behind you one hundred percent. And I want the same guarantee. I will make an appropriate statement—and then each of you will do the same, clearly and distinctly, so that we can trust one another. Then and only then will we discuss the hanging sword: the possibility that one of us"—a glance at Avior—"is our enemy."

"That's exactly what I suggested!" Tey complained.

"Except sane," said Canopus.

Lindo leaned in, forearms bracing on the table, muscles tense, nostrils flaring. "I agree," she said. "Let us proclaim ourselves together, once and for all."

"I agree too," said Hemmel.

"So do I," said Tey, "since it was my idea to start with."

"Fine," said Canopus.

"If we must," said Silvertip.

"I hate this," said Batata. "Yes, yes, I'll do it. But I hate it."

"Hmm? I—yes? Is that the right answer?" said Fjordland, when prodded.

"Edenfield will go first," Avior decided. "And, since Tey has the grace to doubt me, I will go second."

I had the stage, or the stage had me. I wasn't nervous about that part of it. As it so happens, I've always been comfortable on stage. It was more that I was struck by the sudden notion that Sr. Nordfeld might have been wrong about the prefects. Maybe regicide wasn't what they were after. Maybe I was about to make a grave error.

But no, that was absurd. I had proof, many times over proof of what they intended. And ... and, admittedly, after reading Torben's document and hearing what the other prefects had to say, it made a sick sort of sense. If I could trust their reports, there was definitely something wrong in Carina. Akter and Vela were making aggressive, inappropriate moves, and the king didn't appear to be doing anything about it—or even responding to the reports. I could understand how, in desperation and frustration (on Edenfield's part), regicide might seem like a necessary response.

Personally, though, I wasn't convinced that the king was the problem, let alone that killing him would solve that problem. I saw it like this:

Point One: Someone else might be interfering with royal decrees; and if so, murdering the king would only worsen the problem.

Point Two: If the king wasn't being interfered with, he might be keeping his cards close to his chest as a purposeful strategy to maintain the element of surprise. In that case, killing him would substantially weaken Carina's position.

Point Three: Even if he were the problem, I wasn't convinced that the problem was desperate enough to justify killing—or that killing him was the only or best solution.

Point Four: If the prefects succeeded in killing Emil II, the end result would be Prince Emok as a puppet king controlled by Canopus or Silvertip's wife or some other individual who should really, really not have that sort of power.

What a bizarre circumstance I'd landed in, that I found myself making a mental point-by-point list of why *not* to murder someone even while I was standing, making eye contact with each prefect in turn, and proclaiming with perfect enunciation:

"I, Mercedes Cartier, acting Prefect Edenfield, for the benefit of my prefecture and my nation, declare King Emil II incompetent and negligent of his duty. I therefore hereby bind myself to my fellow prefects in seeking his death—and to, with them, executing him at this conference by any means necessary."

Then I shut my mouth and sat down, the thudding of my pulse heavy in my ears. I imagined I could hear the whirring of the spy device Sr. Nordfeld had so carefully planted, that everyone must have been able to hear it. But that was nonsense; it didn't use tape.

A beat elapsed, and then a relieved sigh traveled around the table as the prefects relaxed. I'd gotten it right, and after only an eternity or two, Avior stood to take his turn. He had to clear his throat twice before beginning. "I, Lucio Winter, Prefect Avior . . ."

He followed my formula. Most of them did, although Prefect Fjordland kept getting confused and having to be prompted. Tey launched into a passionate speech that none of us wanted to hear, and Prefect Lindo said simply, "I want Emil dead, the bastard. He killed my sister."

Lindo was the last. It was quite the note to end on. No one knew what to say next. Silvertip tried an awkward, "See? Told you she knew."

"And now we know," Canopus murmured.

"We're doing this," Tey breathed. "This makes it real."

They said these things, and a few other things besides, but not one was the right thing to say. I made no effort to help them. I had the recording, which was what mattered. All I had to do was sit tight until dinnertime, collect the memory card, and scarper. I'd email and call it ahead and take a physical copy by hand.

Francis, you idiot, I thought. *We have what we need. If you hadn't lost your temper—*

But let that go. It was inconvenient that Francis wasn't listening in, but it wouldn't matter: I was in plenty of time. The king wouldn't be leaving his palace for another twenty-four hours. No problem. And once the palace knew what was up, the king would free Sr. Nordfeld and Francis, arrest the prefects and Torben—and maybe put my mind to rest on a few pressing issues. Then I could go home again.

Back to life as usual. Maybe I'd manage to keep my job, although I'd have to break it to Sr. Nordfeld gently that most of his elaborate plan had been unnecessary. Poor man! He doesn't deal well with the humiliation of being wrong. Well, who does? But I would be kind, and he'd be glad that everything had worked out despite our various mishaps, and then—then maybe things would even be better than before. Maybe—

Anyway, I was indulging such pleasant and optimistic fantasies about what would happen next that, in retrospect, it was no surprise that everything went down the toilet.

"Don't get comfortable," Lindo warned Avior. "I want to hear what this is about you double-crossing me. I warn you, if it's true—"

"You heard my statement," Avior interrupted. "What more do you want?"

"Statements aren't worth much if you've turned king's evidence."

"I haven't." Avior didn't seem upset by the accusation. "You're imagining things because you're stressed, but if you think clearly, you'll recall that killing him means as much to me as it does to you—more."

"Because you want to summon a 'demon'?" Lindo snorted. "Haven't you given that nonsense up?"

"Never."

"Really," said Lindo. "Then why haven't you been pestering me to return your 'expert'?" She was addressing the other prefects as much as Avior. "Lucio found some hack who promised to help him summon a demon—without even checking whether he was an employee for the CSS, which he was. I arrested him, naturally. And since then, Lucio has barely mentioned him! He certainly hasn't begged for him back. Is this the man he wants us to think he is? The man who'd do anything rather than let his one chance at summoning a demon slip between his fingers?"

"Wait, we're not doing the summoning?" Tey asked. "I thought that was, like, a thing."

"We are doing it," Avior said, cold fire burning behind his eyes, "if you want my support. I haven't been pestering you for Jon back, Graça, because I have a replacement—someone almost as good." He twirled his hand my way. "Jon's apprentice."

The room erupted into a mass of confused questions, shocked exclamations, and suspicious mutterings:

"Her?"

"What does she have to do with anything?"

"Prefect *Edenfield's* into demonology?"

"I thought she wasn't your agent. Does this mean she *is* your agent?"

"So we have another crazy prefect. We were only ever going through with this summoning thing to appease Avior—why not appease her, while we're at it?"

I coughed into my fist until I got their attention. "I believe," I said, "that I know what Lucio is referring to. As many of you are aware, I worked alongside of Jon Nordfeld for several years in his capacity of cryptanalyst. Unfortunately, that's where the difficulty comes in. You see, in my opinion, Jon Nordfeld is the last man in the world to be involved with demonology. He certainly never mentioned it to me, and he is, besides, an eminently respectable individual."

"Demonology is perfectly respectful," Avior said.

I flatted my lips to indicate that it certainly was not, even as I said, "Be that as it may, it is my belief that Avior's expert contacted him under an assumed name—Sr. Nordfeld's name—to protect his identity."

"So why were you expecting him here?" Lindo shot at me.

I blinked at her. "Why," I said, "because he told me that Prefect Avior had invited him. He was quite honored. I assume," I said, with perilous humor, "that Prefect Avior didn't tell him the reason for his invitation. What a nasty shock he must have gotten! He guards his reputation terribly, and this *will* be a blow."

"So we're *not* doing this pretend demon-summoning thing?" Tey pressed.

"It's not pretend!" Avior snapped. "You don't have to believe in it, but you do have to do it—that was the deal. And if you renege, you'll find yourself a greater enemy than you can imagine!"

"What grown man believes in demons in this day and age?" Silvertip wondered. "And if he doesn't believe, why insist on the summoning? What does he get out of it?"

"A demon?" Tey suggested, and tittered.

"No," Canopus said, staring hard at Avior. "He gets us. He gets us, in the time and place of his choosing, making a treasonous declaration. That's what he wants: evidence. Something to put on record."

"That's what Nordfeld was for," Lindo realized. "An eminently respectable individual, and a member of the Carinan Security Service, to witness. Maybe he has a specialized recording device; maybe he doesn't need one. The word of a CSS man must be worth a lot, when paired with a prefect." Her eyes narrowed. "My knights didn't find anything when they searched him, which means Avior must have been planning to pass the device on . . . or, more likely, record the meeting himself."

"None of that is true," Avior protested. "You know I don't care about the politics or any of the rest of it: I want my demon, and you promised me you'd help me summon one. You *promised.*"

"I don't believe him," said Canopus. "Do you?"

"No," Lindo said, "I don't."

"Neither do I," Hemmel put in.

"This seems strange," Fjordland murmured. "Why are you attacking Lucio? He's a good boy."

"If Nordfeld's not available, is there any harm in doing the summoning?" Silvertip wondered. "If that's what Avior actually wants, let him have it. He gets his way (if that is his way), and we get ours. Problem solved."

"But I can't do it without my expert!" Avior protested. "You, Edenfield, why didn't you tell me you couldn't do it?"

"I did," I said, but I didn't think Avior was listening any more this time than the last time.

"That plan solves nothing, you blithering idiot," Canopus spat at Silvertip. "He's betrayed us. What if the king already knows, and this was meant only as the final proof? Or what if he runs off to warn him?"

Avior crossed his arms. "I'm not going anywhere until I get my summoning."

"Then we keep Avior and Nordfeld where we can watch them until after we deal with the king—obviously," Silvertip told Canopus. "Why do you have to blow everything out of proportion?"

"We *will* summon my demon," Avior insisted.

"Why don't we—" Hemmel began, but no prefects heard the rest of the sentence; they were too busy shouting at one another.

I sat back and watched them. Batata caught my eye and rolled his, but I looked away.

"SHUT UP!" Lindo bellowed. "EVERYONE, JUST SHUT UP AND LISTEN TO ME!"

No one shut up, and no one listened. No one but me paid Lindo any attention whatsoever except Hemmel, who looked faintly ashamed for her. I'd witnessed that more than once, over the past couple of days: that the other prefects dealt with Lindo's irrationality by ignoring it and hoping it went away—and that, for the most part, it did. I was therefore not overly shocked when, after her first few attempts to bellow herself into prominence, she pulled out her phone and began texting furiously.

How weird would it be if I went for a bathroom break? No, they were too suspicious. *Francis, you idiot,* I thought again, and stopped there, because I was the idiot who'd told my sleep-deprived brother about Torben . . . and had made no effort to get Francis back afterward.

I could just imagine how pleased Francis was with me, after more than thirty hours locked up in the knighthouse. Maybe if I apologized *really sincerely—*

Lindo slammed her phone down on the table. She didn't bother with yelling again. She grabbed Avior's chair, dragged it back and, when he tried to stand, slammed him down with a hand on each shoulder. "You want us to believe you're innocent, you're going to have to prove it," she informed him.

We heard her this time. We could've heard a tack drop.

Avior was more peevish than impressed. "How am I supposed to prove anything when you've kidnapped my expert and that woman"— a finger jabbed my way—"refuses to help?"

True, but not fair. "I *told* you—"

"Excuse me, I was talking," Lindo interrupted.

I was quite impressed with myself, the way I chomped down on my response and gestured submissively for her to continue.

Avior wasn't so politic. He grumbled, "If Jon were here, I could show you. You had no right to keep him away from me. And she"— glowering at me—"didn't tell me until too late that she was useless . . . could have broken him out if I'd known she wasn't going to help . . . still could . . ."

"Do stop whining," said Canopus.

Lindo slammed her fist down on the table. "If any of you would *listen* to me, you'd know that Jon Nordfeld *isn't in Lindo.* He's in the woods, camped out with my women."

Avior's complaints died off, leaving his mouth open.

"My knights started traveling the moment I left," Lindo went on, satisfied that she finally had our full and undivided attention. "They arrived Monday night. I knew I'd need them, and I wanted them on hand. I've just ordered them to move in. Edenfield Manor will be under my complete control in twenty minutes."

The others started yelling again at that—

"You brought your knights here? *Here?*"

"Are you insane?"

"You did *what?*"

—but I was slower. A train of thought chugged through my brain, hooting and whistling, lights flashing, wind whipping the moisture from my tongue.

I'd been content to play Bo's stand-in, to relay everything back to him (or back to Torben's sheaf of papers), but I was more than Bo's voice in the conference. I wore the ring of Edenfield Prefecture. I *was* Prefect Edenfield, not just acting, but the actual prefect, until such a time as Bo returned, with all the powers and duties that entailed. And the number-one priority of any prefect is to protect the sovereignty of her prefecture—and thereby protect her citizens.

I was Prefect Edenfield, and another prefect had, without permission, brought her knights into my prefecture with the intention of taking control of my manor, my seat of power. She had done this, furthermore, for the purpose of preventing me from acting freely.

That was bad enough on its own. But for another prefect to do this during the conference, when the king was on his way, was absolutely—was beyond—was—was simply not acceptable, and it was up to me to stop it. And I had to stop it here, because fine knights though Olaf, Roald, and Torben *undoubtedly* were, no way could they beat back the full power of Lindo Prefecture.

I stood abruptly, rocking the table. "If you're declaring war on Edenfield," I said, voice sturdy and furious, "have the decency to do so *before* you invade."

"Sit down, Edenfield," Lindo snapped. "This isn't about you."

She was taller than I, but I'd had more practice. I shot her a double-barreled glare through my glasses and kept my shoulders back, my head up. "This is my prefecture," I said. "Your knights are not permitted here without my explicit permission."

Lindo snorted. "Having proper backup is more important than stroking your piddling pride."

"I have backup."

She laughed at me. She wasn't the only one.

"After spending an hour complaining about how stretched thin you were?" Hemmel said, in between chuckles. "You were *begging* for reinforcements!"

"I haven't seen a single knight since arriving," Tey put in. "Do you think she has anyone except those ancient servants?"

"How could she fit any, in that tiny knighthouse?"

The two of them might have really hurt my feelings, if I cared what they thought. As it was, I let them prance and otherwise expose themselves. I wouldn't look at them, wouldn't acknowledge them, wouldn't engage with them.

I said, "Prefect Lindo, I forbid you to bring knights into my capital or to my manor. I demand that you remove all knights from my prefecture at once."

"Or what? Face your displeasure?" Lindo rolled her eyes. "Sit down, Edenfield. You've no more power here than Batata, and it's high time you realized that."

"Maybe she'll try to arrest you, if you don't do what she says," Silvertip told Lindo, snickering. Had even he lost his fear of me?

"I have sworn to protect Edenfield from hostile forces, and that includes those from other prefectures. Remove your knights, prefect," I said, still focusing solely on Lindo. "I will do what is necessary to fulfill my duty."

"What's necessary is you calming down," said Avior.

Lindo looked down her nose at me. In another of her unpredictable shifts, she was not out of control now—not now she felt she was in control. "My knights aren't hostile toward you unless you act against me," she said, as one speaking to a child. "And before you try," she warned, "know that, as a precaution, my people have disabled local phone and internet access."

Knocking out communications: the first task of any hostile force intent upon invasion.

"Sit down, Edenfield," Hemmel said.

"You're taking this too seriously," Canopus said.

"Go cool your head," Tey said.

There's nothing quite as infuriating as being told you're overreacting . . . except possibly when you wonder if you are . . . except when you know that, regardless, you can't do anything about the situation.

I've tried my best, throughout my life, to never show my anger when I can't follow through on it. Lindo had looked absolutely ridiculous, throwing a fit that no one listened to and no one took seriously—

and that she hadn't the power to enforce.

Real power doesn't require fits, and if I started yelling, I'd only be demonstrating my level of powerlessness. Absolutely the only reason to do that would be if I wanted to make myself look ridiculous—and how would that help me with my end goal? I needed to get back to the children's room, pick up the recording, and escape, not deal with this.

But oh, how it burned.

I sat and said stiffly, "I'll expect an apology from you over this, Prefect Lindo. In the form of favorable trade negotiations."

"I don't see that I have anything to apologize for," she said.

I smiled pleasantly and fantasized about throttling her. "Maybe not," I said, "but our fellow prefects may wish to consider the precedent you are setting."

"Let's get back to what's important," said Avior. "Jon Nordfeld. I want him. I insist on having him. And I insist that everyone uphold our bargain. We summon the demon, or I'm out."

The other prefects didn't tell *him* to shut up. Unlike Edenfield, Avior had money.

"Here's what I propose," said Lindo: "we bring Nordfeld here. My knights will search him again before he arrives to ensure he's not carrying any illicit technology. Once he does his summoning—regardless of whether it works—we lock him up until everything's finished. In the meantime, we search Avior to make sure *he's* not carrying anything."

Avior put his phone on the table. "Now I'm not," he said, and stepped back. Without being asked, without a hint of bashfulness, he stripped to his underwear and let Silvertip and Hemmel pat him down while Lindo went through his pockets. She found a few tissues, a wallet, a bit of lint—and absolutely nothing that could be used as a recording device. She pocketed the phone herself, presumably to be returned at some later date.

"Clear," Silvertip pronounced.

"Get dressed," Lindo told Avior. "My knights will arrive soon with Nordfeld—and I don't want anyone to give the game away. When Nordfeld gets here, Avior will ask him where he wants to summon the demon. Once he gives his answer, we'll search his chosen room. If we find anything out of place, we'll know he's a spy and treat him accordingly."

"And when you don't find anything, you'll go through with the summoning," said Avior.

"*If* we don't find anything."

Avior beamed at us as he buttoned his shirt, serenely confident. "You won't."

Chapter 29:

APOSTASY

Prefect Lindo's knights were admirably quick and efficient and reached us two minutes earlier than expected. That gave me plenty of time to worry about them finding the spy equipment in the attic but not nearly enough time for me to figure out a satisfactory plan for turning such a discovery to my advantage.

Or to figure out how to stop them from jumping from that find to wondering whether, maybe, there might be spy equipment planted somewhere else as well. Such as in the conference room.

The knights arrived. Tey pulled aside the curtain, and we looked out to the west, toward the tree line on the opposite side of the manor from the knighthouse. Knights swarmed out of the woods in orderly jogs and spread out in every direction, gushes of turquoise and charcoal gray. Dozens of them, and likely dozens more I couldn't see. The vast majority were women: stocky, compact, and in peak physical condition. Not one showed a flicker of feeling that it was, perhaps, not *entirely* appropriate for them to be taking over Edenfield Manor.

I watched them, prefects crowded on either side of me, and thought that if I *had* tried to escape, back when the prefects had been arguing, I wouldn't have made it far.

The door opened behind us, but it was only Prefect Lindo stepping out for a moment to speak with her knights. When she returned, she brought Sr. Nordfeld with her.

His suit was rumpled, his face tired, his complexion unhealthy white over pink. He looked every one of his thirty-five years and entirely out of his element. He belonged in a comfortable office, solving a puzzle or raising his eyebrows at me over the edge of his newspaper, impeccably attired with a cup of tea by his hand. He didn't belong here, dirty and fatigued, being drooled over by scheming and treacherous prefects.

Yet here he was, because it was his duty.

He saw me as I saw him. I loosened my arms and gave him a hint: "Jon," I said, smirking. "How nice to see you."

His expression, already impassive, went completely and carefully blank. "Mercedes, what is this?" he asked. He glanced around at the company I was keeping and asked lightly, "Have you become a prefect in my absence?"

I extended my hand, showing off the ring. "Excellent guess, sir."

"So he didn't plan it," Avior murmured. "Interesting." He didn't interrupt us, though, and neither did the others; they were busy watching Sr. Nordfeld with intense and unhealthy attention.

Sr. Nordfeld's eyes traveled around the room, taking them in: Avior's satisfaction, Batata's resignation, Canopus's contempt, Fjordland's vague geniality, Hemmel's patience, Lindo's aggression, Silvertip's knowing amusement, Tey's anticipation . . . and the normal Edenfield's absence.

Again, he addressed himself to me. "Has something indisposed Lord Holst?"

"He had to leave."

"Of his own accord?"

"By his own power, out of necessity rather than preference."

"And his head knight—Captain Nass, I believe—did not take his place?"

"There aren't many qualified applicants for the position of Edenfield head knight, and Bo thought Torben more essentially placed where he was."

"Ah." He took in the room again, and I could guess a fraction of what he was thinking. For a prefect to assign someone aside from his head knight as temporary prefect was unorthodox and irregular though by no means unheard of; but Bo had no reputation as either unorthodox or irregular, and certainly not as the sort of man who handed over his prefecture to a total stranger without a very, very compelling reason. "I can see," Sr. Nordfeld said sagely, "that there is much I do not yet know."

"You bet there is," Silvertip burst in, laughing. He only laughed harder at Sr. Nordfeld's reproachfully raised eyebrow and downturned lips. Hemmel started to laugh with him, but stopped when no one else joined in.

"This is your demonologist, Avior?" Canopus asked, looking Sr. Nordfeld up and down with undisguised disdain. "He looks like an accountant."

"He's a cryptographer for the CSS," said Lindo.

"Cryptanalyst," Sr. Nordfeld and I corrected as one, and then grimaced at each other.

"Whatever," Lindo said, waving this away.

Sr. Nordfeld looked pained. "I break ciphers, not design them."

"Usually," I muttered.

He inclined his head.

"Some crypt*analyst*," Silvertip jeered. "You never even figured out your assistant was Edenfield's spy!"

Sr. Nordfeld nodded. "Mercedes is a puzzle to be reckoned with," he said gravely. I bit my lip to hide my smile.

"Jon," Avior said, stepping forward, "we are ready to begin the summoning immediately. Please tell my esteemed colleagues where we ought to hold it."

"Careful," I said; "we'll judge you severely on your choice!"

"Shut up," Canopus hissed in my ear.

I pressed my lips together and zipped them shut. A silly gesture by a prefect tickled pink by her own stupid joke.

Sr. Nordfeld pretended like he didn't notice—or that if he did notice, my words were of no consequence whatsoever. The prefects couldn't have known that he had only two modes: absolute concentration on the task at hand and absolute awareness of everything around him.

He really did look like an accountant, if you didn't see his eyes. Or if you didn't know what you were looking at, when you saw those eyes.

"The ideal location for a summoning depends on the design of the building," Sr. Nordfeld explained in his most pompous manner. "I have not been here before, and am not familiar with the layout. I had planned," he added, lips disapprovingly thin, "for Lindo Manor, not Edenfield. Perhaps Prefect Edenfield can tell me of potentially appropriate locations." He focused on me again, frowning slightly, one professional to another. "We need an open space, large enough for the ten of us to form a comfortable standing circle. When possible, I prefer an atmospheric location. Any room will function in a pinch, but an ordinary one will make things more difficult and the outcome less certain. Does this manor have such a room? Perhaps an attic or a cellar?"

The prefects looked at me. I shrugged. "Both." They kept looking, and Sr. Nordfeld motioned for me to continue, so I said, "I haven't been in the basement, but I've smelled it, and it's pretty rank and looks dark and creepy. The attic's light and dusty. Either should have enough space."

Sr. Nordfeld nodded. "We will try the cellar first; the atmosphere sounds more promising. If we find it is unsuitable, the attic it is. Please, Prefect Edenfield, lead the way."

I led the way, noting the strategically located Lindo knights posted throughout my manor. Lindo collected half a dozen of them as we passed, and they fell in without a word. They knew the score.

As I observed this, I kept up a light conversation with Sr. Nordfeld—"Are you really a demonologist, Jon? Lucio said you were, but I couldn't believe it."

"I have many areas of interest."

"I know, but this doesn't seem quite . . . quite like you."

He turned his face on me then, and I hoped it was for the benefit of the prefects that his expression turned alien and stark. "Edenfield's spy," he said, "why should I have shared my secrets with you?"

The basement entrance was right by my bedroom door. I hadn't poked my head in since that first excursion, in the dead of night, to plant the spy equipment. Walls of dank air are not my friends, and have I mentioned that I hate basements? Because I hate basements.

I opened the door, and the stairwell breathed out cool, damp air, heavy and close. I switched on the light and got a good glimpse of what we were in for: concrete walls and stairs leading to more concrete below. The basement floor sprawled away from the stairs in every direction. Upon descending, I saw that the stairs themselves were not along the cliff but near the center of the manor. About twenty feet to our left, the wall was rough and rocky, having been blasted out of the hillside instead of poured.

The foundation was vast—much larger, I thought, than the ground floor of the manor. Whatever the intention for it had been, it clearly had never been fulfilled. Maybe I could thank the damp for that: damp stains crawled over broad concrete support pillars and clustered around their square bases. Brackish water bubbled and oozed through cracks and spread paper-thin and green-black over the floor. Low fluorescent ceiling lights flickered and buzzed over us, their sterile light splotched and speckled with grime. The basement should've been shadowy, but the dim, soft light bleached away light and dark and left only lifeless gray.

The atmosphere thickened as we walked. Sr. Nordfeld led now, footsteps echoing hollowly. Sweat blossomed beneath my blouse, irritating cuts and bruises. Batata sneezed.

At the far end of the basement, where two concrete walls met, we stopped. It was less damp here, away from the hill, and without as much standing water. Sr. Nordfeld hadn't been leading us randomly past pillars; he'd followed the basement's gentle slope to its highest point. Strange that said point was away from the hill rather than snugged tight against it, but I'm no architect.

"Here," Sr. Nordfeld announced, voice bouncing flatly off concrete until water sucked it in.

"Check it," Lindo ordered the half-dozen knights she'd gathered. They snapped off bows and immediately swarmed over the area, touching every surface, squinting at the concrete, poking at the cracks. They radiated outward from Sr. Nordfeld, methodical and professional.

"Hunting for smoke and mirrors?" Sr. Nordfeld suggested.

"For spy devices," Avior said, disgusted. "Lindo's paranoid."

"I take it she searched you also?"

"No," Lindo said, "Silvertip and Hemmel did. He wasn't carrying anything, and you aren't carrying anything, and it's clear that my knights aren't about to find anything. That leaves one final possibility." She fixed me with a look, and the others followed suit.

I rolled my eyes. "Let me guess! You think I might have magically hoodwinked you and am secretly—gasp—working against you. Maybe I'm even a demon in disguise. Guess the only way to prove I don't have horns is to give you a strip show à la Avior. Is that it?"

Batata cleared his throat and shifted from foot to foot. "Surely, Graça, that wouldn't be necessary."

"Especially in front of these perverts," Canopus agreed. She smirked at me. "We women have to stick together. How about a pat down? No," she told Lindo sharply. "I'll do it."

While I was submitting to Canopus digging through my jacket pockets and taking my phone away, Lindo's knights returned.

Canopus pronounced me clean. "Not," she added, "that you're likely to stay that way down here. I'll never be able to wear these shoes again."

"I love suede, but it doesn't last," I commiserated.

"Anything?" Lindo asked her knights.

"No electronic devices down here except those we brought in, my lady," replied the knight.

"Then go wait outside the door. And close it. Don't let anyone in; this meeting is private."

The knight bowed, gave her subordinates a brisk order, and they quick-marched out.

Sr. Nordfeld waited until he heard the thud of the closing door. Then he hitched up his wrinkled trousers, and squatted. Lindo's knights had evidentially not taken everything from him, because he pulled a finger-sized piece of chalk from his inner jacket pocket and began drawing.

Sr. Nordfeld's writing is, as a rule, immaculate. Chalk isn't as easy to use precisely as a black liquid ink fine tip, and a dirty, uneven floor isn't the ideal drawing surface, but he must've had some practice, because the end result was quite credible: a near-perfect circle six feet in diameter, with a nine-pointed star inside. Each of the star's points protruded exactly three inches beyond the edge of the circle, and bore not a single break or waver anywhere. And he did all this without the benefit of a ruler or a compass.

While Sr. Nordfeld worked, and on his instruction, Avior directed us to stand around the circle, one at each point of the star. He commandeered the southernmost point of the star for himself and the space to his right for Fjordland.

Once we were arranged to his satisfaction, Avior accepted a bag from Sr. Nordfeld and went around giving out small plastic-wrapped packages. As he handed one to each prefect, he murmured something, and I was uncomfortably reminded of a minister handing out Communion bread with a benediction.

When Avior stopped at me, I stiffened at the unholy gleam in his eye, the ghastly sheen to his skin. *These* were not due to the dreadful fluorescents. "Thank you for standing in for Bo," he said breathlessly. "I know you've had your doubts"—sure he did—"but there can be no more doubt after this." He pressed the little package into my hand and moved on to Tey.

The package was soft, rubbery clear plastic, like the kind in which you get eyeglasses repair kits. Only, instead of a miniature screwdriver, there gleamed a sharp silver sewing needle nestled on a cotton pad.

"Didn't you take these away from him?" Canopus was asking Lindo in an undertone.

"I'm not an idiot," Lindo hissed back. "But, obviously, I had to give him back everything he said he needed for the summoning."

Avior took his place at the head of the star, feet planted on either side of his point, toes nearly touching the circle. He jittered with excitement, eyes greedily upon Sr. Nordfeld's every movement.

Sr. Nordfeld didn't hurry as he finished drawing, pocketed the chalk, and dusted off his hands. You'd have thought he was perfectly calm, if you didn't know him.

I desperately hoped he wasn't counting on me to stand in for the demon. *He must have another plan*, I told myself. Sr. Nordfeld wasn't a man to accept that he was going to fail, and there *were* other possibilities. He never had told me the extent of Cipher's capabilities.

"The needles you hold are new and sanitary," Sr. Nordfeld told us. "Use your needle to prick your skin and smear the blood on the cotton pad. This will be your offering. Once you've finished, toss your cotton into the center of the star, being careful not to smudge the chalk. After the summoning begins, do not pass the chalk lines. Drawing blood will be easier if you massage your hands first."

He gave his instructions as if they were perfectly reasonable, and I found myself obeying almost before he'd finished. Most of the other prefects did the same; only Hemmel and Batata hesitated. Attack of Christian conscience over communing with demonic forces, however little they believed it would work? Squeamishness? Whatever delayed them, it didn't last long.

I pricked my forefinger, dabbed the blood, and dropped the cotton pad as far into the center of the star as I could reach. I was careful not to step over the line of chalk, but Tey, who stood next to me, did so purposefully. He had enough respect not to smear the lines, but I saw his cynical, disbelieving smile as he turned back.

"Think Avior plans to blackmail us with our DNA?" Tey murmured to me when he saw me looking. "None of us can back out now!"

I was too dumbstruck to answer. DNA evidence! That was brilliant—if Sr. Nordfeld could get away with it. He didn't know what I'd captured on the memory card, after all. But how was he going to work it? Did he expect me to do anything? Scoop up the cotton pads and make a run for it, maybe? No, no—that had too many variables. Sr. Nordfeld preferred definite outcomes.

"Is everyone ready?" Sr. Nordfeld asked.

"No," Lindo said. "I don't want you present for the summoning."

Sr. Nordfeld gave her a tolerant look. "And how are you going to do the summoning without me?"

"He's the last link," Lindo told Avior. "I don't want him here. He's set us up, fine. Can't you take over?"

Avior's outrage gave way to pleasure in an instant. "That could work, couldn't it?" he said to Sr. Nordfeld, vibrating with eagerness. "Tell me it will work. Tell me what I should do, and I'll do it. Anything."

Sr. Nordfeld's eyes flickered to me and then, for good measure, across the other prefects. "As you wish," he said, the lines radiating from his jaw announcing how unwise he thought this.

I suppressed another smile. *Brilliant.* Getting him out of sight so he could ready whatever he had planned—or, better, so he could go find the memory card from where he had instructed me to hide it. If he could manage to get past Lindo's knights. . . .

With his accustomed unhurried movements, Sr. Nordfeld withdrew a small notebook from his jacket, and spent a half minute writing. Then he carefully tore out the page and handed it to Avior. "Be aware," he warned, "that in my absence, I can guarantee nothing."

"Then if it doesn't work, we'll try again with your help," Avior said. "But this way first."

Sr. Nordfeld never broke his disapproving frown as he nodded.

"Is that it?" Tey asked. "A drawing and a few words? I thought we were going to have to sacrifice a goat."

Sr. Nordfeld turned his way, unruffled. "Not generally goats," he said. "Kids sometimes, but never goats."

"But there's no sacrifice written on here," Avior said, waving the piece of notebook paper. "Do I just say this? It's so short! Isn't there anything else?"

"There is a great deal else," Sr. Nordfeld said, "but nothing I can convey in words save this: take care."

"But this is easy," Avior complained. "What did I need you for? You could've told me what to do at any time!"

"I collect my payment upon your satisfaction," Sr. Nordfeld replied, "and so I wished to ensure you were satisfied." He circled us, gathering plastic packets and used needles. "I will await your return in the room above. The conference room, I believe it's called."

He left then, without waiting for responses, and without hurrying. He walked with an even step—the soft, measured, steady way a confident man walks in expensive shoes.

Chapter 30:

MUTILATION

Fluorescent lights droned, water gnawed at concrete, and the earth and manor weighed heavily upon subterranean air. In time, the black stains of water would deepen into cracks, and the foundation would crumble in on itself, pulling down the manor with it, crushing anyone beneath and smashing anyone above.

Standing under soft, dirty light, Prefect Avior's unhealthy skin gained an extra sickly yellow, nearly as sick as the sheen over his eyes, the appalling eagerness. Holding the fragile notebook paper in both quavering hands, he read in a thick, panting voice:

> "We have a deal for any who will
>   in fair exchange
> for the fresh blood of we nine prefects
>   bargain."

He lowered the paper, gulping stale air. I closed my eyes to shut out the ugly concrete, but I couldn't shut out the buzz, buzz, buzzing of the fluorescents or the damp crawling over my skin. I itched to act, to distract myself, to do *something*. But I wasn't going to be Sr. Nordfeld's demon. Not today.

When I opened my eyes again, the pillars swam. The white cotton pads in the center of the star seemed to glow—ghastly white and stained by specks of blood.

Pad-pat.

I swayed and blinked hard to clear the blur of my vision. The noise sounded dull on concrete—slow, purposeful. Pad-pat, pad-pat.

Footsteps, heavy on the floor, splashing through the shallow water. Not Sr. Nordfeld's footsteps. I know his sound. I know exactly how he moves and how he doesn't move—the energy and the stillness, the steepling of his fingers and the way he tries not to cross his legs, because crossing them crinkles his trousers.

Pad-pat. I shook my head and peered, but the pillars blocked my view and the soft light deceived me, skewed my depth perception. Knights? It did not sound like knights.

Pad-pat. Movement caught my eyes. It was a person, or at least person-shaped. Its long hair hung in wet straggles down to its waist, and its clothes trailed in ragged strips, half eaten away. With every step, the clothing writhed and spread, slithering down legs and arms and multiplying in ribbons like serpents.

I blinked, and the figure wore black military boots, black fatigues, and a snow-camouflage hunter's vest covered in pockets. Sopping hair dried into coppery red and sprang up in magnificent curls. Then those curls crept up the scalp, pulling themselves into a tight ponytail.

The figure was tall, its head not quite brushing the lights. I knew it.

Water and mud sluiced from its fatigues and squelched from its shoes, splattering thickly upon the concrete. Beneath the red hair, its skin was loose and bone-white, blotched with mottled patches of brown, blue, and yellow. Small wriggling things like grains of living rice crept over and under the flesh. When the clothing had first formed, it had been fresh, crisp, and clean; but already mud and water seeped through and stained it. Beneath the vest, the swollen abdomen deflated as it passed me, and I saw the fingernails regrowing. As she stepped into the circle, the transformation completed itself. Theodora looked as she had when I'd first met her.

"Lucio Winter," she said in a voice like a silver bell.

Avior cleared his throat. He jittered more than ever, and his forehead glistened wet. "Demon!" he cried. "Demon, it is I who summoned you!"

Theodora—no. This was no more Theodora than the proprietress had been. The movements were different, more removed. There had been something human about her, when she had called herself Theodora. This was the personification of Deals & Bargains, and "demon" was as good a name for it as any.

Deals & Bargains stooped within its circle and plucked up one cotton pad among nine.

"Demon, speak to me! Tell me about yourself!" Avior demanded, hopping for its attention.

Deals & Bargains said: "I will not have her as part of this bargain."

"Demon, here I am. Over here. I am the one who—"

Deals & Bargains held up a hand, and Avior's voice choked within his throat. Its face softened slowly toward me, though it remained the personification and not Theodora. It extended the cotton pad my way. It said: "I will not have you as part of this bargain. Take your offering and step away."

I licked my lips. "The payment offered was the blood of nine prefects, not eight. I would not have this exchange count as a renege on payment."

Deals & Bargains said: "I will collect my payment, but not from you. Take your offering and step away."

I couldn't read its face. Heaven help me, but I didn't know what it was thinking, if indeed there was any thought behind its demand— anything beyond the personification working by its own rules.

What I did know was that, if I'd suspected for an instant that Deals & Bargains would respond to the summoning, I would never have agreed to take part in it. I accepted the cotton pad and stepped back.

"Demon, I'm the one who summoned you, not her!" Avior shouted, stomping his foot. "Pay attention to me! I abjure you, by the symbol that binds you, speak to me! I wish to make a deal with you!"

Deals & Bargains pivoted his way. It said: "Go on."

Avior withered under its gaze but did not collapse. It was not making itself beautiful now, but terrifying. Shadows gathered about its shoulders like wings, and I was glad I could not see its silver eyes.

I neither moved nor spoke again during the rest of the bargaining session. I never thought to. I think I couldn't, for I had no part in this deal.

Avior squared his shoulders. He cleared his throat, and a prepared speech squawked forth: "We nine—eight—prefects have watched our nation crumble under rule pernicious, and we must rid ourselves of that rule. But if we act by obvious means, we will be rendered guilty in the eyes of the people and will be rendered unable to guide our beloved nation into her golden age."

Deals & Bargains tilted its head, neither believing nor disbelieving—or simply not caring whether this was true. It said: "What do you want of me?"

Avior bared his teeth, and his voice emerged clearer this time. "Give us a way to kill the king!"

Deals & Bargains said: "Have you no pistols? Have you no poisons?"

"Have you nothing better?" he shot back, rocking forward on his toes. "We need an untraceable way to kill him, one no one can blame on us."

Deals & Bargains said: "I do not kill mortals."

No, she blamed them for killing themselves by her hand.

"I'm not asking you to do it yourself," Avior said. "Give us a means, a way to kill the king—but not by our own hands, and so that no one knows we're the ones responsible. Can you do that?"

Deals & Bargains said: "I can."

"Then give it to us and take our blood in payment."

Deals & Bargains raised elegant, feminine hands to its vest. With forefingers and thumbs, it drew from two pockets two dirty, matted messes. It kept pulling, and the mats resolved into hair, followed by faces, shoulders, and arms. It pulled and pulled, until it had drawn out two young children, which it released upon the freezing concrete floor. Filthy, scowling, skeletally thin and wasted, the children cowered against Deals & Bargains's legs.

They were a boy and a girl, shriveled and hideous, their faces untouched by the springtime of youth. The boy folded in on himself, pressing his hands to his eyes, thumbs to his ears, pinky fingers pinching his nose, recessed jaw hanging loosely. The girl swiveled her head, assessing us, eyes deep and round and hungry as two empty wells. Both children were utterly loathsome and wretched, wrecked and revolting, more animal than human. My stomach churned to see them. They aroused no sympathy in me, no maternal instinct. I think if I could have, I'd have killed them then and there and accounted it mercy.

"What are they?" Avior asked, as fascinated as he was disgusted.

Deals & Bargains said: "Children."

"Yours?"

It smiled. "This boy," it said, stroking the child's hair, "is Ignorance. This girl is Want. They are in my safekeeping, but I am willing to bargain them into yours. Do you want them?"

No one could want them, but Avior practically salivated. "Yes."

"You will treat them as your own?"

"I will."

"Then we have a bargain."

Deals & Bargains lifted its hands and stepped away from the children. They released it without complaint and zeroed in on Avior. The boy hurled himself blindly at the prefect's legs, and Avior put out a hand to steady him. The girl latched onto that hand. She stuffed the fingers into her mouth and ground her teeth into them until blood ran across her cheeks and down her chin and Avior screamed.

Theodora didn't stick around to watch. She swept between Lindo and Hemmel and disappeared beyond the pillars, leaving nothing behind but eight scraps of clean white cotton in the center of the circle . . . and the hollow clack of my heels as I sprinted after her.

$$\mathscr{Q} - \jmath \subset \mathscr{L} \cdot$$

I don't think Theodora was moving like ordinary people do. I saw flashes of her walking unhurried ahead of me, but I couldn't catch up. By the time I reached the stairs, she had disappeared entirely. If I hadn't known where she was going, no way could I have followed her.

But I did know.

I tripped, scrambled, and slammed my way up the stairs, through the door, and into the arms of the knights waiting above. Warm bodies blocked my path and firm hands seized hold of me.

"That woman," I panted. "Red hair, just passed. Which way?"

"No one passed us," a knight told me.

"I have to catch her!" I insisted. "Please let me go!" I tried to plunge onward and got about twelve inches.

"No one passed us," said the same knight, a rough-faced woman with narrowed eyes. "What's the hurry?"

"I have to catch her before she gets to my brother. It's important. Please, let me go!"

"I think," the knight said, with deliberate pacing, "that we'd better wait for Prefect Lindo."

Seriously?

I ground my brain to a halt and reset it. Not easy, when it was screeching at me. It kept screeching, even as I straightened as well as I could under the pressure of a dozen hands and adopted a superior tone. "Take your hands off me," I commanded. "I am Prefect Edenfield, and this is my manor. You have no right to restrain me."

Prefect Lindo had not told them about the passing of the title, based on the way two of them laughed and the other four looked at me like I was insane.

"Please observe the ring," I added icily. "I am Lord Holst's replacement. Release me."

Instinct made them glance down and training immediately loosened fingers and snapped back hands. But they didn't move out of my way.

"We apologize for the inconvenience, prefect," said the same knight as before. "We did not know of your elevation. But, respectfully, Edenfield isn't in charge here anymore. Prefect Lindo is, and she told us not to let anyone pass."

I could've screamed at her. "I'm not running away! I need to get to my brother before that woman does! He's in the knighthouse. It's just around the corner. Don't any of you have siblings? That woman is a dangerous psycho, and she's got my brother wrapped around her little finger!"

"Doesn't matter," my new least-favorite knight intoned. "We have our instructions. You'll need to remain here until Prefect Lindo says otherwise."

I was *not* sitting around while Theodora went and destroyed my brother. But even as I worked myself up to do something truly desperate, another of the knights spoke: "I'll take her."

Like the others, this one was female. Though she'd never said it outright, the last few days had given me the impression that Prefect

Lindo didn't trust men.

The other knights gazed at my savior askance. She shrugged. "It's important to keep up good relations ... and I think the prefect wouldn't appreciate it if we stopped a woman from protecting her sibling, do you?"

The other knights shuddered and drew back. My savior took my arm. "Let's go," she said. Her hand tugged on me once, and then she was running by my side. We burst out of the front door together, dashed along the side of the building, and slammed into the knight-house beyond.

Lindo knights had taken over here, too. Four of them crowded into the outer room, which was no longer even remotely neat and organized. Their heads went up as I passed, but no one tried to stop me from barging into the back room. I found two more Lindo knights there, going through the closet under Roald's incensed gaze.

"Francis?" I called. I could see at a glance that there was no Francis here, but I looked frantically over the room again to make sure. "Where are Olaf and Torben?" I demanded of Roald. *"Where is my brother?"*

"He got away," Roald growled, glaring death at the knights. "Olaf was off-duty when they arrived, but they're going to arrest him the moment they find him. I don't know about Torben. He comes and goes as he pleases."

"He'll come here soon enough," one of the Lindo knights said confidently. "And then he won't be leaving again."

Roald snorted.

"My brother," I prompted him. "Tell me about my brother. What do you mean, he got away? When did he leave? Just now? Was he alone, or—"

A dreamy smile stole over the faces of all the knights. "Not alone ..." Roald murmured.

"There was a beautiful woman," said one of the Lindo knights.

"The *most* beautiful woman," corrected the other. "Magnificent red hair, like the fire of sunset."

"Eyes like stars."

Roald sighed. "Body like a candlestick."

"A *candlestick?*"

"You know, the ones that—"

I cleared my throat, and Roald dropped his hands, which had been carving an excessively womanly shape in the air. "We were distracted," he said sheepishly. "She was *very* beautiful. *They* thought so too."

"I'd have thought better of you two," my escort told the other Lindo knights sharply. They looked embarrassed, but the star-struck distance in their eyes emolliated their shame.

"Did you see which way they went?" I asked.

The Lindo knights motioned vaguely, but Roald said, "To the woods."

My heart sank to my boots, urgency replaced by despair and the closed-eyed moan of *Francis, Francis, what have you done?*

"I watched them out the window," Roald went on. "I was surprised the patrol didn't stop them. If Edenfield knights were as lax as Lindo knights, our borders would be overrun in a day. That's what happens when you get fat off the luxuries of the land and the protections of the bay: you lose your edge."

"Like you're one to talk," said a Lindo knight, eyeing Roald's corpulence. "Our prefect insists on top physical condition."

"And if only you had brains to go along with it, maybe you wouldn't have let them slip through your fingers. You're *never* catching Captain Nass."

A knock on the open door, a cough, a new Lindo knight. "Excuse me, Prefect Edenfield?"

I buried my despair and smoothed over its grave as I turned a gracious nod on the knight. "I am she."

"You're wanted," she said. "If you'll come with me, please."

Chapter 31:

PROFANITY

I had spent most of my waking hours in the conference room, over the past few days, and was beginning to know every whorl in the wood, every crack in the ceiling and fold of the curtains. More than that, I had come to know the habits of the other prefects. In the way of church congregants, they had self-assigned seats reflecting friends and alliances, adapted only by necessity when one of their number had brought a visual aid or wanted to make a point. Always, the head of the table had been left vacant for the king.

Avior sat there now, Sr. Nordfeld to his left, the children behind and to the right. Someone had fastened a heavy leather belt around the girl's head to hold her mouth closed. The buckle pinched the skin of her temple, and the biting leather pinkened the skin, but she made no move to adjust the belt.

In the better light of the conference room, I could see that both children wore dirty sackcloth, the kind we use to transport thirty pounds of moonlight potatoes. Its extremely coarse knitting had rubbed sores onto their shriveled arms and legs, and their feet were bare. Beneath the dirt and matting, I thought the children must be naturally blond—that very fair blond that's almost white. It was hard to tell without seeing more of the boy's face—he still pressed his hands over it, blocking eyes and nose and ears—but I thought the children might be siblings.

I wondered how Theodora had acquired them. And why.

"Prefect Edenfield," Avior said, unsmiling. "You ran away."

He did not look well. His eyes shone feverishly bright, brighter even than in his anticipation in the basement, bright as delirium. His skin had gone yellower and more haggard than ever, his black hair limp, and someone had bandaged his hand. He seemed to have expanded, as if going over the edge into his delusion and (as he saw it) being vindicated had given him permission to fill his own space.

"I did not run away," I rejoined. "I ran *toward.*"

"Toward your knighthouse."

Interesting: the other prefects were letting Avior run this interrogation by himself. By this time yesterday, at least three others would have jumped in. It seemed I wasn't the only one who perceived Avior had gone up in the world. How long the prefects would remain wary was another question, and I wondered what I had missed in the basement, that had led to this and to the belt around Want's head.

"That's right," I agreed, tracking the shifting gazes and nervous tics of the prefects in my periphery. "I ran to find my brother, who happened to be in the knighthouse."

"How convenient," Avior said flatly. "You made no mention of a brother before, but suddenly you remember you need him—right in the middle of a delicate operation."

He was not bursting into insane cackles or crowing, which was somewhat of a relief. He was talking almost as normal, except for the lilt in his voice, the set of his shoulders, the wariness of the other prefects.

I looked to Lindo. She met my gaze defiantly, maybe expecting another attack on her methods, her knights, or her invasion. "I know the demon Avior summoned," I told her, "because she has her claws into my brother. I brought him here with me to get him away from her, and locked him in the knighthouse. You understand that when I ran after the demon, I did so knowing how it would look and not caring how it would look—because I'd do anything to protect him. But I was delayed, and I was too late. She took him."

The blood drained from Lindo's face, and her lips parted in horror.

"I knew they must know each other by what the demon said," Silvertip explained. "That was too weird, the demon singling Edenfield out like that."

"Is that why my demon refused to deal with you?" Avior asked me. "Have you already made a deal with her? Did you succeed in summoning her?"

"Not exactly," Sr. Nordfeld said. It was the first time he'd spoken, and the prefects turned to him. He soaked in their attention, unruffled. "That was professional courtesy."

I shot Sr. Nordfeld an admiring look while the others waded through the mayonnaise of incomprehension.

"Explain yourself," Canopus snapped.

Avior narrowed his glittering eyes and tilted his head, examining me anew.

Sr. Nordfeld leaned forward to rest his wrists against the edge of the table and steeple his fingers. The diamond sharpness of his mind revealed itself, slicing through the room, effulgent with brilliance and beautiful to behold. He did not look like an accountant now. "I am no fly-by-night specialist who can be consulted and disposed of," he said. "The cliché of clichés is the man who orders a weapon of indomitable power and then tests it on its creator. Loose ends must be tied up, and I was not inclined to help Prefect Avior summon a demon without insurance.

"It has, I am sure, crossed your mind"—he inclined his head to Avior—"to test the abilities of these children upon me. Thus far, only wisdom has prevented you from so acting—for it is not wise to destroy the only one who might be able to assist you if something goes wrong with your deal. And yet no doubt—*no* doubt—you feel yourself increasingly capable of dealing with the demon you summoned. You begin to believe that if something goes wrong with your current plot, you could summon her again without difficulty and make another deal and thus solve your problem.

"You are inclined to dismiss the true reason there are no practical amateurs in the field of demonology: that those who try do not survive long."

Avior leaned back contemptuously. "I'm not an amateur."

"No? Then why did you hire an expert? Why did you not perform such a summoning long before? Regardless," Sr. Nordfeld went on, before Avior could respond, "I prepared for your pride. I bought my insurance." He waved a hand at me. "Or do you still believe that Mercedes here is the ordinary brand of personal assistant?"

A beat passed. Not a friendly one, either.

"You planned this," Lindo accused him, grimly satisfied. "I was right about you: you weren't on the level. You were the one who changed the conference location. You've been manipulating the situation from the start."

"There were two possibilities," Sr. Nordfeld said, "of what would happen when you went through with the ritual I designed to be used at this time and this place: either you would summon Mercy or you would summon one of her colleagues. In the first instance, I could be guaranteed safety by my previous arrangement with her; in the latter, she would provide insurance against my harm."

Avior laughed. "You make me want to use you as a test more, not less! These children against a demonologist *and* a demon? I like that. I like that very much indeed. Children—"

"Before you strike," Sr. Nordfeld interrupted, "it would behoove you to listen. Mercy?"

I curled my fingers and hooked them before my naval, stood ramrod straight, emptied my face of human expression, and recited, in my best Avior accent, "'I, Lucio Winter, Prefect Avior, for the benefit of my prefecture and my nation, declare King Emil incompetent and hereby bind myself to my fellow prefects in seeking his death—and to, with them, executing him at this conference by any means necessary.' I have the other confessions as well." I looked to Prefect Lindo. "Your knights didn't knock out the internet soon enough. I recorded the confessions live online, with a twenty-four-hour delay lock. If I don't renew the lock before the end of those twenty-four hours, the recording will be made public in two dozen different forums and social media sites, and emailed to media outlets around the country—as well as to my various contacts within the palace."

I stopped there, to allow each prefect to express his outrage and horror by whatever ways best suited his disposition. I bore the abuse with admirable grace and a small, polite smile.

In the end, they didn't do anything worse than yell at me. I hadn't actually betrayed them—yet—and I swore to them that I wouldn't, as long as Sr. Nordfeld and I remained alive, unharmed, and free.

Only Avior and Fjordland didn't join in the abuse. Fjordland looked mildly offended by it, and Avior was just plain fascinated. *"You're* a demon too?" he breathed. "You mimic humanity so well! How long have you been pretending? What's it like?"

"I knew it all along," Silvertip proclaimed. "You were too compelling, too convincing. No wonder you could manipulate the darkness of my bedroom that way. No wonder you could seal my wife's lips. Of course you were a demon!"

"But what of your background?" Avior asked me. "It's flawless! Family, schooling, job history—everything in place, everything ordinary!"

"Of course," said Sr. Nordfeld. "She could hardly work for the government—or be useful to me—if her cover were anything but perfect."

"And then there's your brother—the one who's here!" Avior smacked his lips. "Is he—"

I gave him my hardest, blankest look. "Off limits."

"But why? Because you love him? Can demons love?"

Lindo was listening in on this one, and I picked my words with care. I said: "Your assumption is based on a faulty premise."

"That he's really your brother?"

"That I have any reason or desire to explain myself to you."

That took him aback for a moment, but he rallied. "In that case," he said, "I will provide you with motivation." He stood and crossed to the door. The prefects quieted, more interested in watching him than in insulting me. Want and Ignorance stayed where they were, but their heads turned to follow the movement, and Want never blinked away from his back as he talked briefly and quietly to the knight outside the door, or as he returned to his chair.

A minute later, the door opened again, and Francis was pushed in: sleepless, disheveled, and foaming mad.

"Francis!" I exclaimed, stepping forward and holding out my hands automatically. "Francis, how—"

I never saw his fist coming. I was abruptly flat on my back, struggling to breathe, knowing I'd lost time but not how much. I tried to say his name again, but nothing came out. I was vaguely conscious of knights dragging him back before he could hit me again, and then Sr. Nordfeld was helping me to my feet and stabilizing me upright.

"You bitch!" Francis screamed at me, struggling against the knights. "You fucking bitch! You killed her! You dragged her to the river and murdered her!"

"He's crazy," Fjordland quavered. "Insane! Why is an insane person in here?"

I touched my temple and shook my head slightly, trying to get a hold of myself. I nearly fell as Francis lunged at me again. I had cringed away from him, which I'd never done before. But then, I've never been afraid of Francis in a temper before. I've always known he would never actually hurt me. Not like he meant it.

Not like this.

Spittle flew from his panting jaws, and his eyes peeled back. "I saw you!" he screamed at me. "I saw you! I saw you shoot her and mutilate her and throw her into the river! I saw her cut off her head with my knife!" he yelled wildly at the prefects. "It wasn't enough to let her die with dignity—she had to cut her into pieces! Oh Theodora, Theodora!"

I could feel the laser of Sr. Nordfeld's attention cutting into my cheek, the volcanic heat burning my skin, the mountain's weight on my heart. I tried to keep my face expressionless as I looked at the prefects, but their eyes bore judgment as they saw my guilt. "'Theodora,'" I told them, in what was meant to be a level tone, "is the name by which he knows the demon you summoned. I told you she had her claws into him, and now you see it for yourselves. She can make him believe anything she wants." I extended my palms. "I tried to prevent this."

It sounded convincing. It was true, which helped. But Sr. Nordfeld knew what Theodora really was, and he had drawn back from me. He understood, and I could not take that understanding from him.

"You *liar!*" Francis spat. "You're always *lying.* And I believed you! I trusted you! I came here to help you! I opened my heart to you and you betrayed me and murdered her!"

"Hardly," I drawled. "We saw your ex-girlfriend alive, healthy, and psychopathic not twenty minutes ago. You must have seen her alive too, for her to spin you this fantasy."

"I saw her spirit, you honey-tongued viper! Her ghost!"

I didn't take his insult as willingness to flyte. That would have indicated forgiveness. And that he didn't mean every word he said.

"Perhaps I can explain," Sr. Nordfeld said. The others must have thought him unperturbed despite the violence. Poker face, cipher face.

Fury.

If I threw myself at his feet and begged him to forgive me, to not think badly of me . . . if I explained . . .

But this wasn't the time for tears. Long past. Ages too late.

That, too, was a sacrifice I had been willing to make in order to rid the world of the proprietress's evil.

Except that I had failed.

"Theodora Banks," Sr. Nordfeld said. "Demon, fairy, proprietress, Deals & Bargains, the red-haired woman with silver eyes. She has many names but only one function: to make and fulfill bargains. What many people do not know—one of the things I hinted that you did not know, Prefect Avior, that could hurt you—is that unfulfilled bargains create a form of ownership. If you owe her, she, in a manner of speaking, owns you."

I blinked and tried to focus on him rather than on the frantically struggling Francis. This logic sounded familiar. Was Sr. Nordfeld getting it from me?

"Although I have never personally witnessed this," he went on, "it stands to reason that in times of crisis, she would use this ownership to, if you will, pass on her death. When she is killed, someone in her debt dies in her place. She herself can die only when everyone who owes her has either paid off his debt or died.

"Technically speaking, therefore," he informed Francis, except that he was really informing me, "if Mercedes did indeed decapitate, shoot, and drown Theodora, she was not killing her—she was killing the poor fools who had unfulfilled bargains with her. My guess is that if the prefects did not summon their demon when they did, Theodora would have eventually run out of replacements and herself died. But she was summoned, and so she did not die."

Ages too late.

"You're her boss," Francis realized bitterly. "Jon. Mercedes said you were *terribly* clever. I didn't recognize you from her description. Probably because she didn't mention you were old and fat."

"That is the problem with assumptions," Sr. Nordfeld said equitably, not rising to Francis's gross exaggeration. "They lead you astray."

Francis snarled at him, fists clenching but making no attempt to lunge. "Smug, self-satisfied, bureaucratic lump," he said. "I can't imagine what my sister sees in you."

"No," Sr. Nordfeld agreed, "I suppose you cannot. But I am not bothered by the opinions of a man who takes the word of a beautiful and beguiling stranger over that of his intelligent and perceptive sister."

"You don't know anything about it!"

"And yet I know more than you, because I have been in Theodora's auction house, and I have seen the evils she kept there."

"She didn't keep anything there! That building had no basement! I saw for myself. I drove there and looked at the ruin and walked over it and examined the foundation. The auction house did not and could never have had a basement!"

"A woman who can be shot, decapitated, and drowned without dying," said Sr. Nordfeld, "can surely hide evidence of a basement from a man who sees nothing, hears nothing, and understands nothing."

"Oh, *I* get it," Francis sneered. "You *like* murder. You *like* the fact that my sister goes around shooting innocent women. What a wonderful assistant she must be, if she's willing to do that for you. Well, she's willing to do everything else for you, so why not? You sicken me."

"You were already sick," said Sr. Nordfeld, "with a greater sickness than you know. But I can help you, if will you allow me."

Francis spat on his shoes.

"Enough of this," Avior said, shaking off the ennui of fascination. "Knights, take Mr. Cartier away and lock him up. We can deal with him later; in the meantime, we have more important business."

"Don't let him hurt himself," I begged the knights, as they pulled my brother away. "And if a red-haired woman comes by, don't let her in. Don't speak to her—and whatever you do, don't make any deals with her."

Chapter 32:

BAITING

The last thing I expected, after so much drama, was to go right back to ordinary conference business, but that was exactly what happened. Sr. Nordfeld was given freedom to roam the manor but not to leave, and I suggested that he take the children's room, since Francis clearly wouldn't be using it.

"Gina Gulbransen can help you with anything you need," I told him, "including fresh sheets. You'll find her in the kitchen, unless Prefect Lindo's knights are interfering there too."

"Thank you," Sr. Nordfeld said. He'd brought up his shields more solidly than ever, and nothing beyond somber professionalism made it into his voice. "I will."

Once he was gone, we sat back down and went on discussing fishing rights and lumber sales, nice as you like, nothing changed except for the presence of the two wretched figures lurking behind Avior and the way Avior's nearest neighbors edged away from him—and the way mine edged away from me. We spoke formally, as necessary, with no personal remarks or jokes or confidences. The other prefects called me Edenfield. They had reverted utterly to the mundane—or to whatever shreds of duty they felt toward the conference and their country. Maybe it made them feel better, to pretend.

I saw Sr. Nordfeld again over dinner. He had cleaned up in the intervening time, and although he wore the same charcoal-gray suit and tie, they had been freshly washed and pressed into crispness. He once more looked exactly as I had always known him; and although I strained to see the signs of his incarceration in his face and movements, he had hidden them too well.

By accident or design, Sr. Nordfeld ended up at the opposite end of the dinner table from me, sandwiched between Avior and Tey. From what I caught of their conversation, the prefects were pressing Sr. Nordfeld on information regarding demons—their abilities, classifications, vulnerabilities, and habits. Since Sr. Nordfeld genuinely had become an expert on demonology in order to effect his meeting with Avior, I had no doubt of his ability to answer anything put his way. In any case, he never looked to me for help.

I caught myself watching him and turned my attention back to Prefect Lindo before she noticed it had strayed. She'd grabbed me as we'd exited the conference room and hadn't let go of me since.

"You said you admired me, but I'm the one who admires you," she was telling me at the moment, intense over asparagus. "The way you take charge. When my sister . . . I suppose you know about that."

"I've heard stories," I admitted. "Rumors, really. I don't know if they're true."

"They're close enough." Lindo squeezed her eyes shut, fingers strangling her fork. She'd thoroughly mangled the greenery on her plate by this point, and had taken one or two fierce bites, but that was it. I placed my hand on her arm and murmured consoling nothings while she concentrated on breathing. "It's my fault," she whispered, voice breaking over the words like water over rock. "I should have stopped her. I should have stopped him."

Which *him?* I wondered. The king or the lover?

"I should have taken matters into my own hands, like you did with your brother. I should have taken him out of the equation, made sure he couldn't interfere—couldn't hurt her.

"But that's just me being foolish again, isn't it? I should know by now that nothing ever goes right for me. That's my life: as soon as something good comes along, someone is determined to ruin it. The universe hates me, Mercedes."

"It doesn't hate you," I told her. "Look at how much you've accomplished."

Lindo blew air out of her nose. "I shouldn't have expected you to believe me. No one ever does. Why should they? I'm not like you. I'm not a powerful personality. No one ever listens to me."

"I'm listening," I pointed out. "I believe you are worth hearing."

I kept listening, too. All through dinner. To her constant moaning. I was terribly sympathetic, which I accomplished by dint of banishing from my mind the constant reminders of how she'd imprisoned Sr. Nordfeld, invaded my prefecture, and plotted to assassinate my king. In fact, I concentrated on her so thoroughly that I was almost surprised by Sr. Nordfeld as he brushed past me on his way out—as well as by the micro memory card he pressed into my hand and the packet of used needles he slipped into my pocket.

~ 2

The sun was setting when I arrived back in my room, which was exactly right. I wasn't going to wait until the middle of the night to sneak out—not this time. Any knights worth their salt would be more likely to expect someone to sneak out in the full dark of 2 a.m. than the gray uncertainty of 8 p.m.

Not that it was 8 p.m. quite yet; but then, I wasn't going out quite yet. I turned out my bedroom lights, let my eyes adjust to the darkness, and tweaked my curtain aside.

I would've had a better view from the children's room, situated at the building's northeast corner, but what I saw of the patrol patterns from here was depressing enough.

Lindo certainly hadn't stinted at bringing knights and assigning patrols. From my east-facing window, I could see three stationary knights planted along the side of the manor and in the trees beyond the lawn. Then there were regular patrols of pairs of knights. Based on what I'd seen earlier today, I'd say Lindo had brought close to a hundred knights all told, at least half of whom were on duty at any particular time.

I made a face and let the curtain fall back into place. No chance of driving away; they'd catch me for sure. I'd have to walk to Gjerde to find a vehicle or—on the off chance they weren't watching the station—the train. Maybe further, if Lindo had posted knights around town. It was so quiet there, any disruption would draw them to me in an instant.

The problem was, Edenfield was so sparsely populated that I wasn't sure I *could* make it to the next town—or into an area where my mobile phone would work—before it was too late. So I might have to improvise.

I changed into a forest-green turtleneck sweater and chocolate-brown skirt, transferred everything I really needed to take with me to the bed—IDs, credit cards, cash, phone, pepper spray, and lip balm—and then went to visit the bathroom.

How does a head knight sneak into his prefect's locked bedroom in the middle of the night? Through a secret passage, of course. It'd have to be on the south wall, against the hill, easily accessible, and preferably out of view of the door. That meant the bathroom. And oh my, wasn't that an unusually wide full-length mirror. What a stroke of originality!

Statistically, "password" is the most common password in the world, followed by "123456" and variations thereof. "Dragon" is the seventh most popular password. You'd be amazed at the number of supposedly intelligent spies who use "trustno1" as their cipher keys no matter *how* we try to train them.

People will be people, I guess. So I wasn't terribly surprised when I ran my fingers around the mirror rim and found a latch that swung the mirror inward.

Beyond the mirror door lay a space of about the same dimensions as the bathroom, paneled on three sides with local beech wood and piled high with emergency supplies. On a small round table, where you couldn't miss it no matter how you hurried past, waited a prepacked backpack.

I wasn't in that much of a rush. I took the backpack into my bedroom and sorted through the supplies, then repacked it with what I wanted. In addition to the items from my purse, this meant space blanket, whistle, multi-tool pocketknife, flares, first-aid kit, energy bars, water bottles, more cash, compass, and flashlight.

Not the lightest pack to hike with, but it'd do. I returned the rest of the supplies to the secret room, and added camouflage coat and black beanie, gloves, and scarf to my ensemble. No telling how cold it was going to get or how long I was going to be stuck out there.

Edenfield's escape route wasn't a multi-level masterpiece like Silvertip's. Beyond the secret room, the tunnel split to run right and left, following the line of the hill. I jogged down the left-hand tunnel first.

As I'd rather suspected it would, after about a quarter mile, the tunnel let off in the woods behind a bush, a stone's throw from an old dirt road. The diminished moon didn't provide much in the way of light, especially through the trees, and I didn't want to turn on my flashlight and be seen. I listened for several minutes, but heard nothing but the sounds of woods at night: the twitter-pated conversations of birds, the dancing swish of a light breeze through the fall foliage. Starlight rendered the magnificent leaves of flaming yellow and orange a study in grayscale, and cold froze the earthy, brown and green scents in my nostrils.

This . . . was a possibility. Gjerde's train station might be watched, but the border station surely wouldn't be, and if Edenfield prefects past had had any brain cells to rub together, that's exactly where this road would lead. That might be beyond the phone outage; and if not, I could definitely take a train north to the capital and hope I wasn't stopped at the Gjerde station when they realized I was gone . . . or I could take a pony to Akter or Vela, hope I could get in without a passport, hope I could get internet access, hope no one thought I was defecting, hope I didn't get blown up by an apparently common landmine . . .

But if I went this way, I'd have to take the road—any further east, and I'd run into the mountains. And I didn't trust the road not to be watched.

I stepped back into the tunnel and headed for the other end. Ten minutes returned me to my starting point, and another ten led me to a second split. A very narrow, rough tunnel ran due south, presumably to let out in the howling wasteland that was Plisp. It struck me as horribly claustrophobic and not very useful to my present situation, although terribly useful to any Velan or Akterian spies who stumbled across the exit. Which probably meant that it was full of booby traps. Bo would know the safe way to get through, but he'd neglected to pass that information to me.

I continued on along the side of the hill until the main tunnel ended, like the first, behind a convenient cluster of boulders and shrubbery. Then I clicked the flashlight off, pushed aside the weeds, and stepped out into the night.

I'd grown up under a sky decorated with spots of darkness between the stars. In books, I'd read about skies like vast cloaks of black velvet; but gazing up from a potato field with no artificial light for fifty miles, I hadn't understood. The sky wasn't coal-dark: it was dusky red, yellow, purple, blue. Not until much later, after I'd visited places cloistered in their own light pollution, had I understood why Carina's flag was black with white stars.

Carina's flag, by the way, is called the Keel, and its stars form the constellation Carina: nine nine-pointed stars in the shape of an old-fashioned ship's keel. Carina is one of only three constellations visible from our country year-round. Along with Vela the Sails, and Puppis (which translates to Akter) the Stern, it makes up the compound constellation of Argo Navis.

There are a lot of stories of how our three nations took the names of constellations as their own, but there is something fitting about it. We are an island settled by sailors who became lost and could not escape our treacherous waters; and *Argo* is the ship sailed by Jason and the Argonauts. I like to think that we have treasures as fine as ever the Golden Fleece was.

But I was getting distracted. I shook my head and trotted north, ears perked.

The woods here were a lot easier to move through than the thick forests of Silvertip. The beeches—*Northofagus carini*, I'd learned over the past couple of days, along with more about their lumber than I ever needed to know—were massive and formed shadowy tunnels beneath crinkling autumn leaves and between their ancient trunks. Someone must've kept up the woods, because there weren't the fallen branches and rotting logs you'd expect; there were only short, fragile weeds and dirt. Beneath the canopy, I got flashes here and there of vibrant sky, which was enough to make good time, and my feet had remembered how to traverse uneven earth, so that I hardly stumbled once.

I'm not sure what made me stop. Some instinct, I suppose. Some sound or lack of sound that stuttered my feet and prickled my skin. I strained my eyes into the many layers of shadow that swathed the woods and clustered into tree trunks and hanging branches, softened my breathing, and waited.

A chill breeze ruffled my hair, blowing wisps across my nose, but I didn't pull them back. I stood and breathed in the peaty air and waited.

The sound of footsteps rewarded me. Not Theodora's heels or boots: faint, patting steps. Not stealthy, just lightweight. One shadow detached from the others and a small, thin, warped figure padded forward until it stood a scant five feet in front of me.

Under a clear patch of sky, its pale skin glowed gray-white and contoured its features. But I didn't have to be able to see it clearly. I knew it by the way its emaciated arms bent to press bony fingers against its eyes. *Ignorance*, Theodora had called the boy. But where was his sister?

"Hello," I said, injecting my voice with the cadence of adults speaking kindly to young children. "We've met before, although you probably don't remember me. My name's Mercedes, but you can call me Mercy, if you like. It's easier. I'm Prefect Edenfield. You've been staying in my manor, and these are my woods."

The boy didn't answer. Maybe he couldn't. Maybe he didn't understand Plishan ... or any other human language. Maybe he couldn't hear me past his closed ears.

"Have you wandered away and gotten lost?" I asked. "Do you need someone to take you back?"

He still didn't answer. I shifted from foot to foot, pretending I wasn't unnerved, and glanced around for his feral sister. She could be hiding behind the nearest tree, and I'd never spot her unless she moved. I didn't dare use my flashlight, not until I was much further from the manor.

"I can see you're happy standing there," I said. "I'll stop bothering you. Have a nice night."

I planned to circle him, give him a wide berth before continuing on my way. I walked to the right, and he followed me: step for step, five feet away, facing me, altering his position only to circumnavigate tree trunks. He stumbled over shrubs and must've scratched up his bare feet—but it was so cold, I doubt he could feel the injuries. Beyond that, he stayed in a line parallel to the manor, in between me and escape.

I said, "Excuse me. I need to get past."

He didn't respond. By that point, I'd have been surprised if he could. So I didn't bother talking to him again. I feinted backward and forward, side to side. He continued moving with me. When I went toward the manor, he followed five feet away. When I tried to move further from it, he blocked my path.

Herding me back, I thought. *Like a sheep.*

The thing about sheepdogs is, though, they don't just have pointy teeth—they're also faster than the sheep they herd. And there was no way this shrimpy kid with his hands covering his eyes and ears and nose could run more quickly than I could.

I took a few steps toward the manor to lull him and then bolted away at an angle, staying parallel to the manor until I'd gotten well ahead of him and then veering north. I didn't look back to check on him: I put my head down and sprinted, ducking around trees, arms and legs pumping.

The boy came out of nowhere. One moment, a clear path before me. The next, a boy standing calmly, hands dangling by his sides. I threw myself aside to avoid running into him. I must've tripped over a root, because the next moment I was sprawling forward, grunting as unhealed flesh tore open again and bruises redoubled.

The boy bent over me—in concern, I thought—and took my hand to help me up, and—

And why was I running away? To save the king? To stop the prefects? None of that was any of my business. Why had I stuck my nose in? I'd only made a fool of myself. I was nobody, a personal assistant in a dead-end job, a woman whose life revolved around whether her boss wanted tea or coffee. I should've left that job months ago, when I'd had the chance, but I'd clung to him instead. How utterly pathetic.

I shriveled to think of it. I cringed. I wished I could just forget the whole thing.

Could I forget? I could, now that I considered it. In fact, it would be easy: I would simply convince myself I knew nothing. Then no one would want to hurt me and no one would expect anything from me. That sounded excellent: I'd forget what I knew, return to my bedroom, and put my head under my pillow. Before I knew it, I'd be home again.

My feet turned of their own accord, and I walked toward the manor, my mind a milky fog. And as I walked, I let go of what I knew. The present left first, fading into the fog. Then the past. Then understanding. Then basic skills. I forgot how to drink from a cup, how to control my bowels, how to walk—

My knees collapsed, and I toppled over. I had not yet forgotten how to breathe. I couldn't; I had forgotten how to forget. So I breathed. I breathed in prickly shrubs, trees and earth, night air.

There I lay. There I might have stayed forever. There I might have died.

But though the milky fog clung thick and opaque, it wasn't thicker or more opaque than scent. These smells were the smells of childhood camping trips, of wrestling with my brothers, of innocent adventures. My brothers' voices came back to me first, shouting, intermingled. Then their faces. Then the feel of their hands, helping me up or pushing me down, grabbing me and letting me go. Remembering these things, I remembered how to squirm away from them, and so I successfully rolled onto my back.

My eyes were open—I had forgotten how to close them—and my glasses askew, so I remembered what it was like to see clearly even as I saw only blurriness and blobs. I remembered getting my glasses, putting them on for the first time. I remembered seeing the rows and rows of perfectly detailed, shining glasses frames and mirrors, and how I had never seen a sight so beautiful. I remembered how to cry.

I knocked my glasses back into place and looked up at the stars, marveling and marveling, for they too were beautiful.

I lay there for a long time, marveling at the wonder of vision and the gift of beauty, and maybe I would have lain there until I starved had I not suddenly remembered that I had pockets and put my hand into one. There was something tiny, hard, and foreign in there, and the edge of it bit into my finger. I brought it before my face and, in the starlight, gazed upon it.

Then I laughed. A micro memory card! How funny, to have forgotten a memory card. And in laughing, I remembered what laughter was and about the things that caused laughter—about jokes and jibes, playful antics and flytes, silly noises and sillier walks.

I no longer remembered why I had made myself forget, and I

didn't want to. I wanted to keep remembering, to keep discovering anew what I had once known. I remembered and marveled and examined until suddenly, with no more transition than between on and off, the fog dissipated, and beyond it gleamed in splendor everything I had thought I'd made myself forget.

I stood up, put the memory card back in my pocket, and saw Ignorance. His hands were back over his face, and he did not speak. I had somehow made it onto the main road leading from Gjerde to Edenfield Manor. The boy guarded one side of the road, and I was not so foolish as to again attempt to pass him. I swayed on my feet, looking to the manor and back to him, lost in indecision.

The boy turned slightly to the road, and I stepped sharply back. On the far side of the paved strip—hunched forward, stick-insect arms bent and wrists loose—stood the girl. Want. Unlike the boy, who reveled in stillness, she twitched constantly—reacting to the night sounds, watching me with hungry eyes. The belt had gone from around her head, freeing her jaw.

I stepped away, along the road toward the manor, and the children stepped with me.

"I am going back," I said, enunciating around thick saliva. "I am not trying to escape. I am going to follow this road straight back to the manor. I was only going for a stroll to clear my head. You didn't have to stop me. You don't have to worry about me."

The girl gnashed her teeth, but she approached no closer. Not through lack of desire or force of self-control, I thought: she'd been ordered to behave like this. The boy, too. The children stayed far enough away that if I reached out my arms and they reached out theirs, we would not quite touch.

I backed up and kept backing up, staying on Ignorance's side of the road. The children stayed with me until we rounded the last curve and hump, and the manor came into view. Then they melted away into the woods, one guarding each side of the road.

Chapter 33:

INVASION

The manor loomed dark, vast, and formless against the night. Orange glowed dimly over the main door and again at the knighthouse. Beyond that, nothing. If there were any other lights on, they had been masked by curtains.

This was the dark before the dawn, not the dark before midnight. I had lost so much time.

I averted my eyes from the orange glow to preserve my night vision and scanned the area. I knew where the guards outside my window were, if they hadn't changed their routine since evening, but I hadn't planned to come back this way—and I suspected that haring off into the woods to try to find the secret passage entry would be an exercise in pointlessness, even if the children didn't appear again. So it'd have to be a frontal approach.

I had one major advantage—or, rather, the knights had made one major mistake: they had driven to the manor. Lindo Manor no doubt had plenty of pavement for a hundred knights to park on, and the knights could've come and gone with the absent king none the wiser. But the Edenfield parking loop was barely large enough for a dozen cars, and so the knights had crowded their vehicles onto the grass on either side of the loop and down the road.

I crawled among the vehicles until I'd come right up to the gravel loop, and no one saw me. In fact, I didn't see a single knight stationed further out than the edge of the loop. Not how I would have positioned my guards.

Maybe not how Lindo had positioned hers, either. If those children...

It was easier to spot the knights while creeping along like a caterpillar, because their greatest movement was in their legs. They paced or rubbed one foot along their shins or adjusted their weight to keep off cramp. Movement alerted me to guards at each corner of the building, at the edges of the woods, and in the regular patrols going two by two like animals into Noah's ark. The patrols themselves helped me spot the stationary knights, because they stopped to check in and receive an all-clear. There might, I reminded myself, be more knights watching through the windows. The lights above main door and knighthouse would not work in my favor if I aimed for them.

If I could see the knights best when they moved, it stood to reason that the same was true in reverse. If I went very, very slowly, it was remotely possible I'd be able to snake my way through the grass to the edge of the building, but what then? I wouldn't be able to get through a door or window without being spotted. It'd also look terribly suspicious. If all I wanted was to get inside, my best bet was to simply walk in. The knights were there to prevent people leaving, not coming back, and I was a prefect. There would be questions, but none I couldn't bluff my way through.

Unless they searched me, which would be bad.

I was looking at this the wrong way around—what was possible rather than what should motivate me. What was my number one priority?

Warning the king.

How could I do that?

Either digitally—in which case I'd need access to a working phone or internet—or personally—in which case I needed a car plus Want and Ignorance out of the way. I did not have to do it myself, if I had a competent ally.

I grinned. I knew exactly where to find one.

There were plenty of knight vehicles around, but I didn't trust them not to have alarms. Besides, they might have ammunition stored in them, and I wanted to cause a distraction, not a slaughter. I likewise dismissed most of the prefects' cars as being too likely to be locked or alarmed. I trusted Batata not to lock or alarm a car, but I didn't remember which of the rentals was his. That left Hemmel's as my best bet: an ancient, beaten brown truck with as much pride taken in it as a neglected dog takes in its fleas. It didn't matter if Hemmel had remembered to lock it, because he'd left the window cracked a couple of inches. The crack might have looked small to Hemmel, but I could've stuck my arm far enough in to unlock the door.

Creating a diversion wasn't the reason I'd brought the flares, but I couldn't think of a nobler way for them to die. I popped the caps off all three, struck them alight, and shoved them through the crack. One after another they tumbled onto the seat. One rolled and stayed there, and the other two bounced to the carpeted floor, already catching the material alight.

If the knights hadn't heard that, they'd see it soon. I scuttled and ducked to the eastern tree line, where I could wait for the fireworks.

It took about four minutes for the knights to realize something was horribly wrong and another four before the truck's interior had transformed into a glorious blaze of sound and light. In between all the running and shouting, I could've probably waltzed across the green without any of them giving me a second look. But frankly, I had better things to do.

I made straight for the knighthouse, yanking my pepper spray from my belt. The door had opened, and a turquoise-and-gray-clad Lindo knight run out, but another knight inside had pulled the door closed behind her—I'd been watching carefully. So I whipped the door open, shoved my scarf over my nose and mouth, and burst in. Three knights stood in a clump, speaking in low, worried voices. They turned toward me as one, but I already had the pepper spray aimed and activated.

My pepper spray has a range of ten feet and lasts nearly half a minute. It's reeve-grade stuff, guaranteed to make you regret your poor life choices for a full twelve hours and leave you with an unattractive UV stain to boot. I aimed at eyes, noses, and mouths, and the knights collapsed, clawing at their faces and choking. Hopefully, Lindo checked for asthma when screening her personnel. I prefer to avoid manslaughter when I can.

Squinting through streaming eyes and holding my breath despite the scarf, I tried the door to the back room. It was locked, but a second's glance revealed the key dropped carelessly on the desk. I unlocked the door, ducked in, and slammed it closed behind me to keep the fumes out. My eyes burned and watered already, and I didn't envy the Lindo knights.

Francis raised his head to stare at me. Bags had taken over his under eyes, and he didn't make any move to attack, unshackled though he was. I showed him the pepper spray in my hand to discourage bad behavior and checked around the rest of the room. Roald and Olaf were back here too. They'd been sitting and, no doubt, bemoaning their fates, but my unconventional entry had brought some interest back to their lives.

"Torben do a runner?" I asked, privately gleeful. Bad timing for trying to take over the prefecture, sir. Very bad timing.

Roald shook his head. "Not a chance of it. What's going on out there?"

Even from in here, we could hear shouts and the roar of fire. "I created a diversion," I said, and focused on Francis. "Have you explained what's going on?"

Francis flicked his teeth at me. I ducked my chin at him, to let him know how childish I thought he was being, and turned back to Olaf and Roald. "There isn't time to explain fully. The short version is that the prefects are conspiring to murder the king—"

"So Torben was right," Roald observed.

"Torben is always right," said Olaf.

I sighed. "The problem is, it's all gone wrong. I have the evidence"—I held up the memory card—"but no way to get it to the king. You probably noticed that there's no phone or internet service. Well, it gets worse, because I just tried to sneak out of here and found out that Avior's put some sort of weird defense around the perimeter. For the record, I left the manor around eight p.m., and it's now—what?"

"Nearly four," Olaf said, checking his watch.

I groaned. My exertions in avoiding the children and getting to the knighthouse had gone a long way toward warming me up, but a deep chill lingered in my bones. If I had not been so well dressed—and had tonight not been milder than my first visit to Edenfield—things could have been so much worse. "So I lost seven hours, or thereabouts. And I was lucky."

"Then we'd better get to work," Roald said. "What's on the card?"

I explained quickly about how I'd tricked the prefects into confessing. Roald and Olaf would need to get on a computer and find the relevant section, but afterward, even playing the clip over the phone ought to be enough. "Not that there are any phones available," I grumbled.

"We don't need phones," Roald said. "Their radios still work—Lindo's, I mean. We can send the signal outside the blanket and have them relay it to the capital. The sound will degrade, but it should be enough. Olaf?"

Impish glee lit up the young knight's face. "I could get creative."

So now we'd see if I was right in trusting Edenfield knights. I handed the memory card and blood-stained needles over. "I recommend tying something over your face if you want to go into the main room," I said. "It's pretty . . . atmospheric."

The knights wrinkled their noses. Yeah, I guess they could smell it from in here.

"And you'd better do something with the Lindo knights I sprayed," I added as an afterthought. "They'll recover eventually, and they may be able to finger me as their assailant."

"We'll deal with it," Roald promised. "Olaf?"

"I think I can find some old gas masks. Wait, where are you headed?"

I paused with my hand on the doorknob, scarf ready. "Someone has to deactivate the perimeter weapon," I pointed out—then shot them a quick grin, gulped down fresh air, and darted away.

૨, ૯ ૪ ૦૨ ,

Hemmel's truck blazed as magnificently and distractingly as ever. No one tried to stop me; no one even noticed me, as I traced the building around the corner to the children's room. The window lock hadn't improved any in the past couple of days, and it was the work of a few seconds to pry the window open and crawl in.

"What on earth—?" Sr. Nordfeld cried. He was awake and sitting up in his narrow bed, curiously vulnerable in blue flannel pajamas. As I pulled the window closed behind me, he got up, barefoot, to watch.

I twitched the curtains closed and turned the flashlight on. "Sorry about this," I said, obscurely embarrassed and determined to pretend I wasn't, "but I need your help."

Stillness descended on him, the same stillness that distanced him from me whenever he was thinking I-knew-not-what. "You should not be here," he told me, the stillness in his voice the greatest rebuke he could have given. "You were supposed to leave hours ago."

"I did leave hours ago," I said, "and I got past the knights easily, but the children stopped me. Look—"

I tried to rush through an explanation, but that sort of thing never works with Sr. Nordfeld. He made me slow down and tell it properly—otherwise, he said, how would he have the necessary information to make a sound decision?

I could hardly argue with that logic, so I let him walk me step-by-step through what had happened since he'd left the basement. What, exactly, had Avior asked the demon for? How had Deals & Bargains phrased it, when she'd announced the children's names? And the girl, Want—she did not attack you in the woods?

"Ignorance didn't either, until I tried to get past him. I think he might have been herding me toward Want, though, not just back toward the manor." I shuddered, remembering what it was like to forget, the shame and despair that had made me *want* to forget. "I was almost lost. I think—I think if he'd been trying, I wouldn't have had a chance. I would have forgotten how to live."

"Most likely, if he turned the full force of his will against you," Sr. Nordfeld agreed. "That would explain his name."

I cocked my head questioningly.

"I have various theories regarding personifications," he said, "and, unfortunately, only a limited pool from which to draw information. In my experience, however, personifications tend to embody not concepts in abstraction but elements related to human endeavor. 'Deals & Bargains' is the making and keeping of deals and bargains. 'Cipher' is the making and solving of puzzles. 'Ignorance' by itself is not a human endeavor; it is a state of being that describes a lack. 'Willful ignorance,' on the other hand, includes the aspect of endeavor."

"And 'Want'?"

He grimaced, tapping his thigh. There was still that strange vulnerability, but it struck me less painfully, since he had become distracted from it. "Grasping greedily, perhaps," he said—"but that is only a guess. You must understand, I have not seen either of them in action, not seen them at all save when they stood dumbly awaiting further orders."

I shrugged. "Your guesses are as good as most people's conclusions. Care to guess at their weaknesses? I need some way to stop them."

His tapping fingers curled and uncurled, restive, uncomfortable, unconscious—and belying the slow steadiness of his next words. "By 'stop,'" he said, "do you mean 'kill'?"

Perhaps some of that despair from Ignorance lingered, or perhaps I was right in having given up my job, knowing he would never allow me back whatever I said. Perhaps I wanted to sever that last tendon of his respect for me, and so make it easier to leave. Or perhaps the hard detachment that had carried me through so many difficult decisions simply had no use for kid gloves when the lives and freedom of an entire nation were at stake. In any case, I made no attempt to soften my, "Preferably."

His head jerked away, and the tapping increased.

"They're not actual children," I reminded him. "They're more of Theodora's monsters. If you'd seen them—"

"I hope," he interrupted sharply, "that you know better than to judge by appearances."

"On the contrary," I said, "I am judging very thoroughly by the appearance of Want biting nearly through Avior's fingers and slavering at me in the woods; and at the *appearance* of Ignorance draining my mind. I am judging without pity the fact that no human would be able to do those things any more than a human could survive being decapitated."

"And are you also judging," said Sr. Nordfeld quietly, "that no human could twist space into a Möbius loop? That no human could see patterns and puzzles in ordinary objects or warp a street system simply by living nearby?"

I rolled my eyes. "Coconuts and bananas. You know you're different."

"Am I? Why? Because I was fortunate enough to bear the mantle of one personification instead of another? Or because I happen to be on your side?"

"Because you're not a crazed psycho."

"Ah! And humanity is based on sanity, is it?"

"You don't *eat people.*"

"And yet we have a word for cannibalism."

"Yes," I agreed. "And when people go that far, we call them *in-human.*"

"Like Theodora." Even in the indirect rays of the flashlight, I could see his face flush. He stalked away from me, stopped abruptly at the door, and snapped back. He'd cast his face in shade, but I could see the glittering of his eyes, the hardening of lines that had always remained comfortably soft. It struck me that I was seeing Cipher at that moment—or the echo of it. He said: "Not all of us were fortunate enough to be born with our personifications, Mercedes. You cannot know what it is like."

"What does that have to—"

"I was eighteen when Cipher came to me. In my first year of university. I was sitting in class when it descended. Out of nowhere, it invaded my mind—an alien and parasitic intelligence crushing me, filling my eyes and ears with sounds and shapes, battering me with patterns, patterns, patterns. Impossible, maddening!

"Do you think it was easy to deal with it, because I seem well-adjusted to you now? I have had nearly two decades to trap and tame and force my personification to do my bidding, and yet it still slips from my grasp. The more I tamp it down, the more it sprays out the edges, distorting space. Never, Mercedes, *never* do I know for certain if what I see is what others see. If it is real.

"And despite all that, I was lucky. Deeply, terribly lucky. I was suited to my personification and it to me. Already, I had stretched and exercised my mental capacities in many directions, when it came to me. I was flexible and I had unusual mental power, and so I was able to develop techniques to cope with that initial influx. I did not drown in the flood of Cipher—or not entirely.

"Have you never wondered why I am permitted to keep a personal assistant in a secured government facility? None of the other crypt-analysts can. Have you never wondered why you were the ninth personal assistant I hired over the course of two years, and why I kept you around when I dismissed the others, many of them with far greater qualifications? It was because my sister, my dear sister who works for the crown and who interviewed you, chose my first eight assistants herself and tasked them with one duty: to keep an eye on Jon and tell her if he'd gone crazy again."

". . . Again?" I whispered.

"I warned her that I would not keep you if she did the same with you. I can tell, you see, by the way people look at me, whether they know. Well, she had finally learned her lesson, and so she decided to take a chance. She trusted," he said, suddenly vicious, "that you had the brains to pick up on it if something went wrong with me again.

"Yes, Mercedes: again. How could I *not* be admitted to a mental institution after telling everyone I met about the endless patterns, the patterns that filled my new world? The secret messages on billboards and cereal boxes; the way the wallpaper whispered secrets as it watched me; the getting trapped in a straight hallway and walking forever without getting anywhere. If my family hadn't taken me to a mental institution, I would have checked myself in. Eighteen is not an unusual age for schizophrenia to set in, and I knew enough to diagnose myself. I was *glad* when my family hauled me in and the psychiatrists drugged me and told me that I would get better.

"Except that I did not get better. If anything, I got worse. It is a terrible thing, Mercedes, to know you are insane."

He shrank back another step, and I kept the flashlight down, allowing him to hide his face in darkness. When he spoke again, his tone was softer but no less angry. "I would still be there if my personification had not asserted itself in more tangible ways. Drugged as I was, I had no power to prevent it leaking out and warping the space of the ward, trapping patients and staff alike in impossible mazes and loops. That was proof enough for the head psychiatrist that I was not simply ill. She stopped the drugs and began in on intense mental workouts, teaching me—helping me teach myself—how to keep my mind under *my* control—not Cipher's."

He waited for my response, watching me, but I could whisper

only, "I didn't know."

"If you had found out," he rejoined, "I would have fired you. I have no desire for an assistant who is constantly watching me, gauging whether I have gone over the edge—again. My sister does not want me even driving myself. What if I have an episode behind the wheel? She thinks I have 'episodes.' She doesn't understand . . . but it does not matter. What does any of that matter to Mercedes Cartier, judge of who lives and who dies? Jon might as well die. It is not as if he is human."

"Sr. Nord—"

"How old would you say those children were, Want and Ignorance? Do you think they have gotten psychiatric help while being carried around in a pocket? By what kindness do you think Theodora acquired them? What deal did their parents make to get rid of their horrifying, dangerous, inhuman children? Because heaven forbid any wretched creatures like that deserve happy homes and loving parents and *life*."

I could hear him panting in the darkness, over the distant yells of knights and the windy roar and crackles of a burning truck. "I'm sorry," I said, because I had to say something. But the moment the words emerged, I knew they weren't nearly enough—either as a response or as an excuse. "You know I think the world of you," I clarified, "and so I'm sorry. I'm sorry that you've suffered, and I'm sorry that they're children. I'm sorry of what you must think of me. And I'm sorry that none of this changes the situation—because I will not sacrifice the king's life or mind—or everyone else's lives and minds—because I feel sorry.

"I told you the deal Avior made with the demon: that she would give him a way to kill the king so that no one would know. *No one.* It might not be the boy's *fault* that he's Ignorance and going to wipe the minds of everyone who might guess at what the prefects have done, and it might not be the girl's *fault* that she's Want and is going to murder the king and anyone who gets in the way—but that doesn't change the fact that they're going to destroy all of us and that they must be stopped. Will you help me?"

"I will not."

Simply spoken, with no room for argument and no intention of further explanation. A plain man in bare feet and flannel pajamas who would not be moved.

I wondered, as he must have known I would begin to wonder, whether this immovability was one of the things he'd learned in the mental institution.

"If you will not help me," I said, "then I will do what must be done on my own. Do not attempt to interfere."

"I will do what I think right," he replied.

I had expected nothing less. I bowed my head and passed him without further comment.

INTERLUDE

King Emil squinted at the shorter, broader, and darker of the strangers standing before him. He understood why the other man, the Edenfield knight, had come, and he was gratified by his loyalty. But what business had a Silvertip construction worker at the prefects' conference? Why had he made it his business to help convey the memory card? The man had barely contributed a word, and he struck Emil as disrespectfully distracted.

"Explain," Emil said to the knight, "how the woman on this recording came to be the new Prefect Edenfield. We haven't been informed of any injury to our appointed prefect; nor have we approved any new appointment."

"The replacement is temporary, sire," the knight—Roald Steensen, he remembered—said. "Lord Holst had to, um, leave. There were threats against his life, and he didn't want to endanger the other prefects or you by staying at the conference."

"We were not informed of any such threats," said the king, annoyed. "Tell us again this woman's name."

"Mercedes Cartier," Steensen replied, nodding to the construction worker. "Francis's sister."

This roused the construction worker enough that he stomped forward. King Emil had to check his instinct to rear back.

When the worker spoke, however, his voice was a surprisingly golden tenor and oozed deference rather than aggression. "Mercedes figured out what was going on. She went to Edenfield to catch the prefects at treason and interfere. She has a talent for that sort of thing."

Emil did not want to believe him. He tried hard not to believe him, to dismiss his evidence even as he had dismissed every other piece of evidence placed before him. He had resisted when his chancellor had rushed these strange guests in and insisted on playing the recording, but he had not been able to deny, even to himself, that he recognized Graça Silveira's voice among the others. He wanted to claim that she didn't mean it, that she'd been playing along with the others to trick them—but there was no mistaking the viciousness in her phrasing, the hideous fury thickening her voice.

How awkward he felt in his curtain suit, in his own home, in the seat of his power, the chancellor's judgmental eyes upon him. He looked to his royal secretary, hoping for salvation from that quarter, but none came. The royal secretary was gazing somberly upon their guests, and so the king turned his attention back there. With what preening was the knight congratulating himself! And that construction worker should never have been allowed in the palace.

He loathed manual laborers. They were made of such coarse and heavy materials that it was a wonder this one's very presence didn't crush his beautiful glass. And the man's sister must be even worse.

Feeling his self-control evaporating, and conscious of the presence of outsiders, King Emil gathered his royalty about him like a cloak. "Thank you for bringing this matter to our attention," he told his visitors. "You will be fed and cared for. Lord Chancellor, Lord Secretary, attend us." He swept to his feet and strode off, not looking back.

Out from under the strangers' observation, an ikari dragon exploded in the king's chest. Its foul breath scorched his throat, and its sinewy, reptilian body squirmed in his belly. Every thrash of its tail struck against the memory of his conversation with Prefect Lindo in the rose garden, of her brief but formal renewal of vows.

This was how she repaid his lenience? This was how she responded to his trust? He had forgiven much in her sister's memory, but he would not forgive this. Not when he had heard her voice, her very own voice.

And yet . . .

The king faltered mid-step, not noticing his companions' alarm.

And yet, what if he made a mistake? No one would really want to murder him, would they? Carina was a civilized nation. He shouldn't have to worry about things like murder and treason and other savage crimes.

"Sire?" The chancellor's voice broke through Emil's paralysis. "Sire, shall I contact the high marshal?"

"Don't be hasty," the royal secretary scolded, twirling his cape around his arm. "You know His Majesty prefers to consult the Tree before making any major decisions. You must not rush him: it may not yet be time for action."

"You take hesitation too far," the chancellor shot back. "If now is not the time for action, when we have every proof, when we are within hours of the treasonous attempt, then when?"

The royal secretary smirked. "A wise strategist considers his timing—he doesn't take impulsive action the moment he receives news."

Some part of the king's mind noted once again how greatly his advisors' mutual dislike seemed to have deepened, but most of his mind spiraled into the far distance. *The Tree,* his thoughts echoed. *The terrible, terrible hanging tree. You may trick them, but you won't trick me. You are mine, as I am yours.*

"How is this impulsive?" the chancellor snapped. "We've known what they were up to for months. We've only been waiting for irrefutable proof, and now we have it!"

"We agree," said Emil, although he had little idea of what either of his advisors had said. "There is something afoot, and we intend to find out what. We fear the prefects have been misled—even that they may have turned against us—but we will not act prematurely. All may not be as it seems. Where is our seidkonur?"

The royal secretary bowed. "On her way, Your Majesty. I took the liberty of summoning her to await you—as, no doubt, my lord chancellor took the liberty of contacting your high marshal."

"You are mistaken," the chancellor corrected frostily. "I would never take liberties with His Majesty." He fell blessedly silent then, falling in step behind the king and beside his rival.

Before long, they arrived at the central courtyard. Nothing ever changed in there, neither with the season nor with the passage of years.

The bare cobbles remained bare; the sorry attempts at grass cringed and withered far from the Tree. And the Tree itself—the Tree! The looming Tree, its limbs reaching out as if to sweep a glass king from his feet! Its branches snakes of Medusa's hair, frozen by her stony glare. The malaise of its presence like fog upon the ground. There stood the Tree. It had stood for hundreds of years, and it might stand for hundreds more.

There, waiting by the trunk—nearly touching it, but not quite daring—stood the seidkonur. And, for some reason, the skald.

"Your Majesty," said the seidkonur, coming forward the moment she saw him. Emil beheld her in turn, approving that she had made herself ready on this occasion—unlike her hurried entrance of last time. She wore a flowing, old-fashioned velvet dress as white as her hair, and her fingernails and toenails had been painted to match.

As she approached him, the skald followed, carrying the seidkonur's staff and satchel. So she was feeling her age today, Emil thought. "You haven't come to bombard us with more rhymes, I hope," he said to the bard distastefully.

The young man, balancing his load with the ease of long practice, swept a bow. "I come only to be of service to my king and his seidkonur," he assured Emil. Since he restrained his cheeky grin and lowered his sparkling eyes, Emil accepted this explanation and forgot him.

"Madame Seidkonur," he said. "We have come on an urgent matter, having received most disturbing intelligence, and we seek the Tree's guidance. Commune with it on our behalf. Ask it to give us a sign if the time has come for us to move against our prefects."

With an accepting bow and a few murmurs of assurance, the seidkonur took up her staff. It was curiously plain, that staff: six feet long, dowel-straight ashy wood no larger than the circle of her thumb and forefinger. No mystic signs adorned it. No polish had touched it, save for the natural polish of use and wear. And yet it seemed absolutely a part of her as she took her place beneath the Tree.

A whirl of white beneath dusky boughs, she danced. Her bare feet swam in plumes of dust; her staff spun precise figures; her cloudy eyes shut against distraction. Emil watched raptly—staring first at her and then at the Tree behind her. It seemed to him that the branches danced in time with her movements—no. Not *seemed*. They *were* dancing with her. The razor edges of twigs minced the air—slivers of movement never before seen in that dead, windless place.

Color shifted, the dirt surrounding the Tree darkening with mois-ture. Liquid oozed up, staining the seidkonur's feet red, squelching and tugging at her until she staggered and slowed. Above her, branches creaked and protested under unaccustomed weight, under the looped ropes cast over their petrified bark.

A fresh breeze of ages past swept the courtyard. Beside and before and behind Emil, men shouted and grunted with effort, and ropes scraped the branches harder, wild with desperate thrashing. Emil caught flashes of kicking feet, bulging eyes, loose fabric. Then living movement stilled and there was only the gentle swaying in the wind. Fabric and flesh rotted and fell away, and bones bleached under the memory of ancient sun.

Time sped by, and the sky closed into a roof. The earth dried, and the dust settled. There were no ropes, no hangmen, no corpses. The Tree brooded motionless and empty.

The seidkonur leaned on her staff, blanched and shivering with astonishment.

"Well," said the skald. "I guess that's a 'yes,' then."

Chapter 34:

CHILD ABUSE

By morning, you'd never have known anything untoward had occurred in front of Edenfield Manor. The knights' vehicles had been hidden and the prefects' cars—minus Hemmel's, which had been carried into the garage and abandoned there, stinking of smoke—had been driven onto the grass, leaving the gravel loop clear for the king. Unlike the prefects, the king traditionally brought a small party with him, both for his protection and to suit his royal status.

I came last to breakfast. My frozen sojourn down memory lane, courtesy of Ignorance, had left me unexpectedly rested, but I still wanted to catch whatever hours I could. It wasn't like I'd miss anything by not pulling myself out of bed before eight-thirty, and I wanted to be at my best.

Besides, there's nothing like being late for making an entrance.

I dressed in sunny yellow cashmere, on the theory that yellow was the last color anyone associated with sneaking around the woods in the middle of the night, and threw open the dining room's double doors. "Good morning!" I proclaimed. "Everyone have a restful night? Quite the fireworks we had."

The other prefects groaned or answered, according to how much sleep they'd managed, how full they'd stuffed their mouths, and what they thought of me. I went to the sideboard to pick out some eggs scrambled with unidentifiable fish, a slice of bread, and a bit of cheese.

A hearty breakfast that my stomach didn't want, but I sat and stuffed it in my face despite the internal objections. Today of all days, I needed my energy.

Sr. Nordfeld sat at the far end of the breakfast table, on Avior's left. Want and Ignorance, as before, waited behind Avior's right shoulder. Upon reflection, I wasn't surprised they were back from patrolling; no doubt Avior preferred to impress the other prefects.

And, I thought, no doubt he'd prefer they not know what he'd been up to.

"Your children look dreadful, Lucio," I said, when I'd shoved about as much cheese down my throat as I could manage. "Positively starving. Have you forgotten to feed them?"

Avior didn't have to say anything; the revelation on his face screamed his answer.

"You haven't fed them?" Batata cried, outraged.

Having such a lowly prefect question him was too much. Avior straightened and sniffed. "Relax. These aren't actual children; they are demon spawn. They don't work by the normal rules. Not like the rest of us."

Sr. Nordfeld's brow furrowed. "Actually—"

My snort overrode him, and he broke off in astonishment. I kept my attention on Avior. "What do you think they live on, air?" I demanded. "It's bad enough that you expect them to work after not letting them sleep a wink last night."

Avior started. "What?"

"It is bad enough," I said, exaggerating my diction, "that the children did not get any sleep last night because they were busy, on your orders, patrolling the woods."

"How do you know that?" he demanded. "How could you possibly know that?"

"Piffling question," I replied, waving a dismissal. "Important question." I inclined my head to Prefect Lindo. "How many of your knights have gone missing?"

Flawed Prefect Lindo was, but stupid she was not. Her hands had fisted on the edge of the table, her back ramrodded, her jaw clenched. "Eight," she ground out.

I nodded, forestalling a rant as I calculated. There were the three

I'd pepper sprayed, which I assumed my knights had taken care of. That left five unaccounted for. Had my knights been busy? Or had some of Lindo's wandered a little too far from the manor?

I put that puzzle aside and moved on to Prefect Hemmel. "I saw the blaze. I'm sorry it happened on Edenfield property, and I'm sure Lucio here would be happy to reimburse you."

Prefect Avior scowled. "Now wait a second—"

I cut him off with a look. "We don't live on air, Lucio. They're hungry, and you haven't fed them. What did you expect? Prefect Lindo, if you have any knights in the kitchen, I highly recommend you clear them out. I would hate for the children to get . . . carried away."

What a lot of uncomfortable shifting that comment elicited. But more importantly, from my perspective, it got Lindo to stomp thin-lipped to the kitchen and order everyone out. No doubt, it'd soon also get Lindo into a nice, distracting screaming match with Avior.

"Lucio," I said, "release the children into my care long enough for me to feed them." In my periphery, I couldn't help seeing Sr. Nord-feld's uncertainty, the way he wondered what I was up to and whether he should try to stop me. Was this a trick? Was I trying to impress him with this public show of repentance? *Don't try anything,* I silently begged him—and could see him deciding that pleasing him would be the most important thing in the world to me.

Well, he had plenty of evidence to go by, didn't he? That was the face I'd always tried to show him.

"I decide whether they get fed or not," Avior said, "assuming they need feeding, which I'm not convinced of. They're mine, and I—"

I was by his side in an instant, fingers tucking inside the knot of his tie, pulling his face close to mine. The children stirred but did not interfere. "Let's get this straight," I growled. "Your deal is with the red-haired witch, not with me. Screw with the children, and I'll *let* you be the one to feed them."

Avior's fingers clenched the table to support his weight, to keep from choking on his own tie. He was made of stouter stuff than Sil-vertip, though, and said, "Jon won't let you hurt me."

"My loyalty to Jon Nordfeld," I said, releasing Avior and stepping back, granite-faced and marble-voiced, "stretches so far and no fur-ther. But out of what loyalty and respect I can be said to have, I will ask politely once more. Prefect Avior, would you please permit me to borrow these children from you for the purpose of fueling them that they might better serve you?"

The dining room connected to the kitchen through two sets of doors: the first leading to a little connecting passage, where staff could enter and exit without giving guests an unsightly view of the kitchen; and the second leading from the entry area to the kitchen itself. Prefect Lindo flapped through the passage and paused in the doorway. She cleared her throat harshly. "The kitchen," she told me, "is clear."

I nodded and thanked her, letting the brief interruption reset the atmosphere. I was uncertain how much Avior cared about saving face, but he took the opportunity sure enough. "Go with her," he told Want and Ignorance. "We want you at your best."

I offered a hand to each child, ignoring Sr. Nordfeld's grateful look. Ignorance took my left hand without complaint—and, indeed, without looking at it. He kept his opposite hand over his face, and it was a wonder he knew anything that was going on. Want took my right hand and immediately tried to shove it in her mouth, but I torqued our wrists sharply, pressing our joint hands to her cheek. "Patience," I warned her.

Whether she reacted to the words or to the tone, I don't know, but she didn't try to bite me again as I led her through the dining room and the closet-sized connecting passage to the kitchen.

Once both doors shut, I dropped the children's hands and pulled two prep stools up to the central island counter. One at a time, I boosted them onto their stools. "If you eat your breakfast like good children," I told them, "you can have ice cream for dessert."

Want clasped dirty hands before her mouth, eyes round, breath hiccupping. Ignorance made neither sound nor movement.

This kitchen was much older than the one in the auction house, and its wood structures and cast iron tools had not been converted to a sea of stainless steel. I'd gotten to know it a little, during my rabbit roasting experiment. It had a small, homey, used feel to it, but the pantry was plenty large enough to hold food for the conference, and the walk-in freezer had one half put aside for meat. Evidently, someone connected to Edenfield liked to hunt.

I set plates before the children, then a loaf of bread. It took a minute to find butter and marmalade, and by the time I turned back, holding them, the loaf of bread was gone. Not a crumb of it remained on its paper, nor on the prep table, nor on the lips of the children. Want stared at me with wide, ravening eyes and parted lips. Beside her, Ignorance chewed slowly. As I watched, he swallowed and his mouth fell open again. Not to eat more—the way he constantly plugged his nose necessitated it. That explained the receded jaw of a perpetual mouth breather, and I wondered if he shut his nose against smells even as he slept—if he slept.

"All right," I said slowly. "I saw some rolls." I put the butter and marmalade before them, but this time I watched. Want immediately snatched up the brick of butter and dug out a pat with her fingers. She placed the pat in her brother's mouth, and he shut his lips around it. As he sucked on it, Want stuffed the rest of the butter in her own mouth. It shouldn't have been possible, for that big brick to fit in that child's mouth, but she swallowed it in a bite. The marmalade went the same way, every sticky blob scooped into her mouth before Ignorance had finished with his butter. The marmalade was gone in a literal two seconds, and then Want stared at me, trembling for more.

In a daze of horrified fascination, I got her more. I put out boxes of cereal, leftovers, cheese, condiments, and desserts. When they were gone, I tried raw meat and flour, and they disappeared too. It worked the same way for each item: I placed the food on the table, Want put the first bite in Ignorance's mouth, and then she ate the rest herself. Around the point we got to a gingerbread house that looked about a year old, Ignorance turned away, full and content.

Want kept eating. She ate and ate until there was nothing left in the cupboards, but her belly never grew fuller, and her face never lost the strain of desperate starvation.

"You've done a good job on your breakfasts," I praised them, stomach churning. "You've more than earned your ice cream. Why don't you help me pick it out?"

Want leapt off her stool and helped her brother down. Hand in hand, they joined me outside the walk-in freezer. I unlocked the door and held it open, letting them enter first. It was negative forty degrees inside there—not bad to stand in for half a minute when you're overheated from working in a hot kitchen, but I wouldn't want to vacation in there. Our breath froze in midair, and the children began shivering immediately and prancing so their bare feet didn't stick to the frosty floor. They clearly wanted to leave, but the possibility of ice cream was too tempting.

"There it is," I said from the doorway. I pointed at a shelf in the back, where two tremendous tubs of chocolate and strawberry ice cream waited. "I'll hold the door for us, because it's pretty heavy. Go ahead and choose the one you'd like."

Want raced to the tubs. They sat level with her head, twenty pounds of heavy cream and sugar. She grabbed the plastic of the chocolate tub with both hands and tried to pull it off the shelf, but the container was slippery with frost and iced in place, and it didn't budge an inch. She elbowed her brother to help her, and he reluctantly lowered his hands from his face to put them next to hers.

I stepped back quietly, into the warm kitchen, one hand curling around the door handle. I'd told the truth: it was a heavy door. If I let go, it'd swing shut on its own. There was a release on the inside, but that wouldn't lighten the load; and emaciated children who couldn't lift an ice cream tub might not be able to open it. Even if I didn't latch the exterior lock, they'd be trapped.

They say you feel warm before you freeze to death.

My fingers convulsively tightened and loosened. I thought of the way Want had eaten, and of the missing knights. I thought of how it had felt to lose myself to my own mind, at the slightest touch of Ignorance's hand. I thought about what I knew would happen if I didn't act now. I thought about innocent human lives and families and the future of my nation. I thought about the auction house and about doing what was necessary and about the greater good.

As I watched, Want gave up trying to tug the chocolate ice cream down and began beating the outside of the tub instead, in an attempt to rip through. Her fingers were blue with cold.

I was going to regret this for the rest of my life.

I released the door and let it shut behind me. "Here," I told Want kindly, reaching over her head to wrestle down both tubs. "Let me help you with that."

There wasn't much actual conferencing that day. We tried, but the knowledge of King Emil's imminent arrival hung heavy among us. The prefects were afraid. They no longer trusted one another—or me—and they certainly didn't trust Want and Ignorance, who never left Prefect Avior's side, at Lindo's insistence. She had, she said, lost enough knights.

It was almost a relief when one of Lindo's knights radioed in to tell us that the king, entourage in tow, was going to arrive early.

I'd been seeing flashes of Lindo knights all day, as they found places to secrete themselves around the manor—which they now did.

Sr. Nordfeld was waiting for us in the entry hall, and kept his expression entirely blank when Avior handed the children over to him and told him to wait with them in the sitting room by the front door. "And as for you, dear children," Avior told them, scruffing their hair, "be ready. I'll point out which one the king is. He's the one you need to kill."

I met Sr. Nordfeld's eyes over their heads, then turned mine hurriedly away lest we arouse comment. It had been, I supposed, too much to hope that my knights had succeeded in getting a message out. I did know that they and Francis were no longer in the knighthouse, because Lindo had told me so, with many a baleful glance at Avior. Equally gone, she said, were the knights guarding them. She was extremely sorry for my loss and expressed again how brave she thought I was, given the circumstances.

I thanked her gravely and told her I couldn't bear to think about it, so she'd change topics.

I was so utterly focused on what was ahead of me, it didn't occur to me until we were actually walking out of the manor to meet the approaching vehicles that, as Prefect Edenfield, it was my duty to take point. Even then, I expected Avior or Lindo to usurp me, but they didn't. It would have looked too strange, I guess.

The royal knights arrived first, in a rush of black vans. They came and they kept coming, dozens of them, crowding around every gap left by the prefects' cars, along the edges of the gravel loop, and down the sides of the road. I'd expected the king to bring a few kingsmen, not an army. My heart fluttered with hope, and I had to school my expression lest the other prefects read it aright.

Once they'd parked, the royal knights themselves gushed from their vehicles. There must have been nearly two hundred of them: men and women in black uniforms with white stars at their caps and necks and white stripes around their wrists. They spread out with military precision, scouting the immediate area and delving deep into the woods. Several searched the empty knighthouse and then took up position before it. Then I was distracted by a few of the higher-ranking royal knights separating the prefects out and patting us down, swiftly and professionally. It happened so quickly it didn't occur to me to protest until they were done. The other prefects seemed to have been expecting it, and the knights didn't find anything objectionable on them. In fact, the only thing they took away was my multi-tool knife, which I'd kept in case it came in handy.

As quickly as they'd appeared, the royal knights withdrew, stationing themselves in various groupings, both offensive and defensive. All this, they did without a word and with fantastic precision.

Only then, with his patriotic Carinan soldiers in place, did the king arrive. Nine identical white cars drove into the parking loop and fanned out. The king would be in one of these vehicles: neither the first nor the last, but one of the seven in between. There was no telling which of the seven it would be; rumor had it, even the inhabitants of the other eight cars did not know.

The vehicles parked and the engines extinguished, and suddenly everything became very familiar and very formal, exactly like I'd seen it on television. Only, from the comfort of my living room, the array and fanfare hadn't been so overwhelming and confusing. The foremost thought in my mind was that I had no idea how I was supposed to greet the king. Why hadn't Torben included that in his notes?

Kingsmen emerged from their cars, sharp in little white hats with brims to shade their eyes, crisp white jackets and trousers, military-grade white boots. They had black stars at their collars, indicating rank, and at their wrists and on their hats. These were the best of the best, a full complement of eighteen, as utterly and continually focused as air traffic controllers, forming up around the fourth car. One bent back to open the door, and the king himself emerged.

My mind wiped itself as blank as if Ignorance were holding my hand. I've never considered myself impressed by celebrity, but this—

he—

He was at once precisely as I'd seen him on television (and stamps and money and in magazines) and a complete stranger. He stood five feet ten-and-a-half inches, and struck me as both shorter and taller than I expected, because he was so much realer. He had a large build, powerful but neither fatty nor muscular, and an oval face. His chin receded into his neck when he opened his mouth, and his skin was not the poreless wash it became under studio lights. Sloping eyebrows led to a broad forehead elongated into thinning hair. He even dressed as I had often seen him—elegantly suited, with a gold sash across his chest and the sword of state by his side. But though he wore black and white, he did not for an instant blend in with his men. If anything, they blended into the background against the powerful foreground of his presence.

"Prefects," he announced, and his voice, too, was as I knew it and yet not: sonorous, the Canopan accent trained to crispness, deep to the point of buzzing, with the slow rhythm of one accustomed to speaking publicly and making himself heard over a cheering crowd. It was exactly the voice he used in his Christmas and Easter speeches. The voice I associated intimately with royalty, with the personality and confidence to back it up. That voice said, *We are speaking words of vast importance, and thou shalt not interrupt or ignore us.* Every syllable, every intonation proclaimed his majesty; and I thought that even if I had never seen or heard him before, I'd have known him as king from the way he spoke.

That thought snapped me out of my daze. I wasn't here to gape and prostrate myself; I was here to save his life.

Sudden violence has a way of getting people's attention, so I turned, raised my foot, and drove it down into Avior's kneecap. I didn't get the angle right, as I had with Dinez, but Avior still collapsed, wheezing. I stomped my nice spiky heel into his stomach.

"Your Majesty!" I cried. "Beware! These prefects are plotting to kill you! You will be attacked the moment you enter the manor!"

In the way of nightmares, no one responded as they ought to have. The kingsmen did not immediately jump to the king's rescue, throw him into the car, and burn rubber away from here. In fact, they didn't do anything at all.

Neither did King Emil. He said, "We know."

Which explained why he'd brought a small army with him, but not why he'd come himself.

"We have heard your recording, Edenfield," he said. "Two of your men brought it to us. But we knew of the prefects' treason long before that—our high marshal caught wind of it months ago. We had not the evidence to move against our prefects, and so we sent spies to each of our prefectures to learn the truth of it." He motioned negligently. My eyes skipped over automatically and stuck.

There was Torben Nass, leaning in that reedy way of his, light-footed and ugly as ever. His white uniform did nothing to ameliorate his appearance, but it did mark him utterly and indubitably a kingsman.

In retrospect, it was obvious. It should have been obvious. True, Torben hadn't exactly treated me well—but then, I hadn't given him any reason to. I'd been too busy convincing him I was in league with the prefects. I'd gotten rid of and then supplanted Prefect Edenfield, bypassing the usual and legal mode of succession. He'd obviously known from the first that I wasn't the king's spy, that I couldn't possibly be for the simple reason that he was. And if that weren't enough, I'd taken it a step further by acting like a madwoman, flouncing about filling Bo's head with partial truths and gorging myself on rabbit.

But none of that, *none of that*, was as horrible and shameful as the knowledge that I would have realized the truth much sooner had Torben not been so very ugly.

And that he knew this.

He met my gaze steadily and nodded. Not in triumph or in sarcasm and certainly not in friendliness; only in acknowledgment.

I was so busy staring and wishing the earth would just swallow me and get it over with that I missed whatever the king said next. What I didn't miss was the royal knights jogging around and past us, the vast majority of them streaming through the doors and windows of Edenfield Manor like a plague of locusts. They jostled us prefects, surrounding and separating us and holding Avior upright. Canopus and Silvertip had barbed comments for the circling knights, but they kept them brief, and none of the others said anything. Tey looked like he was about to faint or throw up, but Lindo burned sheer hatred at me.

". . . have arrested every man and woman wearing Lindo colors," the king was saying. "Then we can go inside and discuss this like civilized people. . . ."

There was so much going on, I was having trouble catching everything. I had to focus on what was important, and right now alarm bells were bonging in my brain. I cleared my throat, and my voice emerged uncertainly amid the rush of knights. "I don't think that's a good idea," I said.

The king didn't pause his speech. He was used to talking over people. His topic of choice appeared to be scolding the prefects as if they were a bunch of naughty children. This struck me as a most peculiar attitude with which to treat treason. But then, a lot of things weren't making sense.

I caught Torben's eye and shook my head. He leaned my way like a sapling in the wind, curious but uncomprehending. Of course: I had only told my knights about some sort of mysterious weapon; he had no way of understanding about Want and Ignorance. No one here but the prefects knew the truth, and they weren't telling. I couldn't count on Sr. Nordfeld to do anything that might endanger the children, and the knights—they would do what any compassionate and sensible person would do with a pair of piteous waifs: bring them out to the king.

"Sire!" I yelled. I didn't think about it first, and I didn't hold back. That was the only way I could override the implicit command in that voice, the power of royalty. "Sire, listen to me!"

The king glanced at me and kept talking. No one paid me any attention except Torben, whose curious look sharpened. He sidled up to King Emil and swayed in.

The king broke off his speech long enough to say, "Not now."

"Your Majesty," Torben said urgently, "Prefect Edenfield has important—"

A shot boomed from inside the manor, then another. Then another. In seconds, the air filled with the thunder of intense gunfire. I slapped my hands over my ears, and the kingsmen clumped around King Emil, guarding his body with their own. They drew weapons, transformed from guards to soldiers in an instant.

The barrage continued for what felt like ages. My ears rang so much, even through my hands, that I didn't realize the battle sounds were petering off until I could distinguish clear breaks: bursts, then single shots, and finally nothing but the echoes between my eardrums.

No one spoke, not even the king. We waited for more, but there wasn't any more. No light streamed from the windows, because every bulb had been shattered. No one emerged. Under the afternoon sunlight, the manor leered down ghostly white and crosshatched brown.

Maybe four dozen knights had remained outside with us, and one of them jogged forward, dropped briefly to one knee before the king, and reported, "Sire, we've lost radio contact."

"They've probably shot out their own radios," King Emil said dismissively. "Deal with it."

"Sire." The knight snapped back to his fellows and started giving orders. Soon after, every remaining knight quick-marched into the manor, leaving only the kingsmen to guard and separate king and prefects.

"Your Majesty," I called, "they won't be able to—"

"Shut her up," the king said absently, not bothering to look my way. "We would have silence."

"Your Majesty, this is important!"

"If she speaks again without leave," the king said, "shoot her."

I clamped my jaw shut, shocked. I tried to tell myself there was something else going on, that under the circumstances as he understood them, the king was acting sensibly. But I felt betrayed anyway. Hadn't I been the one to send that memory card? Wasn't I trying to save his life? Shouldn't he trust me enough to let me speak?

The other prefects were watching me, their expressions ranging from satisfaction to loathing to resignation. Avior was standing fine on his own, though he was favoring his right leg. The whole situation felt more like a nightmare than ever.

The king had lost his bug for speaking, and we waited in silence for his knights to return.

No shots were fired, and no one emerged. Ten minutes passed, then twenty. Attempts to radio those inside resulted in static. Attempts to call were frustrated by whatever Lindo had done to the phone towers.

Finally, the king turned to Torben in pure exasperation. "What game are they playing, Nass?" he demanded. "You said there were only ninety Lindo knights inside. They couldn't have overpowered my men."

"Certainly not without making any noise," said Torben, and I thought I caught some edge in his bland tone. *He doesn't approve of the king's strategy,* I realized.

Torben went on, "Lindo's knights could be hiding from yours, but that doesn't explain why we aren't receiving any radio communications or why none of them have come out to explain—or why no Lindo knight has attempted to shoot from one of the upper stories. Something else is happening. A hostage situation, maybe."

"Or they're all dead," I said without thinking. "I'm sorry—don't shoot!"

"Don't," Torben agreed sharply, forestalling the kingsmen. "She knows something."

King Emil held up his hand, and guns were lowered away from me. "If the first set of knights were dead," he mused, "the second set would have reported it."

"Unless they're dead too," I said.

"You mean Lindo set booby traps," said Torben. "Or are you referring to the mysterious weapon you told Roald about? Have you not dismantled it?"

"About that," I hedged.

"Mysterious weapon," the king scoffed. "What will you come up with next? Avior managing to summon his demon?"

I didn't answer, I was so surprised.

"We listened to the whole recording of that meeting," the king explained. His eyes trailed over the other prefects, smug in his victory. "And my people have analyzed it. We have known for years of Avior's obsession with demonology, but since he clearly had neither the expertise nor the intelligence to summon an actual demon, we did not interfere. But now it seems he found—or believes he found—an expert. A real one, I wonder?"

The king ... believed it was possible to summon demons? What was this, the Dark Ages?

Or did he somehow know of personifications as well? Was that part of the secret knowledge given to kings?

Regardless, his belief would make my explanation a lot easier.

"He found an expert," I said, "although the fact that the summoning worked surprised even that expert."

Or had it? I wondered.

"My former employer," I explained, "Jon Nordfeld, the one who purchased the recording equipment. He made himself an expert so that he could infiltrate the conference to gather the treasonous evidence you heard."

I was straying too far from my point, and was losing my audience. I hurried on. "Anyway, Prefect Avior and the others managed to summon a demon and make a bargain with her—to murder you."

"Her?"

That's what he focused on? "Yes, her. It took the shape of a woman. And the prefects—Avior was the spokesman—asked her for a way to kill you without anyone knowing, and she gave it to them."

"Really," said the king. "What sort of weapon?"

I hesitated, knowing how absurd the explanation must sound. But I could hardly refuse to tell him. "A pair of children," I said slowly. "Horrible, animalistic creatures with special powers, not ordinary children. She called them Want and Ignorance."

One of the kingsmen laughed knowingly. It was such a distinctive, such an unexpected sound that we all swung around to stare at him. The man straightened and put on his military face. "Sorry, sire. It's just—*A Christmas Carol.*" He flushed as we continued to stare. "The book by Charles Dickens, I mean. *A Christmas Carol.* The Spirit of Christmas Present carries around two wretched children called Want and Ignorance. A girl and a boy, the offspring of mankind. It's, uh . . . meaningful."

I closed my eyes briefly, breath caught in my throat. *Again.* How amused Theodora had been when she'd named the children. When she'd caught me a second time with the same trick.

"Do you take this for a joke, Edenfield?" the king demanded angrily. "A demon disguised as a woman! Children as weapons! Literary references! We have been lenient with you, in gratitude to your good intentions, but this is too far!"

I shook my head, trying to explain, not understanding how I had offended him so badly. "She likes to play tricks, Your Majesty. She likes . . . jokes. I've come across her before."

"We're sure you have," the king said, and laughed abruptly. "Good thing we have a sense of humor, or we'd have you shot on the spot for lying to us. As it is, we would see these children for ourselves."

"Sire—" Torben began.

"Fear not," said King Emil. "We are confident in your ability to protect us from children. But just to be safe"—he nodded snidely to me, then turned to the kingsman who'd spoken up—"tell me, Souza, are these Christmas children meant to be dangerous?"

"No, sire," said the kingsman. "I don't think so. Or only in the metaphorical sense—you know, how poverty and ignorance are dangerous, both for the oppressed and for the oppressors; and how they're caused by immorality and lack of Christian love."

"But these aren't actually the ones from the book," I said. "She just named them after the characters to trick us. She—"

I might as well have been invisible and mute. The king was talking again, making plans and giving orders, and the knights responded and the other prefects turned pointedly away from me. Only Avior bothered to glance in my direction, briefly, his lips flat and his eyes empty.

Chapter 35:

CANNIBALISM

We all went. That was part of the king's showmanship: it wasn't enough for him to stop the prefects; he had to grind them into the dirt. He had to show them and the country and our neighbors that not only was any attempt to move against the king a failure, but it had never had any chance of succeeding.

I understood the mentality. I did. Under other circumstances, I'd have endorsed it wholeheartedly. Putting down a rebellion is only a temporary victory, and possibly the first step in defeat, unless you put it down in such a way as will prevent further attempts.

A clump of kingsmen surrounded the king, scouting ahead, interposing their bodies, and keeping wary eyes on the prefects. Torben hung close to Avior, his restless, leaning energy compressed and focused. Not that Avior was likely to do anything rash while he was getting his way.

I hoped his knee hurt him.

Sweat glistened on Hemmel's forehead, and he glanced repeatedly at Lindo, who ignored him. Tey jittered with nerves, Batata trudged along glumly, and Canopus seemed fiercely angry about something. Such as me.

"Whose spy are you really?" Silvertip whispered to me, and a kingsman prodded him away to join the other prefects.

Although no explicit orders on the subject had been given by the king, the kingsmen had lost interest in me. Maybe Torben had told them to let me go—I'd been enough of a thorn in his foot that he must want me gone. I don't know for sure. I do know that as we walked, I fell back, and they let me. I could have ambled away right then, taken the Silvertip van I'd come in, and driven home. No one would have stopped me. Heck, no one would have even noticed.

I trailed after the others with a creeping, horrible curiosity.

Gunfire had gouged holes, gashes, and slits in the wallpaper, splintered doors and frames, dug crevasses in carpets. The sitting room in which I'd first eavesdropped on the prefects—in which Sr. Nordfeld had been waiting with the children—was empty of everything but destruction: its chairs upturned, the king's portrait lying broken before the barren fireplace.

Further back in the manor were signs of explosives, and thick yellow insulation slithered from broken walls and scorched ceiling. A crossbeam lay lengthwise along the hallway, and two more leaned at precarious angles, their ends ragged, their sides splintered. Slivers of shattered light bulbs littered the carpet, dimly twinkling in indirect sunlight and the flashlights of kingsmen.

In short, everywhere the king went, he found every indication of battle except the ultimate one: humanity. The place was completely and utterly deserted. There weren't even bloodstains. That was only the ground floor, though. The second floor and attic remained untouched, except for disturbed dust where knights had hidden before being drawn out. But not a single one of them was left.

"What is going on here?" asked King Emil. "Where have they gone? Is there a secret room?"

"Not one that could hold three hundred people," Torben volunteered grimly. "Or one any knight would have known about."

"There's a basement," said Avior.

If you ask me, when the bad guy offers up suggestions, the last thing you should do is follow them. Evacuating the building is a much better plan, preferably followed by a spot of arson. Torben was of a similar mind, and aired his opinion immediately.

"Obviously, he means it as a trap," King Emil said complacently, "which is why he'll be going first."

"I highly advise against entering the basement at all, Your Majesty," Torben repeated emphatically. "At least not until we've had a chance to clear it. There could be a toxic gas down there. That would explain how so many knights went missing without making a sound. Let's bring in experts with the proper equipment—or, better yet, send in an aerial bomb squad."

"If there is gas, and it's not lethal, then bombing the building would kill my knights," the king observed.

"Then let me get a gas mask and scout—"

"I'm not going to abandon my knights," King Emil interrupted. He seemed to grow as he spoke, and I saw a hint of the naval commander he must once have been. "Stop babying me, Nass. I'm not a coward, and I won't be treated as one. I'm going down there, and you can accompany me or you can be shot."

No fallen autumn leaf was ever as unreadable as Torben made himself then, as he bowed and said, "My life is at your disposal, Your Majesty." He did not add, *As I am, no doubt, shortly going to prove*, and the king did not add, *As it should be*, but I heard both anyway.

"There isn't any gas down there," said Avior, practically skipping with anticipation, "and I'd be happy to prove it. By your leave?" He opened the basement door. The light over the stairs had been broken, but a few of the ones below had survived, and their faint luminescence gave him enough visibility to proceed down. Like sand through loose fingers, the others slipped after him. The only one who paid me any attention was Torben, who pressed the multi-tool knife into my hand as he passed. Forgiveness? It seemed useless, considering what was happening.

Three hundred: that was the number Torben had given for the knights who had disappeared into this basement. I had absolutely no doubt they were either dead, or in such a state of forgetfulness that death would be an improvement. Three *hundred*. That was the cost of my moment of selfishness. A split-second decision at the door of a freezer.

How superior I had been toward Luc, who prized his softer feelings above that which must be done. What a hypocrite I had been. It was no good pretending I hadn't known what would happen, and this was my reward. My reward, their reward. Sr. Nordfeld's reward. All dead.

I did not want to go into that basement. I much preferred Torben's suggestion of bombing the place, only I'd have locked the doors first, to make sure no one could escape.

What did it matter if there were still living men and women in that basement? They wouldn't be alive long. The basement had already swallowed three hundred knights, the Gulbransens, and Jon Nordfeld. A few more weren't going to give it indigestion. And if I followed them down, it'd only swallow me as well, without a hiccup. Then there'd be no one left to tell the tale. No one left to warn Gjerde before the manor turned inside out and disgorged the children. Would it ever stop?

Maybe. Maybe if I went down there, there would be no reason for Ignorance to continue outward. The deal had only been that no one know the prefects were responsible for the king's death. And if I was the last—

But I wasn't the last. There were Olaf, Roald, Francis, and anyone they'd told in the capital who hadn't come with the king. And not just them: for everyone who witnessed the children destroying those who already knew would know and would have to be destroyed themselves, and on and on and—

I might not be able to save those who had gone before, but there were those whom I could save, if I stopped the children now, made sure they were gone for good. I didn't know how, but if there was a possibility, then I had a duty toward them.

Have I ever mentioned how much I hate basements? Because I hate basements. And I was afraid.

"Prefect?"

I jumped and whipped round. There, his fair hair frizzing and tangled, mud on his boots and streaked along his neck, was Edenfield's youngest knight. "Olaf!" I cried. "But I thought you went to the capital!"

Olaf shook his head. "Roald and Francis went. I hid in the woods, in case they didn't make it; I have a backup of the recording. I heard when the king arrived, but there was gunfire, and I wasn't sure . . ."

My heart thudded and my breath roared. I parted dry lips. Here it was, the opportunity I'd been looking for. The one that stole my final excuse.

I drew on my lying face, serious and unafraid. "I'm so glad you're here," I told my knight. "I have a job for you, Olaf. It will be difficult, but I order you to carry it out for your prefect, your king, and your nation."

"I—" Olaf blinked. I don't know what he saw in my face then, but he didn't argue. He said, "Yes, prefect."

"In this basement," I said, "is a weapon of massive power. It has destroyed every single knight who has gone up against it—three hundred men and women. Look around you, Olaf, and see its destruction. It cannot be stopped by ordinary means, and if it is permitted to escape, it will spread like a virus until there is nothing left of Argo Navis.

"I'm going down after it. I might be able to defeat it—I understand about it more than they did, you see. And I . . . have an idea. But the weapon works quickly, and I might fail. If I'm not out in fifteen minutes, it's because I—and everyone else down there—am dead."

"It would be an honor to accompany you," Olaf said, although he trembled.

"You'd only get in the way," I said harshly. "I have a far more important task for you. The moment I go through that door, I need you to find an accelerant—gasoline, maybe, or gunpowder. Dump it outside the basement door. If I'm not knocking and calling for you within fifteen minutes *exactly*, you must lock the door and burn this manor down."

Olaf swayed slightly, dead white, but there was a hardness and steadiness in his shoulders, and he lifted his chin. "Yes, prefect," he said firmly, and I knew I could trust him in this. He checked his watch. "It's two-seventeen now."

"Then start the fire at two thirty-two," I said. "The biggest blaze you can. Don't hold back and *don't* be late. Go, go! Get ready!"

Olaf bowed and dashed off without another word. As soon as he turned the corner, I stepped through into the damp and the dark of the first stair, and I closed the door behind me.

The king's party had a brief head start, but it hadn't gotten as far ahead of me as I had expected. The kingsmen were taking their time, being cautious—and it had only been two or three minutes, though it felt like much longer. Since absolutely the last thing I wanted to do was traverse the twilit basement alone, I hustled to catch up.

My heels splashed the fetid water, and my footsteps echoed dully, lost in the percussion of tapping feet. How the kingsmen expected to hear a thing through the racket they made was anyone's guess.

I caught flashes of kingsmen past massive, mold-stained pillars as I ran, and thought they must have fanned out to search the area. Too many of the soft lights had died, and the remaining ones didn't stretch far. It must've been fear and claustrophobia talking, but it seemed to me that the basement had grown in my absence and twisted upon itself.

I caught up with the king's group just as it arrived in the far corner: the highest point of the basement, the driest spot.

Driest, but not dry. Damp had seeped into the chalk summoning circle, darkening it and bleeding white roots across the concrete; but the circle remained intact.

And so did Sr. Nordfeld.

My breath caught when I spotted him. He slumped beyond the circle, against the corner. His chest rose and fell, and although his face was slack, it did not bear the total vacancy of Ignorance. Asleep, then. But how asleep, and why?

I edged around the group toward him. Torben beat me there and crouched to check his pulse and eyes. "Alive," he announced to the king. "This was Prefect Avior's demonology expert."

"Turned against him, I suppose," the king murmured, absorbed in contemplation of the circle. "This is where you summoned your demon?" he asked Avior, his voice amused and unafraid. "What do you think, Souza?"

The kingsman shrugged. "Not my area of expertise, sire. Looks like the usual mumbo-jumbo."

"Not a magical portal through which my knights were transported to demonland?"

"I shouldn't think so, sire."

The king's laugh careened off concrete pillars. "Smoke and mirrors, hocus pocus. I'm disappointed in you, my prefects. Here I was promised a really good treason plot, and all I get are children's games! I hope," he said cunningly, "this isn't meant as a birthday surprise.

You're a month off!"

"I can see you don't take this seriously," Avior said. He wasn't offended. I don't think other people's opinions meant much to him. "You don't believe I succeeded in summoning a demon."

The humor dropped off the king's face. "I know what real magic looks like," he said, "and this isn't it. But I always take it seriously when people try to murder me. I came to Edenfield for one reason and one reason only: for proof, absolute proof that I could see with my own eyes, of your treason. Once I have it, you will be transported back to the capital and executed. You won't get a chance to grandstand at a public trial, so you can take that scheming look off your face, Prefect Lindo. I see right through you. I see through all of you. Go on, my faithless prefects: try to kill me. This is your only chance. Try it, Avior, if you're man enough."

"If I don't," Avior said, smiling, "will you let bygones be bygones and forget this whole sorry event?"

"Lucio!" Lindo hissed.

"No," said the king, "but I will have you shot right here and now and save you the shame of being slapped in handcuffs, dragged back to the capital, and publicly executed."

"How very generous," Avior said, the edges of his lips quirking. He folded his hands behind his back and examined the ceiling. "Out of curiosity," he said, "what happened to all your people?"

The king's eyes narrowed, and he growled, "We'll find them soon enough. Locked up in a secret room or wherever you've stored them."

"Oh, not the royal knights," Avior said dismissively. "I meant your other people, the ones we came down with. Your kingsmen who were searching the basement. I can't hear them. Can you?"

We held our breaths, listening. We heard:

The gentle gurgle and drip of water.

The faint buzz of fluorescent lights.

No footsteps or voices.

"This is absurd," the king spat. "Men! Kingsmen, to me!"

Sr. Nordfeld's unconscious breathing.

The weight of earth pressing upon us.

The manor above.

Drip, drip.

I blinked and refocused. The unnatural lighting had messed with my perception, and I'd had the strangest impression that the basement was breathing.

"All right, Avior," the king said, "you've had your fun. Where are they?"

Avior shrugged.

"What have you done with them?" the king insisted.

"I? Nothing," Avior said. "But perhaps—yes. Children!" he called. "Children, come here, please. I'd like to introduce you to someone."

We held our breaths again, and the king looked about to object. But then, as one, we lifted our heads at the sound of small feet pattering on concrete, splashing through puddles. The children came hand in hand. Neither seemed injured in the least, and the boy bore no signs of violence. By contrast, the girl's sackcloth had been ripped long past the point of indecency: no more than a few shreds clung to her neck, waist, and wrists. The men shifted, embarrassed. The remaining kingsmen clearly wanted to act, but their training overrode every delicate instinct.

"So you do have children here," the king said, grimacing. "These are . . . your children?" He sounded doubtful. With their pale skin, fair hair, and narrow features, Want and Ignorance no more resembled Avior than they resembled—well, me.

"They're mine," Avior affirmed. "Children, this is King Emil II. The one I told you about."

Want didn't need to be told twice. She lunged at the king, teeth bared, fingers clawing. A kingsman caught her around the middle and lifted her away. She tore into his chest with small, yellowing teeth: biting and slurping and swallowing with impossible speed, hardly chewing . . . and the kingsman was gone, without even a bloodstain to mark his passing.

Most of the prefects fell back, horrified. The king himself froze, lips parted, lost to shock.

His men were better trained. They whipped out their guns and opened fire. The remaining rags clinging to Want were shot away in seconds, but every bullet mysteriously missed her skin, driving chunks out of concrete pillars, floor, and ceiling.

Ignorance lingered to the side, out of the way of the gunfire. There was something oddly innocent in his appearance, standing there with his hands hiding his face. As I watched, one of the kingsmen tried to sneak around Want from the back and passed too close to Ignorance. The boy's hands lowered briefly, and his finger brushed the kingsman's thigh. The man wavered, staggered, and stumbled aimlessly into Want's waiting mouth.

Scant seconds had elapsed, but I'd already waited too long. I kicked my brain into gear and dove into the summoning circle. The multi-tool was open in an instant, and I nearly fumbled it in my hurry to slice my thumb.

Blood was what I wanted. I pressed the cut to the concrete in the center of the circle. "Theodora!" I cried. "Theodora Banks, Deals & Bargains, proprietress and demon—Lucio Winter has broken his deal with you!"

"Has he."

The scene froze at Theodora's voice, like the still of a photograph: Want hunching over her third kingsman, mouth wide and famished; Torben pulling the king from danger and the king resisting him; the prefects watching with expressions ranging from pride to revulsion. The eyes of each were alive and awake, but their bodies were paralyzed—with the exceptions of Prefect Avior and me.

Theodora joined me in the circle, and I stood to meet her. She was dressed as I'd first seen her, in white pure as new-fallen snow, her eyes like two distant stars, her voice as clear and pure as silver bells.

"Yes, he has," I said. "Look!" I pointed at Ignorance and Want. "Look at these children! Naked, starving, publically humiliated, and weaponized. They had no dinner, would have had no breakfast save at my interference, and spent the night patrolling the woods instead of tucked into warm beds. And now, they're being shot at and abused. In his deal with you, Lucio Winter agreed to treat these children as his own, but I don't see him bringing his offspring here. They're at home: safe, fed, rested, and pampered."

"Interesting," Theodora murmured, and gave me something disturbingly like a conspiratorial smile. Then she reformed into Deals & Bargains and strolled among the paralyzed men and women. She leaned over Want and Ignorance in turn, observing them without noticeable emotion. She touched the guns in the kingsmen's hands and peered at the half-devoured kingsman in Want's arms. Last, she continued on to Prefect Avior.

He squared his shoulders and planted his hands on his hips. "What are you doing here, demon?" he demanded. "I didn't summon you, and I'm busy. Go away!"

Deals & Bargains said: "Lucio Abbacus Winter." It placed a long, manicured hand on his cheek. "Do you have children of your own flesh?"

The muscles in his face strained, and he gasped, but I think he had to answer and truthfully. I think she made him. "Yes," he croaked.

"A boy and a girl?"

"Yes."

"Where are they?"

He struggled to keep his mouth shut, but the words tumbled out of their own accord. "At home with their mother."

"Safe? Indulged?"

"Yes. They have everything they could ever want."

"Ah." Deals & Bargains removed its hand from his face, and he collapsed in a puddle of sweat.

He didn't stay down long. Anger reared its ugly head, and made him as ugly as it. He surged to his feet. "How dare you come here, demon! I did not summon you, and I won't have you interfering. Avant! Be gone!"

Deals & Bargains tilted its head, as if Avior were a mildly irritating specimen. It said: "You broke our deal. That makes you mine." It plucked him up between thumb and forefinger and folded him once over its arm, then again the other way, as easily as one might fold a pillowcase. It kept folding until Avior was small enough to slide into the pocket of its white suit jacket, which it did.

Theodora turned to me then, and the smile was back. "Thank you for bringing this to my attention, Mercedes," she said. "I say 'thank you,' but I do not mean that you have incurred any debt in me, because you acted in your own self-interest. Au revoir."

"Don't forget to take the children," I said.

"You wish to make a deal?" she asked, then shook her head. "No, I don't want them back. You can keep them." She fluttered her fingers at me and, without my ever quite seeing her disappear, was gone.

Chapter 36:

REGICIDE

As Theodora vanished, her spell lifted. Torben kept hauling the king away from Want, yelling at him to stay down. The remaining kingsmen filled the basement with echoing, earsplitting gunfire. Prefect Tey fell to his knees before Ignorance, though the boy wasn't touching him. The kingsman in Want's clutches flopped and blew apart under the gunfire, but Want never paused stuffing herself, whimpering in her need for more, more, more through each mouthful.

"No!" King Emil protested. "No, I will not run. Take your hands off me!"

"Sire—!"

"I said no!" the king shouted, flinging himself free. He marched toward the remaining kingsmen.

It felt like I'd looked away for a scarce moment, but in that pause the gunfire had stopped. Only two kingsmen remained, and they had learned from the others' mistakes. Neither one bothered shooting at Want. Instead, they circled her, feinting, drawing her attention, pulling her aside to give the king time to escape. She snarled and grabbed, but they taunted her, buying precious seconds that the king preferred to waste.

"Face us, demon child!" King Emil bellowed, drawing himself up impressively and filling the claustrophobic space with his royalty. "Face us and know us as your king!"

Want's thin, pointed face turned to him. A kingsman took advantage of her distraction to dart up and slap her shoulder, drawing her attention back to him as he skipped away.

That was his plan, but Want hadn't been as distracted as he'd thought. She caught the hand that slapped her and swarmed up it, teeth snapping. In seconds, there was nothing left of him, but she was as hungry as ever.

"You'll thank me later," Torben said. Amid the king's violent protests, he swung him over his shoulder in a fireman's hold. The load bent him nearly double. The king must've outweighed Torben by a hundred pounds, and he kicked and beat at his savior's back.

Torben lurched grimly onward. I crept after him, not knowing what I was doing, but gripping the slender multi-tool, knife still extended. Not because I thought it would help against Want when bullets did nothing, but because it made me feel better.

Torben stopped short, hissing in alarm. Ignorance waited before him, hands over his face. Though he couldn't have been able to see him, he stepped right or left as Torben did. Without his burden, Torben might have been able to dash past—but the king was simply too heavy.

And then, as I watched, Ignorance's hands peeled back, then dropped. I had seen the face beneath once before, in moonlight not much dimmer than the flickering fluorescents down here. It was not a hungry face, and it had no extraordinary features. If anything, I would have said it looked . . . hunted.

Torben's grip on King Emil slacked, and the king rolled off his shoulder and thudded to the floor. The king grunted and curled onto his side, but he made no attempt to rise. He only lifted his head to stare at Ignorance as the boy stepped forward.

My fingers tightened convulsively around the multi-tool. I glanced down at the slender blade, a fragment of memory coasting around my mind, and a clear thought: Want might be impervious to violence, but Ignorance had avoided the gunfire.

Ignorance stepped forward, hands extended toward the king.

I burst into a sprint, multi-tool hilt planted firmly against the heel of my hand. Torben and the king wilted between Ignorance and me, so I ran at an angle, at a pillar. I hit it at full speed and rebounded in a tackle: one hand bearing Ignorance to the floor, the other pushing into his face. We cracked against the concrete and I somersaulted over his head, out of reach. I was on my feet a second later, spinning around, but the boy wasn't coming after me. He wasn't moving at all, except for the unsteady rise and fall of his chest. His face had lapsed into the blankness of unconsciousness.

The knife hilt protruded from his right eye, angled down over his cheek. None of the blade was visible.

Want screamed. I have never heard such a scream. She abandoned the remains of the final kingsman and launched herself at me, screaming and screaming and gabbling a word that was not language, that was not anything, that could be nothing except the only name she had for her brother. No hunger infected her voice; only pain.

I sank to one knee and braced myself. When her hands clutched at my sweater, I caught her elbows and held them locked together on either side of her chest. Her teeth snapped, neck tendons strained, but she could not reach my hands or my face. She had only the strength of a child, after all. So she kept screaming at me.

"I didn't kill him!" I screamed back, hardly knowing what I said. "He's not dead; he's better! I made him better! He wanted to know nothing, and now he knows nothing! I fixed him! He got what he wanted—and I can give you what you want. I can help you!"

She snarled at me with those yellowing child's teeth, more animal than little girl, and shrieked: "I won't let you kill me too! I'll kill you! I'll eat you up, and then you'll be dead, dead, dead and gone!"

I'd thought she couldn't speak. For that matter, I'd thought she couldn't cry—and here she was, crying.

Souza had given me a clue, but I hadn't paid attention. I'd assumed I'd already understood everything. *Fool. Idiot.* Willfully ignorant.

"Want," I said softly, gently. "Want, Want. I've been thinking of you as the personification of greed and grasping and stealing—but you aren't, are you? You are Need. Desperate Need and Hunger, Purposeful Neglect and Starvation. Not what you do but what is done to you."

Though I held her strongly, I took care that my posture was neither tense nor alarmed. My voice was calm and calming, as I would speak to an abused horse or a neglected dog. And, like many wild animals that do not wish to be wild, she stopped struggling and listened.

"I can help you," I said again, and this time I meant it. "Need, poverty, want. These things hurt, but they can be conquered, and not only by death or ignorance. They can also be conquered by faith and by charity."

"Stop it," said the girl, and I saw that she was crying harder than ever. "I don't believe you. Stop it."

"You need to have faith," I said. "Want isn't a girl's name, but Faith is. It's a pretty name, a name I would give to my own daughter. I give it to you. I give it to you that you might always remember it, and that you might always remember this promise:

"Faith, you will be cared for by charity. You and your brother both. You will have food and shelter. It might not always feel like enough, but it will always be enough. It will sometimes be difficult, but Faith is stronger than Want, and you will be happy. You will go to school and make friends and wear pretty dresses . . . and you will be loved."

I loosened my grip on her elbows, and she tried to wriggle away, but I didn't let her. I put my arms around her and pulled her in, hugging her tightly. Teeth clamped onto my shoulder, but they did not rip in, and they did not devour. After a few seconds, thin arms wrapped around my neck, and Faith turned her head to rest it against my chest.

POSTLUDE

The king had fallen. The king had not shattered.

Dazed, Emil held one hand before his face. It remained glass filled with colored sand, impossibly fragile, easy to smash.

But it had not broken. He had fallen from that man's back, and he had not broken.

His mind reeled. There was something he had to remember, or someone—there. A boy on the ground, a pitiful boy with a knife in his brain. Prefect Avior's boy. The man was not a fit father. Unexpected, a prefect having demon children. The seidkonur had not told him of this. The Tree had not warned him.

Terrible, terrible hanging tree.

How had the skald known? Emil must ask him—

But no, how could he? He was dead. He must be dead; everyone was dead. The world was dead. His high marshal had fallen before his eyes, like so many others. The only living beings left on Earth were these few in the cellar: the spy, a handful of prefects, the demon child, the master demonologist, and . . . yes, there. That must be the demon. A small brown woman dressed in sunshine, embracing the naked girl child he had witnessed devouring his high marshal.

What power must this woman have, if she could control such children? He'd thought he must be afraid of her when they met. He had been afraid, had tried to shut her up lest this sister of a construction worker crush him. But now that he looked upon her, he couldn't help but think her beautiful. She was not as magnificent as glass, but nor was she hard wood or steel. She was smoky quartz, and she put him in mind of his Tree. Terrible, yes. But terrible in his control.

What power must her master have, and how confident he must be, to sleep amidst such destruction. Master, demon, demon children. Loyal, as Emil had seen, to him.

Of course they were. He was king.

He thought he would keep them.

Another memory stirred, and Emil looked again to his hands. They had not shattered. They had not scratched. Not a grain of precious blood-red sand had escaped. How was this possible? How could he have survived? Unless—

White-hot excitement surged through the king's heart, so radiant that he looked about him, expecting to see rainbows escaping from the prisms of his chest. But, of course, his curtain-padded suit would block the light.

Smiling dizzily, King Emil pushed himself upright. He was not afraid of shattering. Not now that he knew the glass of which he was made was bulletproof.

. . . to be continued in book 2.

TRAPPED BY CRIME. FREED BY MAGIC.

When Skate tries to burgle a shut-in's home, she gets caught by the owner—a powerful undead wizard. He makes a deal with her. Now, she'd better find out exactly where her loyalties lie.

Skate the Thief
by Jeff Ayers

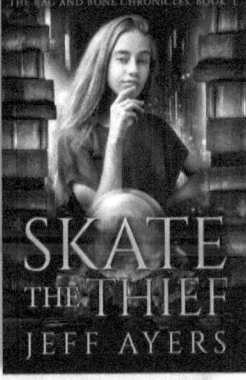

TRUE LOVE. ANCIENT CURSES.

Theodora is determined to unravel the mysterious Seth Adler's secrets. No matter how many thousands of years old.

Painter of the Dead
by Catherine Butzen

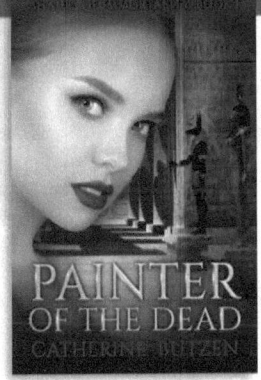

RIDICULOUSLY MAGICAL. MAGICALLY RIDICULOUS.

Crafted as a slave to serve Time, the clockwork man escapes to seek out his imagination, his purpose, and his name.

The Land of the Purple Ring
by Deborah J. Natelson

IT'S TIME TO TAKE OVER

Fodder of Humble Village is a soldier for the plot of each new story, and, frankly, he's really sick and tired of getting speared, disembowelled, and decapitated so the good guys can look glorious. In fact, he's not going to take it anymore.

The Disposable and
The Merry Band
by Katherine Vick

AND YOU THOUGHT COLLEGE WAS TOUGH BEFORE

Try getting bitten by a werewolf. And being hunted by madmen. And being stalked by a very suspicious secret organization.

Hunter's Moon by Sarah M. Awa

THE CLOCK IS TICKING

Plans seldom survive contact with the enemy, a truth thrown at Mercedes when an ordinary trip turns into a battle for survival.

Bargaining Power
by Deborah J. Natelson

ABOUT THE AUTHOR

Deborah J. Natelson was born and raised in Missoula, Montana, USA. She began writing at a very young age, and was soon drawn into editing. After attaining her Master of Theology from the University of St Andrews, Scotland, Deborah worked full time as a line and substantive editor until co-founding Thinklings Books, LLC, in 2019.

At present, Deborah lives in Montana once more—reading, writing, drinking tea, and playing with her Cavalier King Charles Spaniel, Flora.

You can visit her at www.DeborahJNatelson.com

~ Soli Deo Gloria ~